A PROPER SETTING DOWN

She landed in Cole's arms.

The shock knocked the sense out of her. She couldn't describe it any other way. Nothing else could account for the fact that not a single coherent thought remained in her head. He caught her easily, as if he'd done it before. He balanced her lightly against his chest, but that didn't keep her from being acutely aware she was leaning against his body. Heat and tension passed between them like their clothes weren't even there.

"Put me down," she said, finally managing to find her tongue . . . and the indignation that should have boiled to the surface immediately.

"I can't."

"If you don't, I'll punch you in the nose so hard it'll make your eyes water. I'm not in the habit of being manhandled by every passing drifter."

"It's not that," he said. "I—"

She drew back her fist. "You've got exactly one second."

He shrugged and set her down. She felt her stocking feet sink into warm, soft manure.

The Cowboys
Drew

Leigh Greenwood

LEISURE BOOKS   B   NEW YORK CITY

To Heather: If you want to find a good man, get a gun.

A LEISURE BOOK®

May 2000

Published by

Dorchester Publishing Co., Inc.
276 Fifth Avenue
New York, NY 10001

Cover Art by John Ennis
www.ennisart.com

ISBN 0-8439-4714-4

DREW

Chapter One

Drew Townsend settled her rifle at her shoulder. "Pull," she called.

Three clay pigeons rose into the air in rapid succession. Just as quickly, Drew fired three times and shattered all three. The challenger looked on in dismay, disgruntled and angry.

"Let me try again," he said.

"The man wants another chance, Gordy," Drew called out. "Load 'em up."

"Wait a minute," the man said. "I'm not ready."

"Take all the time you want," Drew said.

Drew was the sharpshooter for Earl Odum's Wild West

Show. They were traveling west from New York to the Mississippi River, playing in more than a hundred cities and small towns along the way. When they reached St. Louis, they'd head south to Memphis, then to New Orleans.

The show was laid out in a large field outside the small town of Sunnyvale. Stands now filled with over five thousand spectators had been set up along the east side of the field. The tents that housed the costumes, wagons, stagecoaches, Indian tents, and other props had been set up to the south, the pens holding the horses, cows, and buffalo to the north.

"I don't need a lot of time to get ready to shoot," the man responded angrily. "I just need to be the one to say when I'm ready."

Drew didn't reply. She had been through this hundreds of times. Most men got angry or embarrassed when a woman beat them at a skill they considered their special domain—marksmanship. Even though Drew had earlier demonstrated her ability with a variety of trick shots, there was always one man in the crowd who was convinced it couldn't be so hard if a woman could do it. She had learned to stand quietly, to give them all the time they needed to calm their nerves and take their shots. The outcome would be the same as it was last night and all the nights before that.

She always won.

"You ready?" the challenger called to the man operating the clay pigeon machine.

"Ready," he called back.

The man shifted nervously on the balls of his feet, leaning forward, then rocking back on his heels. Drew knew what was going through the man's mind, why he was taking so much time. He knew he was beaten. He didn't want to shoot and prove it all over again, but he couldn't back down before a woman.

He checked his rifle, changed his balance, and grew still. "Pull!" he shouted.

He missed all three. Earl Odum, ringmaster and owner, broke in to divert attention from the dispirited man. "Once again Miss Townsend proves there's nobody better with a rifle."

As the defeated man turned toward the stands, another man rose from his seat and started forward.

"She may not be as big as her opponents," Earl continued, "but she's huge in talent. There's simply nobody better."

Drew hated it when Earl called attention to her size. She longed to be as tall and strong as a man. She hated being trapped in a woman's body.

The second stranger reached the bottom of the stands. With the easy, fluid motion of a well-trained athletic body, he vaulted over the low wall that separated the performers from the crowd.

"I want to shoot against Miss Townsend," he announced.

"Her act is over for tonight," Earl said. "She'll—"

"I want to shoot against her," the stranger repeated. He was dressed in boots, denim pants that fit his hips and thighs like a second skin, a wide belt around his narrow waist, a chambray shirt that covered broad shoulders, and a broad-brimmed, flat-crowned hat that shaded his eyes. Drew wasn't normally affected by a man's appearance, even one as well formed as this man, but a frisson of excitement ran down her spine.

She decided to ignore it.

"You're too late. We're about to start the trick riding." Earl never let two men shoot against Drew in the same evening. It slowed the show too much and made the audience restless, especially the women, who didn't care about guns. The children, too, preferred the trick riders, even the boys old enough to have their own guns.

"Now," the man said. "I think I can do better than that other fellow."

The defeated challenger had disappeared into the crowd.

"Why can't you come back next time we're through here?" Earl asked.

"The audience wants to see someone go up against her who has a chance to win. What do you say?" he said, turning to the audience.

A round of applause appeared to give him all the support he needed. He came toward Drew. "You're pretty good, aren't you?"

No one called Drew *pretty good*. She was great, unbelievable, unbeatable, or any of several other superlatives. *Pretty good* was practically an insult. Drew made a conscious effort not to let her pride cause her to react. No one had beaten her in the two years she'd been with the show. "I try to give the public a good show," she said modestly.

His gaze blatantly raked her body. "I'd say that was an understatement."

Drew bridled. Her regular outfit was a skirt long enough to reach just below the tops of her boots, a vest, and a shirt buttoned up to her chin. Her favorite color was brown, because it reminded her of buckskin. But no matter what color vest she chose, she couldn't hide her breasts. Buttoning her shirt up to her throat didn't help either. She wore her dark brown hair down in soft curls that billowed in the breeze.

"Are you going to shoot or talk?" Drew asked. She suspected he might be trying to rattle her by his gaze and his rudeness. He would soon learn he was wasting his time. She'd faced hundreds of men, many more rude, more intimidating, more infuriating than he.

"I guess I'd better let my shooting do the talking for me. Do you have a rifle I can use? I don't have one handy."

Drew pointed to the rifle the last challenger had used. He looked at the rifle, and swung his gaze to Drew, then back to the rifle.

"Is there something wrong?" she asked.

"If there were, I wouldn't know, would I?" He turned to the audience. "What do you think, folks? Should I use the same rifle or ask for another?" Several men urged him to use another one. "How about letting me use your rifle?" he said, turning back to Drew.

She knew he meant to imply that the rifle had been fixed so he couldn't win. She handed him her rifle. "Use mine," she said, speaking loudly enough for everyone in the audience to hear her. "I'll use the other one."

It pleased her to see she'd caught him by surprise. Did he really think she'd give the challengers a faulty rifle? That angered her, but her anger subsided quickly. She knew he'd be the one to walk from the ring in defeat.

"Thanks," he said. "That is mighty sporting of you."

"You go first," she said. "I've already established my credentials."

He smiled. She'd scored a hit that time. It was up to him to prove he wasn't all talk and no substance.

He turned back to the audience. "Do you think I can hit the pigeons?"

The men answered with shouts of encouragement. It annoyed her that he was trying to turn the spectators against her.

"What happens if I make every shot?" he asked.

"I'll make every shot, too."

His eyebrows lifted ever so slightly. "You don't think there's a chance you'll miss?"

"If I do, I'll be out of a job by tomorrow." Earl, a small man with feminine good looks, didn't care about his performers, only the number of tickets they could sell.

"Maybe I shouldn't shoot after all," he said to the audience. "I wouldn't want to cause the little lady to lose her job."

Now he really was being insulting, implying the gentlemanly thing to do was to back down so she wouldn't lose her job.

"You can't back out now," Drew said. "You've got everybody's attention. They'll think you're a fake."

She didn't like cocky men, but this man gave the impression of being able to do just about anything he wanted. Drew was certain he wouldn't have come down out of the stands without knowing he had a good chance of beating her.

"I'm no fake," he said.

"Now's your chance to prove it." She gestured to the spectators. "Everybody's waiting."

The man lifted the rifle to his shoulder, checked its weight, its balance, the sight line. "In case you're curious, my name is Cole Benton."

"I wasn't curious," she replied.

14

"I'm a Tennessean by birth, a Texan by adoption, and a cowboy by preference," he announced to the audience, who laughed and applauded. They were enjoying his show.

"I'm sure Texas considers itself fortunate."

"If it doesn't now, it soon will. Pull!"

A clay pigeon flew out of the machine. Cole hit it.

When the crowd broke into noisy applause, Cole turned and executed an exaggerated bow. Then he turned to Drew as though he hadn't done anything unusual. "Your turn."

Drew pulled her rifle to her shoulder and gave the signal. One clay pigeon was propelled into the air and immediately shattered.

"There's obviously nothing wrong with that rifle," Cole said.

"Did you think there was?"

"Not all shows are completely honest."

"Don't you mean you didn't think it was possible for a woman to outshoot a man unless she cheated?"

"All things are possible," he said. He turned to the audience and asked, "What should we do next?"

Several people called for them to shoot two pigeons.

They did. There were no misses

Cole turned to the audience again, but they were already chanting: *"Three pigeons! Three pigeons!"*

"It looks like we've got our orders," he said to Drew.

The results were the same.

"The machine doesn't hold more than three pigeons," Drew said.

"What do you suggest we do next?" Cole asked.

The audience sat in silent, rapt attention. By now Drew

knew she was up against a superb shot. She didn't know if she could beat him. If she went down in defeat . . . well, she'd figure out what to do when it happened. Until then, she was the best shot in Texas, and she meant to prove it.

"Face away from the target," Drew said. "Shout pull, turn, and fire at the clay pigeon."

"That doesn't sound very easy," Cole said.

"It's not. Let me show you how it's done."

She turned her back. "Pull!" As she called out the command, she turned and fired at the pigeon. It shattered. Polite applause from the women.

"Good," Cole murmured. "Very good."

"You sound surprised."

"No, but it's still very good."

He took his position with his back to the machine, shouted the command, turned and fired.

He hit the target. The men and boys erupted with shouts and the noise of stamping feet. He had succeeded in dividing the crowd. That made Drew angry. This was her audience, yet half of them were rooting for Cole. It just went to show a woman couldn't depend on men when the chips were down.

"Two pigeons this time," Drew said. She was tired of this game. It was time to finish up and let the next event begin. Besides, this man irritated her.

She turned her back, called out the command, spun around, and hit both targets.

Cole tried it, missed one pigeon. The men in the audience fell silent.

"Let's try it again," Drew said. Again she hit both targets. The women responded by jumping up in their seats, shouting and cheering.

Again Cole missed one.

He turned to her, and with exaggerated gestures, bowed and kissed her hand. "To the winner!" he called loudly to the audience.

The women in the audience loved Drew's winning as well as Cole's courtly behavior in defeat. They applauded loudly. Even the children voiced their approval.

The men remained quiet.

The band started to play in the background, and Earl began the buildup for the trick riding. Drew turned to leave the ring. Cole Benton walked beside her.

"Shouldn't you go back to your seat?" Drew asked.

"Why?"

"Your family—friends, a young lady, I don't know!—somebody must be waiting for you."

"I don't have any family, and I didn't bring a young lady."

"Everybody has a family."

"I came alone."

Drew didn't like the tickle of excitement that stirred in some dark recess of her mind. Or the one that danced along her nerve endings. She wasn't about to put up with any of this nonsense. She'd stamp it out before anything got started. Cole Benton might be a fine figure of a man, but she wasn't interested in men, fine-figured or not. She had enough men in her family.

"You'll lose your seat," she warned him. "The trick riders are very popular."

"I'm sure they're no more popular than you."

"They're followed by an Indian battle. People fight over seats for that."

"They'll soon be fighting over seats to see you."

17

She stopped and turned without warning. "Why are you following me?"

"I want to talk to your boss."

"Why?"

"I've got a proposition to make."

"Well, he's over there," she said, pointing to Earl. "Now go away. I want to watch the trick riding."

"Why?"

"Because the two men doing the riding are my brothers."

Cole turned to the ring, a look of surprise spreading over his face. The questions would come next. It annoyed her to have to reveal anything to a stranger about her personal life, but there was no other way to explain how her brothers could be a half-breed Indian and a Negro.

"We're all adopted," she said.

"You must have an interesting family."

"I do, but if you're going to speak with the boss, you'd better do it now."

She didn't care if he spoke to Earl Odum or not. She just wanted him to leave her alone. And give her a chance to get rid of this annoying feeling that she might like to get to know something about him. He was an arrogant nuisance. She didn't need to know any more.

She turned away, directing her attention to the ring as Cole walked off toward Earl. The audience always started out a little cool. It made her angry that people weren't just as ready to applaud an Indian or a Negro as a white man. Zeke and Hawk were wonderful showmen, though, and by the time they were done, the spectators would be on their feet cheering. For Drew, that was vindication enough.

"That was a good performance. You ought to do it every night."

Drew turned at the sound of old Myrtle Rankin's voice. She was in charge of the costumes for the show. Her husband helped take care of the animals.

"I couldn't if I wanted to, which I don't," Drew answered. "I don't even know the man."

"He's nice-looking," Myrtle said.

Drew made a face. "You think every man under forty is nice-looking. I sometimes think your only requirement is that they be breathing."

Myrtle chuckled. Her laugh sounded rich and fruity, and came from deep within her large body. She looked like someone's kindly aunt or grandmother. It was hard to believe she'd once been part of a trapeze act.

"When you get to my age, you can't afford to be so choosy," she said. She looked back over her shoulder at Cole. "But this one *is* good-looking."

Drew turned to look at Cole, now in deep conversation with the boss. "I guess you could say he's not too bad," she admitted. She tried to ignore the tickle which now skittered down her spine. It was probably irritation. It would disappear as soon as Cole Benton went away.

"I have several very handsome brothers," Drew said. "I'm not impressed by Mr. Cole Benton."

Twenty-two-year-old Matt was extremely handsome, but nineteen-year-old Will turned heads wherever he went. Then there were Chet and Luke. They had left the ranch, but she could still see their handsome faces, remember their sensuality. She wasn't affected by it herself, but she understood how other women could be devastated.

"I thought you said you didn't know him," Myrtle said.

"I don't, but he told me his name during the shooting, like I was going to want to know it afterwards. The man has a greatly exaggerated opinion of himself."

"Looks to me like he's got good reason."

"Myrtle, will you stop drooling? He might be good-looking, even handsome, but he's conceited. I wouldn't be surprised to find he was trying to talk Earl into giving him a job."

"Well, you have to admit he made the shooting competition more interesting. Usually there's nobody who can come close to you. I still think it would be better if you missed once in a while."

Drew took great pride in her accuracy. Even though she hadn't missed a shot in the nearly two years she'd been with the show, she continued to practice daily, to develop new tricks and perfect them.

"I'm not going to miss shots just to make some man feel better," she said.

"I wasn't talking about the men," Myrtle said. "I meant the show. It would be more interesting if there was a chance someone could beat you."

"They pay to see me hit the targets," Drew said. "Not miss."

"I know," Myrtle said with a shrug. "It's a dilemma."

"What is?"

"How to be perfect and yet seem human."

Drew laughed and pointed to Hawk, who was doing one of his most popular tricks, leaning from the saddle at a full gallop to pick up three handkerchiefs dropped in a row. "If Hawk weren't perfect, he'd kill himself."

"That's why he seems human," Myrtle said. "If he or

Zeke does something wrong, they fall, break an arm or a leg, get trampled on by the horse. If you miss a target, nothing happens."

"You never mentioned this before."

"I guess I never understood what I felt was missing until tonight. The two of you generated a kind of excitement I haven't seen before. The audience felt it, too."

Drew had felt it as well, but she refused to attribute it to anything more than Cole's unexpectedly thrusting himself into the ring and proving himself a very capable shot. Okay, maybe a little had been due to his looks. If he hadn't been so conceited and sure of himself, she wouldn't have had so much trouble admitting she found him attractive.

Drew had been criticized before for not generating enough excitement. The boss wanted to make her more of an attraction. He said she was too mechanical, too lacking in emotional excitement. He wanted her to wear frilly dresses, put bows in her hair, skip about, do acrobatics, even wear a blond wig. Once she'd overheard two women in the Indian massacre say they didn't know why the boss kept such a dull act as a headliner.

"How can I make my act more exciting?" Drew had never asked this question before, not even of Zeke or Hawk. She didn't think she was dull, but she didn't try to fool herself into thinking her act was as thrilling as the real crowd pleasers, the battles between the Indians and the settlers, and the Indians and the army. The audience loved to watch the bloodthirsty fights, with people seeming to die right before their eyes. The women and children screamed at the sound of gunshots when actors fell from their saddles, appearing to be dying from some horrible wound. Everybody shouted encouragement to the settlers or the Army. Nobody rooted for the Indians.

"You could smile more when you go into the ring," Myrtle said. "Audiences like a pretty girl."

"I'm not pretty," Drew said. "I see proof of that every time I look in my mirror." Something she did as seldom as possible.

"Even if you weren't pretty, which you are," Myrtle insisted, "people like watching a woman. You ought to skip into the ring, smiling and waving at the audience."

Drew felt her stomach turn over. "I don't *skip* anywhere. I'd quit first."

"Okay, maybe skipping isn't the best idea, but smiling and waving would make the audience like you more. You look too serious."

Both Zeke and Hawk had told her that, but she couldn't bring herself to grin and wave like a silly female. Acrobats in circuses did that. So did the women who walked the tightrope. And those who rode the elephants. In fact, now that she thought about it, all circus performers smiled and waved.

"I suppose I could smile," Drew conceded. "But I'd feel silly waving."

"My Joe and I have been with some kind of show all our lives," Myrtle said. "Take it from me, you've got to smile and wave at the audience. I'm surprised the boss hasn't made you do it before now."

In a way, Drew was surprised too. Though her act was popular, it was too short to warrant a featured place in the program. Yet Drew's name and picture appeared on the handbills that circulated before they entered a town and on the posters put up after they arrived. The boss had made several suggestions, but he hadn't insisted on her acting on any of them.

"You ought to make more of your figure," Myrtle said. "There's nobody in this show that's got a better one."

"I hope you're not suggesting I wear tights."

"It would appeal to the men."

And make the women angry at her, which was exactly what she didn't want. The women were the major source of her support. They didn't have easy lives. Men held their wives, daughters, even their mothers, in virtual bondage. Drew's victories over the men who challenged her were more for the women of the audience than for herself. The women knew their condition in life wouldn't change, so they liked watching a woman who could meet men in their own arena and soundly defeat them.

That was one reason Drew never considered missing. Secondly, she didn't want to be attractive to her opposition. She wanted to crush them.

"I'll think about your suggestions," Drew said. She turned back to watch the finale of the riding act, the exchange of spears between riders at a gallop.

"They're coming over here," Myrtle said.

"Who?" Drew asked, without taking her eyes off Hawk and Zeke.

"The boss and that man."

"Cole," Drew said, half turning. "Why?"

"I don't know. I suppose the boss will tell us."

Drew reluctantly turned away from the ring as noisy applause broke out. She compared Cole and her boss as they walked toward her. No one could disagree that the boss was better looking. But he was such a pretty man— his complexion and eyelashes were the envy of many a woman—that she sometimes wondered how he kept such tight control over the men in the show, many of whom were nearly twice his size. He looked very much her own height and weight.

Cole towered at least six inches over the boss. His well-muscled shoulders, arms, and legs contrasted with the boss's slender build. Drew felt that tickle of interest stir once again. She angrily banished it. Cole Benton would soon be gone. And just as well. He made her feel uncomfortable.

"I've got good news," her boss announced. "I've just hired Cole to become part of your act."

Chapter Two

Cole could tell Drew didn't like the news. She didn't appear to be one who could—or would—hide her reaction to things she didn't like.

"I don't need anybody in my act," Drew said. "I certainly don't want him."

She said *him* like it was a dirty word. That surprised Cole. Women who went bad were usually interested in almost any man as long as he was attractive. Their need for the company of the opposite sex was well known. If one part of a woman's character was rotten, the rest usually was as well. In his experience, people who lived outside the law did so because they couldn't control the passions that bubbled and boiled inside them.

Maybe Drew Townsend was a different kind of pigeon.

"I don't mean he'll be in the whole act," the boss said.

"Just the part where somebody from the crowd challenges you."

"We don't need him. There's always somebody willing to volunteer," Drew said.

"Cole livened things up tonight," the boss said. "Did you notice how the audience loved it when he talked to them? Besides, he can give you a little competition."

"I haven't found the man yet who can give me competition," Drew said.

"I intend to practice," Cole said. "We can't have you lording it over all the men in the country, can we?"

"I'm not *lording it over* anybody," Drew stated. "I have a skill which I demonstrate through a series of planned shots. The boss is the one who insisted I let any man who wanted challenge me. It's not my fault they can't shoot as well as I can."

"But you need the challengers to make it look legitimate," Cole said.

She bridled. "What do you mean?"

"Like you said, they're planned shots. People might think there's a trick involved, that you aren't really as good as you seem. In fact, you're so good you make it seem too easy to be difficult."

He didn't mind flattering her, especially when he was telling the truth. He hadn't thought more than two or three men in the country could shoot like that, certainly no woman. He'd been stunned to discover she was so young and attractive.

He'd never expected to find himself so strongly attracted to her. She wasn't pretty in the style of the Memphis belles his mother kept pushing at him. Her attraction came from her strength, her directness, her honesty. She was a woman who knew herself and didn't care if people liked her or not. Cole liked that kind of raw strength, the kind he'd found in Texas when he was a Texas Ranger.

But if the evidence against her could be believed, she was one of the cleverest thieves in the West.

He'd known when he stepped into the ring, he'd lose. He was good, the best shot on the force when he'd been in the Rangers, but he didn't compare to this young woman. It hadn't been easy to walk into the ring knowing she would beat him—he did have his pride—but his challenging her had been an essential part of his strategy.

"It was real smart of you to let me use your rifle," he continued. "That removed any doubt that you were as good as you seemed."

"There never was any *doubt* about my ability," Drew stated, her back rigid with outraged pride.

"You can never tell what's in people's minds." He hadn't meant to rile her. He was trying to get in the show, and it would be easier if she accepted him willingly. Every word he said seemed to make her more determined to dislike him.

"I don't care about all that," the boss said. "All I care about is the audience reaction, and they reacted more tonight than they ever have."

"We were talking about that," Myrtle said. "Drew has a few ideas about how to liven up her act."

Cole could tell the old lady was against him, too.

"Good," the boss said. "I'll be glad to see them, but I'm still going to have Cole come out of the stands to challenge her."

"What if somebody else stands up first?" Drew asked.

"Get rid of them as quickly as you can so Cole can move in. The audience really liked him."

"I'm not surprised, considering the way he shamelessly played up to the men in the crowd."

"It was only natural to talk to them," Cole said. "Besides, if I hadn't, you wouldn't have let me shoot."

"Do it again tomorrow tonight," Earl said. "It was great."

Drew turned to her boss. "Do you expect me to stand around every night while he makes a spectacle of himself?"

"I'd like it better if you livened up your part of the act to match his," Earl said. "I've given you one of the top billings because you're really good. You can become one of the real draws for this show, but you have to be willing to make some changes. Myrtle says you're working on some new ideas. Good. Listen to her. She's been around shows for fifty years. She knows what works. I have to go with what we have, and Cole is it. Why don't you two get to know each other?"

"I don't think that's a good idea," Drew said.

Cole hadn't expected she would.

"Why?" the boss asked.

"He's supposed to be a stranger," Drew explained. "The audience will suspect a plant if we act too familiar."

"Then don't act familiar," the boss said.

Shouts of applause signaled the beginning of the mock battle between the Indians and the cavalry.

"I've got to go," the boss said. "Talk it over with your brothers."

Cole looked up to see a half-breed Indian and a black man approaching—the trick riders. He'd almost forgotten them. A foolish thing to do. Drew needed help. She couldn't carry off all those robberies by herself. He'd lay odds these two men were expert shots themselves. The eyewitness accounts hadn't agreed on all points. In fact, sometimes he wondered if people didn't make up things just to get their names in the newspapers. But three things had appeared in every account.

First, the leader of the group was an attractive woman. The second fact on which everyone agreed was that the woman was a crack shot. She was so good she'd been able to disable anyone foolish enough to attempt to stop her by shooting him in the arm, shoulder, or leg. The wounds hurt, but they weren't life-threatening. Because no one had died in these robberies, they hadn't received high priority. Tracking down the robbers had been complicated by the fact that no two robberies ever took place in the same town. When police tried to follow up, the trail had gone so cold it seemed to have disappeared altogether.

The only lead they'd managed to come up with so far was that the robberies occurred when the Wild West Show was in the area or had just left. The authorities had come to the conclusion that the robbers were using the show to take them out of the area before the local police could track them down. Tonight's performance was the last in Indiana. If a robbery took place, the show would be in Illinois before police could organize a pursuit.

Cole Benton, working as an undercover agent for the United States government, had been chosen to get himself hired as part of the show. He was supposed to travel with them and collect information about the suspects. If he could infiltrate the gang, it would be easier to catch them. If not, he was supposed to watch everything they did. If they tried to commit another robbery, government agents would be on hand to arrest them.

"You two put on a good show tonight," the black man said to Drew. "Maybe you ought to do something like that every night."

"The boss has already come to that conclusion," Drew said. "He's hired Cole to be the volunteer from the crowd every night."

"He sure got the crowd going tonight," the black man said. "They were ready for us. We never got such a response before."

"They liked us a lot," the Indian said.

Cole noted he had almost no accent. He obviously hadn't lived with his tribe in a long time. He could easily pass for a white man. It would be equally simple to have the black man wear gloves and a mask. It was possible Cole had stumbled onto the nucleus of the gang first thing.

Cole told himself not to jump to conclusions. It seemed too easy to have identified the gang within minutes of being hired. He had to wait, look at everyone in the show, study their movements, weigh each fact objectively. Still, these three seemed to fit the bill perfectly.

"I Night Hawk," the Indian said, extending his hand. "Half-breed Comanche or half-breed white man, depending on point of view."

Okay, his grammar wasn't perfect, but Cole doubted most people would notice. He sounded like he was trying to make a joke, but there was nothing humorous about his expression. His face remained impassive, his black eyes wide open, his gaze steady and penetrating.

"I'm Cole Benton," Cole said, shaking hands.

"I'm Zeke," the black man said. "You treat Drew right, and we'll get along fine. You do anything to make her look bad, and I'll kill you."

Neither his words nor his expression contained so much as a hint of humor. Cole had no doubt he meant exactly what he said. Cole didn't know a thing about this strange family Drew was supposed to have, but she had two very effective bodyguards. Not that he could see anybody trying to take advantage of her when she could probably shoot his ears off at fifty yards.

"Does that include shooting better than she does?"

"You can't do that, so don't put yourself in a sweat trying. Come on, Drew. We've got to get out of here."

"When are we going to talk about our act?" Cole asked.

"I don't see any need to talk about *my* act," she said. "If I do, we can do it on the train tonight. As far as I'm concerned, the less we have to do with each other, the better."

"Don't be so hard on him," Zeke advised. "He did liven things up. I've been telling you for a long time you had to do something."

They walked away, talking among themselves, the two men agreeing Cole's addition to the show was a good thing.

Cole felt the tug of attraction again. Maybe it was the curve of her hips, the strength of her back, possibly the way she held her shoulders so erect, even her confident stride. He wasn't sure. There was one thing he *was* sure of—she was the antithesis of the women he'd grown up with. He turned to the older woman the boss had called Myrtle. She'd been watching him with Drew and her brothers. "She seems a very determined young woman."

"She's tough as hickory, but she's sweet as can be. I'm Myrtle Rankin. I take care of the costumes. My husband feeds the animals."

"I'm Cole Benton," Cole said. "I hope you aren't against my joining Miss Townsend's act."

"No, but I don't like to see anything upset Drew."

"All her boss and I are trying to do is make the act a crowd pleaser."

"I understand, but you can't expect Drew to like it very much."

"I don't see why."

"You don't understand much about women, do you?"

That startled him. Part of the reason he'd been chosen for this job was his popularity with women.

"Apparently I don't understand Miss Townsend. Why don't you explain her to me?"

Myrtle laughed. "The first thing you have to do is stop calling her Miss Townsend. Drew hates formality."

"She seemed pretty formal to me."

"Cold to you, even angry," Myrtle corrected. "Not formal. Drew doesn't like most men. Doesn't trust them, either."

"She seems to trust those two bodyguards just fine."

"They're her brothers. The couple that adopted Drew raised a whole horde of orphans—eleven, I think. Drew was the only girl."

"Now I understand why she can shoot like a man."

"No, you don't. Drew tries to be better than her brothers, not just to learn from them."

"You seem to know a lot about her."

"Things aren't always easy for an old couple in a show

like this. She watches out for us." She chuckled. "You'd think she was our mother, the way she acts sometimes."

"That'll be a good trait when she marries."

"She doesn't plan to get married. I wish she weren't so set against it, but nothing I can say has been able to change her mind."

"But that doesn't make any sense. She's loyal to her brothers, supposedly to the family that raised her, and she's got such a strong mothering instinct she takes in old couples who ought to be giving her advice."

"Drew will be the first to tell you that as long as she makes her own way, she doesn't have to make sense."

The more Cole heard about this woman, the less he understood her. He guessed he didn't really have to understand her. His job was to get enough evidence on her so he could arrest her, not marry her, but the better he knew her, the better able he'd be to work his way inside her defenses. His captain thought trying to become a member of the gang was his best approach. Cole wasn't so sure of that. This tug of attraction wouldn't go away. Besides, Zeke didn't look like an easy man to fool, and that Hawk character looked perfectly willing to cut his heart out and have it for dinner. Unless he was mistaken, Zeke had been a slave. That meant he hated white men. So why was he a brother to a white woman? Not to mention the half-breed Comanche. Cole wondered if Drew's whole family was a gang of thieves, not a family at all. Everything made more sense that way.

Cole forced himself to laugh. "Since I'm going to be working with Miss Townsend—Drew—on a regular basis, I'll have to depend on you to give me hints. It won't do to have her mad at me all the time. Besides, I have some ideas about how to liven up her act. I need to know how to suggest them so she won't point that rifle at me. I've had ample evidence she knows how to use it."

"I could tell you not to make any suggestions, but I can see you've already made your mind up. Men are like that, determined to do what they want despite advice, even when they've asked for it."

"Am I that bad?"

"Seems like it."

"I'll have to see if I can change that."

"Men never change. They seldom bother trying."

It seemed Drew wasn't the only woman with a poor opinion of men.

"I'll see if I can be the exception."

Myrtle smiled gently. "I wouldn't bother. You're only a walk-on. I don't expect you'll last more than a couple of weeks."

Her harsh evaluation of his chances of making it with the show unsettled Cole. He had to last more than a couple of weeks. He was certain it would take him longer than that to ingratiate himself with Drew. She was dead set against him. It would likely take days just for her to begin to thaw.

Drew had hoped something would happen to cause Cole Benton to change his mind, or the boss to change his, but she wasn't surprised when she saw him enter her car on the train taking the Wild West Show to their next engagement. She was even less surprised when he stopped by her seat.

"Is that seat taken?" he said, referring to the one next to her.

"Yes. It belongs to my brother."

"Which one?"

"Whichever one returns first. The other will sit across from me."

"How about the seat next to him?"

It wasn't taken. It never was. The hard seats were jammed close together to get as many people as possible into one car. When they had to keep the windows closed to protect their clothes from being set on fire by sparks from the engine, the temperature and body odors could become unbearable. Drew was thankful they always traveled at night. The show usually engaged enough space on the train that the people could seat themselves in small, friendly groups. Drew was seldom forced to sit among strangers. It was clear Mr. Benton didn't consider himself a stranger.

And to be fair to him, she guessed she shouldn't either. He was going to be part of her act. She ought to be civil to him at least. And she would be . . . until he left. And he would leave soon. He looked like the kind to wander from one job to the next, staying nowhere long, avoiding putting down roots, making commitments, even making friends. The people who worked in the show fell into clearly defined groups. The regulars like Myrtle and Joe were okay. The show was their life. They were dependable. They'd stick to the end. Then there were people who were building a career. The Wild West Show was only a stepping stone in their climb up to the next rung on the professional ladder. Next came the seasonal workers—

the Indians, Mexicans, cowboys, soldiers, people recruited for a specific job for the season. They would stay until the show disbanded for the winter. Finally, there were the drifters. They drifted in, stayed a few weeks—or days—then drifted out again.

Cole Benton came under the heading of drifters. That was good, because that queer feeling in her gut was acting up again. It was probably heartburn. Drew's mother, Isabelle Maxwell, always said she had heartburn when her husband, Jake, did something she didn't like, or when he wouldn't let her have her way. Drew guessed that was what Cole was doing, giving her heartburn because she didn't like his being here.

"Are you going to make me wait until your brothers get back so I can ask them?"

"Zeke won't sit next to any white man," she said.

"Are all your brothers black or Indian?"

She hated having to explain her family to people she didn't like. "I should have said he won't sit next to any white man not in our family. All my brothers except Zeke and Hawk are white."

"I'd like to hear more about your family," Cole said. "It sounds very unusual."

Her heartburn was getting worse. She wished he'd go away. "I don't talk about my family to strangers."

He sat down across from her without waiting for permission. "Since we're going to be working together, I don't really qualify as a stranger."

"Of course you do. I don't know anything about you except your name. And I don't want to know any more," she added quickly. With the slightest prompting, he'd probably launch into his life story.

"There's not much to tell," he said. "I grew up on a poor cow ranch in Texas. I've been a cowhand, ridden guard on the stage, even did a short hitch in the army. That's where I learned to shoot. But the army didn't pay much. I figured I could put my shooting to better use in a show like this."

"How many shows have you been in?"

"This is my first."

Just what she'd expected. A drifter, going through life with no goal in mind, letting fate and circumstance pilot him willy-nilly from one job to another. Exactly the kind of man she wanted nothing to do with.

"What made you want to join our show, other than a desire to show off by beating me?"

He laughed easily. "I saw a chance to do something I like and am good at. Naturally I couldn't resist the chance to work with you."

"Why? You know nothing about me." She certainly hoped he didn't expect to have anything more than a superficial working relationship with her.

"You're famous," Cole said. "And you're an unbeatable shot. I can learn a lot from you."

She'd ignored dozens of men who were far better at flattery than he. "Do you think I'm fool enough to train my own competition?"

"I'll never be good enough to beat you. But the better I am, the more the crowds will be rooting for you to beat me."

Well, he wasn't as stupid or as bad at flattery as she'd thought. Now if this heartburn would just go away, she could probably put up with him until Zeke and Hawk returned. He might be a worthless vagabond, but he wasn't hard to look at.

Drew usually refused to admit any man was attractive. She wouldn't even say that about Will, and he was beautiful. Cole was attractive in a different way. You couldn't say he was beautiful. His skin was too rough and brown, his hair an ordinary shade of brown. He had thin lips, thick eyebrows, and enough lines in his forehead and around his eyes to have spent the last twenty years squinting into the sun.

But he had beautiful blue eyes, a deep blue, the color of the stones in a necklace Jake had given Isabelle at Christmas. Jake said it was lapis, but she wasn't sure. She never paid much attention to things like that. She had a few pieces of family jewelry her aunt had given her, but you couldn't wear jewelry on the ranch. It would get in the way. Even if it didn't, a woman on horseback would look stupid wearing jewelry.

Unless she was mistaken, it was his smile that was giving her heartburn. It couldn't be sincere. She was certain he used it to charm people into letting him do pretty much what he wanted, which was probably as little as possible. That was why it was giving her heartburn. She knew it was fake, that he didn't mean it. The one thing she hated above everything was a man who made you think one thing when he intended to do something else. But all men were like that, weren't they?

Everybody except her brothers and Jake, that is. If she could find a man like them . . . She let that thought slip away. She had no desire to finish it, no need. Even if she could have found someone exactly like Jake, it wouldn't have made any difference.

"We can probably find some time to practice tomorrow

while you're setting up for the show," Cole said. "You can give me some pointers then."

"The crew sets the targets and the clay pigeon machine in place. I just walk on, do my act, walk off, and I'm done for the evening."

"That's another thing I want to talk to you about. You shouldn't just walk on. There's no energy in walking. No excitement, either. Compared to everything else in the show, it actually seems dull."

He might be a lazy son of a so-and-so, but he certainly was full of opinions. It seemed easier to let him talk and forget whatever he said than to get him to shut up. She was tired and a little sleepy. She had taken an extralong ride that afternoon.

"I suppose you know exactly what will start everybody talking about my act. Plus, get the boss to give me a big raise."

"Once you become the star of the show, he'll have to give you a raise."

"And just how are you going to make me the star? I assume you're not about to teach me how to shoot?"

"No, just help you present yourself differently. Can you ride a horse?"

"Of course I can."

"You don't have to get upset. For all I know, you could have grown up in Chicago or Cincinnati."

"I grew up in Texas. I can ride and shoot just like any other respectable Texas female."

"Can you do both at the same time?"

"Why do you want to know?" She could do both in her sleep.

"I think you ought to enter the ring on horseback," he said, "shooting at targets set all round the ring."

She looked up. Zeke and Hawk had returned. They had their saddlebags over their shoulders. She knew everything of importance they owned was in those saddlebags. The show might consider itself one big family, but Zeke and Hawk had never felt part of the group. Drew hadn't either at first, but once she got to know Myrtle and Joe, everything changed.

"You're just in time to hear how Mr. Benton intends to revamp my act," she said to her brothers.

"Call me Cole," he said.

"*Cole* thinks I ought to enter the ring on horseback, shooting at targets around the ring."

"Sounds like a good idea," Zeke said, sitting down next to Drew. Cole moved over to make room for Hawk. "I've been saying you need to liven it up. You could be a star if you'd just make it more exciting."

"But that's showing off," she said, irritated that Zeke supported Cole. "It's not dignified. What do you think, Hawk?"

"Dignity is for old people. We need to make money fast. You ought to do it."

"Great," Cole said. "We can get started in the morning. Where do you get horses?"

"Joe handles the horses, but I never ride a horse I haven't chosen."

"No problem. I can't wait until they see you come out with pistols blazing. You'll have them jumping up and down with excitement. They won't be able to take their eyes off you until you're finished."

He started describing the entrance as he envisioned it.

Zeke entered enthusiastically into the discussion. Then Hawk was drawn in. Cole didn't hog the discussion. He acted as if he appreciated what the boys had to say. He even asked Drew what she thought.

"I'm listening," she said. "I'll tell you when you're done."

She refused to show even the slightest bit of excitement or approval. She didn't want him to think she wanted his interference, even though he did have a few good ideas. If he and the boys could come up with a plan she liked, she'd probably consider it. But she wasn't making any promises, especially to a stranger who could drift away as quickly as he'd drifted in.

Still, she liked the idea of making her act more popular with the crowds. It would help her make more money, help her reach her goal more quickly. If she was perfectly honest with herself, she liked the possibility she might get more credit for her shooting ability. The Wild West Show was a great success. The audience loved the fights and chases and all the things the Wild West Show brought into town— without the problems prompted by *real* bullets and arrows.

But her performance entailed a level of skill most of the other parts of the show didn't require. She'd tried not to be jealous of the popularity of Indian attacks and buffalo hunts, but she couldn't help it. She didn't want to steal anybody's thunder. She just wanted a little of her own. If Cole Benton could give her that, she just might give him a few pointers on how to improve his shooting.

If she could just get rid of this dratted heartburn. If this was going to happen every time he was around her, she'd just have to give up the idea of being more popular. It wasn't worth feeling like a fire had been kindled in her gut.

Chapter Three

Cole lay awake in his bed in the sleeping car. The noise of the wheels as they ran over the rails, the click as they crossed junctions, the swaying of the car, and the heat all combined to make it nearly impossible for him to relax. He'd spent more comfortable nights on the Texas prairie.

The mattress was too hard and lumpy, the bed too short for his height. Since he wasn't in a closed compartment, he was bothered by people constantly moving up and down the aisles all night. That left him more than enough time to think about Drew.

He didn't know anything about her except what Myrtle had told him. He had no way of knowing how much of that was the truth. There was no reason for Drew to be more honest with Myrtle than with anybody else, but it didn't surprise him that both Myrtle and her husband thought very highly of the sharpshooter. It would be to her advantage to develop close relations with other members of the show. The more the old geezers liked her, the less likely they would be to believe she could be the leader of a group of very clever robbers.

All of the headliners had their own hotel rooms. They could come and go as they pleased without anyone knowing where they'd been or how long they'd been away. They only had to be present for the show itself. In Drew's case, he intended to put an end to that. He planned to start practicing with her every day. He'd decided the best way to spend a lot of time with her, to probe her defenses, was to convince her to let him remake her act. She was very, very good. Incredible, in fact, but the act wasn't exciting. She needed to turn herself into a performer as well as a marksman. She had to learn to touch the audience with her personality, not just her skill. Skill was a cold thing. A brilliant performer could be admired without being adored. He had to find some way for Drew to reach out to the audience, make it important to them that she hit every target, even when she wasn't shooting against anyone.

Myrtle had said Drew had a strong mothering instinct. If so, that ought to do it. If she could convince the audience she cared about them, they would care about her. But maybe that mothering instinct was a hoax, camouflage so people wouldn't see her real nature. He certainly hadn't seen any signs she wanted to mother him. She'd been as cold as a West Texas blizzard.

She hadn't tossed his ideas out the window, but he knew he couldn't take credit for that. If her brothers, or whoever those men really were, hadn't agreed with him, she would have ignored everything he'd said. He had to find a way to get around her dislike of him.

Or a way to change it into like.

That appealed to him more. Drew Townsend might not be the most clever thief in the country, but she was without a doubt the most attractive. Her face wouldn't stop trains, but her body could empty them. That was something else he had to remember. She had to wear clothes that would take advantage of her spectacular figure.

Just the thought of her body clothed in a revealing outfit caused his body to harden. He'd have to watch that. She didn't look the type to be amused by a man's physical response to her attractions. Neither would it do him any good to let his libido overpower his brain. He didn't think that was a possibility—he'd had too much experience controlling himself over the years—but even a brief lapse in control with this woman might be fatal.

Still, he couldn't discount the possibility that a romance might be the best way to allay her suspicions and enable him to enter her inner circle. Female outlaws weren't much different from other women. Even when they knew their lovers couldn't be trusted, they tended to tell them everything they knew. He doubted Drew could be gotten around that easily, but it was something to keep in mind.

But pretending to be romantically interested in Drew bothered him. He knew he had to stop the robberies, that he had to do whatever was necessary to catch the thieves, but his conscience rebelled at pretending to love Drew when he didn't. He didn't know why that should bother him. He'd never felt guilty about lying to a crook before.

Maybe it was because he felt she might be capable of real love.

She acted as cold as a sleet storm with him, but he had the feeling a hot fire burned somewhere deep inside her. Women weren't like men in that respect. If a man seemed cold and hard, that was pretty much what he was like. He usually wasn't anything worth redeeming. You might as well shoot him and save everybody a lot of trouble.

He'd met women who seemed cold and hard on the surface. But no matter what kind of front they tried to put up, they always had a soft inside. It didn't mean they wouldn't fill you full of holes if you did something they didn't like. It just meant they'd be sorry afterwards.

Men changed loyalties easily. Women usually remained faithful for life.

Cole found himself feeling a little uneasy about that. Drew might be a thief and a crook—if so, she didn't deserve the same consideration he would give another woman—but he didn't want to engage her feelings. He wanted any possible relationship to remain on the purely physical level. That would probably suit her just as well.

He turned over in his narrow bunk. The occasional screech of the wheels as they rounded a curve went through him like a knife. He'd have to learn to sleep better if he wanted to be able to shoot well enough to push Drew to her limits.

He wondered how she was sleeping. He'd hoped they'd be in the same car, but he hadn't been surprised when they'd put him in with the cowboys and some of the crew. Their snoring was enough to wake even a sound sleeper.

Drew didn't look as though she ever had trouble sleeping. There was a freshness about her, a luminescence about her skin that made her seem young and virginal. She probably depended on that in her robberies. No red-blooded American male would suspect her of being a thief. The people in the banks, trains, and steamboats she robbed were probably too stunned to do anything but stare in disbelief until they'd been stripped of their gold and Drew's gang had escaped without firing a shot.

If he had been one of the victims, he too would have been left standing with his mouth open, especially if she did something clever like shoot the cigar out of his mouth, or a pen off its stand on the desk. The robber always did something like that. The official opinion was that she did it to keep her victims so stunned, they wouldn't offer any opposition when she made her get-away. That fitted in perfectly with Cole's opinion of women. They might be capable of committing almost any crime, but they stopped short of cold-blooded murder.

But something in his gut told him Drew was different. She seemed to have too much pride, to hold herself to a higher standard than she expected of people around her. Cole had known men and women like that. They would actually suffer before they would let themselves fall short of the expectations they'd set for themselves. He'd gotten that message from Drew almost from the beginning, but he'd discounted it because it ran counter to the information his captain had on the group that performed the robberies. She was the only woman who could do what the leader of the thieves had done.

It had to be Drew.

He experienced a sharp feeling of disappointment. He didn't *want* her to be guilty. If she was, he didn't want to

46

be the one to catch her. He told himself not to be a fool. He had nothing to do with her being guilty. If he discovered it, arrested her, helped to convict her and send her to prison, he was only doing his job.

But something inside rebelled against this assignment. For the first time, he felt dirty, underhanded, like he was spying on an innocent person. She couldn't be guilty. She acted too innocent.

How did he know that? Drew might be the best actress in the world. He'd just met her today. He didn't consider himself a good actor, and he'd been able to pass himself off as an innocent bystander, a drifter who saw an opportunity to make money doing something easy. If he could do it, so could Drew.

But he didn't want to believe she had.

Fisher's Creek, Illinois

Drew did her best to quell the feeling of excitement. Cole's idea for her entrance had certainly livened up the beginning of her act. Even the old people in the show had stopped to watch her practice. They had set up in a field about a mile from town. At the first sound of gunshots, a dozen milk cows grazing in a nearby field had lumbered out of sight.

"It would look better if we moved the targets farther away," Cole said. "Could you still hit them?"

"Yes."

"Be sure. Nothing would be worse than missing your targets on your entrance."

"If I couldn't hit a still target from a horse, I couldn't call myself a sharpshooter."

"From the saddle."

"Yes."

"Standing up?"

"Do you mean standing up *on the horse*?"

"While it's moving."

"I guess so. I mean, I haven't done it in a long time."

"Good. It'll make an even better entrance."

"Come on," Zeke said. "I'll hold the horse for you."

Drew wasn't so sure about this. "Doesn't this get into the area of acrobatics?"

"Sure," Cole said, "but that makes it more exciting. You'll have to take off those boots. Your horse won't appreciate your heels digging into him."

Drew was losing control of her act. She had accepted the idea of making her entrance on horseback. She even liked it. But this business of standing up on a moving horse was something else.

"Why don't you ride around the ring a few times," Cole suggested.

Drew felt her spine stiffen. "You don't think I can do it, do you?"

"You said it had been awhile. It'll give you a chance to get the feel of it again."

He didn't fool her. He didn't think she could do it. Well, she wasn't sure either, but Cole Benton wasn't going to make her look bad. She sat down and pulled off her boots.

"I haven't tried a stunt like this in a long time," she said to Zeke.

He laughed. "I remember you doing it just to prove you could."

"I didn't have to hit targets then."

Zeke removed the saddle and the saddlecloth from the horse. She would have to ride bareback. She wouldn't have anything to hold on to, not even the reins.

"Here, let me give you a hand up," Zeke said.

Even though she'd been around Zeke for ten years, she kept forgetting how big and tall he was. He virtually lifted her off the ground and placed her on the horse. Using his hand to steady herself, she stood up on the broad haunches of the animal. She wouldn't have any trouble getting a foothold, but standing up and shooting straight might be a different matter.

"Do you want me to walk him first?" Zeke asked.

She moved her feet about, testing her balance, waiting to see how the horse reacted to her weight. He acted as though he didn't even know she was on his back. Her balance felt good, secure.

"Let him go," she said. "Let's see how much I remember."

Hawk had picked out a horse trained to canter in a circle around a ring. As soon as it started forward, she remembered the feel of haunches rising and falling beneath her feet. She smiled at the familiar sensation, the ease with which she fell into the rhythm. She exulted in the sense of freedom, of lightness, of being detached from anything that kept her earthbound. She remembered the feeling she'd had when she first tried it, the excitement, the sense of accomplishment, that she could do anything she wanted to, as long as she was not afraid to try.

She felt her spirits soar, her body light enough to fly. She felt like a child again, when there were no limits and all things were possible.

As the horse made its circuit around the ring, she felt herself smiling as she looked at the faces around her, faces that reflected surprise, pleasure, even amusement. She noted in all of them an element of pride in her accomplishment, of shared community.

"Toss me a pistol," she yelled. She felt invincible. She could do anything. Cole tossed her his. She caught it.

"We ought to try it that way sometime," he called as she cantered past. "The crowd would love it."

She wasn't thinking about the crowd. She was thinking about the expression she'd seen on Cole's face. He smiled at her as though he *liked* to see her do something he hadn't expected her to do. There was no jealousy, no resentment. Maybe a little bit of pride.

She jerked her thoughts from his face. She was approaching the targets. She dropped to a half crouch, and fired three shots.

She hit all three targets, but only one bull's-eye.

"Good," Cole called out.

But one bull's-eye out of three was terrible. She was used to perfection, and she wouldn't settle for anything less. The targets were in a straight line, but her horse was running in a circle. Each target represented a different angle, with almost no time to readjust.

"Position the targets in a curve, to match the ring," she called to Cole. By the time she'd circled around again, he had the first three targets repositioned. She fired her last three shots. Two bull's-eyes, one off center. Not good enough.

"Toss me your pistol," she called to Zeke. "I've got it figured out now."

By the time she came around the circle again, Cole had

arranged all six targets in a curve that exactly followed her horse's path. She drew the pistol and fired at the six targets as she made her pass. She hit all dead center.

"Unbelievable!" Cole called. "I didn't think you could do it."

She hadn't been entirely sure herself, but she wasn't about to tell him. Nor would she tell him about the warmth that spread through her at his compliment, his obvious pride at what she'd accomplished. She couldn't account for it. Jake and the boys had always been proud of her accomplishments. Isabelle had encouraged her in everything she'd tried. She was used to encouragement. She was used to people being pleased with her success.

Why should Cole be any different?

Probably because she'd expected him to want her to fail. She'd even suspected he might be hoping to get her job. She'd been wrong. He only wanted to find ways to make the act more exciting.

Damn! Her heartburn was back. Worse than ever this time. She didn't know why he should have this effect on her. But if it kept up, she would have to find ways to avoid him. She didn't like this peculiar feeling. When combined with the warm flush that spread to every part of her body, she felt quite unlike herself.

"I'm going around again," she called out. "I want to make sure I've got it down."

Zeke tossed her a new pistol. She put Cole and his smile out of her mind and focused her attention on the targets. She hit the bull's-eye on all six.

"Did I hit the center of every one or just inside the circle?" she asked Cole. The trick had to be perfect, or she wouldn't use it.

"Center on two, close on the others," Cole said.

"That's not good enough," she called out. "Set up new targets, and I'll try again."

She ran the trick three more times.

"Perfect on all six," Cole called after the last one. "I think you're ready for tonight."

"I want to see the targets." She meant dead center, not close. She couldn't be sure Cole would hold her to the same high standards she set for herself. The horse circled again. Zeke caught him and brought him to a halt. Drew sat down on the horse and slid off.

She landed in Cole's arms.

The shock knocked the sense out of her. She couldn't describe it any other way. Nothing else could account for the fact that not a single coherent thought remained in her head. He caught her easily, as if he'd done it before. He balanced her lightly against his chest, but that didn't keep her from being acutely aware she was leaning against his body. Heat and tension passed between them like their clothes weren't even there.

"Put me down," she said, finally managing to find her tongue . . . and the indignation that should have boiled to the surface immediately.

"I can't."

"If you don't, I'll punch you in the nose so hard it'll make your eyes water. I'm not in the habit of being man-handled by every passing drifter."

"It's not that," he said. "I—"

She drew back her fist. "You've got exactly one second."

He shrugged and set her down. She felt her stocking feet sink into warm, soft manure. Zeke burst out laughing as she looked up at Cole, a fire cone of fury rising up within her.

"I tried to warn you," he said.

"You should have seen your face," Zeke said, then went off on another gust of laughter.

"Here, I'll carry you over to the stands, where you can sit down."

"I can walk," she said.

"I'd let him carry you," Zeke said. "No telling what else you might step in."

Drew had no intention of letting herself be carried anywhere, but Cole took the decision out of her hands. "If you'll get me some water," he said to Zeke, "I'll see what I can do about washing her feet."

Zeke went off chuckling while Drew found herself once again in a very strong, very unsettling, very *male* embrace.

"Do you always plop women down in manure so you can carry them off?" she asked. She couldn't decide whether she would look sillier walking out of the ring in her soiled socks or being carried in Cole's arms. By the time she'd made up her mind to walk and be damned with the mess, Cole was setting her down on the lowest seat in the stands set up for the throngs who would crowd into the arena in a few hours.

"I can't recall doing anything like this before," Cole said. He looked at her feet, sniffed, and wrinkled his nose. "I can't say that I recommend it."

"I should hope not." She couldn't recall when she'd heard a more foolish statement. "What are you doing?" He'd taken hold of her leg, rested it across his own.

"Taking your socks off," he said.

"No you're not."

"They're ruined."

"I can see that."

"They've got to come off."

"I know that, but you're not going to do it."

"Who is?"

"I am."

"I wouldn't advise it."

There he went again, trying to seem as if he were doing her a favor when she knew he was doing just the opposite. "I don't care what you advise," she snapped. "They're my socks, and I'm taking them off."

She didn't like the way he looked at her, as though he'd just told her something that was good for her, and he couldn't help it if she insisted upon doing the wrong thing. An uneasy feeling circled around the edges of her outrage. She might think he was doing this just to be aggravating—she might even be *certain* of it—but ignoring him moments ago had gotten her into this mess.

"Why wouldn't you advise it?" she asked.

"It would be improper."

He looked like butter wouldn't melt in his mouth. He was up to something. "What would be improper about taking off my socks?"

"Maybe improper isn't the right word."

She thought so. He was bluffing.

"Maybe I should have said embarrassing."

"Why should I be embarrassed?" She was losing patience with him.

"Well, you're wearing a short skirt."

"Of course I'm wearing a short skirt. Have you ever tried to stand up on a moving horse in a long skirt?"

"No, ma'am. I don't recall ever having occasion to wear a long skirt. But if I had, I'm sure I wouldn't have tried to ride a horse at that time."

She was going to hit him. Just as soon as she got back on her feet.

"You can't reach your sock without pulling your leg up under you," he said. "If you do that, I think you might show more than you want."

She hadn't noticed that several of the cowboys had come to lean against a fence to watch her. She felt the heat in her cheeks as she thought of what they'd do if she raised her leg enough to be able to reach her socks. She felt anger, too.

"You're enjoying this, aren't you?"

"No, ma'am."

"Don't lie to me, and don't call me ma'am."

"Well, it is a mite funny, if you see what I mean."

"I don't." Now she was lying. "I mean, I can see why *you'd* think it was funny, but I don't see how you can laugh and call yourself a gentleman."

"I'm not laughing."

She stared hard at him.

"Well, thinking about it," Cole confessed, "but not doing it. Besides, nobody's ever called me a gentleman. Which, on the whole, is kind of a relief. Being a drifter is a lot easier to live up to."

"You don't care if people consider you worthless?"

"I didn't say I didn't care, but not having people expect anything of you makes life a lot easier. Besides, I don't think anybody ever said I was worthless. Well, not *completely* worthless."

He was laughing at her. She couldn't say exactly how she knew this. His expression seemed sincere enough, but she was absolutely certain. It made her furious. It also made her determined not to show she even suspected. She didn't want him to think she cared a snap of her fingers for his opinion.

"I see Zeke coming with a wash pan of water," Cole said. "You going to let me take those socks off?"

She started to say she'd wait for Zeke, but changed her mind. Zeke had finally come to accept his role in Jake's family, but the wounds from his years of slavery were still close to the surface. She couldn't ask him to kneel at her feet and remove her dirty socks.

"You let your fingers wander more than a quarter of an inch above the top of my socks, and I'll notch both your ears," she told him.

"You don't have a gun."

"I will tonight. That ought to make my act real exciting."

He grimaced, then grinned slyly. "Too exciting. You can set that water down right here," he said to Zeke. "And don't go off. I want you to watch, to make sure I don't touch her leg. She's threatened to shoot off my ears if my fingers stray so much as a quarter of an inch."

Zeke flashed one of his rare grins. "It would take a shotgun to get me to leave. It's not often anybody gets Drew at a disadvantage. Hawk's going to be mad as hell he missed this."

"You tell a soul, and I'll notch your ears, too," Drew said.

Zeke offered her his pistol. "Fire away, honey. This is too good to keep to myself."

Chapter Four

Drew was furious at Zeke, the horse, herself, and the manure, but she was most angry at Cole Benton because of the look on his face. It could easily be called a cat-who-swallowed-the-canary look. He'd got her in a corner and she couldn't do anything about it. Well, she could, but not without making an even greater spectacle of herself. She promised herself she would remember this. Sooner or later she would get a chance to repay him.

"All right, Mr. Benton," she said, "you may remove my socks. Just remember I won't be unarmed tonight."

"I'm not likely to forget that."

He didn't look the least bit intimidated. Generally men took her threats seriously. It seemed Cole Benton thought he was an exception. She would have to clear up that mis-understanding soon.

"I've been thinking about your boots," Cole said as he rolled down the tops of her socks. "You shouldn't wear them at all."

He didn't touch her skin, but sensations traveled through her cotton socks with the speed of lightning and the intensity of an electric shock. Her skin prickled at his feathery touch. His closeness suddenly seemed solid and tangible. She felt her body stiffen as though in preparation for a shock. Never had anything so trivial assumed such importance.

"I can't go barefoot." She managed to retain enough control over her senses to make a coherent reply.

"I didn't mean that."

He rolled the sock under her heel and slipped it off her foot. A tiny shiver raced through her when his fingers brushed her instep. No man had ever touched her foot. Until this moment, anyone who'd tried would have been shot. She didn't understand why she didn't want to shoot Cole.

"You need shoes with soft soles," he said.

She didn't know where she could find shoes that would fit this description. She couldn't think with his hands on her feet. She'd never known anything could be so disconcerting. She thought for a moment her heartburn had returned—it felt like it—but this was different. It was a nervous feeling deep in her belly, something much more disturbing than heartburn.

Cole removed the second sock. Before she could draw a good breath, he placed the pan of water beneath her feet. "Put your feet in the water," he said.

Instinct caused her to jerk her foot back. She hoped her outward bearing was stiff and proud, but her spirit was in chaos. What had happened to the calm, levelheaded young woman of yesterday? How could such a little thing throw her off balance?

All the things that had happened since Cole arrived had been little. But all of them together were enough to unsettle her completely.

"You don't have any soap," she pointed out. "Nor anything to dry them with."

"I can wash them with my hands," he said. "Dry them with my bandana."

Zeke chuckled softly. She'd have something to say to him later. It was downright traitorous for him to enjoy her embarrassment.

She eyed Cole suspiciously. "Do you always have an answer for everything?"

"No, but it's real helpful when I do."

"Well you can bend your mind to the problem of finding shoes that fit your requirements. In the meantime, you'd better wash my feet if you're going to. These boys have to get their work done sometime."

The several men leaning against the fence watching grinned self-consciously. So much for the wonderful feeling of being accepted into the show's family. On the whole, she preferred her privacy. And washing her own feet.

"I'm sure you have work to do," she said to the men, "so go about it."

They stayed where they were.

"Throw me your gun, Zeke," she said.

He tossed her a pistol without hesitation. In an almost continuous motion, she fired several shots in rapid succession at the gaping onlookers. Their hats flew off like they'd been caught in a hurricane wind. The men's startled looks indicated they hadn't anticipated such a reaction to their stares.

"I don't like to repeat myself," she said.

The men scattered to gather up their hats, stared in surprise at the neat holes in the brims, then hurried away, mumbling among themselves.

"Do you always insist upon getting your way?" Cole asked.

"I don't like being stared at."

"That's a strange attitude for a performer."

She couldn't—wouldn't—tell him that she liked having her skills appreciated, but she didn't like having to show them off in public. It made her feel like a trained bear. She intended to leave the Wild West Show as soon as she got enough money to buy her ranch, but she didn't have to tell Cole Benton that, either.

"Performers need privacy, too, Mr. Benton. I consider washing my feet a private action."

"Then I'm surprised you haven't shot my hat off."

"You're not wearing a hat," she countered. "I'd have to shoot you."

"Couldn't you just part my hair?"

The dangblasted man wasn't the least bit afraid of her. He looked up at her now, his expression bland enough, but laughter danced in his eyes. She was tempted to do exactly what he asked, but he was so close, he'd have powder burns on his forehead. There was no fun in that.

"I considered it. I still might if you don't behave yourself. But you caused me to step into that horse manure, so you might as well wash my feet."

"You ordered me to put you down."

"You didn't tell me there was manure under my feet."

"You gave me one second to put you down."

This was a foolish argument that only made her look childish. "That was my mistake, and I'm paying for it. Now if you mean to wash my feet, get going."

She should have insisted upon washing her own feet, but for some perverse reason she hadn't. She didn't like Cole doing it, but she liked seeing him kneeling at her feet. She wasn't under the illusion he was *really* kneeling at her feet, but it would do for the time being.

She lowered her feet into the water. It was cold. Not at all like a warm bath at the hotel. Not that she was really conscious of the cold. She couldn't think of anything as ordinary as hot or cold water with Cole's hands all over her feet. She had never known her feet had so many nerve endings. There seemed to be millions, and every one was on full alert. No, they'd passed alert and gone into alarm stage.

That irritated Drew. She didn't want her body reacting that way to the touch of a man, especially Cole Benton. He was too brazen, much too satisfied with himself. He had no sense of when he was wanted and when people would have been much happier if he'd just disappear. He acted as if everybody ought to be glad he was telling them how to make things better. She didn't need Cole Benton, or any other man, to tell her what to do.

"If you're going to spend the morning looking at my foot, maybe I'd better wash it myself."

"It's a lovely foot."

"It's a foot like any other," she said, aggravated that she wanted to believe there could be something special about her feet. "If feet were all that pretty, people wouldn't keep them hidden away in shoes."

61

"Not all women do. In some societies it's the custom to go barefoot."

"They obviously don't work around horses or cows."

"When they have to protect their feet, they wear sandals with only tiny straps to keep them on. They even paint their toenails bright colors."

Drew didn't know about sandals. She'd never seen any, and wouldn't trust any shoe to be held in place by a single strap, but she did know about women who painted their toenails. Her brothers had told her only loose women did that. She cocked her pistol and pointed it directly at Cole's forehead.

"You compare me to one of your fancy women again, and I'll do more than part your hair."

Cole's look of innocence would have done justice to her brother Will's look when he actually *was* innocent. "I'd never do that. Quite respectable women wear sandals."

Drew wasn't sure she believed him. Isabelle never wore anything like that, and she'd been raised rich. Neither did Marina or Buck's wife. Naturally none of the women in the Wild West Show did. She'd have to ask her aunt when she got to Memphis. Maybe society women were different. But until she found out for certain, she wasn't going to let Cole Benton put anything over on her.

"You forget about your sandals and get on with washing that foot before I have my next birthday."

"A girl as young as you must look forward to each birthday."

If he kept on like this, she *would* part his hair. She might be only nineteen, but that was practically an old maid in Texas. She was certain Cole knew that. He was just saying all the silly things men said to women. It was about time he found out she wasn't some giddy, scatter-brained female who would swoon and go all foolish when a handsome man started to pay her some attention. She had no use for that kind of man.

She unknotted the handkerchief around her neck, jerked her foot out of his grasp, and started to dry it herself.

"I haven't finished," Cole protested.

"Yes, you have." She moved her other foot about in the pan of water, drew it out, and started to dry it. "If I waited for you to finish, I'd still be here when the show started."

"There are worse ways to spend the day."

"I can't think of any at the moment. Hand me my boots."

He looked as though he wanted to refuse, but changed his mind. "I've been thinking about something else."

"Anybody ever tell you you think too much?" she snapped.

"No."

"Well, they should. And while they're at it, they ought to tell you you talk too much, too."

"I've heard that one."

Why did he grin like a little boy who knew he was being just the slightest bit naughty and was enjoying it nevertheless? He was a grown man, even if he didn't act like it. She guessed drifters were like that.

"I've still been thinking," he said.

It was obvious he wasn't going to hand her her boots if she didn't let him talk. She could get up and get them herself, but she'd get her feet dirty. She resigned herself to letting him talk. "What have you been thinking?" she asked.

"How are you going to get down from that horse?"

"I'll sit down and slide off."

"You might hurt yourself."

"I've been getting on and off horses since I was three. I won't get hurt."

"I have a better idea."

"So do I. You hand me my boots. I'll put them on and leave you here to think of all the ideas you please."

She was sure he grinned just to irritate her. "Mine's better."

"Save it."

"It'll make the show more interesting."

"The show's interesting enough already."

He didn't say anything, but she could tell he hadn't accepted her rejection. She could also tell he was going to keep bringing it up until she listened to him.

"Okay, hand me my boots and tell me how you think I ought to dismount."

He handed her one boot. "You ought to jump."

"That's basically what I'm doing."

"Not slide. Jump."

"That's crazy. I could break my leg." She shoved her foot into one boot and reached for the other.

"Not if I caught you."

Her hand paused in midair. "You want me to jump into your arms in front of thousands of people?"

"It's more exciting."

"Give me my other boot." She couldn't talk to him while she was barefoot. She felt at a severe disadvantage. She took the boot, shoved her foot inside, and stood. "I have no doubt you're right," she said. "I expect the audience would love to see you manhandle me just about as much as you'd like to do it, but if you try it, I'll do more than part your hair." She turned and started across the arena.

"You don't have a very good sense of theater," he said.

She stopped and turned. "Maybe not, but I have a good sense of what it takes to keep my self-respect. Jumping into a strange man's arms isn't on the list."

"If we got to know each other better, I wouldn't be a stranger."

She turned and continued walking away. That remark was too hackneyed to deserve a response.

"Okay, don't jump into my arms. Get one of your brothers to help you."

She didn't stop walking. "They're in the next act."

"They'd have plenty of time to get in place."

"I don't need to jump into anybody's arms. My shooting is exciting enough."

He didn't respond, and she smiled to herself, glad to have finally left him with nothing to say. But almost immediately she began to have doubts. Maybe he hadn't responded because her shooting *wasn't* exciting enough. Maybe audiences did expect something extra, more movement, more spectacle. Maybe they didn't realize how much skill it took to hit a target while moving. Most people lived in cities and bought their food in the market. They didn't have to fight Indians or wild animals. They looked upon shooting as entertainment. They probably thought anybody could do what she did with a little practice.

Why did Cole have to come down out of those stands last night? She'd been perfectly satisfied with her act. Zeke and Hawk were satisfied. Even though the boss kept asking her to do something to make it a little more exciting, he had continued to increase her salary. The audiences enjoyed her show. She always got plenty of applause, especially if a man from the audience challenged her. She always won. The women liked that.

She'd show him. She'd shoot faster tonight. She'd shoot more clay pigeons. She'd nail every target dead center. She'd be so phenomenally accurate they'd be in awe. When she finished, the whole audience would jump up with one great cheer.

Never again would Cole Benton be able to say she was dull.

The show went even better than she'd expected. She could hear the surprised intake of breath when she entered the arena standing on a horse. She heard the hushed silence followed by enthusiastic applause as she drilled every target dead center on her first pass. She made a second pass with the horse going faster, and she drilled them all again. The applause was even greater.

She dropped down on the horse and got jarred rather badly. She waited a moment before sliding to the ground.

She picked up her pistols and proceeded to knock over a series of moving ducks. She'd borrowed that trick from a traveling carnival. It always impressed the audience. It did tonight as well. She finished up with the clay pigeons, shooting one at a time, then two at a time, and finally three.

She never missed

Her act was spectacular, but short. She bowed to the audience, the applause greater than usual. She looked around, pleased, as Earl invited anyone from the audience to challenge her.

"Nobody here is that big a fool," one man called out.

"They're scared of being beaten by a woman," a female voice announced.

"You're damned right," came the reply. "Couldn't face myself in the mirror after a thing like that."

But one man did stand up and start down out of the stands. Drew didn't recognize him. She'd hoped Cole would stand up first. At least he could shoot.

"Sit down," someone yelled at the man coming to challenge Drew. "She'll make you look like a fool."

As if to underscore the spectator's remark, Drew called for three more clay pigeons. She shattered all three effortlessly. The man didn't react, just kept coming. His body looked like Cole's, he even moved like Cole, but the face was all wrong.

To keep the audience entertained, she shouted "Pull!" and once again shattered three clay pigeons. At a spur-of-the-moment inspiration, she laid down her rifle, picked up a clod of dirt, threw it in the air, snatched up her rifle, and shattered it before it could hit the ground, earning another round of applause.

The man kept coming. He stepped into the ring and walked up to Drew. Startled, she recognized Cole—in disguise.

"What are you doing?" she whispered.

"You don't want them to think it's the same man every night, do you?"

The train bearing the Wild West Show to its next stop, Meridian, Illinois, lumbered through the night to the accompaniment of wheels grinding and occasionally screeching against the endless rails that stretched across the dark landscape. Occasional clearings in the trees revealed glimpses of the Ohio River looking nearly black on this cloudy, moonless night. The nip of fall was in the air, but the hot exhaust and steam from the toiling engines ahead occasionally made its way through the windows, dusting the passengers with soot or an occasional cinder, and enveloping them in clouds of stifling humidity.

Drew leaned back in her seat, relaxed, her eyes closed, waiting until she was tired enough to climb into bed. She hated sleeping on trains. It was worse than camping out on a trail drive, but there was no alternative. The only way the show could keep its schedule was to travel during the night. They had accommodations in the very latest Pullman car. A sleeping berth came down from the ceiling above where they were seated. That was where she slept. Hawk and Zeke rearranged the seats and slept below. They never let her travel anywhere unless they were within hearing distance. Both Isabelle and Jake had insisted on that.

"How do you think it went tonight?"

Drew opened her eyes to see Cole standing in the aisle. Zeke, sprawled in the seat across from her, opened a wary eye. Hawk, napping next to her, showed no sign he was aware of Cole's presence.

"I got the biggest audience response ever," Drew answered. "I guess coming in on that horse was a good idea."

"Letting me catch you would be even better."

"I'll settle for tonight's success."

"Don't you want to improve your act?"

"Not like that."

"I've been thinking."

"You're *always* thinking."

"I can't help it if I have an active imagination."

"Use it on your next disguise."

"I've already got that figured out. This idea is for another trick."

"Well, sit down if you're going to talk. I'll get a crick in my neck if I have to keep looking up at you."

"He's not sitting next to me," Zeke stated. The look he gave Cole brooked no argument.

"I don't need to sit down," Cole said.

"What's your next trick?" she asked.

He grinned in that sly, sneaky, self-satisfied way she was learning to distrust. "Meet me tomorrow morning as soon as the arena's set up, and I'll show you."

She sighed in frustration. Why didn't he find some other sharpshooter to annoy? "It would be a lot easier if you'd tell me now. I could be thinking about how to set it up."

"I've already done that. It's practically ready to go."

"Except for the small problem that I'm the one who has to do the shooting and I haven't the slightest idea what you're talking about."

"You can hit any target under any circumstances," Hawk mumbled. "Send him away so I can sleep."

"Don't forget, in the arena, as soon as it's set up," Cole said. He winked at her, then moved away.

What did he mean by that? Nobody winked at her. She wouldn't allow it. It implied a degree of intimacy, at the very least friendship, that didn't exist between them. They had no relationship, no friendship, only the most superficial knowledge of each other.

"What was he doing winking at you?" Zeke asked.

"I don't know."

"I'll tell him not to do it again."

"I can tell him myself."

"You don't want him winking at you, do you?" Zeke asked, watching her out of narrowed eyes.

"Of course not. You know I've been trying to get rid of him ever since he walked down out of those stands."

"He's still here."

"Earl thinks he livens up my act. You and Hawk said the same thing."

"He does, but that doesn't mean he can wink at you."

"I'm a grown woman, Zeke."

"Jake told me and Hawk to keep an eye on you."

"I know, and Isabelle told me to look around for a good man. She said if I found one to tell both of you to go to the devil."

"You're not thinking about hooking up with Cole, are you?"

"No!" She hadn't meant to practically shout the word at him, but the idea was so unexpected it burst from her all on its own. "I'm not looking for any man."

"Lots of women say that, then turn around and run off with the first handsome man they see."

"I'm not running off with any man, handsome or otherwise. But you can bet your last dollar I'd *never* take up with a drifter like Cole Benton."

"You been acting mighty friendly."

"It's better than fighting. And since everybody seems to think my act is better than ever, I figure I'm stuck with him for a while."

"I just wanted to be sure. He seems to know what he's doing, but I don't trust him. You keep your eyes open. He could be a dangerous man."

"Cole?" Drew asked, with a derisive laugh. "I can handle him with one hand tied behind me."

"Don't be so sure. I got a feeling about that man, and it ain't good."

"I have a feeling that's not good, either. It's because he's a drifter, without ambition or pride. He'll float through life as long as his handsome face will let him. After that I imagine his glib tongue will smooth his path. I wouldn't be surprised if he doesn't end up married to some rich widow. I think he practices his smile in front of a mirror just to make sure it's sexy. I know he thinks it's irresistible."

"You just remember to tell him not to wink at you," Zeke said. He closed his eyes. "Jake won't like it if he finds out."

"I'll remember."

But she wouldn't tell him not to smile at her. Even though he was a no-account vagabond, she couldn't deny she liked it when he smiled at her. It seemed warm and genuine, especially when she did a trick very well. It did smart a bit that he seemed surprised by her ability, but his smile took away the sting. She might say she didn't like men—and she didn't—but she wasn't immune to them. She just didn't plan to get hooked up with one for life. With ten brothers, she knew more than enough about men to last her for the rest of her life. He'd need more than a smile and a wink to make an impression on her.

But his smile *had* made an impression, one she couldn't quite categorize. It wasn't that it made him seem almost handsome. He was handsome, even by her standards. She liked his smile because it somehow made her feel better. She didn't understand that, and it worried her. She hated it when she didn't understand things.

She'd decided as a little girl, long before her parents were killed in an Indian attack, that she didn't want to be married. Her parents had fought for as far back as she could remember. All these years later she could still recall the fear, the nausea, the times the fighting made her ill. Fights still made her feel queasy. Jake and Isabelle argued, even though they were deeply in love. If they couldn't get along without fighting, nobody could.

Drew once asked Marina Dillon about it. She was the wife of Ward Dillon, the doctor who lived close by. Ward and Marina were Jake and Isabelle's best friends. Marina said it was impossible for two people as strong-minded as Jake and Isabelle to live together without arguing. She said they adored each other, that arguing was their way of working out a compromise.

But Drew felt sick all over again every time it happened. Fights had caused her parents to separate time and time again, but they were even more miserable apart than together. They'd just gotten back together after one of their separations when they were killed.

Drew knew she was strong-minded. Everybody said so. She also knew she was spilling over with opinions. On top of that, she had argued with her brothers from the day Jake coaxed her out of that ravine where she'd hidden after she stole and killed one of his cows. As much as she'd come to love her brothers, she couldn't imagine living with any one of them.

If she couldn't live with them, she'd never learn to live with a stranger, certainly not one like Cole. He argued with her all the time. She'd have to shoot him before the first week was out.

Myrtle came up and dropped into the seat next to her. "I didn't know you were so friendly with that Cole fella."

"I'm not," Drew said, fearing she was going to have to repeat the same conversation she'd had with Zeke. "I don't even like him."

"Then why would you tell him he could go through your luggage?"

Chapter Five

The click of a firing pin being drawn back brought Cole out of a dead sleep. The feel of cold metal against his temple kept him lying perfectly still in his bed.

"Give me one good reason why I shouldn't scatter your brains all over this sleeper car."

He recognized Drew's voice. She didn't sound happy.

"I can think of several," he replied, as calmly as his rapidly beating heart would allow. "The first being that I have a right to know why you want to kill me."

"Snakes don't have any rights except to be crushed underfoot," she hissed. "Sneak thieves don't have any rights except to know their sins have caught up with them."

"Which category do I belong in?"

"You know what you are, you scum-sucking, possum-eating, rat-baiting, low-down dog."

"For a nice lady, you sure know a powerful lot about cussing."

"I know even more about shooting, especially about shooting belly-crawling snakes."

Cole took his first deep breath. He wasn't out of the woods, but he was certain Drew didn't mean to kill him yet. She was mad clean through, but it wasn't a killing mad. It was an I'm-going-to-beat-the-stuffing-out-of-you mad. Though he didn't think Drew could overpower him, he was certain the two figures looming behind her— Hawk and Zeke—were quite capable.

"I say we cut his throat," Zeke said.

"No, better to gut him," Hawk said. "That way he die more slowly, suffer more pain."

They sounded like they were actually looking forward to sending him into the next world.

"Do you mind telling me what I've done wrong?" he asked.

"Tell me, too."

"Yeah, all of us want to know."

Cole had never been so relieved to have nosy neighbors. Every person in the car was sitting up, standing up, or leaning out of bed, curiosity having brought them all wide awake in a matter of seconds. From their expressions, they were actually looking forward to the possibility of a grisly murder. He very much hoped he could deprive them of their entertainment.

"I heard you spent some time in the baggage car this evening," Drew said. "Find anything interesting?"

Damn! He should have known he couldn't touch any-body's baggage without somebody noticing. They were like one big family, all looking out for each other.

"Nothing at all," he replied.

"What were you hoping to find?"

"Something I could use for a new trick."

"So you don't have the trick already set up."

"I know what I want to do. I just don't have all the equipment. I was just seeing if you had anything I could use."

The gun pressed a little harder against his temple. "So you thought you'd take a look-see in my baggage."

"Just the props," Cole said, fervently hoping the tattle-tale who saw him in the baggage car hadn't realized that only moments before, Cole had been going through Drew's personal belongings to see if he could find any-thing that linked her to the robberies.

"Didn't your mama tell you not to go through other people's things?"

"Sure, but I thought those were *our* things. I mean, we are in the act together. Anything needed for the tricks is as much my concern as it is yours."

"No, it's not."

"Of course it is, especially if I'm going to be the one thinking up all the new tricks."

"I say we cut his throat now," Zeke said.

"Gut him," Hawk corrected.

"You can't kill me in front of all these witnesses," Cole pointed out. He *hoped* they wouldn't kill him here, but he couldn't afford to be too confident. He didn't imagine it would be the first time circus people had covered up for each other. "I can explain."

76

"Get started," Drew snapped.

"Can't we go somewhere else? I hate to keep all these good people awake."

"We want to hear, too," one man said.

"It's my business," Drew barked at him. "If I want you to know about it, I'll tell you."

"Sure, Drew, anything you say."

"Why don't you take him outside on the back of the last car?" someone suggested. "Then, if you don't like his answers, you can just push him off. If they find him later, it'll look like he went sleepwalking and fell off the end of the train."

They were all sticking together. If that hard-faced Indian decided to gut him right here, somebody would probably offer to wash the blood out of the sheets.

"Let me get my pants on."

"Leave them off," Drew said. "Then if we push you off the train, our story will add up."

As Cole threw back the covers and got out of his bunk, he ruminated on the speed with which this assignment had gone wrong. He hadn't expected it to be easy, but neither had he expected to find his neck in a noose quite so soon. If he'd kept his mind on business—searching Drew's trunks for possible clues to her involvement in the robberies—he'd have been gone before anyone saw him. Instead he'd become preoccupied with thinking up new tricks. Now he was in big trouble. One false move, and he might not live to think up any more.

"If you need help getting him to talk, let me know."

That from an ex–lion tamer. Cole guessed the man would offer to see if the big cats liked Cole Benton steaks and cutlets. Cole had a sinking feeling they'd like them very much.

He felt the flush of embarrassment and a stab of anger as he was paraded in his underwear through several cars and out the door of the last one. A small porchlike extension with a metal railing formed the end of the car. Cole held his breath until the wind shifted and the soot and cinders from the train's engine drifted away. Then he relaxed and took a deep breath of cold night air.

He would have been able to enjoy the fresh air a great deal more if he'd been out here under different circumstances. A midnight assignation with Drew ranked high on his list of choices. She might be a thief, but she sure was a pretty one. Besides, if she liked and trusted him, she'd be more willing to take him into her confidence.

He could forget the trust part. He didn't need to see her expression to know it looked grim and angry. That pretty well took care of her liking him as well.

"Now, let's hear your tale," Drew said.

"It had better be good," Zeke said. Hawk grunted his agreement.

"Like I said," Cole began, "I was just going through the crates with all the stuff for your stunts. I thought about asking, but you were so anxious to get rid of me I decided it would be better to just go ahead and look."

"What were you looking for?"

"Candles."

"Candles?"

"He's lying," Zeke said. "I say we cut his throat and throw his body over the rail."

"That's the trick I was telling you about," Cole said, hoping Drew wasn't quite as bloodthirsty as her adopted brothers. "I don't have any candles or holders. I was going to have to buy all that stuff first thing tomorrow if I couldn't find something I could use."

"How would I use candles in the act?" Drew asked.

She was still angry, obviously not ready to trust him, but there was a chance he could make her believe him.

"It's something I saw once in New York," he said, knowing immediately she'd think he was comparing her to New York showmen. He was counting on her determination to be the best to overcome her anger. "You light a bunch of candles and shoot out the flame without knocking over the candles."

"That's easy as shooting dead ducks for Drew," Zeke said.

"Maybe, but the audience won't know that. It looks very impressive to have those lights go out one by one without being able to see anything do it. If it's all that easy, we can add it to the act tonight and start working on something else to put in later."

"Like what?"

It was just like Drew to want to know everything now. He hadn't even thought of what he could do next. He'd been too busy trying to figure out how he was going to worm his way into Drew's confidence.

"I'm still working on the candle trick," he said. "There are a lot of ways to do it, with the candles in a candelabra, in a row, even a revolving table. Think you could do that?"

"What's the next trick you have in mind?" Drew asked.

He didn't have to see her expression to hear the suspicion in her voice.

"I hadn't worked out which would be best to begin

with, but I was thinking maybe you could shoot lying down."

"Shooting lying down is not much," Hawk said. "Anybody who's ever been in a gunfight has done that."

"Lying on their back, their head hanging down, shooting at something they're looking at upside down?" Cole asked.

"That might be interesting," Hawk admitted.

Cole had kept his eye on Drew the whole time. The cold steel of the gun barrel pressed against his stomach was not a comforting feeling. He was relieved to feel the pressure lessen, then disappear altogether. Drew might not believe him yet, but she was thinking about it.

"I guess I shouldn't have gone through that crate without asking you first," Cole said, trying to sound apologetic without sounding so much like a yellow-belly he'd choke on the words. "I really thought we were partners, that you trusted me." He tried to sound just a little bit hurt. "I have been doing everything I can to think of ways to make our act more interesting."

"It's *my* act," Drew said, "and you'd better not forget it again. As for looking through the props, do that before we pack up. I won't be very happy if you forget to put something back and I have to cancel a trick. I'm not on very long, so I need to get in all the tricks I can while I have the crowd's attention."

She believed him, or at least she couldn't come up with a really good reason not to believe him. But Cole wasn't about to get careless again. He knew he wouldn't get a second chance.

"That all you going to do?" Zeke asked. "Tell him not to leave stuff lying on the floor?"

"What do you want me to do?" Drew asked.

"Let me and Hawk have him for a few minutes. We'll teach him to forget to ask before he goes through a lady's trunk."

Cole figured Drew would be more successful in getting her brothers to leave his skin in one piece, so he kept his mouth shut. Zeke looked ready to take him apart. Hawk's expression was harder to read, but Cole had no doubt his thoughts were running along the same lines. Besides, he *had* gone through Drew's personal trunks. He thought he'd put everything back exactly as he'd found it, but you could never be sure with a woman.

A man would throw everything into a trunk and worry about what it looked like when he got where he was going. A woman would spend five times as long making certain everything was packed just right so it wouldn't crease. Then the first thing she'd do when she arrived would be to iron everything and hang it up. Drew didn't strike him as overly domestic, but she always looked neat.

"He's a fool, but that's not his fault," Drew said. "If you want to blame anybody for having to put up with him, blame Earl. He's the one who hired him. You can blame yourselves, too, for thinking he added life to my act."

Zeke and Hawk didn't look happy, but it was clear they were used to doing what Drew wanted. Cole got the feeling just about everybody did what Drew wanted. He shivered violently and realized he was cold. Now that he wasn't expecting to be gutted any minute, his adrenaline had stopped pumping and his blood had cooled off. He was standing on the back of a train on a cold September night in nothing but his long johns.

81

"Let him go back inside," Drew said, "before he freezes to death and we have to get rid of his body. Besides, he does keep coming up with good ideas. We can keep him around until he runs dry. Then we can pitch him from the train, preferably when we're crossing a river."

The woman was all heart. He decided to get back to his bed before she could change her mind. When the captain had explained his assignment, he hadn't bothered to mention that Drew came with her own personal bodyguards and support team. Cole hadn't been prepared for that, but he'd better get prepared. Next time they were going to want blood.

And Cole was certain that, one way or the other, there would be a next time.

But as he settled back into his bed and felt his body begin to warm, his feet begin to feel more like they belonged to him instead of being two blocks of ice, his concern shifted back to Drew. He hadn't known exactly what he was looking for when he went through her trunks. He wasn't foolish enough to expect to find masks neatly packed away ready for use the next time they were going to commit robbery.

To his relief, he'd found nothing. The captain hadn't said they knew she was guilty, just that she seemed the most likely suspect. Cole was to check her out and report back. There wouldn't be any difficulty when he reported he couldn't find any evidence to prove she was involved with the robberies. He couldn't produce any evidence to prove she *wasn't* connected with the robberies, but he had a good intuitive grasp of character. Everything he sensed about Drew told him she wasn't the kind of person to commit robberies.

But his feelings went further than simply being relieved. He wanted to stop looking now because he was afraid sometime in the future he might come across some evidence he couldn't ignore. He didn't want Drew to get off scot-free if she was guilty, but he didn't want to be the one to find the proof.

Yet it was even more than that. He didn't want her to be guilty, or to be caught even if she were. All day, after he'd decided he would go through her luggage, he'd been running scenarios though his mind in which he talked her out of committing any more robberies, into giving back the money she'd taken, into going to one of the western territories, where she'd be effectively out of the reach of the law.

This wasn't like him. While serving as a Texas Ranger, he hadn't been involved in any kind of dishonesty. Doing anything to help Drew escape the consequences of her actions would not only be dishonest, it would be against the oath he'd taken as a federal agent.

He couldn't figure out what it was about this woman that worked so powerfully on him. She wasn't beautiful, though she was pretty enough to satisfy any reasonable man. She certainly hadn't gone out of her way to make herself agreeable to him. It wasn't her moral character— he had never known show people to have very high morals. Were Zeke and Hawk really her adopted brothers?

If not, he didn't want to think about what kind of intimacy that implied.

He didn't know what had gotten into him. Maybe it came from trying to catch a female criminal. He could only assume it went against some part of his training as a Southern gentleman. It was a shame that when he left home he hadn't left all that brainwashing behind.

It was foolish to let himself be influenced by the fact that Drew was a woman. He was a strong-minded man. At least he had been until now. He could put aside his personal feelings and do the job. That was what the captain had expected when he gave Cole the assignment. Success would mean promotion, and further proof he'd been right to walk away from his family's expectations.

Meridian, Illinois

Drew was forced to concede that Cole had a natural talent for the theatrical, a real feel for what an audience would find exciting or intriguing. Maybe drifters had to have the ability to see the entertainment value in virtually any situation. After all, if they failed to be amusing, people would stop supporting them and they'd have to actually be responsible, maybe even take a job.

"We'd better hope there's not too much wind tonight," Cole was saying. "It'll blow the candles out."

"I could always shoot the match out of your hand," she said.

"Let's stick with the candles for now."

He probably didn't think she was good enough to keep from hitting him. That piqued her vanity, but she decided to let it pass. He'd only been officially part of the show for two days. He'd have plenty of opportunity to learn to appreciate the extent of her skill with guns, and her willingness to practice to make herself even better. But he seemed determined to do everything he could to make her act the most sensational in the Wild West Show.

Why?

She didn't have an answer to that question, and it bothered her. She didn't like it when she didn't understand things around her, what people were doing, their motives. She took people as she found them. The old regulars in the show were her favorites. They were just what they seemed—honest, hardworking, friendly—and they loved being with the show. They wouldn't consider any other kind of life.

But none of that applied to Cole Benton. He would drift from one place to another using his handsome face and pleasing manner to ease his way. At some point, before his physical charms faded completely, he'd probably sweet-talk some rich widow into marrying him, and be set for life. He'd probably take advantage of her trust, cheat on her from time to time, spend too much of her money, but Drew had no doubt that she'd feel she got a fair return on her investment. Cole Benton looked like just the man to make any woman think having him to herself—even if only part of the time—was worth almost any price.

"Get those candles ready," Drew called. "Zeke and I can't wait here all morning."

"In a minute."

She didn't like to be unoccupied. All kinds of unwelcome thoughts thrust themselves on her, like what she'd been thinking a minute before. She couldn't recall when she'd ever speculated about any man as she had about Cole. He was exactly the kind of man she despised. Yet now she couldn't stop thinking about him, wondering about his past, his present motives, what he'd do in the future. She didn't like that. It wasn't like her.

"Ready," Cole called.

She fired six shots in rapid succession. Damn! She'd missed one.

"What's wrong?" Zeke asked. "You never miss."

"I was thinking about something else. Light them again."

This time she cleared her mind of every thought and concentrated on what the audience reaction would be if she missed.

"Okay, ready," Cole called out.

She whirled and fired six shots. Six candles went out like clockwork.

"That's better," Zeke said. "I thought for a moment you were coming down with something."

"I'm never sick."

"You never miss, either. I got to go get ready for the riding stunts. You'd better practice a little more, just to make sure."

"I am sure, dammit," Drew snapped at Zeke's retreating back. "Put the candles on the turntable," she called out to Cole.

"That'll make it virtually impossible to hit all of them," he said.

"Put them on the turntable anyway," she said, determined to show him there were no limits to what she could do when she put her mind to it.

It took Cole several minutes to set up the table. All the while Drew fidgeted and fussed and stewed. It was bad enough to have Cole doubt her skill, but it was a major blow to her vanity to have Zeke tell her she needed to practice. Zeke was her severest critic, but he was also one of her most steadfast supporters. He'd been the one to convince Jake and Isabelle to let her join the Wild West Show. He'd also been the one to talk Hawk into working with him so they could join the show and keep an eye on her.

She'd been angry at first. She didn't need anyone watching over her, but now she was glad for the companionship. She wasn't good at making friends. The first few months would have been terribly lonely without Zeke and Hawk.

"How fast do you want me to spin it?" Cole called.

"Try it once and see."

He spun it so fast the candles blurred and went out.

"I guess that was too fast," he said.

He relit the candles and tried again. It was much slower, but the candles still flickered and threatened to go out. She took careful aim and fired.

She snuffed all six.

Cole slowly turned to look at her. "You're damned good."

"Of course I'm good."

"No, I mean *damned* good. I didn't think anybody could do that. How did you manage it?"

She'd always been able to shoot with uncanny accuracy. She didn't know how. She just did it. She'd gotten even better with long hours of practice. This year she hadn't pushed herself so hard until Cole showed up with his ideas for new tricks. Now she'd have to start practicing as much as before. It wasn't enough that she could make the shots when she was concentrating. She had to make them all the time, under any conditions, regardless of distractions, including weather.

And she had to be fast. The audience didn't think there was anything difficult about the shots if she took her time to prepare. But when she went from one trick to another with hardly a stop in between, it left them breathless, and the applause was loud and wholehearted.

"We ought to start with the candelabra first," Cole said. "We can change over to the turntable when they get used to that."

"Nobody knows what I do from one show to the next."

"They will from now on. I intend to see that newspaper reporters are here to see your performances. You're going to be famous. People will come to the show just to see you, expecting to see certain tricks. That's when we'll have to start varying them, making them even harder."

"And how do you intend to drag all those reporters out to the show?"

"I don't know. I just thought of it."

Just what she expected, lots of big ideas but no thought about how to make them work. "You don't have much time. The show starts in a few hours."

"I'll think of something."

"While you're doing that, I'll practice the rest of my act. Then I'm going to watch Zeke and Hawk go through their stunts."

She ran through the act three more times. Everything went perfectly except the dismount from the horse. If she stopped the horse, it slowed the act. If she dropped to a sitting position and then bailed out, it left her feeling off balance. She either had to wait a few seconds while she got her balance back, or fire right away and risk missing some of the targets.

"You ought to have somebody to catch you."

Drew turned in surprise to see that Earl had come up behind her.

"That would give you a speedy and easy dismount," Earl said. "And it would appeal to the audience."

"There isn't anybody out there but me."

"How about Cole?"

"He's in the stands. He couldn't pretend to be a stranger and appear with me earlier. I'd have to get Hawk or Zeke to catch me."

"Okay," Earl said, "but let's practice it now. I want to see how it looks."

"Zeke and Hawk have gone to the stables," she said.

"Then let Cole catch you."

Chapter Six

The surge of energy that jolted through Drew's body was as troubling as it was unexpected.

"No!" She hadn't meant for the word to come out as a strangled shout, but it did anyway.

"Why not?" Earl asked.

"I don't need to practice it now. I can wait until the boys are done."

"There's no need to wait. Besides, I want to see it."

"I can't be jumping into the arms of a man I barely know." She didn't know why Earl couldn't see that. "My mother would have a fit."

"This is show business, Drew. We have to do all kinds of things our mothers wouldn't approve of."

Drew knew that. All the women she knew had either

been born into show business or joined over their parents' objections.

"You don't have to worry about Cole getting fresh," Earl said. "I'll be here."

"I'm not worried about that. He knows I can put a bullet through his heart at a hundred yards."

It wasn't Cole but rather his effect on her that worried Drew. She'd spent her whole life immune to the attractions of the male sex. Since she disliked most men and intended never to marry, that suited her just fine.

"Good. I'll tell him to get the horse."

Drew wanted to call Earl back, but she knew it was pointless. He might be short in stature and too pretty to be a man, but when he made up his mind to something, he stuck to it. She didn't want anyone to catch her when she dismounted from the horse, but she was sure it would be a crowd pleaser. It certainly was an easier way to get down. Dropping to the ground while the horse was still moving jarred every bone in her body.

She wouldn't have minded if she didn't have to practice with Cole. Just his presence was enough to cause her to feel too agitated to sit still. At first she thought it was pure irritation. She didn't want to share her performance with anyone, especially a conceited good-for-nothing like Cole. But she found herself looking for him when he wasn't around, wondering where he was, what he might be doing.

She tried to tell herself she was nervous about what he would come up with next. She was, but she was honest enough to admit she was curious, too. Even worse, she found him attractive, appealing. She hated it, cussed herself for it, but she couldn't help it. She guessed that was what had gotten him through life so far, women who couldn't help being attracted to him, women who'd do just about anything to keep him close by.

She might be as susceptible as other silly women, but she wasn't foolish enough to let it go beyond that. You had to treat a man like Cole the same way you treated a wild stallion. He might be the most beautiful animal you've ever seen, but you had to let him stay wild. It was foolish to think he could be broken to saddle. Cole would always have a crowd of women around him, but he'd never be faithful to any one.

Drew shook her head to clear it of these troubling thoughts. She had to get her mind back on her work. Cole and Earl were heading her way with the horse.

"I found some shoes for you to wear," Cole said as he handed her what looked like a boot top attached to a ballet slipper. "It'll look like a boot but be supple enough for you to stand up on the horse."

"Where did you get these?" She knew he couldn't have bought anything like that in a store.

"I had Myrtle make them out of some old boots and a pair of slippers I found at a pawn shop."

"They're perfect," Earl said, "a brilliant idea. Now let's see Drew jump into your arms."

Drew put it off as long as possible. She first made it clear one of her brothers would catch her in the show. Then she made Earl discuss how Zeke or Hawk would come out, where he'd be while she shot at the targets, how and when he'd leave after he'd caught her. But she couldn't put it off forever, especially since Earl was impatient to get on to his other duties.

"Help her up on that horse," he said to Cole. "I think it'll be a brilliant entrance. I don't know why one of us didn't think of something like this long ago."

"Because we made my shooting the focus of the act," Drew said, "not some theatrical claptrap."

"Audiences love claptrap," Earl said. "This whole show is nothing but an imitation of what really happens in the West. People don't want the real thing, just a comfortable approximation. Now let's see what this looks like."

She stalled a little longer by insisting Cole set up the bull's-eyes so she could make her entrance exactly as she would for the show. But the time came when she couldn't postpone it any longer. The targets were set up, Cole stood ready, and Earl was waiting.

"Hell!" she swore. She swung herself up on the horse and got to her feet. She clucked to the horse, and he cantered into the ring.

Drew drilled her three targets. While the horse was making the circle around the arena, Cole grabbed up the targets and waved them in the air to show the make-believe audience Drew had hit them all dead center. Then he dropped the targets and ran to catch her when she was directly in front of the stands.

"Hell!" Drew said as she jumped.

It was worse than she'd feared.

He didn't grunt or stagger under the impact of her body. He just stood there, smiling down at her, as if he did this sort of thing every day. His arms felt strong, easily capable of handling her weight.

Drew felt her pulse leap and her heart hammer in her chest. Not once since she was a small child had a man held her. Yet she was now cradled in Cole's arms like some sort of fancy woman. She knew she ought to order him to let her down, but she couldn't summon the strength. Or the will.

More than ever she found herself acutely conscious of his virile appeal. She could feel the magnetism that made him so self-confident, made women want to be near him, want to surrender to his charm. She couldn't miss the musky smell of him as he pressed her close. She tried to ignore the pulsing knot that formed in her stomach, but it was useless. She rested firmly in the arms of a strong, handsome man, and she was acting just like a brainless female. She wanted him to go on holding her.

She was an idiot. She should have threatened to quit before she jumped into Cole's arms, but it was too late now. The damage had been done.

She cleared her throat and pretended not to be affected. "You're supposed to put me down immediately," she said. "You don't want to slow down the act."

She was pleased to see he didn't produce his usual snappy comeback. In fact, he looked just about as bemused and confused as she felt. Good. If she was going to be knocked senseless by some useless male, it was only fair that he be just as strongly affected by her.

"Great! Wonderful! Marvelous!"

Cole set her down as Earl came running up, sparing Cole the necessity of responding.

"That was perfect. The audience will be breathless. Everything after that will seem better than ever."

"Good. I'll go over it with Zeke as soon as he's done practicing," Drew said.

"Forget Zeke," Earl said. "Cole is going to catch you. I want him to become part of your act."

"No!" Her response, a desperate attempt to separate herself from the feelings that assailed her when she was in Cole's arms, came before she thought. She couldn't do this every evening.

"Why not?" Earl asked.

She desperately searched her mind for an excuse Earl might accept.

"Being in the arms of a man I barely know upsets me," she said. "I'm not sure I'd be calm enough to shoot well after that. If any of my family saw me, I know I wouldn't."

"Your family's not here, and you've got all the time in the world to get to know Cole," Earl said. "I won't force you to put him in your act, but it would certainly give it a big boost. You could become a real star."

"I'll do it with Zeke or Hawk."

"It would be better with Cole."

"Why?"

It was a stupid question. She knew the answer before Earl said it.

"He's good-looking in a sassy sort of way that will drive the women crazy."

"If he's part of my act, he can't challenge me at the end."

"He's worth more in the ring. Holding up those bull's-eyes was a brilliant idea," Earl said to Cole. "What made you think of it?"

"I don't know. It just seemed the natural thing to do."

"He's got good theatrical instincts. You listen to him, and soon you'll be *the* star of the show."

Drew had endured the comments about her act being slow and even boring, but that was too much. Her temper flew out of control. "Then you'd better let him replace me. I can be out of here before tonight." She turned and started out of the arena.

"I didn't mean that," Earl said, running after her. "People love you. You're a great shot, a great act."

She stopped and spun around to face him. "Then why are you and everybody else trying to change it?"

"If other people are saying the same thing, maybe it's something you ought to consider."

But she didn't want to consider it. She just wanted Cole Benton out of her life.

"I'll talk to Zeke."

"Zeke's a great stunt rider, but he doesn't do anything for the women."

"How about Hawk?"

"Better, but Cole is still the best choice."

She stood there, feeling trapped, knowing Earl was right, wanting him to be wrong.

"If you're uncomfortable around Cole, spend some time getting to know him. He seems like a nice enough fella."

"And what happens if we make him part of the act and he decides to drift on out of here next week?"

"Then you can use Hawk or Zeke until the end of the season. If it works really well, we'll find somebody else for next season."

She'd ask Matt. If Earl wanted somebody to capture the women's attention, Matt was just the man he needed. And if Matt wouldn't do it—he hated to leave the ranch—she'd ask Will. He was young and a little undependable, but there wasn't a more handsome boy west of the Mississippi.

"Practice it a time or two more," Earl said. "You might feel a little better about it then."

She couldn't possibly feel better if she had to jump into Cole's arms two or three more times. She'd probably be so shattered she wouldn't be able to work for a week.

"Okay, but I'm not promising anything."

Earl broke into a huge smile. "Great! I knew you'd do anything you could for the good of the show."

Right now she felt more like a fool about to stick her head into the lion's mouth, and she couldn't come up with one good reason why she wouldn't lose it.

"Are those men really your brothers?" Cole asked Drew. They had finished practicing and were sitting in the stands watching the stunt riders go through their routine.

"I said they were, didn't I?"

"Yes, but—"

"Do you think I'm lying?"

She'd been snapping at him ever since she'd jumped into his arms. He couldn't say or do anything that didn't rub her the wrong way.

"No, but it's hard to imagine how a black man, a half-breed Comanche, and a white girl would end up being adopted into the same family."

"My parents are unusual. What are yours like?"

He didn't want to talk about his family. "Let's just say I'm a misfit who couldn't live up to their expectations."

"What sort of expectations?"

"That I'd be a solid citizen. You know, get a job and go to work every day. Marry, settle down, raise a family. Drink, cuss, gamble in moderation, and carry on all affairs discreetly."

"My family was a lot like that, too. That's why I didn't go back to them."

"I don't understand."

"My real parents turned their backs on their families. Unfortunately they didn't have much in common besides wanting to get away from their kin. They fought all the time. They ignored advice to travel west with a wagon train. They set out alone and were killed by Comanches. I was saved by a man who heard the shooting and came to investigate."

Cole couldn't help letting his eyes stray toward where Hawk was working nearby.

"Hawk had nothing to do with that attack," Drew said. "The Comanche didn't trust him and the white people threw him out. Isabelle found him in an orphanage with seven of my brothers."

"But you just said you had a family."

"My aunt found me about a year after my parents were killed. She wanted me to live with her, but I decided to stay with Isabelle and Jake. I figured if my family didn't want my parents, they wouldn't be too happy with me, either."

"Why aren't you with Jake and Isabelle now?"

"Why aren't you with your family?" she shot back.

"I asked first."

"It's none of your business."

"If we're to get to know each other well enough for you to let me be part of your act, we've got to know more about each other."

"Who said I'm going to let you be part of my act?"

"Nobody, but you know the spectators love me."

"Modest, aren't you?"

"I prefer to call it being realistic."

"How long can I expect you to stay around? If I'm going to change my act to make you part of it, I need to know if you'll be here past the end of the week."

"Why should I leave?"

"You floated in. I figure you'll also float out. Drifters do."

So that was what she had against him, or at least part of it. "How long do you want me to stay?"

"Until the end of the season."

"When is that?"

"The regular season ends after Memphis, but Earl wants to go to New Orleans in November. You'd have to stay until then."

"Okay."

"Just like that, you'll agree to stay?"

"Why not?"

"Suppose you get the wanderlust?"

"I won't."

"Suppose you do?"

"I've given my word. I'll stay."

"Just how good is the word of a drifter?"

He wasn't making much progress at working his way into her confidence. She'd thrown up enough barriers to repel a battalion.

"What do you want me to do?"

"Pack up and leave today so Earl will stop bugging me about putting you in my act."

She said it quickly, looking him straight in the eye, but he saw something else in her eyes, in her stance. She might want to get rid of him, but she was also a little frightened of him. Why?

"I've said I'll stay through New Orleans, and I will. Now tell me why you left Jake and Isabelle."

"Because I want my own ranch and this is the fastest way I know to make the money to pay for it."

Especially if she was using it as a cover for the robberies. The robbers had taken more than a hundred thousand dollars. She could buy a very nice ranch with her share, but thieves didn't normally invest the money they stole. They usually squandered it and had to steal more.

But he hadn't seen any sign Drew was spending money. In fact, he hadn't seen her spend anything at all. Zeke or Hawk neither. Maybe all three of them wanted to buy a ranch.

"I would have thought your parents would help you, maybe even give you some of their land."

She threw him an exasperated look. "I told you, Jake and Isabelle adopted eleven of us. That's too many to provide for. Besides, they have a daughter of their own. We figure after all they've given us, we ought to provide for ourselves."

"That's very noble."

She gave him another look, this one definitely unfriendly. "You don't sound like you think so."

"What about your own family? You said your relatives wanted you to live with them."

"Everything in life comes with strings attached. Let's just say I didn't like their strings."

He could understand that, even if he couldn't believe anything else she said. She'd hardly looked at him, but kept her gaze fixed on the trick riders. She mumbled to herself occasionally and wrote on her pad. She didn't like people messing with her act, but she apparently planned to make several suggestions to her brothers.

If he could believe they were her brothers. It seemed

unlikely to him that anybody would adopt eleven orphans, especially such a mix as Drew described. Yet when he allowed his instincts full rein, they told him Drew Townsend was exactly what she appeared to be, a superb shot who had taken a job with Earl Odum's Wild West Show. She had been adopted, along with Zeke and Hawk, and had formed a very close bond with them over the years. Her brothers had probably been sent by her parents to make sure nothing happened to her.

But he couldn't let his feelings become involved in his work. That was a good way to botch his assignment, an even better way to get killed. He had no doubt in his mind that Drew could kill him. He also had a strong feeling Zeke and Hawk were rather good with guns themselves. It was a perfect setup for thieves, and working in the show a perfect cover.

His captain had said the evidence was mounting, that he was nearly certain Drew was the leader of this gang. Cole had been here only a few days, not long enough to pit his feelings against evidence gathered by several law officers from different states. He had to go with the facts.

"You agreed to tell me about yourself," Drew reminded him.

He brought his attention back to Drew. She had leveled an accusing glare at him.

"You don't mean to weasel out, do you?" she asked.

He didn't know why her descriptions and comparisons always had to be so unflattering. "There's not much to tell. My family had very specific plans for me. When I didn't do what my parents wanted, they made their displeasure known."

"Parents are always expecting you to do or become

what they never managed to do or become themselves. What was so difficult about your situation?"

"Probably nothing. But as you said, I'm the drifting type. I don't like being tied down."

"So you started drifting."

"Yes."

Her gaze remained on him, open, curious. "And now you find you can't stop."

"Let's just say I haven't found a reason to stop."

The corners of her eyes crinkled, and she laughed unexpectedly. It was a soft laugh, easy and liquid. He couldn't remember ever hearing a sound he liked better.

"I bet I know what could stop you, at least for a little while."

"What?" She couldn't possibly mean . . . she'd probably shoot him on the spot if the thought even crossed his mind.

"Some silly woman with enough money to pay for your pleasures and sufficient foolishness to ignore the fact you're a shiftless, conscienceless drifter who would waste her money and be unfaithful to her at nearly every opportunity."

Her evaluation shocked him. True, he'd pretended to be a drifter who thought it might be fun to work in a wild west show for a while, but that didn't make him a womanizing wastrel. It certainly didn't mean he was the type to take advantage of the credulity of some poor woman desperate to trade her money for male attention.

"I don't think I'd be all that bad." He expected her to temper her evaluation.

"You'd probably be worse," she said. "Men always take advantage of women. It's their nature."

"Taking advantage is one thing. Being a scourge on society is another."

She looked him full in the face. "Men can't help being that either."

"You don't like men very much, do you?"

The crinkles around the eyes appeared again. "I like them just fine. I just don't make a fool of myself over them."

"How about your brothers?"

"Zeke doesn't have any family. At least, if he does he doesn't know where they are. Hawk's mother is dead, and his white and Indian relatives don't want him. My family doesn't want me the way I am, so all we have is each other. We stick together because we don't ask anything of each other we aren't ready to give in return."

"What's that?"

"Loyalty. Outside of that, it's everybody for himself."

"That's a pretty harsh evaluation of life. Don't you believe in the goodness of man?"

"Sure. Jake and Isabelle are the best people on earth, but there aren't any more like them."

"What makes them so good?" He was beginning to take this personally. She didn't really know him, but she'd lumped him in with the worst of men. "You've practically said they are the only two decent people in the world. There must be something outstanding about them."

"No. They're just ordinary people."

"Then why aren't they liars and deadbeats like the rest of us?"

"I didn't say everybody was a liar and a deadbeat."

"Yes, you did. What did Jake and Isabelle do that was so wonderful?"

He'd angered her now, but that was all right. He was a little put out himself.

"They adopted all of us when nobody else wanted us. They gave us a home, made us feel wanted, helped restore our self-respect."

"Do-gooders on a monumental scale."

"Don't make fun of them."

"Did they succeed in their lofty objectives?"

It surprised him when she didn't snap back at him. "I used to think so, but most of the boys have left. Now I don't know."

He wanted to explore the issue further. If Jake and Isabelle were real, if they really had adopted all those kids, they might have established a network of gangs all over the South. No telling what a really clever leader could accomplish by adopting kids already alienated from society and teaching them to get back at people who'd hurt them. He wanted to know more about this couple.

"Who are those men over there?" she asked.

"Which men?"

"The ones talking to Carl. Why is one of them pointing at me?"

"Those are reporters. I invited them to come see you give a demonstration. I'm going to make you the biggest attraction in this show."

Chapter Seven

"Who gave you the right to bring them here?" The look she gave him said she'd rather riddle his body with bullets than speak to even one reporter.

"I told you what I wanted to do."

"I never thought you'd do it." She got to her feet. "You asked them here, you talk to them."

Cole grabbed her wrist. "You can't leave. They came to see you, not me."

"Watch me."

Drew pulled hard against his hold on her; he let her go. He didn't understand why she was so set against meeting the press, unless she didn't want anybody to take a picture, for fear somebody could identify her as the leader of the robbers.

"Do you want your act to be a success?"

She stopped and turned to face him, irritation pinching her features. "We've already been through this."

"Do you want to earn enough money for your ranch in one more year, or do you want to keep doing this for the rest of your life?"

"You know the answer to that, too. Get to what you mean to say."

"This is show business. The person with the most talent doesn't always come out on top. You've got to sell yourself to the public, make the audience want what you have to offer. You've got a great gimmick, a woman who can shoot better than a man."

"It's not a gimmick!"

"Sorry, wrong word." She was stuffed with enough pride for two people. "People are naturally curious about guns and sharpshooters. They'll be even more curious about a woman."

"So?"

"So you've got to let people know you're here."

"My name's on all the posters."

"So are a lot of other names. There's nothing to draw attention specifically to you."

"I don't want to draw attention to me."

"Then why are you in this show?"

"To make money."

"Like you said about your family, everything comes with strings attached. To be successful in show business, you've got to advertise. The way to do that is to get people to write about you, to put your picture in the newspaper so the public will know who you are, what you can do. If they make you sound interesting enough, you'll be famous."

"I don't want to be famous."

"Then you'll never make enough money to buy a ranch."

This wouldn't be a very convincing argument if she was saving all the money she got from the bank robberies. But she was thinking about it. He could tell from the angry look she threw him, she didn't like it one bit. That confused him even more. If she was saving her money from the robberies and really didn't want publicity, why was she even considering it?

"What are they going to want me to do?"

"To give them a demonstration."

"What else?"

"They'll want to know something about you. That bit about Jake and Isabelle adopting eleven orphans is perfect, especially after they see Zeke and Hawk."

"I'm not telling them about Jake and Isabelle. They'd hate it. I'm not making oddities out of Zeke and Hawk, either. They're people, not freaks for strangers to gawk at."

"Then let me do the talking for you."

That didn't placate her. "Why should I trust you? You're the one who got me into this mess in the first place. Why didn't you stay up in those stands that first night? Did seeing a woman outshoot a man needle your male pride so badly you couldn't stand it?"

He didn't like letting her think he was that shallow, but it was certainly better than the truth.

"It was a spur-of-the-moment decision. I thought it would be fun."

"You've caused me nothing but misery ever since."

The last person to say that to Cole had been his mother. He didn't like having to add Drew to that list.

107

"Well, it's done and can't be changed now."

"*You've* done it, so you deal with it." She turned and walked away.

"You can't leave now," he called after her.

She didn't answer, but just kept walking. He looked at the approaching reporters, calculating whether he should try to bring Drew back or disappear himself. He decided to face the reporters by himself. He'd brought them here without consulting Drew, so he had to be the one to figure out what to do next. But when he'd done that, he was going to throttle one very stubborn and frustrating female.

He didn't know what he'd expected this assignment to be like when he took it, but it was turning out to be unlike any other.

"They tell us you're Cole Benton," one of the reporters said when he came up.

"You got the right man."

"Where's this dame you were telling us about?"

"Any chance she's the little lady we saw sitting with you when we came in?" another asked.

"Yes, that's Drew Townsend."

The man whistled. "If she can shoot anywhere near as good as you say, we can have every man within a hundred miles fighting for a ticket."

"She wouldn't like that," Cole said, knowing Drew would hate it. "She's a little shy."

"Why?"

"Drew is proud of her abilities, but she doesn't want anybody making a fuss."

"I never met a dame in show business who wouldn't

give her left breast to get her picture in the newspaper," one reporter said.

"Drew is more likely to shoot the pen out of your hand for saying something she didn't like."

"No woman can shoot that good."

"She's even better than that," Cole said.

"How come?"

It was up to him to give them a story that would interest the readers, but he didn't want to stray too far from the truth.

"Her parents didn't know much about getting along in the West," Cole said. "They'd have starved if it hadn't been for the game Drew shot. She was too little to use a shotgun, so she used a rifle. Got to where she could shoot the head off a squirrel, quail, or a rabbit. Since she used a rifle, they didn't have to dig buckshot out of their dinner."

The reporters wrote rapidly on their pads.

"Where are her parents now?" one asked.

"They headed west and got killed by Indians. Drew was taken in by a couple that adopted eleven kids."

"Nobody's fool enough to adopt that many kids," one reporter said.

"They did. Two of them are working in the show, a black man and a half-breed Comanche."

He had everybody's undivided attention now.

"How did she end up in this show?" one man asked.

"She's trying to make enough money to buy her own ranch."

Cole looked up to see Zeke approaching. He looked madder than a stomped-on snake. He had several bull's-eyes, which he handed to Cole.

"Set these up," he said.

"What for?"

"You wanted a demonstration, didn't you? Well, you're going to get one. Drew's coming out on that horse, just like you wanted, only I'm catching her."

He punched Cole in the chest with a long black finger.

"No need to be mad," Cole said. "I'm doing this for her."

"I know you are. That's the only reason I don't let Hawk cut your throat."

"Then why the hell are you so mad?"

"Because you made Drew mad. I don't like it when that happens."

"Well, you must stay upset a lot, because that sister of yours doesn't ever seem to be very happy."

"She was until you showed up."

One of the reporters tapped Zeke on the shoulder. Zeke turned and glared so fiercely at the man, he stumbled back a few steps.

"You that black kid that was adopted with her?"

"Yeah," Zeke growled. "What of it?"

"What do you do in the show?" the man asked.

"Trick riding, some lassoing. I'm thinking about adding knife-throwing."

The reporter backed farther away. "If this is what he's like," he said to Cole, "I don't want to see the half-breed."

"That's good, because he doesn't want to see you," Zeke said. "Now if you want to see Drew's act, get yourself up into those seats," he said, addressing himself to the group.

"Is she going to do the whole act?" Cole asked Zeke.

"That plus some of the new tricks."

Greatly relieved, Cole smiled in spite of himself. Only her pride could have caused Drew to change her mind. She must have figured if she didn't perform, the reporters would write about her anyway, only they would say she was a fraud, that she hadn't shown up because she didn't want to be exposed.

She was going to be about as happy as a coyote after a wolf stole its dinner. He'd forced her to do something against her will to protect her reputation.

"Okay, gentlemen," he said to the reporters, "get ready to be dazzled."

Cole had to give Drew credit. When she decided to do something, she went all out.

She entered the arena standing on her horse, a big smile pinned on her face. He hoped the reporters couldn't tell it was completely insincere. She shot the center out of all three targets. Cole held them up for the men to see, then rushed to put up three more. Three more shots, dead center. She dismounted by leaping fearlessly into Zeke's arms.

Then, without so much as a pause, she shattered a series of targets that ran across a table like ducks in a shooting gallery. She followed that with the candle trick. Then, while Cole relit the candles and started the table spinning, she shattered three clay pigeons one after another. She then turned, shot the flames out of the moving candles, and ended up by hitting more clay pigeons, two at a time, and finally three at a time.

She came forward and executed a curtsey. Then she took a pistol Zeke handed her and proceeded to fire directly at each of the reporters. Their open-mouthed wonder at her performance was nothing compared to the shock of having their hats shot off their heads. A couple went white as sheets. One yelled and dived under his seat. Another jumped up and fled. One—and Cole had to give him high marks for bravery—leaned over, picked up his hat, and looked at the neat hole in the brim.

He looked up at Drew, then back at his hat. "Lady," he said, "that's the fanciest shooting I've ever seen. You must have kept your family's table well stocked."

"I told them your parents weren't very good at living rough, so you had to supplement the menu with game you shot," Cole explained. He wasn't certain she wouldn't turn her pistol on him next. She had one bullet left.

"They never went hungry," Drew answered, giving Cole one last withering look. "Anything else you want to ask? I wouldn't want you to get anything *else* wrong. You there, under that seat," she called, pointing her pistol at the reporter still crouched on the ground. "Come out. If I'd meant to hit you, you'd be dead. And you," she said, indicating the two reporters who hadn't yet regained their natural color, "buck up before you disgrace your parents by fainting."

The one reporter who hadn't seem fazed by anything broke out laughing. "Lady, I've never met anybody like you. I figured if you were half as good as your fella said you were, you'd look like a cross between a fur trapper and the bearded lady. But your fella said you were damned pretty, and he's right."

Drew fixed Cole with a look that promised retribution, then turned back to the reporter. "I'm flattered you like my looks, but if you don't want a hole in your forehead, you'll stop referring to that coyote as *my fella*. I'd as soon be yoked with a longhorn bull. In fact, I'd prefer it."

"Anything you say," the reporter replied, not visibly upset by Drew's threats. "Anything else you do in this act of yours?"

"No."

"We've got several new tricks in mind," Cole said, "but we don't want to show everything at once. We thought it would be better to add one here and there, you know, keep the act fresh, give each audience a little something new."

The reporter looked from Cole to Drew, the faintest suggestion of a smile on his lips. "Is that so?"

"Yes." Her answer was reluctant. "I'll be riding in on horseback for the second time tonight. I don't know when I'm going to add the candles."

"She's never missed one yet," Cole told the reporters, "but she wants to practice it a little more. You can hit a thousand targets and no one notices, but miss one and they won't talk of anything else."

"They'll be talking about something else this time," the reporter said. He looked at his hat once more and shook his head. "I wouldn't have believed it if I hadn't seen it for myself. Come on, guys," he said to the other reporters. "We have stories to write. I don't know about you, but mine is going to be on the street by suppertime."

"Do you mind if we take some pictures?" one of the others asked.

"Come by tomorrow morning about this time," Cole said. "We can set some up then."

"I don't want any pictures," Drew said.

"I told you, Miss Townsend is very shy," Cole said. "We'll have to keep this low-key, and we insist upon approval of all pictures before they're used."

"Certainly."

Cole knew the reporters would agree to anything to get a picture. They'd print what they got regardless of whether Drew liked it or not.

"Come early tonight," Cole said. "Miss Townsend is the first act after the opening parade."

"Is she going to shoot our hats off again?" one of the reporters asked.

A devilish smile appeared on Drew's face. Cole had never seen that look before, but he knew it wasn't a good sign.

"I think it would be a great trick to line all of you up and send your hats into the next county, but I think I'd prefer to use *my fella* as a target tonight." She smiled even more sweetly. "Let's hope I don't pick that time to miss."

Cole decided he just might not enter the ring tonight. There was an old saying about those who ran away living to fight another day. The way Drew was looking at him now, he'd be lucky to make it to another day.

"Zeke," Drew said, "why don't you show these fellas out? I need to talk to Cole."

Cole considered trying to sneak off with Zeke, but he figured she'd shoot the heels off his boots. He stayed and awaited his fate.

"What did you tell them about my shooting game to feed my family?"

Cole breathed a sigh of relief. She might not like what he'd done, but apparently she was more concerned, at least right now, with the background he'd made up for her.

"I told them your parents weren't very good at living rough, so you learned to shoot game to feed your family."

"You didn't mention Jake and Isabelle?"

"I just said you were taken in by a couple who adopted eleven orphans. I didn't mention their names. I knew you wouldn't want me to."

"My not wanting it hasn't stopped you before. Why should it now?"

"Believe it or not, I'm not trying to make you mad."

"You couldn't prove it by me."

"I'm doing this for your own good. I know you don't want to do it yourself because you're naturally shy."

"I'm not shy. I just don't like strangers knowing my business. If I read a lot of stuff in those papers, I'll—"

"You can't blame me for everything they write. You know reporters make up stuff."

"I *can* blame you for their being here in the first place."

"Why did you let Zeke catch you?"

He'd been thinking about that the whole time. She'd said from the first she didn't want to let him catch her, but he felt slighted anyway. He had known she might decide not to use the jump, but he'd figured if she did, she'd let him catch her. It was his idea. It wasn't fair to cut him out of it.

"You were busy with the reporters."

He felt a surge of relief. She hadn't said she hated him and would shoot him through the heart if he so much as laid a hand on her. She hadn't said she'd quit the show before she'd let him touch her. She'd given him an excuse that sounded halfway believable.

"Besides, you're still supposed to be a stranger coming down out of the stands."

"I can't do that now. The reporters know I'm part of the act."

She didn't look surprised. He guessed she'd already figured that out.

"I guess there's no reason not to let you set up the bull's-eyes and the candles."

"Or catch you when you dismount."

"Zeke will do that. He has time to get back to his horse before I'm done."

"It'll be a close call."

"He knows."

Cole decided not to push. With a little luck, Zeke would find he didn't have enough time. Drew's act was spectacular, but it was short. "I've thought of a new trick," he said.

"I think that's enough for tonight."

"You'll need something for tomorrow."

"We'll do the candles."

"Want to go through it again?"

"Okay."

Cole was careful not to smile. Little by little he was working his way inside her defenses. He was convinced she liked him. She didn't want to, but she couldn't help it. He'd never had to trade on a woman's affections before, but the captain had told him it might be necessary to get the kind of information they needed to convict the robbers.

He hadn't wanted this assignment. He didn't like the idea of lying to a woman about his feelings, but he was trying to stop a criminal. He told himself any lie was acceptable if it would lead to the robbers' capture.

But he didn't feel like that now. He felt like a traitor. He felt dirty. He wasn't talking about some unknown stranger any more. He was talking about Drew Townsend, a woman he liked. And despite the facts, the more he learned about her, the harder it was to believe she was a criminal.

But it wasn't his job to argue with evidence gathered by law officers from several states. He was to infiltrate her operation and find a way to betray her. He would do that because it was his job. But if he found she wasn't guilty, he would try his damnedest to clear her name.

Millville, Illinois

Cole looked irritably about him. There wasn't much about the town of Millville to interest a visitor. It looked prosperous enough with its three- and four-story brick buildings and its busy streets filled with people going about their business on a Thursday afternoon. He missed the trees of older, more established towns. It had been his experience that founders of towns were too anxious to lay out lots and sell them to prospective buyers to pay much attention to aesthetics. That usually had to wait for the second generation.

"It looks like a nice little town," Myrtle said to him. She had asked Cole to help her buy some new material. She had meant to ask Drew, but she had disappeared.

That was the real source of his irritability. Last night's show had gone off without a mishap. After the crescendo of publicity that had begun with those first newspaper articles a week ago, the crowds were larger, the applause more vigorous.

Drew didn't seem to be affected by their success or the prospect of achieving stardom. She'd practiced with him each morning in a depressingly efficient manner, speaking only when necessary. This morning she'd disappeared almost immediately afterwards. A diligent search hadn't turned up anyone who knew where she'd gone. No one knew where to find Zeke or Hawk, either.

Cole followed Myrtle into what appeared to be a warehouse containing thousands of bolts of cloth. "Don't panic," Myrtle warned. "I'm not going to look at everything."

"You couldn't," Cole responded. "We're only going to be here for a few more hours." Cole noticed he was the only man in the building. He took that as a bad sign.

"You don't have to look at anything until I ask," Myrtle said. "You can spend your time thinking up more tricks for Drew."

He spent his time being irritated.

He didn't feel that he was doing a good job on this assignment. He was supposed to insinuate himself into Drew's inner circle, but he couldn't do that when he couldn't even find her. If three people could disappear from under his nose, he obviously wasn't qualified for this job. It was no consolation that no one else knew where to find them. Nobody else had any reason to keep an eye on their movements. He did, and he'd failed.

His captain wouldn't be pleased.

Then there was the personal side. There shouldn't have been a personal side, but it was useless to pretend there wasn't. It wasn't like he'd fallen in love or become infatuated, but he had developed a strong liking for Drew. He was ashamed to admit it was rapidly turning into a powerful physical attraction. It was a very inconvenient way to feel about a woman he was supposed to spy on.

It affected his judgment. It made him want to see everything Drew did in the best possible light, thus causing his inner feelings to be at variance with his duty. It was a very uncomfortable and unnerving situation. It had never happened to him before. He didn't like it.

"You'd never know it from the way she talks, but she has a wonderful eye for color," Myrtle was saying. She showed him two pieces of cloth that seemed identical to him. "I can't decide which is the best match."

"Either one looks fine to me," Cole said.

Myrtle laughed comfortably. "But you're a man. Everybody knows men are practically imbeciles when it comes to judging color."

It wasn't his strongest point, but Cole resented the imbecile remark. "If it doesn't match, I'm sure they'll let you exchange it."

Myrtle's frown indicated *she* wasn't certain. "I don't think we'll have time to return it before we leave town." She put the bolts back. "I think I'll wait for Drew. I'm sure St. Louis will have a wider selection."

"I can't see how," Cole said, remembering the confusion of hundreds of shades of blue and purple.

They were doing two shows in Millville. As soon as they could get everything torn down after the show and loaded on the train, they would leave for Wilton Springs. They usually had only one show in a town before moving on to the next engagement, but later in the month they were scheduled to spend four days in Memphis. Cole wasn't happy about that. His family lived in Memphis. He wasn't worried about having to visit his mother. He always did that. He was concerned someone in the show might discover he was a member of one of the wealthiest families in the city.

That wouldn't help him in his work.

"Do you always depend on Drew to do things like help you match material?" Cole asked Myrtle.

"No, but she likes to help. She's taken a real interest in us regulars, especially those of us who have been here for years."

"How so?"

"She's advising us on how to invest our money so we'll have something when we retire. Most of us had just ignored it. But Drew made us realize that's stupid. She's made us start putting money aside."

Cole stopped in his tracks. "Do you mean she makes you give her your money?"

"No." Myrtle chuckled. "Though I think she would have if we hadn't agreed to her scheme."

"What scheme?"

"Each week she marches us down to a bank and helps us deposit our money."

They were approaching the local bank. Cole felt as if a cold hand had suddenly closed around his heart. "Does she know anything about your accounts?"

"Of course. She has all our records. We're not very good at things like that."

Cole had a sinking feeling. He could see all these trusting old people depositing their money year after year, handing over their records to Drew. But when they went to get their money, they'd find their accounts had been emptied long ago.

And their friend Drew Townsend would have disappeared.

"Have you ever deposited any money in this bank?" Cole said, indicating the building in front of them.

"I think so, but I don't remember."

"Let's go inside and find out." If Myrtle had an account, he had to know if the money was still there.

"I don't remember my account number."

"It's okay. All you need is your name."

They entered the building together.

"There's Drew," Myrtle exclaimed. "She can help me pick out the material on our way back."

Seated in the middle of the lobby, like a spider surveying her prey, Drew watched everything going on around her with an eagle eye.

"What's she doing here?" Cole asked.

"Now I know I don't have any money in this bank," Myrtle said. "Drew always checks out every bank before she lets us use it. She says you can't tell about the honesty of a bank until you've observed the customers that come through its doors."

Cole had a different explanation for Drew's presence. A robber could never decide how best to rob a bank until she'd spent several hours observing its operation.

Chapter Eight

Drew wasn't happy that her reaction on seeing Cole enter the bank with Myrtle was to smile up at him. She hadn't been expecting him, or she'd never have let her feelings betray her. She'd been having trouble with her response to him ever since Earl talked her into jumping into his arms. She'd never been in a man's embrace before, so she had nothing to compare it to, but she didn't think she ought to be thinking about him so often. Or wondering if it would feel the same when . . . *if* she jumped into his arms again.

Nor should she have started comparing him to other men and deciding he was more handsome, more charming, stronger . . . well, that was exactly the problem. She shouldn't have been thinking any of that. Zeke was bigger and stronger, but there was no question that Cole was more handsome. Maybe she ought to send for Will. No other man seemed particularly handsome when Will was around.

"I wish you hadn't come to town without telling me," Myrtle said as she approached Drew. "I have to buy more fabric, and you know how I depend on your eye for color."

Drew forced herself to shift her gaze from Cole to Myrtle. Cole's expression confused her. He looked as though he had an unpleasant duty to perform and was going to do it no matter how much he disliked it. She didn't understand why he should direct such a look at her. Everything had gone unusually well recently. The audience response had been so good Earl was planning to make her name bigger on the next posters.

She still wouldn't let Cole catch her, but she'd promised Earl she'd think about it. She even let Cole talk her into a new trick, though it was so easy she hardly considered it a trick. He would pretend to start to juggle six balls, and she'd shatter them as he threw them up. It was a good thing she never missed. He wasn't a juggler.

Drew focused her attention on Myrtle. "Let me see what you bought. Did Cole help you pick it out?"

She peeped at him to see his response, but his scowl remained unchanged.

"I decided to wait for you," Myrtle said. "Cole tried to help, poor man, but you know how men are when it comes to judging colors. Except for Earl, I've never known one who could tell violet from lavender, magenta, or lilac."

"I didn't know there were that many colors of purple," Cole said. "And she tells me there are even more."

"Shades," Myrtle corrected. "See what I mean?" she said to Drew.

"I'm surprised you got him inside the store," Drew said, hoping to ease Cole's heavy frown. "Most men would have headed straight for a saloon."

"I don't deny I felt the urge," Cole said, his expression only slightly less forbidding, "but I had to buy some candles and clay balls. You shot up my entire supply."

"I had no idea it was so hard to find clay balls," Myrtle said. "Cole had to order some made."

Drew couldn't stop wondering why Cole would go to so much trouble for her act. He'd be off doing something else in a few weeks. Maybe some drifters were like that, entering wholeheartedly into one thing until they got bored and looked for something else. The more she thought about it, the more he puzzled her. He didn't behave like the drifting kind of man. He'd attacked the problem of making her act more entertaining with a single-mindedness that reminded her of the Randolphs and their determination to become the richest family in Texas.

"Myrtle tells me you're casing out the bank," Cole said.

"I'm studying it, if that's what you mean," Drew said.

"Why?"

"Because I'm always looking for ways to get more interest on my money."

"You can get that information from an interview with the bank manager."

"I already have, but I like to see for myself what the customers look like. If I see a lot of sour-faced businessmen and frowning farmers, I know it's not a good place."

"Drew always decides where to put our money," Myrtle said. "She hasn't made a mistake yet."

"Every bank has its own personality," Drew explained. "You can see it in the people who work for the bank, and in the customers. I wouldn't trust my money to any bank that didn't have a friendly and open personality."

Drew got the feeling Cole thought she was nuts, or lying. She could understand why he would be skeptical of her method of choosing a bank—men rarely understood why the feel of a thing was so important to a woman—but she didn't understand why he'd think she was lying.

She told herself not to worry about it. She didn't know Cole very well. She couldn't be certain of the meaning of his expressions. There was no point in trying to figure out what he was determined to keep hidden. Nor could she figure out why she should want to. He would be gone in a few weeks. Then it wouldn't matter.

She got to her feet. "I'm done here."

"Is it a good bank?" Myrtle asked.

"I don't think so. I'll wait until we reach the next town. Let's see what kind of bank they have there."

"Why don't you keep your money in one bank?" Cole asked.

"I don't want it all in one place. If one bank fails, and quite a few failed last year, I won't lose all my money."

"None of our banks failed," Myrtle said. "We did what Drew said, and all our money is safe."

That didn't appear to make Cole happy. He was definitely out of sorts, something she'd never seen before.

"I'm ready to go back if you are," she said.

She and Myrtle left the bank. She thought Cole meant to stay, but he came out before they'd gone very far.

Drew didn't like towns. She never went into one unless she felt it was necessary. The walkways were always crowded with people, the streets with wagons, the air with noise, smells of bread and meat, unwashed bodies, and horse manure. People brushed against her in passing without making an attempt to move out of her path. In Texas that would have been cause for taking offense. In a crowded town it was just the way things were.

"I wish I had a horse," she said, speaking her thoughts aloud.

"What would you do with a horse?" Cole asked.

"Get out of this town in two minutes instead of fifteen or twenty."

"I'm glad you don't," Myrtle said. "I wouldn't want to be left behind."

"I'd take you with me."

"Not on a horse, you wouldn't," Myrtle said, laughing and shuddering at the same time. "I'm afraid of them. I don't know how you let Cole talk you into riding one."

"Popularity," Drew said, jokingly. "I couldn't resist the opportunity to draw bigger crowds and make more money. It'll mean I can have my ranch sooner."

Myrtle didn't like that. "But that means you'll leave us."

"Not for long. You'll be coming to live with me in a few years."

Myrtle's doubtful look told Drew she had more work to do in convincing the show people that living on a Texas ranch was a desirable way to spend their retirement.

"It's her!"

The shrill voice from the crowd riveted Drew's attention. She looked around to see who the unseen person could be talking about.

Barely a second later a woman burst from the crowd and strode straight up to Drew. "You're Drew Townsend," she announced. "I saw you in the Wild West Show last night."

Drew had rarely been recognized on the street, and never in such an attention-getting manner. People all around stopped to stare.

"She's a sharpshooter," the woman announced. "She shot all kinds of things last night and never once missed. She's better than any man."

Drew wanted to turn and melt into the crowd, but when she started to back up, Cole put his hand in the small of her back.

"Let her rave about you," he hissed. "It'll earn you more good publicity than a dozen newspaper articles."

"I never would have believed it if I hadn't seen it," the woman said. "My husband read that article about you in the newspaper. He said it couldn't be true. That's the only reason we went." She laughed happily. "He was so furious he hardly said a word all the way home. How did you learn to shoot like that?"

"I don't know," Drew said, miserably uncomfortable at being the object of all this attention.

"You can't teach that kind of talent," Cole said. "It's God-given."

The woman beamed at Drew. "She's sure a godsend to the women of this town. Now the men can't say women can't handle a gun as well as they can. I hope you're going to perform again tonight. Both my sisters are taking their husbands. They didn't believe me when I told them what you did. I hope you're not going to miss tonight."

"I'll do my best." Drew couldn't understand why she felt so uncomfortable talking to this woman. She didn't like talking to strangers, but she could do it. At least she *used* to be able to, before Cole came into her life. A lot of things were different now.

"Miss Townsend never misses," Cole said.

The woman appeared to notice Cole for the first time. Her eyes got a little wider, and her smile grew more pronounced. "You're the man who held up those bull's-eyes, aren't you?"

"Yes, I am."

"You're lucky to have a wife like her."

Shock at the thought of being married to Cole fled when Drew saw the expression on his face. She supposed to a man like him marriage was worse than a prison sentence.

"We're not married," Drew said.

Now it was the woman's turn to look embarrassed. "I'm terribly sorry. My husband says I always talk before I think."

"Don't give it another thought," Cole said, flashing his considerable charm now that he'd recovered from his surprise. "Lots of people who work together in shows like this are married."

"Like my husband and me," Myrtle said. "We've been on the circuit for nearly fifty years."

"I'm sure you'd make a very handsome couple if you were married," the woman said to Drew. "Well, I'd best be going before I put my foot in it again. Remember, don't miss a single shot tonight. After what I said to my Joe, he'll never let me forget it."

Much to Drew's relief, she hurried away. But Drew's reprieve was short. She was recognized twice more before they reached the outskirts of the town.

"I'll never go near another reporter as long as I live," she declared when the open field where the show was set up came into view. "I can't even take a walk without people recognizing me."

"I think that's rather nice," Myrtle said. "No one's ever recognized me. Well, not in a very long time."

"Of course she'll talk to every reporter who wants a story," Cole said to Myrtle. "And she'll smile like she's having the time of her life at the photo session this afternoon."

Drew rounded on Cole. "I didn't give you permission to arrange another one."

"Earl did. He's going to pose with you. He even offered to pay for having new costumes made."

"Earl must intend to make you a really big star," Myrtle said. "He's never paid for costumes for anybody else."

Angry rebellion boiled inside Drew. Once more Cole had railroaded her into something she didn't want to do. But she didn't mean to give in to him this time. She'd talk to Earl. She'd have him cancel the photographers.

"This will be wonderful for everybody in the show," Myrtle said, beaming with happiness. "If we start drawing bigger audiences, Earl will have to raise our salaries. Wait until I tell everybody."

"Myrtle, don't—"

Myrtle waved and hurried on ahead.

"Now see what you've done," Drew said, turning on Cole.

"What?"

"You've forced me to let those men take more photographs. I don't want pictures of me plastered up and down the Mississippi. I don't want any new dresses. I don't want to be the star. But now I have to, because everybody is depending on me to increase their salaries. Why couldn't you have stayed in the stands and kept on thinking you were better than I am?"

"I thought you wanted people to appreciate your skill."

"I do, but—"

"They can't if they don't come see you, and they won't if nobody mentions your name or tells them what a fantastic marksman you are. We usually stay in a town just one night. We're gone before the people who came to the show can tell the people who *didn't* come to the show about you. This way the news can go on ahead of you, start people anticipating you, *wanting* to see you."

Drew started to tell him she didn't want any of that, but she didn't, because it wasn't entirely true. She did want recognition for her skill; she did want people to know she was the very best; she did want them to flock to see her. She just didn't want to have to deal with the results of fame.

What irritated her the most was that Cole Benton had orchestrated this whole publicity campaign without her approval. He'd made it impossible for her to refuse without seeming ungrateful for her good fortune and indifferent to what was best for the show and the other performers.

But maybe the most unsettling aspect of this was the way her feelings for Cole were changing. She was tired of being bossed around, of having him come up with things he thought were good for her act and practically forcing them on her. She was tired of having her comfortable pattern of life constantly overturned by his unbounded enthusiasm for turning her into a famous sharpshooter.

But if she was honest—and she made a practice of being honest no matter how much she disliked it—she was starting to like having him around. It infuriated her, but she couldn't stop herself. She might be irritated by his interference, but she kept putting up with it. She might say she didn't want to have to put up with his attention, remember his smile, or respond to his charm, but she did.

"I suppose my feelings about this are contradictory," she said, "but let me try to explain my reaction." She could tell from his expression he expected some sort of rebuff.

"I do want recognition." She couldn't help smiling. "My brothers say I like lording it over them, that I can't resist showing off when I can do something better than they can. It's true. I'm naturally bossy, and being able to do things better than they can made me feel I had the right to tell them what to do. They spoiled me. They let me get away with it so often I got used to being the boss. So you can see why I'm not happy to have you come in and take my own act out of my hands."

"I'm only trying—"

"I know what you're trying to do. I like it when I'm in the arena. I don't like it when I'm not. I realize that's my problem, not yours, but it's the way it is. You're pushing me along so fast I can't decide if I want to go along or not. This may be just an act, only part of the show, but it's my act. I want to control it."

"Earl told me you'd be glad I was doing all this, that you were too shy to do it yourself."

She couldn't help laughing. "Nobody in my family would call me shy, but I do like my privacy. I also want to be in control of my own life. I saw what happened to my parents. I'll never let it happen to me."

"So what do you want me to do?"

He looked so adorable when he was being contrite. She wanted to cradle his head and tell him everything would be all right. Only she was certain if she did anything so unwise, *nothing* would be all right. Why did useless, good-for-nothing drifters have to have so much charm? Why did he have to be so tall, so strong, so good-looking?

"Maybe you ought to choose another performer to make famous. I'm going to quit as soon as I get enough money for my ranch. The more famous you make me, and the more money Earl has to pay me, the sooner that will be." She sighed in resignation. "At least ask me before you do something else."

That odd expression was back, the one that seemed to say he was hurt she didn't understand and appreciate what he was doing, that said he didn't believe a word she was saying. His look implied he didn't like something about what was happening; it hinted at even more important feelings. But that was always the way with Cole. She could never tell what he was really feeling, nor could she trust what he said to reflect his feelings.

"Okay, I promise to ask. But I don't promise not to push a little when it's something I think is important."

"I'll accept that."

"In return, you've got to stop keeping me at a distance."

She felt herself bridle. "What do you mean?"

"You avoid me. You won't talk to me unless I corner you. You disappear every chance you get. If we're going to work together, we've got to get to know each other so well that each of us can anticipate what the other is thinking."

"Why?"

"Because it'll make the act work better."

She wasn't sure she trusted that to be his only motive. "It's going just fine as it is."

"You heard what that woman said. She was delighted to think we were married, or at least interested in each other."

"But we aren't." She *wasn't* interested. Just curious. That was natural.

"I know, but people like to think they see a romance developing, especially between performers. It makes it more exciting."

"I'm not going to pretend to be mooning over you."

"I don't mean anything like that, just to smile at each other occasionally, like when you make a really spectacular shot."

"I *always* make spectacular shots."

"I know that, but the spectators don't. It'll be more fun for them if they think I'm as proud of you as they are."

Are you? The words nearly jumped out of her mouth. She choked them back, horrified she would even think them. "I don't see why that's necessary."

"Let's try it tonight and see how it works. If you don't get a better response, I won't say another word about it."

"Just what do you expect me to do?" She was on tricky ground. She wasn't used to this man-woman thing, but she had enough sense to know if you let a barrier down, it was going to be hard to put it back up again. She needed to keep big roadblocks between her and Cole. She didn't understand it, and she was very disappointed in herself, but she was definitely falling victim to his charm.

And Drew Townsend didn't like being a victim.

"Just smile at me," Cole said. "Speak to me between tricks, maybe even mention my name, saying you appreciate my help in performing your tricks."

That didn't seem like too much. It shouldn't be dangerous. "Okay, but a smile is all you're going to get."

Drew had thought Cole would stick to his role as helper. He didn't. He played to the audience shamelessly. He dressed up so smartly you'd have thought he was going to a society party rather than appearing in a wild west show. It soon became obvious the women in the audience were paying more attention to him than to her.

She couldn't blame them for being unable to do what she couldn't do herself—take her eyes off Cole. She'd been around very handsome men ever since she was adopted, so she couldn't explain why she should be so attracted to Cole. True, he was tall, slim-bodied, and strong, but so was nearly every man in the show. Cole looked like a cowboy without the rough edge, an idealized version of the real thing. His hair was cut perfectly, he shaved every day, his clothes were clean and neat. The show was full of cowboys with the shaggy look. Cole stood out by comparison

Okay, he had a million-dollar smile and a dapper appearance, but looks didn't make the man. Neither did broad shoulders, narrow hips, or well muscled legs. The clothes he had on tonight fitted him nearly as closely as his skin. If she attempted to wear anything that tight, Zeke would lock her in her room. He was worse than Jake when it came to reminding her she was a lady and ought to dress and act like one. She didn't know what had happened to him when he was a slave—he wouldn't talk about that part of his life—but it had turned him into a puritan.

"You sure you want that man to catch you?" Zeke asked two days earlier.

That man was Cole.

"No, but there's no point in your having to run to be ready for your entrance."

"I don't care."

"I do. So does Earl. If it doesn't work, I'll let you do it, or I'll go back to entering like I used to."

"Horseback is better."

Everybody said that. People always talked during the show, but the noise dropped in half when she entered the ring standing on a horse. Parents pointed for their children to watch. Even the women turned their gazes from Cole. Everyone applauded when she hit the bull's-eyes while on horseback. Their applause grew much louder when Cole held up the targets so they could see she hit them all dead center. Their applause was even greater the second time, still greater when she put out all three candles.

Then, without warning, she jumped into the air and came down in Cole's arms. There was a sudden, swift intake of breath in the audience when she jumped straight into the air. A moment of silence when she landed in Cole's arms, then a vigorous outbreak of applause. Some people even whistled and hooted.

Finding herself in Cole's embrace was just as much of a shock as it had been the first time. It was all Drew could do to remember that she had a show to do. She had prepared herself for the sensation of his arms around her, her body held tightly against his, but she hadn't prepared herself for the brilliance of his smile. That went straight to her belly and started a quivering flutter that threatened to incapacitate her.

Drawing on all her strength of mind, Drew tore her attention from Cole's face and back to the audience.

"Let me down," she hissed when he didn't immediately set her on the ground. "You're not supposed to carry me about like a trophy."

"Have dinner with me tonight."

She couldn't decide whether she was more shocked he was asking her to have dinner with him or that he was doing it in the middle of her act.

"This is no place to ask such a question."

"It's the only place I can get you to agree."

"This is blackmail."

"I know."

She tried to get her arms free, but he held her too tightly.

"If you don't let me down immediately," she said, doing her best to smile at the audience, "I'm going to make a target out of you instead of those clay pigeons."

"Promise."

"I'll consider it."

Cole paraded her about the ring like a prize doll. "She's such a little thing," he shouted out to the audience. "Who'd guess she could shoot like she can?"

"Put me down!" Drew hissed.

"Promise?"

"No."

"She's light enough to catch easily."

The heartless beast tossed her into the air and caught her again.

"Promise?"

"I'll kill you," she said, so angry she couldn't smile.

"Want me to toss her again?" Cole asked the audience. "She might get dizzy, but she can still shoot the eyes out of a squirrel."

"Toss me again, and I'll shoot your eyes out."

The audience was laughing, applauding, calling for Cole to toss her into the air again.

"Promise?"

"Okay, but I swear I'll get you back for this."

Cole set her down. "We have to get on with the show," he told the audience.

Drew went through her act at breakneck speed. Every time she took aim, she thought of Cole. When she tried the very difficult shot of putting out lighted candles on a revolving table, she thought of Cole. When she shot three clay pigeons in the air at once, she thought of Cole.

She didn't miss a single shot.

Performing a flawless routine was easier than having dinner with him was going to be.

Chapter Nine

"I haven't forgiven you," Drew said.

"I know," Cole said. They had finished their meal and were enjoying coffee and brandy.

"I will get my revenge."

"I know that, too."

Cole had had a buckboard waiting outside the arena when they finished their act. The minute they reached the hotel she had stalked off to her room without a word. Once inside with the door locked, she'd paced back and forth, calling Cole every name she'd ever learned from her brothers, calling herself nearly as many for being fool enough to cave in to the pressure and being an even bigger fool to actually consider honoring a promise forced from her.

First she decided to stay in her room for the evening,

but that made her angry because she was being punished for something Cole had done. Next she decided to wait for Zeke and Hawk before she had dinner. But she wouldn't put it past Cole to have told them they needn't bother to return to the hotel until later. In the end she was so full of things she wanted to say to Cole, names she wanted to call him if she lost her temper sufficiently to forget she'd been brought up a lady, she decided to have dinner with him after all. It was the only way she could work off her ire.

"What you did was cowardly. No gentleman would expect a woman to honor a promise extracted under such conditions."

"I know."

"It proves you're not a man of character."

"I know that, too."

It made her furious that he just sat there, smiling like he was as happy as a calf in clover, letting her say anything she pleased, and agreeing with her.

Even the hotel dining room contributed to her irritation. It was a dull little room, the walls covered in a dark wallpaper featuring exotic flowers and vinelike foliage, all made darker by the passage of time and a film of soot and grease. The two pictures of hunting scenes did nothing to improve her appetite. The diners sat in ladder-back chairs and ate at small tables so close together the waitress's skirt brushed against Drew every time she passed. The fact the room was full of diners, all talking, made it impossible to achieve any feeling of privacy.

"How can you let me say all these things?" Drew demanded.

"Because they're true."

"Don't you care?"

"Only if you do."

"Of course I care. I mean, I would if I liked you, which I don't. I couldn't possibly like a man lacking in honor. That is, if I were the kind of woman to go around liking men, which I'm not."

"What's wrong with men?"

"They're men."

"I thought that was our advantage."

"It would have been if you'd been created more useful and dependable than a wild stallion eating locoweed."

"You like your brothers."

"They've got their shortcomings, but Isabelle never put up with foolishness. I'm not sure she could have done much with you, but she'd certainly have taught you not to extract promises from women when you had them at a disadvantage. That's a very ungentlemanly thing to do."

"I know."

She brought her hand down on the table with a bang. "Stop agreeing with me!" She was aware of an abrupt silence, of everyone in the hotel dining room looking at her. "It makes it impossible to get mad at you," she said in a softer voice.

"I don't want you to be angry with me."

"I do. You deserve for me to be furious. And I am."

"Will you stop being furious if I agree I'm the most unprincipled scoundrel in the world and most abjectly beg your apology?"

"You needn't go to the trouble," she said, disgusted. "I'd know you didn't mean it. You'd do it again if you had to."

He grinned that insolent, devil-may-care grin. "Damned right."

"Why would you do that?" It didn't make sense to her. He didn't seem like a flirt, despite the fact he was a drifter and they usually had no qualms about making promises they didn't intend to keep.

"I like talking to you," Cole said.

"Nobody likes talking to me," Drew said. "I'm bossy, argumentative, and I'm always right. Even my family ducks when they see me coming."

He laughed. "Really?"

She wished she hadn't told him that. It made her feel too vulnerable. "They say they already have one mother and don't need another."

"I would consider that a compliment."

"You wouldn't if you were me. It means I'm a pain in the—Isabelle told me I wasn't to use that word ever again."

"And you do what she says?"

She hesitated. "Most of the time. If she found out I used that word, she'd do something terrible. Isabelle was raised a lady, but she can think of awful things to do when people don't do what she wants."

"She sounds like a tyrant you're well rid of."

Drew took offense. "Isabelle is a wonderful person. I couldn't have had a better mother."

Cole looked dubious.

"I still want to know why you insisted we have dinner," Drew said, getting back to her original question.

"I told you, I like talking to you. I like the stories you tell. I never heard of any family like yours."

141

"What you mean is you don't believe my stories."

"Did I say that?"

"No, but I can see it in your eyes. Come on, why did you invite me to dinner? I can't imagine where you got the money. I know Earl doesn't pay you very much."

"I don't want to talk about Earl. It's my money. I want to talk about you."

"What about me?"

"Anything."

"I've already told you everything there is to know."

"What are you going to do when you get your ranch? Myrtle said you'd invited her to retire there."

She'd invited several of the older people to live on her ranch when she discovered they hadn't saved any money and would be destitute, but she didn't want Cole to know about it. It made her seem soft and foolish, exactly what he expected of a female who didn't have enough sense to know you couldn't make a success of a ranch burdened by a crowd of old, useless hangers-on.

"My family raises cattle. I expect I'll do the same."

"Suppose your husband wants to do something else?"

"I'm not getting married."

"Why not? Did somebody jilt you?"

"If he had, he'd be dead," Drew snapped before she had time to realize her reaction made it sound like she had been jilted and was still furious about it.

"You mean Zeke or Hawk would have tortured him to death?"

"I mean I'd have put a bullet between his eyes," she said, deciding she'd already made the wrong impression, so she didn't have much to lose. Besides, it didn't matter what Cole thought of her. She wasn't interested in marrying him, either.

"I imagine all those brothers must have scared off a lot of suitors."

"They might have if I hadn't scared them off first."

"Why?"

"Why do you keep asking me questions I've already answered?"

"Because I find it hard to believe a beautiful woman like you has no interest in men."

"You just demonstrated one of the reasons."

"What did I do?"

"You told a bald-faced lie without blinking. You can't trust a man to tell you the truth, not even when you've got a knife to his throat."

"When did I lie?"

"When you said I'm beautiful. Men are always making stupid remarks like that. You think it makes a woman like you, but it just makes her angry when she knows it's not true."

"But you are beautiful. You'd be more so if you dressed like a woman instead of a female version of Daniel Boone."

"That's another reason."

"What?"

"Men are always saying they like a woman just as she is. But give them five minutes, and they start suggesting ways to improve her."

"Woman are even worse about that."

"Not me. I don't want any man, so I have no reason to want to change him." She pushed back her chair. "Now

143

we'd better get to the train station. I imagine they'll have everything packed and ready to leave by the time we get there."

"Will you have dinner with me again?"

She paused. "Why?"

"I told you—"

"I know what you said, but I don't believe you."

"Then you'll have to give me a chance to convince you I'm sincere."

She stood. "It doesn't matter whether you're sincere or not. You'll soon be gone."

Drew waited in the lobby while Cole settled the bill. She noticed several women looking at her, envy plain on their faces. She felt like announcing that any fool who wanted a charming drifter could step right up. She'd be happy to trade him for a good cutting pony.

But even while that thought was passing through her mind, she decided it would be nice if he weren't a drifter. She wasn't about to lose her head over him, but it was a shame such an attractive and charming man should go to waste. But she wasn't fool enough to think *the love of a good woman* could change Cole Benton.

She didn't know why he'd decided to attach himself to her or why he was working so hard to make her act a hit, but she wasn't going to fight him any longer. He seemed to have a knack for knowing what would appeal to the audience. She didn't have it. She'd been stiff and ill at ease those first few months. Only her spectacular shooting, and the fact Earl couldn't find anyone to replace her, had kept her employed. Now she was comfortable enough to take advantage of Cole's suggestions.

As long as he didn't come up with any more stunts like

having her jump into his arms. Still, it was nice to have an attractive man around who worked hard to please her. Her brothers loved her, put up with her, even defended her. She was proud of them, and was seldom happier than when she could be in the middle of the whole bunch, but that wasn't the same.

Everything was different with Cole.

She was glad she wasn't the kind of woman to fall for his looks or his charm. She knew she wasn't beautiful, but she didn't mind being told she was. She knew she wasn't a scintillating companion, but it was nice to have a man act like he couldn't get enough of her company.

Yes, she could see some of the reasons women let themselves be flattered and captivated by attractive men. She'd enjoy a little flirtation. But that was all it would be. She doubted she'd see him again after New Orleans. If he stayed around that long.

"I haven't seen Drew," Myrtle said. "I don't know where she is."

Cole was completely out of temper. He'd walked the length of the train, but he couldn't find Drew. What was more, he couldn't find Zeke or Hawk. He couldn't believe they'd been left behind. Drew was far too responsible for that. So where were they?

He couldn't very well check every sleeper, but he didn't see how he could have missed all three of them. He finally gave up and claimed a sleeper for himself. He'd find them when they reached Taylorsville. Then he'd ask what had happened.

Cole settled into a sleeper, but he didn't get a lot of sleep. The nagging question of Drew's whereabouts wouldn't go away. But that wasn't nearly as bothersome as her declaration that she wanted nothing to do with men. He could tell himself he was concerned because it compromised his plan to worm his way into her confidence. He could tell himself his increasing interest in her, his efforts to make her act really spectacular, were all part of his plan to stay close to her, to become so necessary she'd have to accept him into her inner circle.

But he'd be lying.

He liked her. No, it was more than that. He'd never met anybody like her. She was so matter-of-fact about everything. She had organized her whole life, knew exactly what she wanted to do, and didn't mean to deviate from her plan. Yet he couldn't rid himself of the feeling that below the cool, calculating control existed a woman just as passionate as Drew was imperturbable. Maybe, like Sleeping Beauty, this woman wouldn't wake until Prince Charming came along.

Instead of lying here trying to figure out how to bring Drew to life, he ought to be trying to figure out how to cool himself down. He'd never gotten this interested in a woman before, and he'd been introduced to some of the most beautiful and charming women in three states. It was pure insanity to let himself become romantically interested in a woman he was investigating.

But in order to convince Drew he liked her, he'd probably have to be at least a little interested in her. Surely a woman as clever as Drew could sense when a man was lying about something as important as that.

Once again the feeling of revulsion rose in his throat like bile. He should never have let his captain talk him into taking this case. It was hard enough to do his job when it was a case of straightforward pursuit and arrest. It was very difficult when he had to pretend to be somebody he wasn't. It was nearly impossible when he had to pretend to feelings he didn't have.

But the very worst, the one thing he wasn't sure he could live with, was to betray what he *did* feel. If he did that, he'd be betraying himself as well as Drew.

He'd never thought much about marriage. The women in Memphis were too soft, those he met in Texas too used-up. But he loved Texas for its wildness, the freedom it offered. He'd never expected to find a woman who could survive surrounded by the wildness and freedom his spirit yearned for.

Then he'd found Drew. She not only survived, she thrived. Her strength only added to her beauty.

He'd spent many a night tossing restlessly in his sleeper, his body hard with thoughts of what he'd like to do to Drew, *with* Drew. But lately there'd been a shift. She seemed more of a partner, more his equal. With that had come respect, and a very different feeling, a yearning for something he'd given up hope of finding—a woman with the strength to bridge the chasm between the world that had produced him and the one that had won his heart.

But unless he wanted to run the risk of exposing himself as a complete fool, he would have to put all these thoughts out of his head. In all probability Drew was a thief. It was his job to find the evidence to prove it one way or the other. It was also a job he'd agreed to do. He'd never backed out of a job before. He couldn't start now.

But having made up his mind to proceed as planned, Cole still couldn't get to sleep. He couldn't stop wondering what had happened to Drew.

Taylorsville, Illinois

"We took a later train," Drew told him when she showed up for practice the next afternoon.

They were practicing in the yard of a farmhouse while the crew set up for the show in a nearby field. Cole was certain every person under twenty who lived within a radius of five miles had gathered to watch. The boys imitated Drew's tricks with imaginary rifles. Their female relatives uniformly made fun of them.

"What other train?"

"We can't always get everybody on one train. Sometimes we travel on as many as four."

Cole silently cursed himself for a fool. He'd let himself get so emotionally involved with Drew, he wasn't paying attention to the obvious. If he'd been thinking at all, he'd have realized there were several other trains during the night.

"What did you want?" Drew asked. "Have you come up with a new trick?"

"I thought you might try a few shots with a mirror." He hadn't thought any such thing. The words came out on their own. He'd spent all his time wondering where she was, knowing the only reason he hadn't gone back to look for her was that she had Zeke and Hawk with her.

"That sounds hard."

"It is, but you can do it."

He had to get himself under control, or he was going to make a mess of this job. If he did, the other agents would never let him forget a woman had outsmarted him. The fact he was becoming more and more interested in her wouldn't make any difference.

"What does Earl think of it?"

"He doesn't care as long as the fans applaud. What I really want you to do is wear some different clothes." He hadn't planned this, either. It just came out.

"Like what?"

She looked suspicious, like she didn't trust him.

"Your outfit is very nice, but brown is a dull color. And those loose clothes don't take advantage of your biggest asset."

"What's that?"

She asked as if she wasn't sure she wanted to know.

"Your femininity. You look like you're ready to ride out and round up a few steers."

"That's how I'm supposed to look."

"Not necessarily. You're a woman excelling in what's usually considered a man's sport. The more feminine you appear, the more remarkable your accomplishment will seem."

"Are you saying I don't look like a woman?"

If he said yes, she'd probably shoot him dead on the spot.

"Of course not. I'm saying you can look more feminine with different clothes. We can look for something as soon as we finish practice."

Cole had done a lot of crazy things in his life, but he'd never taken a woman shopping against her will. Neither he nor the saleswoman was making much headway with Drew.

"I don't wear ribbons," Drew announced. "And I don't wear pink."

"I'm not asking you to wear this for yourself," Cole said, wondering what it would take to convince Drew he didn't mean this as a personal insult. "I'm asking you to wear it for the men in the audience who will respond to you as a beautiful, desirable woman."

"I've already warned you about lying, Cole Benton."

"And for the women who see you as the kind of woman they'd like to be if Mother Nature had only given them the chance."

"Women do like to see a pretty woman look like a woman," the saleswoman said.

"What do you think I look like now?" Drew demanded in a tone so stern the saleswoman nearly swallowed her tongue.

"You look very nice, but . . . well, it's just that . . . I think some other colors would make you look even prettier."

"What she's trying to say," Cole said, driven by frustration to brutal frankness, "is that you'd make a better impression if you didn't look like you'd just come from a winter spent trapping beaver in the Colorado."

"The beaver were trapped out decades ago."

"Good. Now you've got no need to go around looking like your grandpa."

"Both my grandfathers were successful businessmen who would never have been caught dead wearing buckskin."

"Then why do you?"

"Because I like it."

"Fine. Wear buckskin on your ranch. Wear it on the train, at the hotel, on the street if you must, but wear something pretty and feminine when you go into the ring."

"I'm not dressing up queer for anybody," Drew said, looking at the pink dress as though it was a coiled rattlesnake.

"You've got to appeal to an audience any way you can."

"If they don't like the way I dress, they don't have to watch me."

"You'll never get to be a star, thinking like that. You've got to ask yourself what the spectators want and give it to them."

"They want fantastic shooting," Drew said, her eyes bright with anger, "and that's what they get."

"If that's all they wanted, Earl could hire an Arkansas coon hunter or a Colorado mountain man. They want more. They want a show. That means spectacle, making everything bigger than life, making it as bright and exciting as possible."

"Now you're saying my shooting isn't interesting enough to make people want to come see me. If that's the way you feel about it, I'm surprised you bother with me at all."

Cole had been around many women during his life, but never one more determined to take everything he said the wrong way.

"It's exactly like entering the ring on horseback," he said, "shooting the bull's-eyes and candles from horseback rather than on the ground. Those things may not be difficult for you, but they look impossible to the audience. That makes it more exciting."

"Then think up some more *exciting* tricks."

"I will, but changing the way you dress would work better than two or three new tricks."

"We have dresses in lots of other colors," the saleswoman said. "Blue has been very popular this year."

"Do you have something with a white pinafore?" Cole asked.

"Pinafore!" Drew exclaimed like he'd uttered a dirty word. "You expect me to wear a pinafore, like some poor, helpless female who has no more gumption than to do everything a man tells her?"

"You don't like bright colors, you refuse to wear ribbons, you threatened to shoot my ears off when I brought up cosmetics, and now you cringe at the mention of a pinafore. What have you got against looking like a woman?"

"I look like a woman. I'm wearing a skirt."

Cole looked down at the heavy brown skirt that stopped at the top of her boots. She wore a brown shirt over a white blouse buttoned up at the neck, and gloves. This morning she had coiled her hair under her wide-brimmed hat. There was no way anyone could mistake Drew for a man, but her manner of dress effectively diminished her feminine appeal.

"It takes more than a skirt to make a woman look like a woman. You should get rid of that hat, and wear a ribbon that brings out the color of your eyes, a dress that accentuates the shape of your body."

"You're just like all the rest of the men in this world," Drew snapped. "You want to tart me up until I look like one of those women men pay to spend time with. Well, you can mark me off your list. If my shooting isn't good enough, Earl can find himself another sharpshooter. I joined this show to work, not turn myself into a painted hussy concerned only with what men think when they see her."

"I'm not talking about men."

"Indeed, he's not," the saleswoman added, fearful Drew would leave without buying anything. "Women like to see another woman looking pretty and feminine. That way, if she can best a man at something, it makes it all the more exciting. We feel if you could do it, maybe we could, too."

But Drew wasn't listening. She'd turned on her heels and marched out of the store.

"Oh dear," the saleswoman said. "And that pink dress looked so lovely on her."

"Pack it up," Cole said.

"But she said she wouldn't wear it."

"I know, but maybe I can get her to change her mind. Give me two more, something in bright yellow if you have it and that blue dress you mentioned, but no pinafores. That might be too much."

A short time later Cole walked out of the store with three complete outfits. He told himself he was a fool, that he ought to be trying to gain her confidence, not fighting over ways to make her more attractive. But he wasn't nearly so worried about that anymore. He didn't know who could be pulling off all these robberies, but it couldn't be Drew.

She resisted his suggested changes because she felt it diminished her talent and turned her into a woman with a gimmick. She wanted to be appreciated for her talent alone. Nothing else. She'd invited several old people to retire to the ranch with her. She might not want to take care of a husband and children, but she did intend to take care of these retired show people.

That wasn't the description of a woman who robbed banks. This was a woman who, despite her loud protestations to the contrary, wanted to love and be loved. Something had made her think she disliked men, couldn't trust them, but the way she talked about her adopted brothers showed that once a man proved himself trustworthy, she could be attracted to him.

And Cole wanted Drew to be attracted to him.

He'd been fighting his attraction, telling himself over and over again he couldn't let himself become interested in a criminal, that it would destroy his objectivity, make it impossible to bring the case to a suitable conclusion. But if Drew was not responsible for the robberies, he could let his feelings off the leash. He didn't have to be careful anymore.

But he did have to tell his captain they were investigating an innocent woman while letting the real culprit continue unhindered.

Deciding a telegram would be the quickest way, he turned toward the telegraph office in the post office. He took a form, wrote his message, and handed it to the operator.

"I got a telegram for you," the man said when he saw the name at the bottom of the message. "Just came in a few minutes ago."

The captain knew the Wild West Show's itinerary. Cole was supposed to check for messages each day. He'd done that before he took Drew shopping. Cole took the telegram handed to him and broke it open. The message was brief.

ROBBERY AT THE MILLVILLE BANK EARLY THIS MORNING. SAME GANG.

"Give me back my telegram," Cole said to the operator. "I've made a big mistake."

Chapter Ten

"I know you don't trust banks," Drew said to Ben, a man who'd gotten too old to be an acrobat and was now responsible for some of the props needed by the cast of the Wild West Show. "But it's better than putting your money under your mattress and having it stolen."

"Or gambled away," his wife said.

"Banks get robbed all the time," Ben said, ignoring his wife's comment.

"I know, but this bank is part of the Randolph Bank in Chicago. They'll give you back your money if anybody steals it."

"How do you know they'll do that?"

"Because the people who own it are friends of my parents. I've been on cattle drives with Monty and Hen Randolph. If they promise to make good on any losses, they will."

"I never heard of anybody doing that," said one of the men who helped with the horses.

"That's how banks work," Drew said. "You deposit your money. When you want it back, they give it to you."

"I don't know," Ben said. "It doesn't sound right to me."

"Stop arguing," Myrtle said. "Has Drew ever steered us wrong yet?"

"No, but—"

"Then be quiet and put your money in the bank. You're an old man, Ben Oliver. You'll need it before you know it."

For the last two years, almost from the moment she'd discovered that most of the elderly people who worked for the show had no savings, Drew had been urging them to take half of their earnings and put it in the bank. She hadn't been able to convince anybody at first. They didn't trust banks, and they didn't trust her. But when Myrtle decided to open a bank account, others followed suit. Before long Drew was escorting about a dozen people to the bank each payday. Drew kept a record of every account, showing them how much money they had deposited and how much interest it had earned.

At the end of last season, one of the men had been injured by a buffalo. When he was able to withdraw all his money plus interest, the remaining doubters were convinced.

Having reached the bank, Drew went inside and stepped directly up to the teller's window. Seeing her deposit her money encouraged the old people to keep up their accounts. Having made her deposit, Drew found a seat, opened her book, and prepared to enter the new deposits. She was engrossed in her work when Cole entered the bank.

"Have you talked Cole into saving his money, too?" Myrtle asked.

Despite their argument, Drew's immediate response was to look up and send Cole a welcoming smile. She couldn't help being pleased he continued to seek her company.

When she saw his expression, she changed her mind. He looked ready to commit murder. She got up without hesitation and hurried toward him. "What's wrong?" she asked. "Has someone been hurt?"

He looked shocked and hurt, like his best friend had hit him in the face.

"When did your train leave Wilton Springs?" he asked.

Drew had anticipated many responses, but not that one. "Why do you want to know?"

"Answer me! It didn't leave last night, did it?"

He was angry, aggressive, and accusing. She didn't know what was bothering him, but she resented his taking it out on her.

"I don't know what this has to do with anything, but I decided I wanted some time to myself. I knew there'd be another train this morning, so I stayed overnight."

"Did Zeke and Hawk stay with you?"

"Of course."

He looked ready to do something drastic, but she had no idea what, because she didn't know what was bothering him. "What's all this about?"

"Are all these people with you?" he asked, pointing to

the people busy depositing their money. Myrtle had taken over recording the deposits in the book.

"Yes."

"What are they doing?"

"Depositing their money in the bank. What does it look like?"

He looked about ready to attack one of them. Drew didn't know what had gotten into him, but his behavior was making her uneasy.

"Are you sure it's not your money?"

"I've already made my deposit."

"But that would be too much money to deposit at one time without making people suspicious."

Drew laughed. "I don't know how much money you think Earl pays me, but I can promise you it's not enough to raise eyebrows at any teller's window."

He seemed unable to take his eyes off her friends.

"How big is your ranch going to be? You don't need a million acres."

"It's a good thing. There aren't that many acres in the whole valley."

"What valley?"

"Jake's valley in the Texas Hill Country. Ward and Buck already have ranches close by. Isabelle hopes we'll all come back there someday."

"Who?"

"My brothers. Who did you think I was talking about?"

"What is Myrtle doing?"

"Writing down the amount of the deposits for me."

His expression grew even wilder. She'd never seen any sign of it before, but Drew wondered if Cole might have a secret drinking problem. She couldn't think of anything else that could account for such bizarre behavior.

"Why?"

"It's none of your business." She was irritated with his attitude. She didn't understand it or find it excusable.

"Humor me."

"Why? You're acting like a steer with a cactus thorn in its nose."

He walked over, took the book from Myrtle, and looked through several pages. That made her so furious she marched up and snatched it from his hands.

"This is private information."

"Then why do you have it?"

"Because I'm the one who talked these people into starting savings accounts. I keep a record of their deposits, the banks they're in, and the accumulated interest. This way they can see their savings grow."

"Why would you do something like this?"

"They're all reaching the age when they won't be able to work much longer. When I found out they didn't have any savings, I talked them into putting some of their money aside so they won't be destitute. We've had this discussion before."

"They can't save much in so few years."

"I'll transfer the money to one bank."

"Which one?"

"One owned by some friends of our family."

"Who?"

"Jeff and Madison Randolph, if you must know. They nearly doubled the money we invested with them last year."

"You know the Randolph family?"

"Yes."

"How?"

He was treating her like a criminal, demanding answers to questions he had no business asking. "Cole, what's this all about?"

"Just answer my question."

That was it. She didn't care what was bothering him. He could go on being miserable by himself. She was tired of trying to be concerned and having it thrown back in her face.

"My father served in George Randolph's company during the war," she said. "They have a ranch about fifty miles from us. We always send our cows to market together. Now that's the last question I'm going to answer. I don't know what's bothering you, but I resent the way you've treated me and my friends."

He hesitated, as if he wasn't sure what to do next. Despite her anger, she couldn't help worrying. This was so unlike Cole. Something must be badly wrong, but she couldn't imagine what it could be. Or what it had to do with her friends depositing their money in the bank.

He turned to Myrtle. "Is that all the money Earl pays you?"

"Pitiful, isn't it?" her husband said. "And to think what I used to make when I was an acrobat."

"We all made more when we were young," Myrtle told Cole, "but we didn't save anything."

Cole seemed to rock back and forth on the balls of his feet, apparently trying to make up his mind about something. "You're all depositing part of your salary," he said, "nothing else?"

"We've got nothing else," Ben said. "I wish we did."

Cole paused a moment longer before obviously forcing a smile to his face. "Sorry." He turned and strode from the bank without another word.

"What was that all about?" Myrtle asked Drew.

"I have no idea."

"He looked really worried."

"Upset," another said.

"Mad as hell," a third volunteered.

"All of that," Drew agreed.

"I wonder why he wanted to know about our money," Myrtle said.

"From the way he acted, you'd think he thought we stole it."

"Nobody would steal this little dab of money. It's not worth the risk."

But Drew was thinking about something else. The Cole who'd come into the bank was no lazy drifter going from one job to the next with no thought for his future. This Cole had his mind focused on something specific, something that had gone wrong, something that was very important to him.

One thing was certain. Cole Benton wasn't who he pretended to be.

Drew thought for a moment he might have been hired by Earl to make sure nobody stole his money, but she discounted that. That would have explained why he wanted to know where they got the money they were depositing, but Earl had never been robbed. There were too many cowboys in the show, too many genuine Indians, all of whom were excellent shots.

Cole Benton was here for some specific purpose, she was certain of that. Even though she had no idea what it might be, it made her feel better about liking him. She wouldn't allow herself to get truly interested in a man. That would wreck all her plans. It would have been especially foolish to like a drifter. But a man with a secret mission? Well, now, that was something else.

The clack of the train wheels nibbled away at the edge of Cole's nerves, making him jumpy and irritable. At the same time, the noise served as a barrier, cutting him off from conversations around him, allowing him to wallow in the morass of the bleak thoughts that filled his mind.

After their confrontation in the bank, Drew was keeping her distance. Cole was seated with Myrtle and her husband. Other people filled the car with conversation, noise, and the smell of closely packed bodies.

He must be losing his grip. He'd been going around in circles for the last several days, trying to make sense of Drew's activities. No, that wasn't true. He'd been trying to find a way to prove her activities couldn't possibly have anything to do with the latest robbery.

Everything he knew about her character, everything he felt when he was around her, said she was a woman of strong principles. He might not like what she said and did, but she acted according to what she believed.

Then there was all the evidence. She and her brothers had taken a later train, giving them plenty of time to stage the early-morning robbery. And it wasn't as though it was a random choice. He had seen her sitting in the bank observing everything that went on. Myrtle said she did it all the time.

Then there was this business of her herding all those old people into a bank to make their deposits. It could be exactly what she said, an investment club for their retirement, but show people were notoriously improvident. Saving money was the last thing they'd do. Wasn't it possible Drew had divided up the money stolen from the bank and had each of those old people deposit a portion of it in his or her name? There wouldn't be any problem getting it back. They obediently gave her their deposit slips with all the information she would need to take the money out at some future date.

The mention of the Randolph family gave him pause, however. Everybody in Texas knew the Randolphs. Rose Randolph was General Grant's goddaughter. He'd sent General Sheridan to check on them when they were having trouble with rustlers. Monty was making a name for himself as a cattleman, Hen as a gunman, Madison and Jeff as men of business, while George oversaw the whole family enterprise. They all had reputations as tough men to deal with, but everybody knew they were rigidly honest. They wouldn't have had anything to do with robbers.

Of course Drew could have lied about her father serving with George Randolph. Any number of people must have known him in the army, and there were hundreds of ranches in that part of Texas. Cole had no evidence to prove or disprove her story, and he wasn't likely to find any.

But now he had a new worry. Drew had been disappearing regularly the last few days. He hadn't paid any attention to it when he'd first joined the show. He couldn't expect to know where she was all the time, but now everything she did could be significant. The fact that she appeared to be determined to make sure he didn't know where she went was even more worrying. What could she be hiding now?

"You're worried about something."

Cole came out of his abstraction. "Sorry I'm such poor company, Myrtle."

"You've got things on your mind."

"You might say that."

"Are you in love with Drew?"

The blunt question jolted Cole out of his abstraction. "What?"

"She's a lovely girl. I suppose I should say woman, but at my age she seems like a girl."

"She's definitely a woman," Cole said. "But I'm not in love with her."

"It would be all right if you were."

No, it wouldn't. It would be the worst thing that could happen. He was having enough trouble dealing with the physical attraction.

"Drew told me she didn't like any men except her brothers," Cole said.

"Then a handsome young devil like you is what's needed to change her mind."

"She says I'm a drifter, that she can't depend on me from one day to the next. Not exactly the kind of man to interest a down-to-earth woman like Drew."

"Maybe not, but she likes you anyway."

"I haven't seen any sign of it."

"You wouldn't."

"Why not?"

"Because you're a man. I don't know a single man who understands Drew."

"That's all the more reason not to be in love with her," Cole said. "A man should understand his wife."

"I didn't say anything about marriage," Myrtle said. "Drew is dead set against that."

Cole supposed it was his proper Southern upbringing, but the women he knew automatically associated love with marriage. He had assumed all women did.

"In that case, it's a good thing I'm too old to be climbing up a vine-shaded veranda."

"What a lovely picture. Do you have a vine-shaded veranda?"

Damn! He was talking too much. "No, but if I ever get married, maybe I will."

"Drifters never stay anywhere long enough for vines to grow big enough to give shade."

Cole looked up to see Drew standing in the aisle next to him. As usual, Zeke and Hawk were in close attendance.

"Men don't drift forever," Myrtle said, with her sweet, understanding smile. "Some—the very best ones—are just looking for a reason to put down roots."

"Are you looking for a reason to put down roots, Cole?" Drew asked.

Her smile said she was baiting him. Cole didn't like being needled, especially when Myrtle's words contained enough truth to make him uncomfortable.

"The word *marriage* has been responsible for more hasty departures than the threat of a shotgun," Cole said, trying to sound as lighthearted as he could.

"Are you getting ready for a hasty departure?"

"I told you I'd stay through New Orleans. I may be a drifter, but I'm a man of my word."

"Sit down, dear," Myrtle said to Drew. "You're giving me a crick in my neck."

"There's not enough room for all of us."

"Hawk and I will come back later," Zeke said.

Zeke and Hawk moved away and Drew settled down next to Myrtle.

"I'm glad you invited me to join you," Drew said to Myrtle. "The boys are very good about keeping an eye on me, but they get tired of hanging around all the time. Especially when there's a good card game to be had."

"They like cards?" Cole asked. Somehow, he couldn't associate those two with gambling.

"Hawk is a genius with cards. If he keeps it up, he'll win enough money for his ranch before I can earn mine."

"He wants a ranch, too?"

"All three of us want ranches," Drew said, "but Zeke and Hawk aren't very good at saving."

He wanted to ask what they found to spend their money on, but decided that wouldn't be smart.

"You ought to enroll them in your savings program."

"I have, but the kind of ranch they want will take a lot more than we can earn in the show."

So where were they planning to get the extra? She might as well tell him she had to steal to get the money she wanted.

"I suppose gambling is one way to get the extra money, unless you lose it instead," he said.

"I think games of chance are stupid. Life is enough of a gamble for me."

Robbing banks was a horrific gamble. She placed her life on the line every time she did it. "So what do you do when you disappear nearly every afternoon?"

She smiled like a woman with a secret. "I manage to entertain myself."

"Would I find it entertaining?"

"I don't know. Myrtle, do you have any leftover cloth?"

"Lots, dear, but what would you want it for?"

She glanced at Cole, then turned back to Myrtle. "I've been told that if I dressed in something more interesting than brown, the audience would like it better."

"I'm sure that's true, dear. You look very nice, but brown is such a depressing color. It always makes me think of rotting leaves."

Cole had difficulty suppressing a smile.

"I had no idea you disliked my clothes so much."

"I don't dislike them, dear. They're quite nice, but bright colors are much more cheerful. Don't you agree, Mr. Benton?"

"Mr. Benton has already made his opinion known to me," Drew said.

Cole did smile this time.

"If he said you ought to wear brighter colors, I hope you listened to him."

"The saleswoman in Taylorsville showed her several very attractive dresses," Cole said, "but she didn't like any of them."

"Why, dear? If they were pretty . . ."

Drew looked annoyed at the direction the conversation had taken. "I'm not fond of pink."

"It would be perfect with your coloring," Myrtle said, instantly animated. "Why don't we go look for a dress tomorrow?"

"There aren't any good shops in the next town. We'll have to wait until we reach St. Louis."

"You don't have to wait that long," Cole said.

"Why?" Drew asked.

He knew she wasn't going to like what he'd done, but this was the perfect opening. "I'll be back in a moment."

He hurried to the baggage car. It took less than a minute to find the box. He returned to the car with the box tucked under his arm.

Drew looked curious at first, then slightly confused, before realization hit her. Then she looked furious.

Cole considered undignified retreat, but decided to plunge ahead. He resumed his seat, then handed the box to Myrtle. "I hoped she might change her mind, so I bought this."

Myrtle opened the box. "It's beautiful!" she exclaimed.

"You bought that dress after I told you I'd never wear it?" Drew said, her eyes hard and glittering.

Time to confess to everything. Might as well be hanged for several crimes as one. "I bought three dresses. I thought you'd look beautiful in them."

"I've already warned you twice about lying."

"It's the truth."

"It's not."

An idea occurred to him. "Have you got the guts to make a test?"

She looked even more angry. "I've got the guts to do anything, but I'm not going to let you decide what clothes I wear."

"You already know my opinion."

"And you know how highly I value it."

169

Her being snide just made him all the more determined. "But you can't ignore Myrtle's opinion. Or the opinion of everyone in this car. Even Zeke and Hawk."

"They're not here."

"I'll get them."

"What for?"

"I want you to put this dress on and let everybody decide whether it makes you look beautiful."

"I think it's a wonderful idea," Myrtle said.

"Don't be ridiculous," Drew said. She looked uncomfortable, cornered.

Cole got to his feet. "Listen up, everybody!" Conversations stopped, and heads turned in his direction. "Drew is going to try on a dress. She wants us to help her decide if she ought to wear it when she performs tomorrow."

"Sure," some said. Others nodded their heads.

"Okay," Cole said to Drew. "Time to step up to the line."

Drew gave him a look meant to freeze his soul. "You will pay for this."

Chapter Eleven

Drew decided it ought to be legal to shoot men, especially men like Cole Benton. He had backed her into a corner in front of her friends, challenged her courage, and made it impossible for her to refuse to put on this dress. She didn't want to wear anything chosen for her by a man, especially not Cole Benton. Besides, she hated pink. She would have preferred to try on one of the other dresses, but Cole had closed even that small avenue of resistance.

She had to go back into the car and subject herself to the judgment of whomever happened to be there. That irritated her, too. All her life she'd made her own decisions. But Cole had made a habit of making decisions for her. She had put up with it so far; that would come to an end right now. She didn't know what she'd do to get even, but she swore it would be something really wicked.

She left the small compartment and almost ran into one of the cowboys in the narrow passageway. The surprised, wide-eyed look he gave her, answered any question she might have had.

"Is there a party somewhere on this train?" he asked.

She wondered if he hoped she might ask him to go along. "No. I'm just trying on a dress to see if it would be suitable for my act."

"That would be suitable for just about anything," the cowboy said, his eyes glued to the dress's low-cut neck.

"Put your eyes back in your head," she snapped. "This is purely a business decision."

"Maybe," he said with a roguish grin, "but it sure is going to give a lot of people pleasure."

Drew was tempted to take the dress off immediately, but she refused to let Cole know that discovering she could be an object of lust upset her. She was used to being treated with the respect due to a woman, but without all the nonsense that went along with being a woman in search of a husband, a companion for the evening, a dance partner, or just someone to flirt with. She'd made it clear to everyone she'd met for at least ten years that she had no time for that kind of foolishness.

Now Cole was responsible for changing all that. Another thing he had to answer for. His sins were piling up faster than she could think of punishments.

Be honest. You haven't been thinking of punishments for at least a week.

There was no point in denying it. She'd been thinking how much she enjoyed his company, how attractive he was, how charming when he decided to smile, how pleasant it was to have someone so attentive to her.

But he'd gone too far this time. She strode toward the car.

"Okay, here it is," she announced when she stepped into the car. "Be careful what you say," she said, frowning at everyone in sight. "It won't take me but a minute to get my guns."

"Nobody's going to say anything bad, dear," Myrtle said.

"They're not saying anything at all."

"It's because they're in shock," Cole said.

"What do you mean?" She turned on him, suspicion making her edgy. She had endured more than enough already. She wasn't going to tolerate anything more.

"You look beautiful," Myrtle said. "I imagine they're having trouble finding the words to tell you."

"Is that what you meant?" she asked Cole.

"Yes."

"I don't believe you."

"Look around you."

Drew turned in a slow circle until she'd looked at the face of every person in the car.

"Do you think I ought to wear this dress, or one like it, in the show tomorrow night?" she asked no one in particular.

Heads nodded. Several people mumbled words of agreement.

"You look damned pretty," someone said. "Never would have suspected it."

Several people echoed his opinion.

"Nice shoulders," someone said.

She spun around to identify the voice, but people only smiled at her.

"Great bosom, too."

She didn't respond. She knew they were teasing,

maybe even baiting her in return for the rough treatment she'd given them since she joined the show. Though it was nice to be thought attractive—if she could trust them to be telling the truth—she didn't welcome their comments, especially not when they caused Cole Benton to grin so broadly he looked simpleminded.

"I hope you're satisfied," Drew said to Cole.

"I won't be satisfied until you wear that dress for your performance. Come on, fellas," he said to the men in the car. "Don't you think Drew ought to wear this dress tomorrow night?"

Clapping hands, stomping feet, and a few sharp whistles made their feelings unmistakable. Drew had never elicited such a reaction from a male audience before. She'd have expected it would make her furious.

It made her blush.

And that made her furious.

"If the men in the audience are going to act like this, I most certainly will not wear this dress."

"Why not?" Cole asked. "Are you afraid of being treated like a woman?"

"What do you mean by that?"

Cole had never been mean or cruel before, yet today he'd been bullying her from the moment she sat down. She must have offended him in some way, but she couldn't think how. She'd continued to accept his suggestions for her act. She'd continued to let him catch her. She'd even listened to him when he said she ought to smile and wave at the audience, talk to them once in a while.

That had been difficult for her. Despite her bravura, she was uneasy around people who weren't part of her fam-

ily. She could handle any job on the ranch, even recalci-
trant cowhands, but she lacked confidence in herself as a
woman. She'd gotten around her lack of confidence by
divorcing herself from traditional female roles, but Cole
wouldn't allow her that out anymore.

He'd tricked her into putting on this stupid dress, and
now everybody was telling her she was pretty. It was hard
to disbelieve a whole carload of people, but it wasn't easy
to believe them, either. It was frightening to consider letting down her barriers. She'd accepted that she was a
tomboy. She preferred men's activities to those of
women. She had never found a man outside her family
she could like or trust, so giving up the idea of a husband
and family hadn't been a problem. She'd never wanted
one in the first place.

But she liked Cole even though she was sure he'd lied
about being a useless drifter.

"Are you afraid to have men say you're pretty?" Cole
asked.

Yes. Petrified. "Why should I be afraid of that?"

"There's got to be some reason you insist on dressing
in the least attractive manner possible."

"I dress as I do because it's comfortable. Who can
relax in a dress like this? I'll tear it or spill gun oil on it.
Hell, I can't even sit down without wrinkling it."

"It's cotton," Myrtle said. "You can wash and iron it."

She didn't want to know that. She wanted to go back to
her brown clothes and forget about being pretty and having men whistle at her and stare at her bosom. If a man
did that while she was wearing her boots and hat, she
could draw her gun and threaten to shoot his ears off. But
a woman in a pink dress couldn't do anything except

blush and pretend to be too modest to admit she wanted him to do exactly what he was doing.

"I couldn't wear something like this all the time," Drew said. "I'd be a nervous wreck."

"Why, dear?" Myrtle asked.

"Because . . ." It was impossible to say she didn't want to be told she was pretty because she might start to believe it. If she let herself believe that, there wouldn't be any way to stop herself believing in or wanting all kinds of other things. The prospect frightened her. Her life was simple now, and that was the way she liked it. "Because I don't want to," she finished lamely. "I don't like dresses. Never have."

"You don't have to wear them all the time," Cole said. "Just for the show."

Drew looked at Myrtle, but she got no help.

"You look lovely," Myrtle said. "You just wait until tomorrow and see if you don't get more applause than ever."

"If I don't, I'll never put this dress on again," she told Cole.

He grinned the insolent grin that said he knew he'd won. Again. "You'll be a sensation. If not, I promise to buy you any boring brown outfit you like."

"Where does a drifter get enough money to buy clothes for women?"

She thought for a split second he looked startled, but his ready grin appeared.

"I'm not drifting now. I have a job."

"You'd have to have two jobs to pay for all those clothes."

"Unlike you, I have nothing against gambling. I had a bit of luck on a riverboat before I got here."

"I thought gamblers kept going back for more until they lost everything."

"Some do, but I like drifting even better."

He was lying. She didn't know why she was so certain, but she was. She just couldn't imagine what he could be doing that he wanted to keep secret. She came back to the idea that he might be here to protect Earl's receipt box. There had been a number of robberies recently in towns where they had played. Earl might have gotten nervous.

She got the feeling Cole was a man who could take care of himself in just about any situation. If Earl did want someone to keep an eye on his cash box, pretending to be a drifter would be a good disguise for a private detective.

But as far as she could tell, Cole hadn't paid any attention to Earl or his receipt box. Maybe Earl had secretly hired Cole to turn her into a star. Earl had advertised her appearance in the show from the very beginning, more than she thought justified by her popularity. Earl always said a big name star could attract more people than an overall fine show. Drew wasn't sure about that, but Earl had enough experience to know what he was doing.

Drew made up her mind to find out what Cole was really doing in the show.

"Just as long as you don't drift until after New Orleans," she said. "Though if my act goes as well as you think, Earl may want you to come back again next year. Would you consider it?"

The look in his eyes mystified her. It wasn't shock,

confusion, or the panic of a footloose man who sees the prospect of a lifetime of responsibility closing in on him. It was fear. That surprised her. She had assumed Cole wouldn't be afraid of anything.

"That's asking a lot," he said.

He had himself under control now; the charm turned on full blast.

"I might decide to stay in New Orleans. I've heard some mighty tempting stories about the women down there."

"I imagine they're looking for something better than a drifter with shallow pockets."

Her retort shocked her. If that wasn't the response of a jealous woman, she didn't know anything about women. And while she thought women were often remarkably silly creatures, especially when it came to men, she did know her own sex.

"I understand gambling is right popular in New Orleans. Maybe my pockets won't stay so shallow."

She was disgusted at herself for starting this conversation and at Cole for confessing he depended on gambling for his income, at least some of the time.

"I suppose there are women who don't mind hitching their fortunes to the wind, but I can't say I think much of the idea. Now I'm going to get out of this dress."

"Why?" Myrtle asked. "You look so charming in it."

"It's sweet of you to say that, Myrtle, but—"

"You don't have to believe us," Cole said. "Look around. The men still can't take their eyes off you."

"I don't like being stared at."

"Even in admiration?"

"No."

She didn't think she'd mind being admired if she could believe it was genuine, but she was quite resigned to being plain. She really didn't mind it. Jake and Isabelle had been adamant that their children wouldn't grow up thinking looks rather than hard work would bring them success. Drew had received more than her share of praise for her accomplishments. She liked work, and she enjoyed its rewards.

She certainly didn't want men mooning over her just because she had a pretty face. Isabelle always said a pretty face wasn't much good unless it was backed up by good character and a strong back. Besides, men in the mooning frame of mind were practically useless. They couldn't think of anything except dancing and flowers and saying silly things about moonlight, eyes, and hair. Confront them with a steer, and they were liable to get run over before they could gather their wits about them.

Still, a little admiration—just once in a while— wouldn't be a bad thing.

"I promised I'd wear this dress for the show," she said to Cole, "and I'll keep my promise. But the rest of the time, I wear my own clothes."

"Fair enough," Cole said.

"Maybe we can talk Earl into turning her into a mistress of ceremonies," Myrtle said. "Then she'd have to wear a dress for the whole show."

"I've got an even better idea," Cole said. "When we arrive at a new town, she can march down the main street giving demonstrations to work up interest in our show."

"I'm sure the local authorities would love to have me shooting at signs, tree limbs, even birds," Drew said. "The women and children would probably run screaming from the streets, though I have no doubt the men would love it."

"Okay, it wasn't such a good idea. I'll think of something else."

"I'm sure you will. In the meantime, I'm going to change. By the way, I'll pay for these dresses."

"You don't have to. They're my gift to you."

"I don't take gifts from men. Either I pay for them, or you take them back to the store."

"I can't."

"Then I guess you're stuck with three dresses. I'll return this one to you as soon as I can take it off. I'm sure you'll find someone who'll wear them."

For once, she had the upper hand, and Cole knew it. He flashed the grin that was rapidly destroying her self-control.

"Okay, you can pay for them."

Drew left the car, but she couldn't banish the image of Cole's sexy grin. What did she mean thinking he had a *sexy* grin? No such thought had ever crossed her mind before. He wasn't beautiful the way Matt and Will were beautiful. He wasn't sultry like Luke or Chet. He didn't tower over her with bulging muscles like Sean. Most important of all, he didn't have the bedrock integrity and sense of responsibility Jake had. There shouldn't be anything about Cole Benton to make her look twice.

She reached the compartment, locked the door behind her, and started to unbutton the offending pink dress.

Maybe Isabelle was right. There were all kinds of men in the world, some of whom appealed to women for no accountable reason. Obviously Cole Benton was one of those men, but never in a thousand years would she have thought she'd be one of those women. She was too sensible, too aware of the failings of men, too certain of what she wanted to do with her life. Now she kept thinking of Cole as somehow showing up at her ranch and staying . . . forever.

No, she couldn't allow that to happen. If she was acting this silly when she only saw him for a few hours a day, imagine what would happen if she saw him all the time. She'd be as brainless as a newborn calf.

Norton, Missouri

Cole was determined Drew wouldn't disappear again. Every day since they'd left St. Louis she'd vanished right after practice and hadn't reappeared until it was time for the show to begin. It didn't make him feel any better that either Zeke or Hawk—or both—disappeared with her. He'd never been worried about her safety. Anyone would have to be a fool to attempt to harm her with one or both brothers at her side.

Zeke and Hawk weren't like the new breed of cowhands coming to Texas since the end of the war— Easterners soft from living in towns who expected the law to protect them. They were among the last of a breed of men who could ride out into the unknown, confident in their ability to defend themselves, their women, and their property.

But Cole's admiration for Drew's brothers didn't make him any less irritated at being left behind. Even though he was certain Drew wasn't involved in the robberies, he still couldn't explain away some cold, hard facts. Drew had had the opportunity to commit every one of the robberies. There had been another two days ago. It had taken place one afternoon after Drew and her brothers had disappeared. When he'd asked where she'd gone, she told him it was none of his business, that their relationship was restricted to their act.

He wished that were true. He'd tried to make it so, but thoughts of Drew filled his mind at all hours of the day. He'd volunteered to help Earl with the business end of the show. But even becoming involved with the logistics of moving and setting up so much equipment, providing feed and shelter for dozens of horses, cows, and buffalo, not to mention housing and transporting all the people involved in the show—not even all this could drive Drew from his thoughts. His dreams had become so erotic he hardly got any rest, but Cole had only himself to thank. He'd been the one to insist she wear that pink dress.

He'd dreamed of her before, but now he dreamed of her arms and shoulders, of the top of her bosom. He didn't know where Drew had come by the notion she was plain, but it certainly wasn't from a man. She didn't employ the usual feminine bag of tricks, the fluttering eyelashes, the dimpled smile, the coy glance, or the seductive sway of her hips. What she did have appealed to Cole even more.

She had a perfect body, strong, supple, athletic. Every move radiated the sensuous grace of well-trained, beautifully controlled muscles that blended gently with her perfectly smooth shoulders and delicately formed hands and wrists. And no matter how much she might wish to deny it, she was pretty.

How could she not be with big, brown eyes, a smiling mouth—when she wasn't angry at him—and a way of tilting her head to the right when she didn't believe him.

That happened so often she practically had a permanent list.

Her gaze could be direct and paralyzing. It also had the power to make him forget where he was and what he was doing. But it was her smile, especially when accompanied by her laugh, that destroyed his resistance and haunted his dreams. There was an earthiness, a visceral quality about her that was totally missing in the women he grew up with in Memphis. It reminded him of the untamed wildness of Texas.

Without realizing exactly what he'd been looking for in a woman, he'd found it all in Drew.

Yet there remained the fear that despite his instincts, she might be guilty after all. She'd led her motley army of old people to the bank the day after the most recent robbery. He had to find out what she was doing. When she emerged from her hotel room, he was waiting for her.

"What are you doing here?" she said, clearly not pleased to see him.

"Waiting for you."

"Why?"

"I'm tired of working with Earl. I figured whatever you're doing has to be more fun."

"Not fond of work, are you?"

"Not that kind."

"What kind are you fond of?"

"Following pretty women around." She was dressed for riding, just like the female leader of the gang of robbers.

"I haven't seen too many around here, but I'm sure you could find at least one willing to waste a few hours entertaining you."

183

"I'd rather waste them with you."

Her gaze narrowed. "Exactly what are you proposing?"

"I'll leave that up to you."

"In that case, I propose you go find somebody else to annoy."

Cole didn't think she was annoyed. Flustered was more like it. That was a relief. He was tired of being the only one affected by this relationship. He didn't consider himself a lady-killer, but he'd received his share of feminine attention over the years. Drew's relentless cold shoulder was getting on his nerves, as well as doing some serious damage to his ego.

"Sorry, this is my day to annoy you," he said. "I've set it aside especially."

"Your calendar is so crowded."

She was making fun of his rootless condition again. He wondered what she'd think if she knew his real background.

"I make room for whatever appeals to me the most. I'll follow you wherever you go," he said, when it was clear she wasn't going to invite him to join her.

"I don't need you to follow me. I have Zeke."

But Zeke wasn't dressed for riding when he walked up. "We can't go today." He ignored Cole, speaking directly to Drew. "Earl wants to change our part of the show. Hawk and I will have to spend the rest of the day working on it if we expect to have it ready for tonight."

"I'll go with her," Cole offered.

"I can stay here today," Drew said.

Zeke gave Cole the once-over. "I don't suppose he'd be much help in a pinch, but he's better than nothing. You think you can ride with her without falling off your horse?"

Cole grinned despite himself. "I'll tie myself to the saddle just in case."

Zeke didn't look amused. "You let anything happen to her, and I'll kill you."

Cole knew that wasn't an idle threat. It was a sure promise.

"I'll be just as zealous as you and Hawk together."

"You aren't worth Hawk's left hand, but Drew is more than a match for anybody she's liable to meet. I want you back in two hours," he said, turning to Drew.

"Don't be stupid, Zeke. If I go at all, I'll come and go when I want."

"Jake wouldn't like that."

"Jake always lets me do what I want."

"Only because he'd have to knock you out to stop you," Zeke said, irritation mingled with admiration.

"Don't worry. I'll make sure Cole stays out of trouble. Now go get your new act worked out."

Zeke hesitated briefly. "Remember what I said," he said to Cole before turning and stalking off.

"Is he always that pleasant?"

"You're fortunate. He's been in a particularly good mood for several days. Besides, he likes you."

Cole shivered. "Let me know if he changes his mind. Now where are you going?"

"Don't you know?"

"Not yet."

"For a ride in the country. I start feeling jumpy if I stay cooped up in a town for more than a day or two."

Chapter Twelve

Drew didn't know why Cole wanted to ride with her. He obviously had expected to do something else, though she couldn't imagine what. There wasn't much in Ohio, Indiana, Illinois, and Missouri except farms. Most towns were barely large enough to fill the stands for one night. That was why Earl moved the show to a new town nearly every night. It would be a relief to reach Memphis, where they'd spend three days in the same place. But even small towns were big enough to cause Drew to miss the wide-open spaces of Texas.

"Is this what you do every time you disappear?" Cole asked. "Ride through the countryside?"

"What else is there to do?"

"I don't know. I figured you did something more exciting."

"You keep forgetting I grew up on a ranch. None of us likes staying in towns. Even Isabelle, and she grew up in Savannah."

"I'd like to meet Jake and Isabelle. You've talked about them so much, I feel like I know them."

"I'm not sure you'd like them."

"Why?"

"Isabelle has very strict ideas about how people should behave. When they don't come up to her standards, she's not slow to tell them."

"And you don't think I measure up?"

"I know you don't."

He didn't look as though he liked that, but it wasn't her fault he was a drifter, a liar, or whatever he was. Isabelle might not hold being pathetically useless against him. She said some people couldn't help it, they were just made that way, but she couldn't stand lying. Not for any reason.

"Jake is big on responsibility," Drew said. "He never told any of us what to do, but it was always clear he expected us to make something of ourselves."

Drew hadn't been pleased when Cole insisted on riding with her, but she was having a good time. The early fall weather made the day sunny and cool. Her horse had a little spirit, so she didn't feel like she was astride a mule too lazy to put one foot in front of the other.

The fields they passed were mostly empty. Farmers had cut and stacked their hay long ago. Oat and wheat fields were bare. Most crops had been picked or cut. Some fields remained green with late melons, pumpkins, squash, even peas. There was a lot of corn, most of it dry, the stalks turned brown, waiting to be gathered and stored in barns as winter feed for livestock.

Cattle and pigs had grown fat from summer grazing and rooting through the fields for dropped kernels of oats and wheat. Even chickens and geese seemed to be getting as fat as possible before they were slaughtered on the first cold days in October or November. It was the picture of an idyllic countryside, grown fat from the fertile land and the peace and prosperity since the war. So very different from Texas, where the open wounds of war were still visible.

Their visit to New Orleans would be the first time Earl had taken the Wild West Show to the deep South.

"How many brothers are still at home?" Cole asked.

"Two."

"Where are the others?"

"Buck got married and bought a ranch next to Jake's. Sean and Pete left for the Colorado gold fields early this year. Luke left a while back to hire out his gun. Chet followed to keep an eye on him. Bret went off to Boston a few years back, but nobody cared much. Bret was always hard to like."

"Who helps Jake?"

"Will and Matt. I expect Matt will stay even if Will leaves. Matt hates being around strangers even more than I do."

"Doesn't seem like your parents were able to make all of you feel that you were part of the family."

"Isabelle says it's hard for orphans to feel close to anybody. She says they've spent so long being rejected and having to look out for themselves, they're afraid to believe they don't have to any longer. Isabelle was an orphan herself, so she ought to know."

"Is that how you feel?"

"I was never really an orphan. They found me just after my parents had been killed. Besides, I've got family. Too much. Now I'm tired of talking about myself, and I'm tired of plodding along like some fat, lazy tenderfoot who doesn't know what to do with a horse. I'm ready for a gallop. Keep up if you can."

Drew had expected to leave Cole in the dust. He kept up with her without any visible effort. She settled her horse down for a hard gallop, but he still stuck to her side even when they thundered past a wagon heavily loaded with oat straw.

"Where did you learn to ride?" Drew asked.

"I've spent a lot of time in Texas," he said with a grin.

"Doing what?" she asked.

"Riding, roping, drifting about."

"You were a cowboy?"

"You could say that."

"What would you say you were?"

"More like an inspector. My job was to see that things went the way they were supposed to."

"Do you mean you went after rustlers and Comancheros?" She couldn't believe that. You had to be tough and knowledgeable to handle rustlers. You had to be all that and lucky to go after Comancheros and come back alive. Cole had never given her the impression he wanted to work very hard at anything. Still, he could shoot very well. He might be able to do other things she hadn't expected.

"I went after rustlers occasionally."

"I don't believe you."

"Okay."

"You don't care?"

"No."

That surprised her. She'd be furious. "I know you can shoot and ride," she said. "What else can you do?"

He regarded her with curiosity. "What did you have in mind?"

"Can you throw a steer?"

"You want me to prove it?"

She looked around. She saw a few cows in the distance, but they were obviously milk cows. They wouldn't have enough sense not to give up and lie down.

"Can you rope?"

"Can you?"

"I can rope better than anybody except Ward. I had to," she said, remembering past slights. "They wouldn't let me throw the steers."

"Jake probably thought it wasn't suitable for a woman."

"He said I was too light, that the steer would hardly know I was riding his horns."

She hadn't liked being told to leave that to the boys, but Jake could be mighty stubborn when he made up his mind. Once, when she defied him, he picked her up, tucked her under his arm, and deposited her unceremoniously on her bottom at the campfire. She had been very careful not to put herself in the position of having to suffer that humiliation again.

She took up the rope she carried on her saddle. She hadn't expected to need it, but riding out fully equipped made her feel better.

"I'll rope that fence post," she said.

"That doesn't look very hard."

"You do it, too, and I'll find something harder."

After roping angry steers determined to risk breaking their necks rather than allowing themselves to be roped, it was a simple matter to toss a loop over a stationary fence post.

"Your turn," she said when she'd recoiled the rope.

It was apparent from the moment Cole took the rope in his hands that he knew what he was doing. He handled it with the familiarity of an old hand. His loop settled over the post just as easily as hers had.

"What next?" he asked.

Drew looked around her, but she couldn't find anything that offered a challenge. She didn't see any horses or mules, and sheep, if there were any, were just as useless as cows.

"How about one of those goats," she said, pointing to a small herd of goats grazing in a field close to a line of trees.

A smile crinkled the corners of Cole's mouth. "I've never roped a goat before."

A gurgle of mirth began to bubble inside her. "I haven't either. Think you can do it?"

"Sure, but you've got to rope one, too."

"How do you propose to enter the pasture?"

"Jump. You can jump your horse, can't you?"

Now he was being insulting. Without bothering to answer, she rode a short way back down the road, put her horse into a gallop, and easily cleared the fence into the field. Cole executed the jump just as easily. Drew felt the pinch of her competitive drive, the prod that had always forced her to try to be better than her brothers.

"I jumped first," she said. "You get to rope first."

"Afraid to rope a goat?"

191

She refused to rise to his bait. "Embarrassed." Much to her surprise, both of them laughed. "You've got to promise never to tell anyone. Zeke and Hawk would never let me forget it."

Cole uncoiled the rope, then trotted his horse toward the goats. They broke and ran. Cole let out a whoop that would have made any Texas cowboy proud and went after his chosen goat, a female. He roped it without difficulty, jiggled the rope off the panicked animal's head, and calmly recoiled it as he rode back to where Drew waited.

"Your turn," he said, handing her the rope.

"Why did you pick on that poor female?" she asked.

"She was running faster than the others."

Drew made up her mind to rope the big male. He might not be able to run as fast as the younger female, but he was a more worthy target. She worked the rope in her hands as she rode toward the scattered herd. The big male didn't appear interested in running very fast. Drew rode by him a couple of times, yelling loudly each time. Finally, the sluggish brute took off at a decent pace. She brought her horse up behind him and dropped the rope neatly over his horns.

The big male grunted angrily, turned, and charged her horse.

Drew couldn't count the times a longhorn had turned on her. After the first time, it never bothered her. For some reason, maybe the unexpectedness of it, the goat's attack caught her flat-footed.

"Looks like you got a temperamental one," Cole called out.

He was making fun of her, something she'd never allowed before without striking back. But instead of getting angry, she started to laugh. The whole episode was

192

foolish—the one-upmanship that had caused her to challenge Cole, their lassoing fence posts, invading a pasture to lasso goats. This was something adolescent boys might do. Sober, serious adults wouldn't even consider it.

"Let's get out of here before we're battered to death by your victim."

The goat was headed in her direction again. A devilish urge struck her. Instead of jostling the rope off his horns, she spurred her horse forward, cantering across the field just ahead of the enraged goat. Instead of feeling embarrassed at doing something so foolish and irresponsible, she felt an almost childlike elation.

"What do you think you're doing?"

She turned to see Cole riding next to her. "Having a little fun," she replied. "He looks too fat. A little exercise will do him good."

"Probably, but I don't think his owner will agree with you."

"What owner?"

"The one heading toward us with a shotgun tucked under his arm."

Instead of feeling embarrassed, Drew wanted to laugh hysterically. She didn't know what had gotten into her, but she was clearly not herself. "I guess I'd better let him go."

"I don't think that's going to satisfy his owner."

Drew jostled the rope off the angry goat's horns. That didn't appease the goat, who chased her halfway around the field before he gave up. Unfortunately, that brought her practically face-to-face with the angry man carrying a shotgun.

"What are you doing, trying to steal my goat?" he demanded, the shotgun pointing in Drew's direction.

"I wasn't trying to steal it," Drew said, determined to face up to the consequences of her foolishness. "I just roped it to prove I could."

"I roped one of your nanny goats," Cole confessed. "She couldn't stand to be outdone, so she had to go for the biggest goat you had."

The farmer looked at them as though he'd stumbled across two escapees from an insane asylum.

"Drew's from Texas," Cole explained. "She's used to roping savage steers every day. Having been away for about six months, she was getting real homesick. I brought her out here trying to restore her spirits. We tried roping your fence posts, but that didn't do the trick. I thought the goats might work, but it's just not the same."

Drew didn't know whether Cole was trying to spin a story the farmer would believe or make her look like an idiot. It was all she could do to keep from laughing out loud.

"A Texan, you say," the farmer said, giving Drew a piercing look.

"Born and bred," Cole said.

She'd never told him where she was born.

"I've heard about Texans," the farmer said. "Never anything good."

"You can't blame them," Cole said. "It's all that heat. Then there's the ticks."

"Ticks?" the farmer asked.

"The ones that give northern cattle a fever that kills them."

The farmer's expression grew dark. "I've heard about the fever."

"The tick bite doesn't make people sick, but every so

often they start to act a little peculiar. It wears off in about an hour. But while it lasts, you never know what they're going to do."

"Like what?"

Drew couldn't tell whether the farmer believed Cole or not, but he obviously wanted to know what strange things Drew might do while under the influence of this dangerous tick.

"Once she wanted to lasso a buffalo."

"A buffalo!" the farmer repeated. "Did she do it?"

"Sure. Drew can lasso anything, but buffalo have thick necks and short horns. The rope wouldn't stay on. Besides, buffalo have bad tempers. It chased us from San Antonio all the way to Fort Worth."

"Is that a long way?"

"That buffalo chased us for a week. We wore out half a dozen horses."

Drew bit her lip. That was a trip of nearly three hundred miles, two and a half weeks on a cattle drive.

"But that's not the worst," Cole said. "She lassoed a pig once. Not just an ordinary pig, but one of those great big boars with tusks that can rip a horse's belly wide open. Then she put a saddle on it."

"A saddle! What for?"

"So a monkey could ride it."

The farmer's eyes grew wide. "A monkey! Where'd she get something like that?"

"From a circus passing through town," Cole said. "She stole the poor little critter from its cage, tied it to the saddle, and raced the two of them right through the middle of town. Women screamed and fainted all around. Horses reared, riders fell in the mud, and wagons crashed into each other. You never saw such a mess. We had to get out of town before they arrested us."

Drew could have sworn she noticed a twinkle in the farmer's eye.

"Does she do stuff like this often?"

"No. But when the fit gets hold of her, there's nothing to do but ride it out."

The farmer subjected Drew to a good looking-over. "She seems like a sweet little thing. You'd never suspect she was subject to such peculiar fits."

Now Drew knew the farmer hadn't been taken in by Cole's story.

"I take her out into the country when I sense one coming on," Cole said. "She can't do as much damage out here. Besides, we don't want people to hear about it. They might not want to come see her in the show."

"What does she do?"

"She's a sharpshooter," Cole said, "the best there is."

The farmer looked at her with renewed interest. "You're not spinning a tale, are you?"

"I wouldn't dream of trying to fool you," Cole said. "Come to the show tonight and see for yourself."

"I don't have money for that kind of foolishness," the farmer said. "Nor the time," he added.

"You don't have to worry about the money. I'll leave word at the gate that you're to get in free."

"I wouldn't think of going to a fancy show and leaving the wife at home. Or the children."

Drew knew Cole realized they were being squeezed, but his smile never faltered. "And how many children would you be bringing?"

The man rubbed his chin as though thinking hard. "Would thirteen be too many?"

Drew saw Cole choke back an appreciative chuckle. "Thirteen is fine, as long as no more than two of them are older than you."

The farmer grinned. "Just one."

"What name do I give the ticket taker?" Cole asked.

"Warner," the farmer answered. "Jim Warner and family."

"Done," Cole said. "The show starts at three o'clock. Don't be late, or you won't get the best seats."

"I'll remember," the farmer said. He turned his gaze to his goat, which was cavorting about the field.

"I don't know if old Billy will ever be the same," he mused. "I hope he has enough energy to breed the rest of the nannies."

Drew recognized an effort to squeeze more blood from the turnip, and decided enough was enough. "Maybe you ought to chase him about the field once in a while to get his blood going," she said. "It might make him feel younger in a lot of ways."

As though to prove her point, the billy showed a sudden and very pointed interest in a nanny. Drew couldn't hold it back any longer. She started laughing, and Cole joined in. After only a slight hesitation, the farmer laughed as well.

"Looks like we've done you a favor," Cole said.

"I'd rather you didn't do me any more."

"I think I can safely promise that," Cole said. "We need to get back, or we'll be late."

"Don't forget the passes," the farmer reminded him.

"I won't," Cole assured him.

He and Drew jumped their horses back onto the road.

"How dare you make up such an absurd story about me," Drew said once they were on their way back to town. "You made me look like an idiot."

"Neither one of us looked particularly intelligent. It's a safe bet he saw us roping those fence posts. I was hoping he'd let us go because he thought we were crazy."

"He knew you were lying."

"That was the other choice. Make him laugh so he wouldn't take it too seriously."

"And gouge you for free admission to the show."

"For him and every one of his relatives if I'm any judge."

"I expect so. What are you going to say to Earl?"

"Nothing unless asked."

"What were you going to do if he had taken it seriously."

"Sacrifice you and run away as fast as I could."

They both laughed, but she knew he wouldn't have done any such thing. He'd come to her rescue with that silly story without a moment's hesitation. He had a sense of honor behind that lazy front. Though nothing they'd done was very difficult, he clearly knew how to handle a horse and rope. What had he really been doing in Texas?

Neither surprise nor curiosity was her strongest feeling. Rather a strange warmth spread through her. She knew it had to do with Cole. She appreciated his coming to her aid so quickly. She also liked the fact he wasn't as useless as he pretended to be. But most surprising of all, she'd laughed.

Drew had never laughed much. Her family often teased her by calling her old sobersides, but she rarely saw anything funny in the things her brothers did. Will regularly reduced their family to hysterics, but he made Drew want to shake him and tell him not to be a fool. Which she had done. Many times. Jake would laugh and say he was a hopeless case. Isabelle would ring a peal over his head, then end up cooking his favorite dessert. That made Drew madder than ever.

She wouldn't have been able to put up with Jake's restriction of having at least one brother work in the show with her if Zeke and Hawk hadn't been the choices. They were as serious as she. In fact, she couldn't remember more than a dozen times either one of them had smiled in nearly ten years. Until this afternoon, that had suited her just fine.

She had absolutely no reason to have laughed. She and Cole had been caught doing something childish. She'd have scolded Will for at least a week, reminded him of it for months, but all she had done was laugh. What was worse, she *still* wanted to laugh.

"I don't think your company's good for me," she said to Cole. The dratted man smiled at her. She had to fight to keep from smiling back at him. "I've been riding through the countryside of nearly a dozen states, and never had a minute's trouble. I ride with you one afternoon, and I'm roping goats."

"It does sound ominous when stated like that."

She could see the amusement in his eyes. She struggled to remain serious.

"You forgot to mention the fence posts," he said. "And practically running down that hay wagon. Did you see the driver's eyes? I thought they were going to pop out of his head."

A bubble of laugher formed deep inside her. "He did look rather startled."

"Not half as startled as when we galloped around him."

"I didn't look back."

"His cheeks turned bright red. He looked like he'd put his face too close to the fire."

The bubble of laughter surged a few inches closer to escape.

"But you should have seen him when you roped that fence post."

"What did he do?"

"He whipped his horses into a lather, and the hay wagon went off down the road, shaking like a fat lady in wide skirts."

That was too much for Drew. The bubble escaped, and she gave up the fight. "You made that up," she accused as soon as she recovered her speech.

"You weren't looking. You can't know."

"But I know you, Cole Benton. You can tell the most incredible lies with a straight face. I can't believe a word you say."

"Not a word?"

"Not even a little one."

"Good. I was about to say you're enchanting when you laugh."

Chapter Thirteen

All desire to laugh left Drew. Nobody had ever called her enchanting. Her brothers would have hooted if anyone had. She was a good hand, a stalwart friend, a loyal sister, a severely honest critic, a dependable worker, but no one had ever called her enchanting. Come to think of it, no one had called her pretty before Cole. It was a good thing she knew he was a liar. As for liking her, that didn't even warrant consideration.

"If I was to start believing things like that, I'd be worse than a tenderfoot at a horse sale," she said.

"You don't like being compared to a tenderfoot, do you?"

She didn't like the look he gave her, as though he knew something about her she didn't. "I can do nearly anything as well as a man. Some things a lot better."

"You're proud of that, aren't you?"

"Why shouldn't I be?"

"No reason."

His look said something else would have been a better answer. "You probably think a woman should sit around in pink dresses, looking helpless, and hanging on every word out of some man's mouth."

His spontaneous laughter wasn't the response she'd anticipated.

"Heaven preserve me from women like that. I've seen enough to last a lifetime."

"Then what do you like? Don't answer that," she said quickly, horrified she'd asked such a question.

"Why not?"

"When I decided I didn't want to marry, I realized it didn't matter what kind of women men preferred."

"You never have told me why you decided not to marry."

"You never asked."

"I'm asking now."

"It's none of your business."

"Probably, but you brought it up. It's rude not to explain."

"There's nothing wrong with being rude, especially when people want to know things you don't want them to know."

"You don't ever explain yourself to people?"

"No."

"That must leave you few friends."

"I don't need friends. I've got plenty of family."

Friends would just be a responsibility. She intended to

devote all her energy to her ranch. She was determined to be just as successful as Jake.

"Then you'd better tell all your old people who're planning to retire to your ranch," Cole said. "I don't think they're the type to turn into top hands."

"They're not my old people. I'm just trying to help them save up some money so they'll have something to live on when they're too old to work."

"So you told them they could come live on your ranch."

Damn! Why did he have to know so much about her? He must have been questioning everybody he met.

"I told Myrtle she could come. I suppose some of the others thought they could come, too." That was bending the truth, but he didn't have to know that. "I don't expect any of them would want to live in Texas. It's too hot."

"It's not hot in the Hill Country. I found it very pleasant when I rode through."

Either Cole Benton knew too much, or he could make stuff up faster than she could figure out whether or not he was telling the truth.

"Why should you care what I do?" she asked.

"I didn't say I cared. I'm just curious."

The hurt was unexpected. She didn't want him to care very much, but she did want him to care a little. She liked him despite herself. It was only fair that he like her in return.

She didn't want to get into a philosophical argument with him. "Why do you want to know?"

"Because I think it's a crime for a lovely young woman who obviously cares a great deal for other people to shut herself away from the very thing she cares most about."

"But I don't care for other people."

"Yes, you do."

"I don't. I never have. Isabelle complains about it all the time."

"I imagine she complains about your compulsion to try to run other people's lives whether they want you to or not, but I doubt she ever said you didn't care for other people."

"You're wrong. She's always saying I don't care for people's feelings."

"Why did you bother to help those old people? They've been getting along for decades without you."

"I can't stand it when people don't behave sensibly."

"But isn't sensible and logical a matter of opinion?"

"Not when it comes to having a roof over your head and enough food to eat."

"Why should that bother you so much?"

"Because my parents weren't sensible," she burst out, unable to hold back any longer. "They were always fighting, yet they cut themselves off from their families. They headed west when they couldn't survive a month without help. When they did get their hands on a little money, they wasted it celebrating at an expensive restaurant, buying new clothes, or moving into a fancy hotel. We were thrown out of more places by the time I was ten than you have been in your whole life."

Now that her burst of temper was over, she regretted telling him so much. It wasn't just that she was ashamed of the way her parents acted. She was embarrassed to be their daughter. They had failed at everything they attempted. Even worse, they hadn't seemed to care.

"I've never been thrown out of anyplace," Cole said.

"Good for you," she snapped. "It's no fun."

"That isn't to say I didn't sneak out *before* someone could call the sheriff on me."

He flashed his grin again, the one that made her want to like him so much she'd tell him anything he wanted to know, but she didn't believe him. He might actually be a drifter—she wasn't sure of much about him anymore—but she was certain Cole Benton hadn't ever run away from anybody or anything.

"I don't like uncertainty," Drew said.

"Nothing lasts forever."

"That's why I'm not getting married. People let you down."

"Not always."

"I'm not taking the chance."

"What about your Jake and Isabelle?"

"They're different."

"Why can't others be different?"

"Maybe they can for somebody else, but not for me."

"Why can't you trust anybody?"

She pulled her horse to a stop, and turned to face him. "My parents had me by accident. They dragged me around behind them like forgotten baggage. They never once thought about how what they did would affect me. It was worse with my brothers. Sean's aunt left him in an orphanage because taking care of him might have interfered with her career. Hawk's white and Indian relatives threw him out. Zeke was a slave. He doesn't even know who his parents are or where to find them. Buck's father sold him to pay a debt. Matt's uncle sexually abused him."

"Judas! And Jake and Isabelle adopted all these boys!"

"Now you know why they're different."

Cole nodded. "So now you're trying to pay them back by adopting all the Wild West Show's castoffs."

"I'm not adopting them."

"You might as well be if you mean to let them live on your ranch."

"If any of them do want to live on the ranch, I'm sure they'll be able to do something to help support themselves."

"Such as?"

"I'm not going to worry about that yet."

"That's because you don't have any answers."

"If you're so smart, why don't you come up with one?"

"It's not my problem."

"Good. Then neither of us has a problem."

"Then there's no reason you can't have dinner with me tonight."

His invitation was so unexpected, she could almost believe she'd heard him wrong.

"What do you mean, will I have dinner with you tonight?"

"You know, eat food together."

"When you ask somebody to *have dinner* with you, you mean more than that. Why?"

"Do I have to have a reason?"

"Yes."

"Why are you so suspicious?"

"You drift into my life like a dandelion seed, but you stick to me like a cocklebur. You think up tricks for my act, buy me dresses, and harass me until I rope a goat. You say you're just wandering around, amusing yourself, but no drifter I ever knew works as hard as you do. And you still haven't told me where you got the money to pay for those dresses, dinner, the balls and candles for the act."

"You're not a very trusting person."

"I prefer not to be a fool."

"I told you I like you. I think you're pretty. When you give yourself a chance, you can be charming, too."

"Oh, I forgot. You're a liar as well."

He grinned again. She had to get him to stop that. She wondered why the scamps and scallywags of this world had to have all the looks and charm. Why couldn't they be ugly and mean-tempered?

"Considering what you think of me, I'm surprised you agreed to ride with me," Cole said.

"*You* are riding with *me*. And I feel safe because I can shoot better than you. Look, are you serious about dinner?"

"Why wouldn't I be?"

"You're hardly ever serious about anything. Why should this be any different?"

"Because I'm serious about convincing you men find you attractive."

"Why should you care?"

"Because I like you."

"So now you're a Good Samaritan?"

"Dammit, Drew, why are you so difficult? All I asked you to do was have dinner with me."

"That's not true. You asked me to believe you like me, that I'm pretty—at least when I wear that pink dress—that I can be charming and desirable."

"I didn't say desirable."

"Sorry. A slip of the tongue."

"But I was working up to it," Cole said. "I didn't think

you'd believe that until you at least thought you were pretty."

"I'm glad to see you're not totally stupid."

"Thanks for the vote of confidence." His tone was sarcastic.

"I didn't mean it like that. Look, Cole, Isabelle had a very large mirror in her bedroom. I saw myself in it more than once. I know what I look like."

"Not to me."

"Why should I look any different to you?"

"For the same reason a mother thinks her child is beautiful when everybody else thinks it's an ugly little pug."

A spurt of laughter escaped Drew. "So now you're looking at me like a mother. Really, Cole, you have depths I never suspected."

"Me either. Only I'm referring to homicide. If you don't stop intentionally misunderstanding me, I'm going to choke you and leave your body in that field back there for the goat to abuse. Not everybody sees things the same way. I bet Isabelle used to tell you that you were pretty."

"She was my mother. She's supposed to say things like that."

"I got the feeling Isabelle wasn't the kind of woman to mouth empty phrases."

"She's not. She's— All mothers think their children are beautiful and smart."

"Look, are you going to have dinner with me or not?"

Drew wanted to dine with Cole. She wanted to believe all the things he said, but she didn't dare.

"I'll have dinner with you if you promise not to tell me I'm pretty, charming, or desirable."

Cole laughed. "I'll bet this is the first time in history a woman has agreed to dinner on those terms."

"Take it or leave it. I intend to swallow nothing more than my food."

"Okay, on your terms. But only for tonight. I give you fair warning that before the show leaves New Orleans, I'm going to make you believe you're much more than pretty, charming, and desirable."

"What more is there?"

"Beautiful, enchanting, and irresistible."

Much to her chagrin, Drew discovered that beautiful, enchanting, and irresistible were exactly what she wanted to be.

At least to Cole.

"This has been a very nice evening," Drew said to Cole.

"Is this your way of telling me it's over?"

They'd had dinner in the small hotel that served the town of Norton. Cole had apparently spoken earlier to the waiter to reserve a quiet corner table, and to the cook to guarantee beef of sufficient quality to satisfy her Texan taste buds.

He had dressed in a black suit, white shirt, and bow tie. It was very plain dress, nothing like the fancy clothes Earl wore when he went on the town, but Cole looked absurdly handsome. Drew had given in to a fit of vanity and worn Cole's blue dress. And shoes instead of boots. She was pleased to see the look of heightened interest in Cole's eyes. He'd better like the way she looked. He was the one who'd goaded her into taking a chance that men really could find her attractive.

If she failed, it would be his fault, and she'd never forgive him.

"We've finished our meal, had dessert, I've had coffee while you had a brandy," Drew said. "What else is there? And what's a drifter doing drinking brandy?"

Cole laughed softly. He'd been doing that a lot this evening. She wished he wouldn't. He looked like a man who took life as it came, enjoying the good and ignoring the rest. As much as that went against her beliefs, Drew couldn't help wishing once in a while she could be like that.

"Most no-goods have expensive tastes. Fine women, fine food, fine liquor. It's what keeps us broke."

"I never said you were no good."

"As good as."

"I'm sure you could be quite successful if you wanted to."

"What makes you say that?"

She wished he'd stop demanding explanations of nearly everything she said. She didn't want him to know she'd spent enough time thinking about him to be able to come up with answers.

"You say you're a drifter, but you've worked very hard since you've been here. Earl says you've been a godsend when it comes to getting the show from one place to the next. And even though I don't like to admit it, you keep coming up with good ideas for my act."

She thought he looked a trifle disconcerted.

"That's the closest you've come to saying something nice about me. I'll have to invite you out to dinner more often."

Now it was her turn to feel uncomfortable.

"I didn't say that as thanks for dinner. I don't know why you're doing what you're doing. I suppose you have a reason, though it's been my experience men seldom need a reason other than wanting to do something."

"For a woman who keeps insisting she loves her brothers, you sure have a low opinion of men."

"I never said a man had to be perfect for me to love him."

"I'm glad to hear that. For a minute there I just about lost hope."

The bottom fell out of her stomach. He'd been saying ridiculous things all evening: that she was pretty, enchanting, irresistible. She knew they weren't true, but she'd let herself think they might be.

But she wanted nothing to do with love. It scared her to death. Her parents had vowed they loved each other passionately, that they couldn't stay apart. Yet they made each other miserable. Drew had never found a man, no matter how handsome or capable, who didn't irritate her within twenty-four hours. She had no intention of making her parents' mistakes.

She forced herself to smile as if she were sharing a joke. "If you're going to fall in love, you need to find somebody with money. That way you won't have to work at all, and you can have all the fine food and whiskey you want."

"How about women?"

"I imagine you could find a woman who'd let you run about on a pretty loose rein just to be able to call you her own."

"I don't suppose you'd be that kind of woman."

"I'm not the kind to fall in love. If I were, I'd expect my husband to be faithful."

"You do mean *husband*, not lover?"

Drew wished she'd gotten up five minutes ago. "If I were to get involved with a man, it would have to be marriage. I can't imagine putting up with some man for years, or months, and having him up and walk out just when I'd gotten him into decent shape."

"You wouldn't do the same?"

"I told you, I'm not getting married."

"But suppose you loved a man."

"I wouldn't."

"Just suppose, for the sake of argument, that you did."

"If I did, for the sake of argument, I'd be faithful to him. Falling in love is a stupid thing to do. But if you're going to do it, you might as well do it right."

"And right is getting married and being faithful to each other for the rest of your lives?"

"Yes."

"Like Jake and Isabelle."

"Well, yes."

"But not like your parents."

"I suppose they were faithful, but they were mismatched in just about every way. My husband would have to like all the things I like, want all the things I want, think about things the way I do."

"Wouldn't that be boring?"

"Since it'll never happen, there's no point worrying about it. Now, I'm ready to go. You're welcome to sit here for the rest of the evening."

"I suppose your husband would have to be ready to leave the table when you wanted."

She stopped. For the first time, she truly thought about the answer. "If I really loved him, I'd probably sit and lis-

ten to him all evening even if he were talking drivel.
Which is another reason I don't intend to fall in love. I
would hate myself if I were to turn into a silly female
who nods agreement with every statement that comes out
of a man's mouth regardless of how inane."

"I can't imagine that happening to you."

Cole stood and held Drew's chair while she got up.
That hadn't happened in a long time. It was nice.

"It didn't happen to Isabelle," she said as they left the
restaurant. "She adores Jake, but she will argue with him
for weeks if she doesn't agree with something he's
doing."

"Does Jake give in?"

"Sometimes. He respects Isabelle's opinion, but he's
pretty strong-minded himself."

"It sounds like a lively household."

"It is." They reached the lobby. She turned. "Thank
you for a lovely evening."

"It's not over yet. Accepting a man's invitation for dinner automatically implies acceptance of a walk along the
river afterwards."

Drew wasn't about to fall for something that obvious.
"A gentleman never extends an invitation and intentionally leaves part of it unspoken."

"Who says I'm a gentleman?"

"It's written all over you. You couldn't be more proper
if you'd been born and bred into an old Southern family."

He clearly didn't like that. She wondered why. Probably because he *had* been born into a Southern family, and
they'd thrown him out on his ear.

"I forgot there was going to be an exceptionally fine
moon tonight."

Drew couldn't stop the bubble of laughter. "You can think up a suitable lie for any occasion, can't you?"

"I'm hurt," Cole said, his eyes dancing with mischief. "You there," he said to the clerk at the desk, "what kind of moon do you have tonight?"

"A full moon," the man answered. "Half the town will be walking along the river tonight."

Cole turned back, smiling in triumph, but Drew wasn't going to be drawn in that easily. "I'd rather judge for myself."

"You'd better get your coat," Cole said. "Once you see that moon, you won't want to come back to get it."

"I'll take my chances," Drew said.

But the moment she stepped outside, she was struck by the biggest, brightest, most romantic full moon she'd ever seen.

"Now may I talk you into a walk along the river?" Cole asked, his voice soft and entreating.

She'd challenged him and lost. It was only sporting to give in. "For a little while."

"You won't need your coat," he said when she looked back at the hotel. "I'll keep you warm."

"I don't think I'll need that kind of help."

Drew realized she'd seldom thought of the moon except as a means of seeing cows at night, certainly never as a reason to take a walk along a river with a man. She'd never been asked. She supposed men had kept their distance because she'd always made it plain she had no time for romance. She'd said all the same things to Cole, but he'd asked her anyway. There had to be a difference, but she couldn't decide which was more surprising, his asking her or her accepting.

"It's a beautiful night," Cole said.

"The boys wouldn't have any trouble riding herd," Drew replied. "Nothing could sneak up on them in all this moonlight."

"Is that what you think of when you see the moon?"

"What else is a moon good for?"

"See those couples," Cole said, pointing out people walking hand in hand, their arms around each other, or sitting quietly. "I'm sure not a single thought of herding cattle has crossed their minds."

"Then they didn't grow up on a cattle ranch."

"I would be willing to bet it wouldn't make any difference."

"If they had, they'd know that looking after cows is the only reason a sensible cowhand would leave a comfortable, warm bed."

"Well, I'd appreciate it if you could forget about cows for a few minutes."

"And think about what?"

"Me."

"Why?"

"If I have to tell you, I don't suppose there's any point."

"I've been thinking about you all evening," Drew said, a little peeved. "I watched you eat for nearly two hours. I told you more about myself than I've ever told anybody. What more do you want?"

"A lot more. But this will do for a beginning."

Then he took her in his arms and kissed her.

Chapter Fourteen

No one had ever kissed Drew. The only cowboy who'd dared put his arm around her had found himself flat on the ground, the barrel of a gun only inches from his forehead, his eye rapidly swelling from the impact of Drew's fist. Drew had no desire to knock Cole down or draw her gun on him. In fact, she felt as though she was the one who'd received a body blow.

She was unable to judge the nature of the kiss. She couldn't tell if it was the kind of kiss a man gave a woman who was his friend, though she doubted that. She'd never seen any man attempt to embrace Isabelle, and she had lots of friends. It didn't seem likely it was of a more amorous nature. Cole had told her she was attractive, but kissing was a whole lot of steps beyond pretty compliments.

Or maybe it wasn't. Maybe other people kissed all the

time if they liked each other. It seemed like a silly thing to do, but then she thought most people were silly, especially when it came to anything having to do with romance. Mooning about when they were afraid their love wasn't returned, talking about each other like there was no one else in the world, making lifelong decisions based on naked animal attraction. From everything she'd seen, romance brought on a dangerously unbalanced mental state, a condition she intended to avoid at all costs.

But the kissing part wasn't nearly as bad as she'd expected. Neither was being held real close. It was a bit uncomfortable at first, but soon a very satisfactory warmth surged through her. And excitement. Or nervousness. She wasn't certain, this being her first time. She hoped she wasn't so nervous she did everything wrong. She supposed people got evaluated on this. Even though she didn't plan to do it again, she didn't want Cole to put her down as the last person he'd ever kiss twice.

About this kiss . . . well, she didn't really know. She had been adamant she didn't want any man's mouth on hers. It sounded very unsanitary, as well as a downright silly thing to do—after all, two people standing around like they were sucking on the same grape, well, it just looked silly. She'd seen Jake and Isabelle kiss a thousand times without being able to understand the attraction.

But it felt entirely different from what she'd imagined. Cole's lips were soft, yet strong. The taste of his brandy lingered. The pressure was gentle yet insistent.

She felt her body relax, lean into Cole's, felt her lips respond to his kiss. Then, almost as though she'd been pitched into water above her head, a feeling swept over her that defied description. It made her want to be even closer to Cole, to kiss him harder, to put her arms around his neck and hold on tight.

Before she could summon her limp muscles to respond, Cole broke their kiss. She looked into his face and saw reflected there the shock she felt.

"Now do you understand why I wanted you to think about me?" he said, his voice lacking its usual vibrant timbre.

"Why did you do that?" she asked.

"Because I wanted to."

"Why?"

"Haven't you ever wanted to kiss anyone?"

"No."

"Haven't you wondered what it was like?"

"I thought I knew."

"And?"

"I was wrong."

"Better or worse?"

He seemed unusually anxious over her answer.

"Better." Drew realized Cole's arms were still around her, their bodies still pressed together. A feeling of awkwardness overcame her, and she pulled away. "I'd better go back."

"You haven't seen the river yet."

After his kiss, neither the river nor moonlight seemed very significant.

He took her hand. "You can't go in yet. I promise I won't kiss you again if you'll just walk with me."

Drew realized she wouldn't have minded being kissed again. The first kiss had caught her so much by surprise she couldn't really judge how she felt. She wondered if the results of a second kiss would be the same. Isabelle once said kissing Jake got better each time. If their first time had been as pleasant as Cole's kiss, then considering the number of times they had kissed over the years, the kisses must have become so intense as to be nearly unbearable. Drew could hardly imagine anything that wonderful, but her whole body shivered at the thought.

"Okay."

"It's a beautiful night," Cole said.

She couldn't ask him to kiss her again, but her mind was definitely not on moonlight and water.

He held her hand firmly in his. "I can remember many nights like this when I was a boy, and I *wasn't* herding cattle."

She wondered if he'd spent them kissing the girls who agreed to walk in the moonlight with him. She wondered if he remembered any one of those kisses as clearly as she was certain she would remember this one.

"I like herding cattle," she said. Jake said she was good at it, that she didn't upset the cows the way some of the boys did.

"Forget cows. Think of how pretty the moonlight looks on the river."

She had seen moonlight on the water many times before, and it had never struck her as anything special. She'd always been too busy to give it much thought. But now that she looked at it, it was rather nice. The moonlight spilled across the water in a wide streak that was creamy white in the center and silver along the edges. The surface of the river rippled gently as the water moved slowly downriver.

"It is nice," she agreed.

"It's beautiful," Cole said. "There wouldn't be so many people out if it weren't."

There weren't exactly hundreds of people out, maybe a

dozen couples, and most of them paying scant attention to the river. Some walked hand in hand and talked quietly. Others had settled on benches provided for those interested in quietly watching the river go by. One couple stood in full moonlight, kissing. They seemed so casual about a phenomenon that had shaken her down to her foundations.

"Is that the way you kiss when you take a woman for a moonlight walk?" Drew asked, indicating the kissing couple.

Cole seemed a little surprised by her question. "Sometimes."

"There are other ways?"

"Lots."

They walked a little way in silence. "Did you take a lot of girls walking in the moonlight when you were young?"

"A fair number."

"Did they like it?"

"I never had any complaints."

He looked out over the river, preventing her from seeing his expression. "Did you kiss all of them?" she asked.

"No."

"Why not?"

He turned to face her, amusement and curiosity mixed together in his expression. "I didn't want to."

"I thought all men wanted to kiss women."

"We do, but we don't want to kiss *every* woman. I expect women feel the same way about men."

She'd never thought about it. She rarely saw any women other than Isabelle, Marina, and Hannah. Marina had married Ward, a doctor who was Jake and Isabelle's best friend. Hannah had married Buck, the only one of the orphans so far to get married. She was certain none of them would consider kissing another man the way they kissed their husbands. The thought came to her that she would never consider kissing another man the way she'd kissed Cole.

Did that mean she felt about Cole the way Isabelle, Marina, and Hannah felt about their husbands?

That was impossible. All three of them were miserable when they were separated from their husbands for more than a few hours. She could go for days without thinking about Cole.

You haven't stopped thinking about him since that first night.

Of course she hadn't. He'd dogged her heels practically every minute. That was just like a man. Once they set their minds on something, they were like a dog after a bone, determined to have it until they got it. Then, half the time, they dropped it and walked away. A woman would never do that. If she set her mind on one special quarry, it would be impossible to think of giving him up.

"I expect women are a lot more careful with their kisses than men," she said.

"You're probably right."

"Are you careful with your kisses?"

He laughed. "I haven't always been, but I think I probably will be from now on."

"Why?"

"You have to answer a question first. Have you always been careful with your kisses?"

"That was my first kiss."

"Your absolute first?"

"Yes."

"What was wrong with the cowboys who worked for your father?"

"We didn't hire hands. There were enough of us to work the ranch until recently. One tried last time I was home. I punched him in the face and told him I'd shoot his ears off if he touched me again."

"It's a good thing I didn't know. I'd have been too afraid to lay a hand on you."

It hadn't escaped Drew's notice that Cole managed to do quite a few things he knew she didn't want him to do.

"Do you always hold hands when you walk a girl in the moonlight?"

"Why so many questions about what I do when I'm with other women?"

"I've never done any of these things. I'm sure I'll never do them again, but I just wondered."

Cole stopped, turned, took her other hand in his. "Why wouldn't you want to be kissed again? Was it so unpleasant?"

"N-no. It wasn't *unpleasant*."

"But you didn't like it."

"No. I—"

"What?"

"Is it always like that?"

"Like what?"

She couldn't think of words to describe how she felt that wouldn't sound foolish to a man who'd kissed dozens of women hundreds of times.

"I thought I wouldn't like it, that it would be uncomfortable. But it was really nice."

Cole took her hand and started walking again. "It's supposed to be nice. It's one of the things men and women do when they want to show how much they like each other."

"Why should you want to be nice to me? You hardly know me. I argue with you all the time."

"I like you."

"Why?"

"Do I have to have a reason?"

"Everybody has reasons for what they do. Sometimes they don't want to admit to them, or don't look hard enough to find them, but they're there."

"That's not a very romantic way to look at things."

"Romance encourages people to see what they want to see rather than what is."

"And that's bad?"

"No matter how much you hate it, you have to face reality."

"Did your parents?"

"No, and they paid for it with their lives. It almost cost mine, too."

"You're a strange woman, Drew Townsend. I've never met anybody like you before."

"I'm no different from everybody else." She didn't like being told she was strange. It didn't sound like a good thing.

"You try to do everything better than men, but you're very feminine despite yourself. You say you don't like love, don't trust it, yet you love your family and believe in Jake and Isabelle's love. You say you don't like people, yet you invite half the show to retire to your ranch. You don't think you're attractive when even the worst mirror will confirm you're very pretty. You say you're shy, yet you choose show business as a way to make a living."

He stopped and pulled her to face him. "I don't think you know what you want. Or maybe you *do,* but are afraid of it."

223

"Now you're the one not making any sense."

"It's your fault. I used to be extremely logical."

"So you gave up being a gentleman to become a drifter. That's not a sterling example of logic."

"It's as good as liking a woman who's determined never to like me in return."

"I like you. I didn't want to at first, but I do."

"What caused you to change your mind?"

"I've been trying to figure that out. It worries me that I can't."

"Is it my handsome face, my sparkling wit, my manly physique?"

She couldn't help laughing. "Don't be ridiculous."

He looked disappointed. "I wasn't."

"You're handsome enough, but I've got several brothers who're better looking. As for manly physique, Sean has more muscles in one arm than you have in both."

"I never realized what a problem it would be to court a woman with ten brothers, all from different gene pools."

"Are you courting me?" The word had stopped her in her tracks.

"Maybe that wasn't exactly the right word."

"Good, because I don't want any man courting me."

"Okay, *liking* a woman, wanting her to like you. It's difficult when you can't measure up to her brothers. Isn't there anybody in that corner of Texas who's an ordinary mortal?"

"Sure, but—"

"Not in your family."

"You might be better looking than Pete. And I suppose you have more muscles than Will. He's the most trifling child you've ever met, but—"

"Don't strain yourself trying to compliment me."

"I was going to say you have a kind of charm and persuasiveness that none of them have. You keep talking me into things I don't want to do. I can't even stay mad at you. And there's something very nice about your smile. I keep thinking of the innocence of a little boy who's about to get into mischief. He knows he shouldn't do something, he knows he's going to get into trouble, but he can't help himself."

"Is that it, I'm like a little boy?"

"No. You lie beautifully. If I were the least bit impressionable, you'd have me believing I was beautiful, that men were practically standing in line for a chance to spend a few minutes in my company."

He muttered something she couldn't understand.

"And the attention you've given to improving my act is very flattering. Zeke and Hawk tell me I haven't been very gracious about it, that I ought to thank you for—"

Without warning, he grabbed her and kissed her, hard and fast. She felt the world spin, throwing her completely off balance. He broke the kiss, held her at arm's length.

"That's what I want from you, not thanks. I don't want you to think of me as a cross between a priest and a choir boy. I'm a grown man made of flesh and blood, with all the wants and needs of any other man. Call me dangerous. Call me ugly if you must, but don't call me boyish and charming."

Drew had never expected anything she might say to Cole to unleash such a fierce reaction. She'd tried to say things she thought would please him, but she couldn't tell him the truth.

If she were to tell Cole how powerfully he affected her, she'd have to admit it to herself. She didn't want to do that. He had already weakened her resolve to have nothing to do with men. He'd managed to make her revise her opinion of kissing. She dreaded to think what else he might be able to do if given free rein. She had already learned if she gave Cole an inch, he'd take a mile so fast it made her head spin.

"I didn't say you were boyish or innocent," she said, trying to sooth his bruised ego. "I just said you made me think of a boy."

He growled something inarticulate.

"I can't help it if you're charming and gentlemanly and thoughtful."

He growled again, but this time she had no trouble understanding the curse he uttered.

"You're just like my bothers," she said. "If you can't be rough, tough, and completely without sentiment, you think you're a failure."

His expression lightened a little. "Maybe not quite that bad, but men do like to feel they're at least a little bit dangerous. Hell, how can we protect our women if we're powder puffs?"

"I can protect myself. You, too, if it comes to that."

He sagged, like a defeated man. "That's even worse. No man who needs to be protected by a woman can call himself a man."

"That's ridiculous. If you care so little about society's rules that you choose to be a drifter, why do you subscribe to such a silly notion?"

Instead of answering, he picked her up.

"What are you doing? Put me down!"

"Not until you admit I'm bigger and stronger than you."

"Don't be absurd. Put me down."

"I can run faster, throw farther, and climb higher."

"Cole, put me down. People will stare."

"Admit it. I'll hold you off the ground until you do."

She couldn't tell whether he was joking or serious, upset or fooling her.

"Okay, you're bigger and stronger."

"What else?"

"All the rest. Faster. Anything you want. Now let me down."

He lowered her until they were nose to nose, but Drew wasn't thinking of her nose. She was thinking of her body touching his along its whole length, of her breasts pressed hard against his chest, of the churning sensation that suddenly turned her belly into a roiling sea.

"Put me down this minute."

"Only if you kiss me."

"I've kissed you twice already."

"No, *I* kissed *you*. Now it's your turn."

"This is blackmail."

"It's your punishment for reducing my ego to the consistency of cornmeal mush."

The comparison struck her as funny. "Surely not that bad."

"I'll probably need several kisses to restore it to health."

The churning sensation increased. She could flatly refuse and demand he put her down, but she wanted a chance to try it again. It really didn't make sense to argue with him. He was bigger and stronger. He could hold her off the ground for as long as he wanted, and she couldn't do anything about it without making a scene. It would be much more logical to do as he wanted.

227

"I'm only doing this because you're forcing me to," she said.

"Beggars can't be choosers."

"I've never kissed a man before, so you can't blame me if it's not very good."

"I'll just keep holding you until you get it right."

She leaned forward and kissed him lightly on the lips. She'd expected him to do something. He didn't. His lips remained perfectly still.

"You've got to help," she said.

"Why?"

"Because I don't know what I'm doing."

"Just keep doing what you're doing."

She kissed him again, but this time she put a little more energy into it, made it last a little longer. Cole's limbs quivered in response. Maybe she'd learned more from watching Jake and Isabelle than she thought.

Then she bit him.

Not hard. Just a nip. It wasn't planned. She didn't even know what she was going to do until she did it. It surprised her as much as it surprised Cole.

With a deep-throated growl, he let her slide down his body until her feet touched the ground. Then he wrapped his arms around her body, pressed her to him so hard she was afraid she couldn't breath, and kissed her ruthlessly.

Drew discovered kissing wasn't a difficult skill to acquire. She didn't even have to try hard. Cole seemed more than anxious to do all the work. Which was just as well, as she was having a very difficult time keeping up with what he was doing, as well as its effect on her body.

She liked the feel of his mouth on hers. He was a little rough, and he was making strange groaning sounds. It was difficult not to be pleased when you could have such an effect on a man. He seemed to be trying hard to prove something. She didn't know what just yet, but she was willing to hang around until she found out.

She tried very hard to keep her mind on his kiss, but her body was acting up in ways it never had before. Her stomach was in full flight, doing dips, twists, figure eights, and just plain churning itself into a state. Her muscles seemed weak, flabby, unable to support her weight or control the movement of her limbs. Her legs threatened to go out from under her at any moment. To protect against that, she slipped her arms around Cole's neck.

That produced a satisfactory arrangement for her, but it resulted in Cole making a whole series of louder and more urgent noises. It also resulted in his pressing his body more firmly against hers. She hadn't spent the last nine years surrounded by boys growing into young men without anticipating what happened very soon thereafter. What she hadn't anticipated was its effect on her.

In the welter of sensation that engulfed her, she gradually became aware that her nipples had become extremely sensitive. Being pressed hard against Cole's chest had turned them into two points of boiling sensation that sent sparks and shivers radiating throughout her body. She yielded to the urge to press even harder against him and was rewarded by another groan.

Drew was finding it harder and harder to get her breath. She felt swept away, sucked into a maelstrom—

She felt Cole stiffen. The click of a cocked gun was unmistakable.

"Get your hands off her, or I'll drop you where you stand."

Chapter Fifteen

The feel of cold steel against his temple caused Cole to go rigid. The sound of Zeke's voice only partly reassured him his life wasn't about to come to an immediate and messy end. Having Drew to himself for a whole evening, having her in his arms, kissing her, had caused him to forget that Zeke and Hawk had been sent to be her watchdogs.

Breaking their kiss, releasing Drew, stepping away from the warmth of her body, he felt as though part of him were being torn away. It didn't help that Drew stared up at him with a combination of surprise and bemused wonder in her eyes. She might have spent the last several years trying to convince herself she wasn't interested in men, but the last minute or so had knocked that notion right off its foundations. And clearly no one was more surprised than Drew.

"You can put your gun away," Cole said, without turning to face Zeke. "I didn't force your sister to let me kiss her."

"I don't believe you," Zeke said, keeping the gun hard against Cole's temple. "Drew never lets anybody kiss her. It took Buck forever to get her to let him kiss her when he comes to visit."

"This wasn't exactly a brotherly kiss."

"I noticed. I also noticed you kissed her out in the open, where anybody could stand and stare. Drew would never do that. She hates being stared at."

Drew didn't say a word, just continued to stare at Cole, her eyes wide with wonder.

"You'd better say something to your brother," Cole said. "He seems to think I forced you to kiss me."

"You did."

Cole cursed Drew's habit of responding with the literal truth. He cursed it again when he felt the gun press harder against his temple, heard Zeke's angry growl.

"If you hurt her, I swear I'll kill you on the spot, no matter how many people are watching."

"Drew, for God's sake, speak to your brother before he does something all of us will regret."

"I won't regret it," Zeke said.

"I'll regret it enough for both of us," Cole replied.

Drew seemed to snap out of whatever trance she'd fallen into. "Put that gun away, Zeke," she said, sounding like her old self. "You'll have everybody staring at us."

"As if you standing here kissing Cole, your bodies

wrapped together as tight as vines, isn't going to be noticed!"

Drew blushed. "I forgot where I was."

"Forgot where you were!" Zeke repeated in tones of disbelief. "Do you happen to remember what you were doing?"

Drew turned her gaze back to Cole. Her expression went all soft and dreamy. "Yes. I remember what I was doing."

"You said he forced you, but you don't look like it," Zeke said.

"He said I insulted him by comparing him to a boy. He picked me up and wouldn't let me down until I kissed him enough to restore his self-respect."

"That was a damned stupid thing to say. I can't believe you fell for it."

"None of you ever liked being called a boy. I can remember—"

"This isn't the same, Drew. You're grown up now, and this man was kissing you in public. That's practically the same as saying you're engaged."

"It was just a friendly kiss," Drew said. "There's nothing wrong with that."

Zeke looked from one to the other, an expression of disbelief crossing his face. "Lord, nobody's going to believe this. Drew has fallen in love. And with a drifter. Isabelle is going to kill the three of us."

"I'm not in love!"

"Then why were you kissing this river rat in full view of anybody who happened to pass by?"

"I told you."

"That was no excuse."

"It's the only one I've got."

"Then you'd better not tell anybody. They'll think you're crazy."

"If you're going to be angry at anyone," Cole said, "be angry at me. It was my fault."

"It sure as hell was," Zeke shouted, "and you can be sure I'll get to you soon enough."

"Fine, but leave Drew alone."

"You're not going to tell me you're in love with Drew, are you?" Zeke demanded.

"Would you believe me if I said I was?"

"Hell, no."

"Then I won't bother answering your question."

"I might believe you'd try to marry a rich man's daughter, but I sure wouldn't believe a drifter has fallen in love with a woman who wants nothing but her own working ranch."

"If you want to know the truth, I like your sister. She's a fabulous shot and good with horses and goats. And she's pretty in the bargain."

"What's this about goats?" Zeke asked, bewildered.

Cole smiled at Drew. She smiled back.

"Nothing important. Now unless you want to attract even more attention than you have already, you'll put that gun away."

Several couples had interrupted their courting to watch the unexpected confrontation. Cole was certain they were disappointed it hadn't ended in a shooting. Nothing exciting ever happened in little towns like Norton. A shooting would have given people something to talk about for weeks to come.

"Drew's coming with me," Zeke said.

"Is that want you want?" Cole asked Drew.

"It's better this way," Drew said. "I had a good time. Thanks for dinner."

"See you tomorrow morning."

"No, you won't," Zeke said. "We're heading for Memphis tomorrow."

"We'll need to practice," Cole said.

"I'll let you know," Drew said. She looked back once. Cole thought she was going to say something. Instead she waved—a small motion with her right hand—turned, and walked off into the night with Zeke.

A fierce battle raged inside Cole as he watched Drew disappear. He wanted to go after her, demand the right to accompany her back to the hotel, demand the right to ask if she really did like kissing him, ask if she'd do it again.

Another part of him held him back, saying he was a fool and he ought to thank his lucky stars Zeke showed up before he did something stupid like tell Drew he loved her. Or worse still, make love to her. He reminded himself he'd been sent to collect evidence to prove Drew was behind the string of robberies. Though he hadn't found any direct evidence, he couldn't ignore the growing circumstantial evidence. He'd found it without really looking. If his captain called upon him to defend his performance in this case, he'd have a hard time doing it.

He might think Drew was innocent, he might have a conviction that went right down to the core of him, but he didn't have any proof. What's more, he didn't have the first bit of evidence—not even a well-founded suspicion—who might be behind these robberies.

He'd fallen down on the job no matter how he looked at it. All he'd managed to do was become infatuated with a woman who might be a master criminal. For the first time in his career, he'd failed to carry out an assignment. He was a disgrace.

Cole turned and walked down to the river. He didn't dare go back to the hotel yet. He knew he'd go looking for Drew, and right now he had to do some serious thinking, the kind of thinking he couldn't do when Drew was occupying his thoughts, or when he remembered how she felt in his arms, how wonderful it was to kiss her, to have her kiss him back. He'd half expected her to refuse his dinner invitation after the disaster with the goat. Just remembering it caused him to smile.

Somewhere inside that tightly wound-up woman was a another woman struggling to get out. He didn't know what she was like, but he was certain she wasn't dead set against men or marriage. She probably wasn't ashamed to admit she had a soft heart, one that would cause her to invite a bunch of old people to come live with her if they didn't have anywhere else to go. She was also perfectly capable of admitting she loved her brothers and came close to worshiping Jake and Isabelle. She would also admit she wanted and needed love to feel complete.

Cole knew he had no right to stir this woman from her long slumber. That was a job for some young man who could approach Drew with an honest and open heart, who could come to her believing in all the goodness of which she was capable, absolutely certain she could never do any wrong.

It certainly wasn't a job for a man who had lied to her from the very first.

Cole watched the water flow by, wishing it would carry him to some place where he felt none of this indecision, none of this distaste for the work he had to do, for what he'd already done. He was caught between his duty and his desire to get to know Drew better, to become part of her life. But as much as he fought the battle over and over again, he knew the outcome had already been decided. He'd begun in one camp. It would be impossible to change to the other now. No matter what he said to himself, regardless of the excuses he might make, he knew he'd already compromised any chance he had with Drew. The sensible thing to do—the only thing, really—would be to get on with his job and leave as quickly as possible.

It would be better for him. Better for Drew, too.

He wondered what she really thought of him. She was so determined she could never feel anything more than a tepid friendship for any man that she wouldn't admit to herself she might actually be fond of Cole. He didn't dare use the word *love*. Just the sound of it frightened him. The loss and pain it implied were too great to think about.

He could be putting himself though all this agony for nothing. Maybe she didn't feel anything more than a mild liking for him. Maybe she had been mesmerized by the kiss, not the man behind the kiss. That wasn't a very flattering thought, but Drew had made it perfectly plain on many occasions that she was less than impressed by Cole Benton. It was quite possible she had let him ride with her, accepted his invitation to dinner, walked down by the river because she was tired of resisting, not because she'd learned to like him.

Then why would she say he was charming, gentlemanly, even sweet and boyish? It wasn't the kind of compliment a man wanted to hear, but it was exactly the sort of thing a woman would say, especially one who seemed to believe it was her role in life to take care of everyone she met.

It was time to find out if Drew truly liked him, to decide whether his feelings for her were merely infatuation or something deeper. Once he knew that, he could decide what to do. He didn't know what that might be, but at least he would be doing something to clarify his situation, instead of sinking deeper and deeper into a morass of questions, doubts, and worries.

He'd never acted like this in his entire life. He'd always known exactly what he wanted to do. He remembered his mother's words when he'd left home.

"A woman will bring you to your knees one of these days," she'd called after him as he walked down the steps to his waiting horse. "She'll make you bow your head and beg. I'm just sorry I won't be there to see it."

Cole had been absolutely certain his mother was wrong. Now he wasn't so sure.

Memphis, Tennessee

"What do you mean she's gone?" Cole said to Myrtle.

"She's not here."

"But everybody from the show is staying at this hotel."

"We can if we want, but we don't have to."

"Where did she go?"

"She didn't say."

Cole was more than frustrated. He was angry. Drew had disappeared. Zeke and Hawk, too. They had four days in Memphis and only one show, a wealth of free time. He'd been hoping to spend it with Drew.

"Did she say anything about meeting me for practice?"

"No. We didn't have a chance to talk. She left directly from the train. She said she'd see me in a few days."

Myrtle seemed surprised Cole didn't know Drew's plans, but he wasn't about to explain that though Drew had accepted him in her act, she hadn't accepted him in any other part of her life. He believed she wasn't the thief, but her disappearance did nothing to reassure him. He couldn't prove her innocence as long as she closed him out of her world. If she were with him just once when a robbery took place, it would go a long way toward removing suspicion from her.

That wasn't the only area in which he needed reassurance—or more information. He'd hoped to discover the extent and nature of her feelings for him, if she felt anything other than irritation and weary acceptance. He'd also hoped to learn more about the extent of his own emotional involvement. Cole had left home rather than be forced into a kind of life he hated, and into marriage with a kind of woman he couldn't respect. Drew gave every indication of being the kind of woman he'd spent the last ten years looking for. Falling in love with her might be the worst mistake of his life, but turning away before he knew whether she could love him might be even worse. Most men weren't lucky enough to find the perfect woman. Cole thought he might have. And he couldn't turn his back until he knew whether she could love him.

And if she were responsible for the robberies . . . well, he'd figure out what to do about that if the need arose.

But he was getting ahead of himself. He'd been doing that ever since he met Drew, which was probably a good indication he ought to keep his distance. It would be safer, but he knew he couldn't.

A day later he found a reason to change his mind. A well-known business firm in Memphis, one of the few to keep large amounts of cash reserves on hand, was robbed. The description of the thieves was the same as in all the previous robberies. Cole couldn't make himself believe Drew was responsible, but he had no proof. He couldn't put it off any longer. He had to talk to his commanding officer.

"I want to be taken off the case," Cole said when he'd been ushered into his captain's office.

"No greetings? No how-is-your-family? No stories to tell?"

Cole felt some of the stiffness leave his body. "Sorry, Ben. This case has got me so wound up, I don't know what I'm doing."

"In that case, we'd better start with a drink. Whiskey okay?"

"Fine."

The office was small, bare, and lacking the comforts afforded most officers of Captain Benjamin Wattle's rank, but the government didn't spend much money on its covert operations. Ben was lucky to have an office. He'd had to provide the furniture himself. Since he came from a modest background, he'd limited himself to a desk and a chair, a chair for his guest, and a cabinet that held his records as well as his liquor. Two Audubon prints and a plain white curtain at the single window were the only touches of decoration.

"You can sit down," Ben said. "This isn't a military review."

Cole settled into the chair across from Ben's desk and accepted a glass of bourbon whiskey, but he didn't relax despite the fact that he and Ben had known each other for nearly a dozen years. He felt that he'd failed his old friend, failed himself as well, and he didn't like it.

The captain poured himself a drink and settled back in his chair. "I had expected to get regular reports from you," he said, sipping his drink. "I haven't heard anything since that first week."

"There hasn't been anything to report."

The captain's eyes narrowed. "You'll have to explain that remark."

"As I told you, there was no problem working my way into the show. I became part of Drew Townsend's act that first night."

"But you were only coming out of the stands at the end of the show to shoot against her. You couldn't learn much like that."

"The boss wanted to spruce up her act, so I started coming up with ideas for things she could do. She didn't like it at first, but it gave me a reason to meet her at practice every day, for us to work together in every show."

"That still leaves a lot of time."

"I couldn't come up with an excuse to spend all my time with her, but I tried to make sure I saw her or her brothers as often as possible."

"What brothers?"

"According to her, she and ten boys were adopted by this couple in Texas. When she decided to join the Wild West Show, they insisted two brothers go along to make sure nothing happened to her."

The captain didn't say anything, but Cole could tell

from his expression he was already questioning what Cole was telling him.

"Whatever else might be right or wrong in this case, the watching over her part is right. I stumble over her brothers all the time, especially an ex-slave called Zeke. I can't decide whether he hates my guts or just all white men."

"I'm not interested in Zeke."

"You would be if you saw him. Her other brother is a half-breed Comanche."

The captain began to show more interest. "The reports say the men in the robberies wear masks."

"And there are always two, never more, never less."

The captain took a sip from his drink. "Go on."

"Three robberies have taken place while I've been with the show, one when the three of them took a train the next day, one when they stayed a day late, and one here in Memphis after they disappeared."

"What else have you learned?"

Cole explained about Drew sitting in the bank, studying everything that happened, about the old people depositing money.

"Why do I get the feeling you're about to tell me something I don't want to hear?" the captain asked.

"I don't think Drew has anything to do with those robberies. The timing is purely coincidental."

The captain's eyes grew a little wider, but he showed no other outward sign that Cole's words surprised him. "There's more, isn't there?"

"Yes. I want you to take me off the case."

"You said that when you came in. Now tell me why."

"I don't think she's guilty."

"I don't want to know what you think. I need facts. Either you have proof one way or you have it the other."

"I don't have proof either way," Cole admitted, "but that isn't the reason I want you to take me off the case."

"Then what is?"

He'd worked out exactly what he was going to say last night, but now it sounded like something a new recruit would say.

"I've lost my objectivity," he said.

The captain's gaze narrowed. "How come?"

Cole swallowed hard. "I've become interested in her romantically."

Silence. Long and uncomfortable.

"I did everything I could to keep it from happening, but I couldn't stop it. Don't think Drew has somehow figured out who I am and seduced me. She didn't want me near her and did her best to keep me out of her act. She has lost no opportunity to tell me she doesn't trust men and has no intention of letting one into her life. She thinks I'm a useless drifter."

The captain flashed his first smile. "That seems a very unlikely beginning for developing a relationship."

"I didn't say we had a relationship," Cole admitted. "I can't tell you how Drew feels about me."

"But you think she's innocent?"

"She's not the kind of person to lie, cheat, or steal. She won't let anybody do anything for her, not buy things for her or give her gifts. I realize this is no kind of proof, but it's all I have to offer. That's why I'm asking you to take me off the case."

"Who do you think I ought to put on it? Hodges? Willis?"

Both men were known for being hard-nosed, even brutal in their pursuit of evidence. They were also known womanizers. There'd be trouble with Zeke or Hawk within twenty minutes. Though Cole often wished her brothers would find another interest in life, he had to respect them for their loyalty to Drew and their determination to protect her.

"How about Bill Walker?"

The captain grinned. "Bill should have been an accountant. He's good for fraud, but useless with anything like robbery. Hodges and Willis are better."

"They're the kind of men you send after confirmed criminals when you want to bring them in dead or alive, not after someone like Drew."

"Why not someone like Drew?"

"Because she's too innocent to suspect what they'd be up to. They'd think nothing of trying to seduce her to get her to tell them what they want to know."

"Could they?"

It was an insulting question, one that caused him to rise halfway out of his chair. "You're baiting me. Why?"

"I don't like to see a good officer go bad."

"I'm not going bad. I just want off this case."

"It's all the same. It doesn't matter why you can't finish the job."

"I'm trying to tell you, Drew isn't behind the robberies. You're on the wrong trail."

"That's not what the evidence says."

"Then the evidence is circumstantial."

"Maybe, but there's a lot of it. We'd have a good chance of getting a conviction on what we've got now."

Cole knew he was bluffing. All Drew needed was an

alibi for one of the robberies to blow the government's case out of the water. He didn't know what Drew had been doing or where she had gone, but he was certain she was innocent. If she weren't, she was too smart to have forgotten to provide herself with an alibi that would be hard to disprove.

"We both know you don't have a case," Cole said. "You're trying to back me into a corner. What do you want me to do?"

"Stay on the case," the captain said. "If she's not guilty, find out who is. Until you do, I can't let off the pressure. She's the only real suspect we have."

"I can't be around her, knowing I care for her, trying to persuade her to care for me, knowing all the time I'm looking for evidence that might put her in jail. That's a lousy thing to do to any woman."

"I'll give you three days to make up your mind," the captain said. "If you turn down the case, I'll assign it to Hodges. Why don't you go visit your parents while you're thinking about it? I know they'd like to see you."

Chapter Sixteen

"You can't go to this party dressed like that, Drucilla. I don't see why you won't wear clothes that enhance your natural beauty."

"I don't have any natural beauty, and don't call me Drucilla. You know I hate it. My name is Drew."

"You were christened Drucilla Eloise Taylor Townsend," her Aunt Dorothea Rutland stated. "I know because I was there."

Jake had filled his ranch house with comforts for Isabelle, but even their elegant sitting room paled in comparison to the luxury of the suite Drew's aunt occupied in Memphis's finest hotel—silk-and-velvet-covered beds, chairs, and windows, an Aubusson carpet on the sitting room floor. The suite had been furnished in the Louis XVI style, in gold, white, and blue. Jake and the boys wouldn't have sat down for fear of breaking some of the fragile-looking furniture.

Drew stayed with her aunt every time they happened to be in the same town. Each time she prepared an excuse as to why she needed to skip this visit, but she never had the heart to use it. Her aunt was a widow without children. She'd been heartbroken when her only sibling, Drew's mother, ran off to marry a man the family disliked. She'd been devastated by the news her sister and niece had been killed by Indians.

She had found Drew less than a year after Jake and Isabella adopted her. She had done everything in her power to induce Drew to come live with her. She wanted to introduce Drew into the world of high society, to see her married to a suitably rich and socially prominent man, then to sit back and enjoy Drew's children.

Drew had refused point-blank to leave Jake and Isabelle or be introduced into society. Her only ambition was to have her own ranch alongside that of her adopted family. Her aunt was horrified when Drew joined the Wild West Show. Not even her most tearful pleadings— or offers to purchase the whole state of Texas for Drew if she wanted—made Drew change her mind. Rather than give up on her crusade, Dorothea forsook the society of New York several times a year to travel to the cities where Drew appeared.

This was their sixth visit this year. Usually Drew could stay only a few hours, maybe overnight, but this time she was stuck for three days. Drew loved her aunt. She was a truly genuine person whose concern for Drew was deep and abiding. But no matter how many times Drew explained why she wanted to stay in Texas, her aunt simply could not understand how her niece could prefer a cattle ranch to the salons of the wealthy and privileged. Nor could she stop trying to convince Drew of her mistake.

"I know what I was christened," Drew said, "but I don't feel like a Drucilla, and I don't look like one."

"You would if you put on a decent gown, let me fix your hair, and wore some pearls."

That was something else Drew didn't like. Every time she visited her aunt, she presented her with a new dress. Drew had enough dresses she'd never worn to fill several closets. That didn't count the shoes, hats, and everything else that made up the wardrobe of a well-dressed young society woman. The clothes were tight, confining, and exposed too much of her shoulders and bosom. What's more, they were meant to be worn only inside. Drew didn't understand why any woman would choose to close herself up inside a house all day.

"You can't go about in polite society dressed like one of those crazy Texans," her aunt had declared. "I'd be a laughingstock."

But Drew held firm. She'd go dressed in a simple white blouse and plain brown skirt or she wouldn't go at all. She considered giving up her boots sacrifice enough.

"I don't know how you can stand to dress like that," Drew said of her aunt's elaborate mauve silk gown, feather headdress, and elaborate jewels. "It would take me the better part of a week to get myself tarted up like that."

"Honestly, Drucilla, I don't know why you insist upon talking like a loose woman."

Drew clenched her teeth and tried not to mind being called by her full Christian name. She was sensible enough to know her aunt would never change. There were times, and right now was one of them, when she was certain she couldn't stand it another minute. But her soft heart always stopped her from leaving. Even without Isabelle gently pointing it out, Drew knew she was the only family Aunt Dorothea had left.

"This is what all ranchers wear," Drew said. "And please don't start in about going into society. I told you from the beginning all I wanted was to stay in Texas and have my own ranch."

"Then let me buy you one so you can stop performing in this terrible show. *Theater people!*" her aunt exclaimed, as though they all had some fatal and communicable disease. "I don't know how you can stand to consort with them."

"Most of them are very nice," Drew said, "though you wouldn't like them. You have nothing in common."

"I should think not. I can't understand what you find that's so interesting about them."

"They take care of each other. They even take care of me."

"Thank goodness for that. I shudder every time I think of you alone among strangers, traveling to strange towns."

Drew couldn't help laughing. "I'm not alone. Hawk and Zeke look after me."

Drew knew her aunt found it impossible to accept that a young woman of her family should depend upon a black man and a half-breed Indian for protection. Drew wouldn't allow anything to be said against Zeke and Hawk, but her aunt nearly had apoplexy every time Drew called them her brothers. They had agreed not to talk about it.

"I still say you shouldn't be doing anything so unlady-like as traveling in a wild west show." She spoke the words in a half whisper, as though she were afraid the maids would hear and broadcast her disgrace all over town.

"I like being in the show. I like it when people applaud my skill."

Her aunt shuddered. "Please don't mention that you shoot guns. I can't imagine how any female could do that without suffering an attack of nerves."

"If females didn't shoot guns, they'd be killed by Indians, thieves, wild animals—"

Her aunt covered her ears. "Don't say another word. You'll make me think of what happened to your poor mother. I'll have nightmares for a whole week."

"I won't talk about guns and Texas if you promise not to criticize what I do or the people I work with."

Drew had grown weary of this conversation. They had it every time she came for a visit, but Dorothea never really gave up. She was just as stubborn as Drew.

"I was delighted when I heard you'd be here for three days," Dorothea said. "Even though I hardly know any-one here, I managed to secure an invitation to another party, our second in three days."

Her aunt was greatly pleased to have scored such a tri-umph. Drew felt she'd been consigned to purgatory. Her aunt lived in New York and Chicago, but she had connec-tions in every major city from Boston to San Francisco. Usually Drew's visits were too short to allow her to attend balls, parties, or even dinners. This time she had no excuse.

"Maybe you'll meet a young man you could like."

That was the real reason Drew dreaded going to parties. Her aunt was convinced if Drew met the right young man, she'd give up the Wild West Show and her idea of owning a ranch, and settle happily into the role of wife and mother. It was utterly beyond her realm of understanding that any woman could actually *want* to avoid marriage and motherhood.

Drew fixed her aunt with an unwavering gaze. "I've promised to go to this party. I've even promised to try to behave so I won't embarrass you. But if you insist upon shoving me into the arms of one idiot after another, none of whom have anything to recommend themselves except their fathers' money, I'll cause a scene that will send all of your young bachelors running for the first wallflower they can find."

"I don't know where you learned to talk like that!" her aunt exclaimed, more upset by what Drew said than her manner of saying it.

"I learned it being around men in the dust, dirt, sweat, and heat of working with stubborn, cantankerous cows. Believe me, I can say things that would turn your ears pink."

Her aunt covered her ears with pudgy hands. "Don't. My nerves would be ruined for a week."

"Then promise you won't force any more men down my throat."

"Drucilla, darling," her aunt said with the resigned attitude of a woman who didn't expect the request she was about to make to be heeded, "do you have to express yourself in such a manner?"

"It's the way I talk. You wouldn't want me to edit everything before the words came out of my mouth, would you?"

Her aunt looked as though she'd be profoundly grateful if Drew would do exactly that. "Please don't talk that way tonight. If you do, nobody in this town will invite me anywhere ever again."

"Why should you care? You don't live here."

"Bad news travels fast, especially if it's something socially embarrassing."

"Gossip," Drew said. "That's the trouble with the people you know. They lead useless lives. If they had something to do, they wouldn't have time to worry about what I wear, how I talk, or that I work for a living." This was another old argument. Drew hadn't meant to let herself be drawn into it again. "Sorry, Aunt Dorothea, but you know how I feel about that."

"It all comes from your mother marrying *that man*," her aunt said. "If she hadn't——"

"If she hadn't, I wouldn't have been born, we wouldn't be having this conversation, and you wouldn't have to worry about such an unsatisfactory niece as myself."

"I don't mind worrying about you, and you're a wonderful niece."

"But one who disagrees with you in practically every way."

Her aunt sighed. "I don't see why your father had to take your mother to Texas. There were so many other places he could have gone."

"I don't know either, but I'm glad he did. I love Texas. It's the perfect place for me. Now let's not argue about it anymore." Drew stood. "It must be time to go to this party of yours."

"It's okay to be a little late. In fact, it's more fashionable."

"To hell with fashion," Drew said. "I want to get this shindig over with."

"I don't know why you insist upon dragging me to things like this," Cole said to his mother. "You know I hate them."

"After running off and leaving me, the least you can do is escort me to a few parties when you're home," his mother said, a complaining edge to her voice. "You have no idea how hard it is to convince people you haven't turned into one of those savages you go after."

"I don't work in Texas anymore," Cole said. "I do undercover work for the government."

His mother grimaced as though she had a bad taste in her mouth. "So you consort with criminals instead. Do you know how embarrassing that is to me?"

Cole cursed under his breath for at least the one hundredth time since he'd been home. He never passed near Memphis without stopping to visit his family. He had no qualms about turning his back on the kind of life his family expected of him, but he couldn't ignore his family.

They had just entered the home of one of Memphis's most prominent society hostesses. After climbing wide, shallow steps to a porch with wrought-iron railings, they stepped into a wide central hall that ran the length of the house. On the left, a double salon gleamed in candlelight dispersed from two enormous chandeliers. Chairs had been placed along the wall, and the carpets rolled up to allow dancing. A small string orchestra struggled to be heard above the din of conversation. Servants served wine cups, cooled with last winter's ice, at the back of the hall. The men were directed to the library if they wanted something stronger to drink.

Everyone looked overdressed and overanimated.

Cole hated the continuous round of social events that made up his mother's life. He would have much preferred to stay home, but he'd learned through experience it was easier to go along than to fight. Because he was an only child, his mother had never accepted his decision to turn his back on the way of life she considered superior to all others.

"Don't worry. I'll probably do something else soon," Cole said.

"Something even more embarrassing." His mother looked pained. "I wish you would come home and behave yourself."

Cole didn't reply. There was nothing to say that hadn't been said many times before. He'd already decided he wouldn't tell her he'd joined the Wild West Show. As far as his mother was concerned, people in show business were common, immoral, and probably criminal. He couldn't think of a way to tell her about Drew that wouldn't bring on a fainting spell.

"Maybe you'll find a nice girl," his mother said. "Once you have a wife and family to think of, you'll feel quite differently about associating with such unsuitable people."

Cole didn't reply to that, either.

"I hope you're not going to refuse to dance tonight," his mother said.

"I don't like dancing."

"But you do it so beautifully. You're always the most

handsome man in the room. All the young women want to dance with you."

His mother meant they wanted to dance with the Benton fortune. The fact that Cole wasn't plug-ugly was a secondary consideration. "I don't dance," Cole said.

"Then talk to them."

"How? They have nothing to talk about but parties they've been to, parties they haven't been to, and the people who went to both. They never want to talk about things that interest me."

"Most people find it very difficult to be interested in savages and criminals."

His mother's tone and expression implied that such things could only be of interest to the lower classes. Cole didn't reply to that, either. He had stopped trying to explain himself to her years ago.

"I will try not to embarrass you," Cole said. "But if Sibyl Owens corners me again, I'll leave her standing, even if it's in the middle of the room."

"She's a beautiful young woman," his mother said. "Her family is the oldest in Memphis."

"She's also in search of a rich husband."

"It's so sad to see such an old family fall on hard times."

"They wouldn't be having such a hard time if her father and brother would stop drinking and gambling and pay some attention to their business," Cole snapped.

"You don't understand—"

"No, I don't," Cole said, "so let's not—"

Cole stopped midsentence, the words choked off in his throat. "Who is that woman?" he asked. He had to be dreaming, sleepwalking, or simply deluded, but unless his eyes betrayed him, Drew Townsend had just entered the room.

"Who?" his mother asked.

"That young woman who just entered."

"I don't know."

"Everybody knows everybody at this sort of function."

"I've seen the older woman before, but I don't know anything about her. Doreen," she said to a matron nearby, "do you know anything about the two women who just entered?"

Doreen Cutchins was one of the reigning dowagers of Memphis society, one of the hostesses of the party.

"That's Dorothea Rutland and her niece. Mrs. Rutland is a wealthy widow who showed up here for the first time last year. She didn't stay long, but she hired the biggest suite in the hotel. She seems to have an unending supply of money."

"I can't believe you would send her an invitation without knowing more about her."

"She presented impeccable letters of introduction. Imagine, she has a letter from a Vanderbilt! Well, how could I refuse her after that, even if I wanted to, which I didn't. Herbert is taking me to New York this winter. I plan to ask her for a letter of introduction to Mrs. Vanderbilt."

"What about the niece?" Cole asked.

"I don't know anything about her except that she dresses with a deplorable lack of taste and is very stand-offish. She was rude to poor Hunter Ashby last night, flat refused to dance with him, said she wasn't going to waste her time on a dried-up melon rind that probably hadn't been any good when it was ripe. Have you ever heard anybody say such a thing?" Doreen asked, her substantial bosom heaving with indignation. "There have been Ashbys in Memphis for more than a hundred years."

Despite his surprise, Cole couldn't help smiling. That sounded exactly like something Drew would say.

"Molly Franks thinks they're forcing their way into society in hopes the young one can catch a husband. If she expects to have jewels like the ones Mrs. Rutland wears every time I've seen her, she'll need a very rich husband."

"Jewels won't be the only expense," Cole's mother said. "If that dress is any example of the rest of her clothes, it'll take a fortune to supply her with a wardrobe."

Seeing Drew at a society party had stunned Cole. That she should have an aunt of sufficient wealth and social connections to be able to procure an invitation was even more perplexing. Everything was in direct and glaring conflict with what he knew of Drew.

Or thought he knew. A hideous explanation presented itself almost immediately. Unfortunately, it fit the situation much too well.

Suppose Drew was behind the robberies, after all. Suppose she was using the money to support herself and her aunt in this extravagant lifestyle. If she was introducing herself to society in various cities—that would account for Mrs. Rutland appearing only now and then and staying at hotels—she was most probably scheming to catch a rich husband.

Cole didn't want to consider this new possibility. He'd convinced himself Drew was innocent. He'd even tried to convince his captain. Maybe he was a stupid, infatuated fool who couldn't believe the evidence right before his eyes. Every time he decided Drew couldn't be responsible for the robberies, something happened that pointed the finger directly at her once again.

It was about time he woke up and started doing his job. He hadn't been able to come up with an explanation for a single one of the facts that pointed to Drew's involvement. The fact that the leader was a female who was an excellent shot, that she was accompanied by two heavily masked men, that the robberies always took place in or near the towns where the Wild West Show was performing, that he didn't know Drew's whereabouts at the times of the robberies. Then there was the fact she studied the workings of every bank she could, that she had all these old people depositing money in bank accounts that she controlled. And now, despite her modest clothes, she was attempting to enter a society well beyond the grasp of even the wealthiest Texas rancher.

Maybe the captain wasn't bluffing when he said he had enough circumstantial evidence to convict her.

"I'll go over and introduce myself," Cole said.

"You can't talk to her!" his mother said.

"Why not? You wanted me to dance."

"I want you to dance with a nice girl."

"How do you know she isn't?"

"I don't know anything about her."

"I'll ask," Cole said, knowing such behavior would horrify his mother. "Anything you particularly want to know?"

"Cole Benton, if you tell that woman I want to know so much as one thing about her, I'll refuse to acknowledge you're my son."

"Promise?"

He knew he shouldn't tease his mother so, but her snobbery irritated him.

His mother ignored his remark. "You can't just walk up to her without a proper introduction."

"That's the advantage men have over women. They don't have to be so careful of their reputations."

But he had to be careful to use his head, he told himself as he started across the room. So far his heart had decided what he'd think, how he'd act. He couldn't afford to do that anymore. He might feel sure Drew wasn't responsible for all those robberies, but feelings didn't count. Facts did, and he had gathered precious few.

"I do declare, it's Cole Benton in the flesh."

Cole recognized Sibyl Owens's voice before he turned to see the blond beauty bearing down on him. He recognized her gown as one he'd seen before, made over to appear new. He felt sorry for her. He knew the humiliation a woman suffered when she had to wear an old gown, even one so cleverly disguised, but he wasn't willing to sacrifice himself to restore her to the style of living into which she'd been born.

"Your mama didn't tell me you'd stopped chasing your savages long enough to come for a visit."

"I don't chase Indians or rustlers anymore," Cole said.

"How disappointing," Sibyl said, presenting her cheek for Cole to kiss. "I was dying to hear about some of your adventures."

"Mama says my adventures aren't suitable for feminine ears, especially the ears of refined, unmarried ladies."

"Don't remind me," Sibyl said, making a face. "I'm so

long in the tooth I'll probably be considered on the shelf before the evening's out."

Cole had to admire Sibyl. She'd marry him for his money in a flash, but she didn't hide the fact her family had fallen on hard times or that it was her duty to find a husband rich enough, *and willing*, to pay off the family debts.

"I think you'll manage to stay in circulation a bit longer."

"You want to walk me around the room and make all the young things so jealous their smiles will crack?"

"You forget about my *unsuitable adventures*," Cole said. "I'm more likely to make them head straight for the protection of their mamas."

Sibyl hooked her arm in his. "Don't pretend to be modest. You know you're the best-looking man in the room."

Cole knew that wasn't so. No one could pretend he was as handsome as Hunter Ashby, but every female in Memphis knew the Benton family fortune was several times larger than the Ashby fortune. Everyone also knew money improved a man's looks several times over.

Sibyl tried to steer Cole in the direction of a group of young couples heading toward the dance floor. "You'll have to excuse me tonight," he said. "I've got to see that young woman over there."

Drew had hung back as her aunt greeted one hostess after another. She kept her head high, but she seemed to see no one in the room. Cole's heart felt lighter, his mood more buoyant. It was an unlikely attitude for a woman determined to insinuate herself into society, but it was entirely consistent with the Drew he had come to know.

"Have you succumbed to the charms of the newest heiress, too?" Sibyl asked, her face tight with her effort to keep desperation at bay.

"I don't know. That's not the role she was playing the last time I saw her."

Sibyl's expression eased; her grip on Cole's arm didn't. "Does this have something to do with your mysterious job? I've asked your mother to tell me about it, but she refuses."

"Mother is ashamed of me."

Sibyl took a moment to give Drew a complete going-over. "She doesn't look like a savage or a criminal."

"Looks can be deceiving."

"You really have to talk to her?" Everything about her expression and voice said she hoped he would change his mind.

"Yes. Right away."

Not being fool enough to push when she knew it was useless, Sibyl released her hold on Cole's arm. "Then I won't detain you any longer. But you must promise to hurry back and tell me every delicious detail."

"You know I can't do that."

Sibyl pulled a face. "Nobody here ever has anything interesting to say." She flashed him a brilliant smile. "I was depending on you to rescue me from a very dull evening."

"How can it be dull when you're the most beautiful woman here?"

"Very easily when you're also one of the poorest. Go chase after your mystery woman. Maybe she's got a gun hidden in her purse." She giggled. "Maybe she'll shoot you. That ought to liven up the evening."

"Nothing nearly so interesting."

Cole hurried across the room before anyone else could waylay him. He came up to Drew while she was being introduced to a matron and daughter who obviously felt Drew was several notches below them on the social scale. He waited until the women had left, then tapped Drew on the shoulder. She swung around to face him.

"I never expected to find you in a place like this," Cole said.

"Cole!" Drew exclaimed.

Cole saw excitement in her eyes and pleasure in her expression, heard welcome in her voice.

At that moment, he was lost.

Chapter Seventeen

"I never expected to see you at a society party," Drew said. "How in the world did you manage to wangle an invitation?"

"I could ask you the same thing."

"My aunt dragged me here."

"I thought your family was in Texas."

"This is my *real* aunt, my mother's sister. Every time I visit, Aunt Dorothea does her best to drag me off to some affair like this. Thank goodness you're here. It's a relief to have someone to talk to besides people who obviously think they're better than I am. We can be outsiders together."

"Why would your aunt bring you here?" He hoped she'd deny the rumors, the gossip that had caused suspicion to spring up in his heart yet again.

"She's convinced if I meet some nice young man, I'll give up my crazy idea of owning my own ranch. She can't understand why anyone would want to live in Texas."

"I didn't realize you were part of society. What do they think about your being in the Wild West Show?"

"They don't know, but it doesn't matter. I'm not part of society and don't want to be. Besides, I'll probably never see any of these people again."

"But if—"

"My aunt lives in New York, but she follows me around the country trying to convince me to give up my foolish ways."

"You've got me confused. I thought your family was killed, and you were adopted."

"They were, and I was, but my aunt found me a year later. She wanted me to live with her, but I wanted to stay with Jake and Isabelle. Now she follows me everywhere. I see her practically every month. Please don't say a word about New Orleans. Jake and Isabelle are coming with some friends of theirs, George and Rose Randolph, and I want to spend my time with them."

"You didn't tell me your aunt was rich."

Drew seemed to stiffen. "What difference does that make?"

"If your pearls are real, that necklace alone could buy a dozen ranches. Why are you working in a traveling show?"

"I intend to pay for my own ranch," Drew said, a sharp edge to her voice. "I wore these pearls to keep my aunt from breaking into tears and ruining her makeup. She tried to give them to me, but I wouldn't take them. Jake and Isabelle wanted to give me a ranch, but I wouldn't take that, either. I mean to be entirely independent."

"Is your independence that important?"

"More important than anything else. My parents were so determined to be independent they ran away, even though it cost them their lives. I guess it's in my blood."

Cole could feel a ball of tension in his stomach unravel. Drew didn't sound at all like a young woman stealing money to have the means to thrust herself into society so she could find a rich husband. On the contrary, she seemed determined to turn her back on a life of wealth and privilege.

"My aunt's coming back," Drew said. "Pretend you've come to ask me to dance."

"But I don't want to dance."

"I don't either. But if I don't dance with you, she'll drive me crazy until I dance with one of the stupid young men she picks out. Last night it was a fool by the name of Ashby. I forget his first name."

"Hunter."

"That sounds right. I really don't care what his name is. Oh God, he's here tonight. I don't want him to see me."

"I've never seen you afraid of a man before."

"He's not a man. If he were, I could shoot him."

"Is that the only way you know to handle men—to shoot them?"

"It works."

"If you want to drive them off."

"What else would I want to do? Now stop arguing and let me introduce you to my aunt. And no matter what you do, don't mention that we work in the show together."

Cole found it surprising, but amusing and comforting

as well, that there was someone in the world Drew couldn't run over without a backward glance.

"I see you've managed to capture the most attractive man in the room already," Dorothea Rutland said when she approached. "I told you you'd find a nice man."

"He's an outsider like me," Drew said. "That's the only reason I'm talking to him. He used to work in Texas. You can't imagine how happy I was to find him here."

Cole told himself not to attach too much importance to Drew's words. Or her smiling welcome. She didn't see him as a lover, only a kindred soul in the foreign world of high society.

Dorothea looked Cole over from head to foot. "He doesn't look like a cowboy to me."

"I'm not," Cole said. "I worked with the Rangers."

Dorothea looked horrified. "That's worse than being a cowboy."

"I quit," Cole said.

"What do you do now?" Dorothea asked, still withholding her approval.

"I've just quit my old job. I haven't begun anything new yet." It was close to the truth. He had quit trying to prove Drew was a thief and was about to start trying to prove she was innocent.

"What is your name?"

"Cole Benton," Cole replied.

"And we're about to dance," Drew said before her aunt could ask another question. "You can interrogate him later." She practically dragged him out on the floor.

"I told you I don't like to dance."

"Hunter Ashby is coming our way. Unless you want me to create a scene, you'll dance with me."

For a moment, Cole was tempted to see what would happen. The thought of what his mother and her friends would do caused him to chuckle, but he chose the safe way out. His mother would never forgive him if he was involved in a scandal.

"You dance very well," Cole said after a few moments.

"You sound surprised."

"Since you despise everything most women enjoy, I thought dancing would be included."

"I had ten brothers. Isabelle insisted they all learn to dance. I was the only sister, so they danced with me."

"You dance like you had a professional dance master."

"Isabelle was brought up in society. She had the dance master."

"I'm glad to know she put her knowledge to good use."

"The boys didn't think so. You should have heard the complaining. But that stopped when Jake told them there weren't many chances for a man to hold a pretty woman real close without some male relative putting a gun to his head and asking his intentions."

Not being one to miss an opening, Cole held Drew a little closer. "Your Jake sounds like a very practical fella. Intelligent, too."

"Jake is just about the smartest man in the world."

Drew didn't seem to mind his holding her close. He figured if he could keep her talking, she might even rest her head on his shoulder.

"Smarter than me?" Cole asked.

"Lots smarter," Drew responded without hesitation. "A bunch of low-down farmers just about cleaned him out while he was away at the war. He not only outsmarted them, he now owns more than a hundred thousand acres.

Jake says you can't afford to squat on land anymore. If you don't own it, somebody will steal it out from under you."

Cole found it difficult to concentrate on Jake or be interested in his economic policies. He'd managed to hold Drew so close her breasts rubbed against his chest. The contact was slight and fleeting, but the results were significant and lasting. He hadn't forgotten the feel of her body against his own that night down by the river. Nor had he forgotten the taste of her kisses. He wanted to crush her in his embrace and smother her with kisses. He wouldn't have cared if all the self-important guests had been outraged, but he knew Drew would be mortified. He had all evening. He would find some way to steal a few moments alone with her.

The music came to an end. Cole had some idea of dancing with Drew again—in fact, he wanted to monopolize her entire evening—but his mother had other plans. She sent Sibyl to intercept him almost before he left the dance floor.

"Cole, darling, your mother needs you this instant. I'm not certain she's entirely well."

His mother was never well when people weren't doing what they wanted them to do. It was a ploy she used often. Unfortunately, it still worked.

"I'd like you to meet Miss Drew Townsend," Cole said to Sibyl.

"How do you do, Miss Townsend. I don't mean to seem rude, but Cole needs to return to his mother immediately."

"Of course," Drew responded. "I wouldn't think of keeping him. I'm tired of dancing anyway."

"But you've only danced one dance," Sibyl pointed out.

"One too many as far as I'm concerned," Drew replied. "You'd better hurry to your mama, Cole. I'd have been long gone if Isabelle had taken a bad turn."

Cole knew it was pointless to attempt to explain that his mother's bad turn was merely bad manners. "Save me another dance," he said.

"She just said she doesn't like to dance," Sibyl reminded him. "It's rude to force a girl when she doesn't want to."

"I doubt the men here will allow her to languish in a corner. I just want to make sure I get my share of dances."

"If you see Hunter Ashby heading my way, get over here as fast as you can," Drew said, looking about her like a pursued animal. "I considered hiding a gun in this dress, but the danged thing doesn't have a pocket. I could have put one in my leather purse, but my aunt said it was *unsuitable*. You can't even hide a pocket gun in this thing." She held up her evening purse. Her expression clearly said she considered the elegant cream silk reticule worse than useless.

"What an odd thing to say," Sibyl said.

"Miss Townsend grew up in Texas," Cole explained. "She's used to defending herself against rustlers and other marauders."

"How terrible. I'm sure you're relieved to be in Memphis."

"I can't wait to get back to Texas," Drew said.

Sibyl's smile was as broad and brilliant as it was insincere. "I hope you'll be able to return soon. Now, Cole, you really must go to your mother."

"Tell her I hope she feels better," Drew said.

"What a quaint girl," Sibyl said as she watched Drew

walk back toward her aunt. "I can't imagine who she expects will marry her."

"Apparently Hunter Ashby has designs in that direction."

"His mother would never let him marry a female of that type."

Cole came to an abrupt stop. His hand shot out, grasped Sibyl by the arm, and spun her around. "And exactly what type of female is she?"

Sibyl reacted with surprise and outrage, but she quickly got her anger under control. Cole figured her family's financial situation must be truly desperate. Sibyl was known for her imperious temper.

"I would have thought that was obvious," she said. "She might fit into Texas society—I'm glad to say I know nothing of it—but she obviously could never belong here."

"She doesn't want to belong here."

"How fortunate for everyone concerned."

Cole told himself not to waste time bandying words with Sibyl. He didn't care what she thought. "Where's Mother?"

"In the sitting room. She felt weak and had to lie down."

She always felt weak when something happened that she didn't like. Cole felt a sudden revulsion for a society where people didn't say what they meant, where they hid behind subterfuges and small lies to keep from being honest. If Drew didn't like something, she said so. If she was confused or unsure, she demanded an explanation. You always knew where you stood with her because she made no attempt to hide her feelings. The society he'd grown up in had developed an intricately woven pattern

269

of behavior and carefully worded phrases designed to hide a person's true feelings. It took a lifetime to fully master it. Cole had forgotten how much he hated it.

"Have you called for a doctor?" Cole asked.

"Your mother was afraid calling a doctor might destroy everyone's pleasure."

He hadn't expected his mother to change her lifelong habits, but he couldn't stop hoping. He found her just as he expected, lounging on a sofa and looking radiantly healthy.

"Cole, I hated to tear you away from the party. I'm sure you were enjoying yourself immensely, but Sibyl insisted upon fetching you."

"What's wrong this time?" He hadn't intended for his words to sound so harsh, so abrupt, but if he'd followed his inclinations, he wouldn't have come at all.

"I'm just feeling faint. I'm certain if I remain quiet for a while, I'll feel much better soon."

"If that's all, you don't need me here."

His mother looked shocked, then hurt.

"You can't leave your mother alone," Sibyl said.

"Why not? It's not like I'm leaving her on the street. Besides, you're with her."

"But she's your mother."

"You don't have to stay long," his mother said. "Just sit for a few minutes."

Cole didn't want to sit down. He knew once he did, the few minutes would stretch into half an hour. It would stretch even longer if he didn't do what his mother wanted.

"I don't see why you're in such a hurry to get back to the party," his mother said. "You always swear you don't like to dance."

"For a man who doesn't like to dance, you were quick enough to dance with that woman," Sibyl said. Her expression wasn't pretty. But then jealousy was never attractive, not even on the face of a beautiful woman.

"I hope you will at least dance with Sibyl," his mother said. "She's been so kind and thoughtful to me."

Cole knew he was being cornered, and his temper flared. "Do you want me to stay with you, or do you want me to dance with Sibyl?"

"Don't make him dance with me if he doesn't want to," Sibyl said.

"I don't see why he shouldn't dance with you," his mother answered. "He's already danced with that woman's niece."

Now Cole understood. "Miss Townsend is a stranger in town. You always said we should take care of guests first, family later."

His mother knew she'd been boxed in and didn't appreciate it. "I know nothing of that young woman or her aunt," she said. "I don't know if they deserve such consideration. Besides, I wouldn't expect you to dance with her when you won't dance with a young woman I love as though she were my own daughter."

His mother was resorting to broad hints early in the evening. He wondered what she would say if she could hear Drew's opinions of men and marriage. "It's always best to do the right thing first," said Cole. "You can't regret it later."

"Well, you've done your duty. You can now devote the rest of your evening to Sibyl."

"I'm certain Sibyl would prefer to dance rather than remain here with you and me."

"I wouldn't think of leaving your mother while she's feeling unwell," Sibyl said. "I couldn't look myself in the mirror if I did."

Cole sat down. "I'll give you fifteen minutes. If you're not better by then, I'll take you home."

"I would hate to keep you from the dance."

"You wouldn't. I'd come back as soon as the doctor arrived."

His mother looked horrified. And furious. "I can't believe that woman has enslaved you in less than fifteen minutes."

"No woman has ever managed to enslave me in fifteen minutes. Or fifteen hours."

It had taken Drew nearly fifteen days.

"Why won't you dance with any of these young men?" Dorothea Rutland asked her niece.

"Because I don't like any of them."

"How can you tell? If they even try to talk to you, you drive them off."

"They're silly, boring, and I wouldn't hire one of them to work on my ranch. I certainly wouldn't consider marrying one of them."

"I'm not asking you to marry them, just dance."

"I don't like to dance."

"You've danced with that Cole Benton three times already. Any more, and people will start to gossip about you."

"I don't care what they say. Besides, I'm just trying to make him feel comfortable. He's more of an outsider than I am."

"How do you know?"

"He's a drifter. I don't know how he got in here. Maybe his mother is a poor relation of some of your fancy friends." Drew giggled. "I wonder if they knew she'd bring Cole."

"I could ask."

"Don't. I'm not going to marry him either."

"I should hope not. If he's a drifter, he could disappear one day."

Drew laughed. "You don't know much about drifters, Aunt Dorothea. They can stick to a woman as long as she's willing to spend her money on him and turn a blind eye to his catting around."

"I know he's handsome, and he seems quite charming, but you don't want a husband like that."

Drew laughed again, but this time the laugh wasn't quite so easy. "I have no intention of falling in love with him. He just wandered into the show one night and wormed his way into my act."

Drew's aunt looked horrified. "He's one of your show people? I wonder if Doreen knows." From her aunt's reaction, you'd have thought Drew had accused Cole of being a swindler or a rapist.

This time Drew's laugh was genuine. "Have you noticed that a different young woman comes to fetch him every time he dances with me? I think somebody's afraid we'll discover who he is and tell everybody. Or maybe his creditors have followed him here. He spends money he doesn't have without a blink."

At that moment Cole came through one of the doors on the opposite side of the room.

"He's coming this way," her aunt said. "Do something, quick."

Dorothea sent out urgent and desperate signals to several men nearby to join them, but none seemed willing to risk another embarrassing dismissal, not even for the chance to dance with the niece of an obviously very wealthy woman. Cole reached them without competition.

The whole evening had been rather confusing for Drew. She hadn't wanted to come. She had intended to refuse every invitation to dance, but she hadn't offered a single protest when Cole drew her to the dance floor. He wasn't the tallest, most handsome, or most personable man in the room, but there wasn't anyone whose company she preferred. And when he came through that doorway and headed in her direction without a moment's hesitation, she had felt a surge of excitement, a flush of pleasure that was as unfamiliar as it was unwelcome.

She could hide behind any excuse she wanted, but the bald truth was she was glad to see him again, even more pleased that he sought out her company rather than that of some beautiful, rich, and more socially acceptable young woman. She hadn't expected to enjoy this evening. And with the exception of her dances with Cole, she hadn't. It was the exceptions that concerned her.

"You can't dance with my niece again," Dorothea said the moment Cole reached them. "You'll start people talking."

"I'm going to start them doing more than talking," Cole said, taking Drew's hand. "I'm going to start them speculating furiously."

"What are you talking about?" Drew asked.

"Dance with me, and I'll tell you."

Cole wasn't acting the least bit like himself. On many occasions he'd been irreverent, irrational, or spontaneous, but he'd never looked harassed, harried, or reckless. Now he looked all three.

"Young man, you can't—"

But Cole whisked Drew away to the strains of an energetic polka.

"I can't follow your steps," Drew complained.

"It doesn't matter. We're going outside as soon as we reach one of those doors."

The party was being held in a double salon that extended the length of one side of the house. Two sets of double doors opened onto the main hall. Cole danced Drew through the set nearest the front of the house.

"Hot in there," remarked one of the men smoking a cigar in the spacious hall.

"Boiling," Cole said as he danced Drew right on through the front door and onto the porch that ran across the front of the house.

"It is cooler out here," Drew said.

"I'm not escaping the heat," Cole said. "I'm escaping my mother and her endless string of potential brides."

"Do you mean they'd agree to marry you even though you're a drifter?" She gave him a stern look. "You haven't told them, have you?"

Cole tugged at her hand until she followed him down the steps that curved on either side of the porch to the garden below. "I haven't told anybody anything, because I'm not marrying any of them."

"Where are you taking me? My aunt will have a fit if I disappear."

"We're not going out of the sound of the orchestra. I just want you to myself, where your aunt won't be sending young men to break in on us and my mother can't attack me with an armada of unmarried females."

Drew laughed. "Cole Benton, I never would have guessed it, but you're a coward."

"If you're trying to say I'm running away, you're right."

He led her around the side of the house to the garden directly beneath the windows of the double salon. "Now we can dance without danger of being interrupted."

"I thought you didn't like to dance."

"I was wrong. I love it."

He took her in his arms, and they began to move slowly through the moonlight and shadows of the garden.

"I thought I didn't like it either," Drew said.

"Confess, you like dancing with me."

Drew didn't want to confess to such a weakness. It seemed to her that she'd already confessed far too much when it came to Cole Benton. She didn't know why she shied away from this particular confession, but she didn't trust him.

"It's not nearly as dull as I thought," she said.

"That's not the answer I was looking for."

He suddenly picked her up and whirled her around.

"That step's not in this dance," she said.

"Give me an answer I like."

"Are you threatening me?"

"Yes."

"Why?"

"Because I feel desperate."

"Why?"

"Can't you guess?"

"How can I? I don't know your mother, or the women who're supposedly chasing after you. I would have thought a man with your charm would be able to twist any woman around your little finger."

Cole paused in the dance. "You think I have charm?"

"Yes. I've told you that."

"No, you haven't."

"I'm sure I did."

"You didn't."

"Well, I'm telling you now. You're charming, too much for your own good, I would guess."

He gave her a quick kiss, picked her up, and whirled her around. "What other attributes do I have that you've failed to mention?"

"Stop that."

"I will when you answer my question."

"You're a drifter, you—"

"You've mentioned all the uncomplimentary ones far too often. Isn't there something else you like about me?"

That was part of her trouble. She could think of far too many things she liked about him. "I like it that you're taller and stronger than I am."

"That's not much." He seemed offended. "Nearly every man is stronger and taller than a woman."

She was finding it difficult to think with him holding her so close, his face so close to hers, his lips . . .

"Do you think I'm nice-looking?"

"I suppose so."

"Is that the best you can do?"

"If you ever meet my brothers, especially Will, you'll understand."

"I never tried to impress a woman with ten brothers and a perfect father before. Isn't there anything I can do better than they can?"

"No."

He looked devastated.

"Yes, there is," she said, glad to have thought of something. "You can think of better shooting tricks for me to perform. And I never knew anybody with a better understanding of what would work with an audience."

That didn't appear to lift his spirits.

"I don't know you very well," she said. "I'm sure if I did, I'd be able to come up with a dozen different things."

He grinned, and she was relieved to see the old Cole back. It bothered her to say things that hurt him.

"Don't talk," Cole said. "Just dance with me."

"Don't you think we ought to go back inside?"

"No."

She began to feel uneasy. Cole wasn't acting like himself. He made her think of a discontented lover.

"Is something wrong?" she asked.

"Yes."

"Are you still worried about your mother sending those women after you?"

"No."

"Then what is it?"

"I'm trying to figure out how to tell a woman who doesn't like men, who doesn't intend to get married, and who has ten brothers and a father who can do everything better than anyone else in the world, that I love her."

Chapter Eighteen

Drew felt as if she'd been butted in the ribs by an angry cow. Cole couldn't be in love with her. Nobody had ever been in love with her. She wouldn't allow it. She didn't want it. She had set her goals long ago, and she didn't intend to let anything get in her way. Nor was she going to be deflected, even momentarily, by something as pointless as some man falling in love with her.

"You can't be," she said.

"Why not?"

He kept dancing, faster and faster, so much faster she was having difficulty thinking. She needed time, space, quiet, stillness, and she had none of them.

"I don't want you to be in love with me."

"Too bad. I already am. Are you in love with me?"

"No."

"I didn't think so."

"I told you I don't like men."

He turned her in circles until she was dizzy.

"Stop! I can't think with you whirling me around like a weather vane in a storm."

"That's what I feel like. And the wind is blowing harder and harder."

She pulled against his embrace. "Let me go."

"You aren't going to run back inside, are you?"

"No."

"Promise?"

"I'm not a coward or a foolish woman."

He let her go reluctantly. "No, you've never been foolish. Sometimes I wish you were."

"Why?"

"You wouldn't understand."

"Probably not. I don't understand half of what you say."

"I love you. It's that simple."

"But you're a drifter."

"Drifters can fall in love."

"But what happens when you want to drift somewhere else?"

"You could come with me."

"And if I didn't?"

"Maybe I wouldn't want to drift anymore."

"You don't even like me. I'm stubborn, opinionated, and I shoot better than you do."

"I know, but I love you anyway."

Drew could feel the panic closing in around her. Something truly peculiar was happening to her. She didn't understand it, but she knew she didn't like it.

"I thought you liked kissing me," Cole said.

"I do."

"Let's do it again."

"Now?"

"It seems like a good time."

It seemed like a terrible time. Absolutely the worst. She couldn't decide whether to stay or flee. Cole didn't give her a chance to decide. He took her in his arms and kissed her with barely restrained passion.

His kiss didn't feel the way it had the last time. She experienced none of the surprise of discovery, the delight in a newfound pleasure, the breaking down of a long-held taboo. Like a boulder that comes crashing down the mountain through your house, destroying everything in its path, this kiss shattered Drew's notions about men and love. Like an avalanche, it knocked her flat, leaving her prostrate and defenseless.

She pushed away from Cole.

"What's wrong?" he asked.

She didn't know what to tell him. She wasn't sure she knew herself. "Everything," she muttered.

"How can everything be wrong? You've got a rich aunt who wants to satisfy your every wish, you're the star of the show, and you've got a perfect family. You're a beautiful woman being kissed in the moonlight by a man who loves you."

"I don't want a rich aunt, I don't want to be the star of the show, and I don't want anybody to love me."

But even as she spoke the words, she was aware of an ache in her heart. She had prepared herself to do without love, even convinced herself she didn't want it, but it would be nice to have just a little bit. But then the realities of love and all that it would entail sprang to life in her imagination, banishing the newly budded wish for the chance to experience just a little of that sweet-tasting nectar.

"You just want your ranch and your perfect family."

"My family's not perfect."

"Maybe not, but in your mind you've turned them into paragons. You're safe from love because no man can measure up to the sum of so many."

"That's nonsense. Why should I do something as silly as create a man in my mind who doesn't exist?"

"To protect you in case you were tempted to fall in love."

"I've never fallen in love."

"But you've been tempted."

"No."

"You've been tempted so much you're scared you might give in. Are you afraid of being in love, of being loved?"

"I'm not afraid of anything."

"Then why are you so afraid you might love me?"

"I'm not afraid. I could never love a drifter."

Cole gripped her arms. "Drifters are just people looking for something to give their lives meaning. When they find it, they don't want to drift any longer."

Drew struggled to break his hold. "I don't want to give anybody's life meaning. I just want to be left alone."

Cole's grip tightened. He pulled her closer. "You can't turn your back on love."

"Yes, I can."

"I don't believe you. I think you want to love and be loved. You've just told yourself you don't for so long, it's hard to change your mind."

Drew fought against his hold. "You may have succeeded in telling me how to run my act, but don't you dare try to tell me how to think."

"I don't want you to think," Cole said, slipping his arms around her. "I want you to feel."

"I'm feeling, all right. I feel—"

He silenced her with a kiss that infuriated her at the same time it melted her bones. His body felt hard and tense against her. She could feel the heat of his passion, his anger, his . . . she didn't want to know what he was feeling. She couldn't handle her own feelings.

She wanted to push him away, deny that his kiss meant anything. Yet she felt her body sag against his, her arms go around his neck, her lips respond to the pressure of his mouth. Her whole being seemed to spring to life in a way that vitalized every part of her. She felt more than pleasure and curiosity in his kiss. She felt need, and that caused her to panic.

With a tremendous effort of willpower, she forced herself to break their kiss, to pull away from him. "Let me go."

His hold on her didn't loosen. Her panic threatened to become hysteria. "If you love me as you say you do, you'll let me go this instant."

She thought for a moment he wasn't going to respond. Then his arms fell to his sides and he stepped back.

"What are you going to do?" he asked.

"Go inside."

"We've got to talk."

"We have nothing to say," Drew said, backing away. "I don't know if you love me—or why you should love me if you do—but I don't love you. I'm going back to my aunt. You're not to come near me for the rest of the evening."

"Drew—"

She half turned. "I won't dance with you. I won't even speak to you. I don't want to be in love!"

She turned and ran back to the house. By the time she reached the steps to the porch, her heart was beating so fast she felt as if she couldn't get a breath. She forced herself to stop for a moment. She took several deep breaths, then climbed the steps to the porch. Before going inside, she looked back. Cole hadn't followed her. She told herself she was relieved.

Then why did she feel ready to cry?

Cole stood stock still, staring after Drew's retreating figure, wondering how he could have been so stupid as to have gotten himself into this fix. He hadn't known he loved Drew until the unguarded words came tumbling out of his mouth. He knew what she thought of men in general and men like him in particular. It would take a great deal of work just to prepare her mind for the idea of falling in love.

Yet he'd dragged her away from the party and out into the garden— a move guaranteed to make her an object of curiosity and possibly censure—and thrown the declaration at her from out of the blue. Then, when she reacted with shock and surprise, he wasn't smart enough to back away and give her a chance to get used to the idea. No, he'd practically forced it down her throat, kept on pushing her into a corner until she broke and ran.

Any fool could have predicted what would happen. Why couldn't he have seen it?

Because he was an idiot. The conflict between his duty and his emotions had robbed him of common sense. Now he was acting like a fool, desperate to convince Drew he really did love her, equally desperate to prove she wasn't a robber. Trouble was, he'd made a total mess of the first, and hadn't even started on the second. Some crackerjack undercover agent he'd turned out to be. If his boss could see him now, he'd surely yank him off the case.

He looked up at the light coming through the windows of the double salon. It seemed cheerful and inviting. It beckoned him to return to its friendly warmth. Only it wasn't friendly. As a younger man, he hadn't been able to reconcile his own goals with the empty social world his family valued so highly. He realized now he never would. He wouldn't ignore his family, but as the years went by, it would become less and less a part of his life, until he would find it difficult to remember he had once lived in that world, content with his life and the people around him.

Then there was Drew. She represented the kind of life he wanted. She was strong, direct, honest, a woman who knew her own worth and didn't need anyone or anything else to give her value in her own eyes. She stood on her own two feet, willing and anxious to earn whatever she wanted.

And he had driven her away.

He couldn't believe he'd done anything so stupid. He'd always been considered the smartest of the agents, the one who could control a situation and solve problems by using his brain rather than a gun or his fists. Now, when he needed his brain more than ever, his feelings had taken over, making him act as foolishly as the most inept agent.

Okay, so he'd been stupid, acted foolishly, made a terrible mess. At least he'd accomplished one thing—no, two. He no longer doubted he loved Drew. That in itself was a tremendous relief. Secondly, he was absolutely positive she wasn't guilty of the robberies, and he was going to prove it.

But before he could do either, he had to get himself under control. He'd spooked Drew. She'd be as nervous around him as a newborn colt. He would have to reassure her he wasn't going to pressure her to love him. Neither was he going to force his love on her. It wouldn't be easy. He wasn't a man to deny himself what he wanted once he knew what it was, but he knew Drew was more important to him than anything else. If he didn't manage to control his feelings, he might lose her forever.

If he didn't solve these robberies, he might lose her anyway. His preoccupation with his feelings for her had kept him from exploring other possibilities. If Drew and her brothers weren't the robbers, then who was? It had to be someone connected with the Wild West Show, someone using Drew's presence as a cover. It was about time he started living up to his reputation as a clever agent rather than proving that, when in love, he could be as much of a fool as any other man.

"I can't imagine why you'd do anything as foolish as leave the party with that man," Drew's aunt was saying to her as the carriage carried them back to her aunt's hotel. "You could be ruined socially."

"I don't care about that," Drew said, trying hard not to shout at her aunt. "I'll never see any of those people again. It wouldn't matter if I did. I don't care what they think."

She couldn't think about strangers when her whole life felt as though it were falling to pieces around her. She didn't understand it, she didn't like it, and she was trying her best to keep it from happening.

"Drucilla, honey, I know you don't like society. I don't understand it, but you've told me so many times that I've got to believe you at least *think* you know what you're talking about. But you may not always want to live on a ranch. If you make yourself notorious, society's door could be closed to you forever."

"How could going into the garden with Cole make me notorious?"

Why had she let him talk her into leaving the salon? She knew it would upset her aunt. She also knew the nosy witches at that party would make trouble. They didn't like outsiders, even rich ones.

"A single woman should never disappear with a single man. Even if everyone knows nothing happened, you'll get a reputation for being fast."

She already had a reputation for being fast—with a gun. She was as slow as molasses in winter when it came to men. What had happened that was so terrible she felt as if she wanted to die? Cole had kissed her. True, it wasn't as much fun as before, but that was probably because she was upset. It still sent delicious chills all through her, made her want to kiss him even harder, longer.

Then there was the fact that he loved her. She didn't love him, and she had told him so. He didn't like it, but he was a gentleman. Nothing bad had happened. It was over, done with, forgotten.

Only she couldn't forget a single word Cole had spoken.

"You don't have to worry about my reputation, Aunt Dorothea. I'll disappear into Texas in a year or so, and everybody will forget about me."

"Society is a small circle. There aren't many rich people in the South since the war. You're an heiress. Everybody will remember you."

"I don't want your money," Drew said. "Give it to somebody else."

"I don't have any other relations except my husband's Yankee cousins. And they have too much money already."

"Then give it to charity. I'm going to earn everything I get."

Much to her surprise, the thought of owning her own ranch didn't send her pulse racing as it usually did. The prospect of seeing her own brand on her own cows, of deciding when to start the roundup, of ramrodding her crew, of building her own house—none of these gave her the feeling of satisfaction or accomplishment she'd always had before.

"I don't know what you'll do with my money," her aunt said, "but you'll inherit it when I die."

"Then I hope you live to be a hundred."

"If I have to keep chasing you all over the country just to get to see you for a few days or hours, I probably won't live to see my next birthday."

"You shouldn't see me at all. It always makes you unhappy."

"I couldn't stop seeing you even if I wanted to. I'd feel I had deserted your mother. I don't know what I could have done, but I've always felt partly responsible for her death. Maybe if I'd encouraged her to confide in me before she met your father, she'd have told me what was bothering her. I don't know that I could have helped her, but I could have tried."

"Please, Aunt Dorothea, don't feel guilty about my mother. You couldn't have done anything to change things. Neither of my parents ever listened to advice."

"When I think of how close you came to dying, it makes me want to shoot your father all over again."

"Mama wanted to go west even more than Papa. They rebelled against all rules of society. I can't remember seeing them happy except when they were spending money they didn't have." Maybe her parents' disregard for money was the reason she was so determined to pay her own way, to avoid any kind of debt, financial or emotional.

She wondered if they had felt as miserable as she did now, if she had inherited her mother's temperament and would be miserable for the rest of her life. No, she'd been happy with Jake and Isabelle. Her brothers irritated her from time to time, but that was to be expected in any family. And though she didn't exactly like show business, she had enjoyed her time with the Wild West Show. It helped establish her independence, her ability to support herself. No man would ever expect her to stay home and look after his babies. She was going to do everything a man could do, and she was going to do it just as well.

That assertion didn't give her much satisfaction either. Being one of the most successful ranchers in Texas suddenly seemed lonely and uninviting, and she knew who was to blame.

Cole Benton.

If he hadn't opened his mouth about being in love with her, she wouldn't be sunk in the corner of her seat, ignoring her aunt's lecture on propriety and the role of women in society, watching her dream of a ranch of her own grow tarnished and uninviting, thinking about a grinning mouth, twinkling eyes, and strong arms. If he had just kept his mouth shut, she would have spent her last night with her aunt in relative peace and returned to the Wild West Show with a smile on her lips and a skip in her step.

Now she was miserable enough to give a grinning fool the blue megrims.

"I wish you weren't leaving tomorrow. I'm going to miss you."

"You could come to the show to see me off."

"You know I can't bear the thought of you being in that show."

She wondered if Cole would be there. She'd gotten so used to him, she didn't know if she could do her act without him. It certainly wouldn't be nearly as exciting for the audience. Or for her.

She might as well admit that that was the problem with the ranch. It didn't seem nearly so exciting without thinking of Cole being there with her. Only now did she realize that she'd gradually come to think of him as part of her life.

She wondered if he would go to her ranch with her. She wondered if she would have the courage to ask him.

"Where does your season start next year?" her aunt asked.

"I don't know yet."

No, she wouldn't ask him. She *couldn't*. It wouldn't work.

Why not? Jake and Isabelle had made it work. So had Ward and Marina, Buck and Hannah, even Rose and George Randolph. If they could all manage to love each other, why couldn't she and Cole?

Did she love Cole already?

No, but she liked him too much to consider never seeing him again. She liked being with him. Until tonight, she'd never fallen into a bad mood when she was with him. She had already admitted she liked his kisses, his strong arms holding her. She didn't believe she was beautiful, but she liked to think he thought she was. She liked the pride he took in her achievement.

"Why don't you spend the winter with me?"

"I have to go home. Jake and Isabelle are expecting me."

Maybe she could fall in love if she gave herself a chance. There were a lot of men she liked and admired. She'd always assumed she didn't want to have anything to do with a man, but now that she thought about it, she'd been surrounded by men for years, dozens of them. She was used to it.

She *liked* it. It was women she had no use for.

Did she want to have a man in her life, in her house . . . in her bed? The answer came fast and clear. Yes, and she wanted that man to be Cole.

"I'm sure they would understand. After all, I am your only living relative."

"Isabelle wouldn't. She still gets depressed when everyone can't be home for Christmas."

The swiftness of the answer, the certainty that the man couldn't be anyone but Cole, nearly knocked the little remaining sense out of her. How could she have come to like Cole so much without realizing it? She wasn't an idiot. She hadn't been sleepwalking. It should be impossible for a reasonably intelligent woman to miss something like that.

Yet she'd missed it, because she'd been telling herself for years she didn't want love, didn't want marriage, wouldn't even consider the idea. She'd become so accustomed to feeling no attraction to men, to being certain it couldn't happen to her, she hadn't recognized it when it did.

Now she was on the verge of falling in love with a drifter.

"Do you think you could talk Jake and Isabelle into spending the winter in New York?" her aunt asked.

"No."

"New Orleans?"

"It's too far from home."

"I wish you'd stop calling that ranch home."

"But it is my home. The only real home I've ever known."

"It wouldn't have been if you'd come to live with me."

"It was too late."

"You were only eleven. You could have learned."

Drew reached across and took her aunt's hands. "You've got to accept that I'm different from you. I *like* the ranch. I like cows and dust and sweat. I don't like dressing up and going to parties. For your sake, I wish I did. But I don't. I never will."

Her aunt sighed deeply, and gave Drew's hands a squeeze. "It's not that so much. It's just that I miss seeing you. I love you, Drucilla. I want to see you married and settled with children."

The image caused Drew's throat to close convulsively.

"I can't learn to like ranches," her aunt said, "but maybe I can meet you halfway. Do you think you could visit me more often if I lived in San Antonio?"

"You wouldn't like it."

"I can like anything if I make up my mind to it."

Something closely resembling a shaft of pain shot through Drew from bosom to belly. Cole might say he loved her—he might truly love her—but he was a drifter. He'd promised to stay through New Orleans, but he'd made no promises after that. Just that he loved her.

Drew knew love would never be enough. Her parents

had loved each other. Their forgiveness of each other was just as tender and sweet as their fights were ugly and violent. Drew couldn't endure the fights, or Cole's coming back from time to time. That would be worse than his disappearing forever. It would keep hope alive, and that would tear her apart.

Why had she done anything so foolish as to let herself become involved with a drifter?

She remembered she had decided Cole had joined the show for a purpose, that he might not be a drifter, but that didn't help. Once his job was over, he would disappear. She was probably entertainment while he did whatever he was doing. She might not be pretty, but she was available.

Drew cursed herself for a fool, because she wanted everything she knew about Cole to be different. She wanted to tell herself she barely knew him, that he could be the most dependable, reliable, responsible man in the country. She wanted to forget he had wandered into her life without the baggage of a past or a future, without family or obligations. She wanted to ignore the fact that if he could walk away from all that, he could leave her behind even more easily.

"When are you leaving?" her aunt asked.

"Tomorrow, immediately after the show."

The show. She'd nearly forgotten the show. She would have to perform with Cole, and pretend nothing had happened, that her life was just as orderly and serene as ever. She wasn't sure she could do that. She was certain if he said one sweet, tender word to her, she would burst into tears.

Chapter Nineteen

Drew was so jittery she couldn't stand still. She prayed Carl would make his introduction longer than usual. It sounded shorter. Maybe the horse would go lame and she could walk in rather than ride. The horse was in perfect condition.

"Why are you nervous?" Zeke said as he helped her onto the horse's back.

"I'm not nervous."

"If you don't calm down, you'll miss shots."

Just what she needed, a real boost of confidence. The music came up, Earl announced her name, Zeke slapped the horse on his hindquarters, and Drew was in the ring and in the spotlight.

She refused to look at Cole. She hadn't been sure he would show up, but he'd set up the tricks as usual. She concentrated on the targets as she rode by. She breathed a sigh of relief when she hit all three dead center. The second pass went just as well. She started to relax.

Too soon. She missed one of the candles. Damn! She'd never missed. She took a slight hop in the air, turned completely around, and quickly fired a second shot. She got it. She stumbled when she turned around to get ready to jump into Cole's arms. She caught Cole's look of surprise out of the corner of her eye.

Hell, she would jump even if she was off balance. She wouldn't give in to nerves, embarrassment, or whatever feelings were turning her into an addlebrained fool.

The jump was a mistake. The feel of Cole's arms around her, her body pressed close to his, the look of entreaty in his eyes, hit her like the sudden onslaught of a fever. Her limbs began to tremble.

"Put me down," she hissed when Cole continued to hold her, carrying her around the ring like a trophy.

"Why didn't you come to practice today?"

"We don't have anything to say to each other. If you don't put me down this instant, you'll ruin the act."

Cole tossed her in the air. She spun around like a top.

"She's light as a feather, folks," he called to the audience, "fragile as a lamb, but she can shoot the eyebrows off a mosquito at fifty yards."

"I'll shoot *your* eyebrows off if you throw me up in the air again," she hissed. "I'll be so dizzy I won't be able to hit a thing."

Cole tossed her again, caught her above his head, and held her there.

"She's so good, she can shoot the target from where she is right now."

She was going to kill him. There was absolutely no doubt about it.

"Show the good people what you can do, Miss Townsend. Give us a clay pigeon!" he called.

Almost immediately a clay pigeon was launched into the air. By some miracle, Drew's bullet smashed it to smithereens.

"Two this time," he called out, and two clay pigeons sailed into the air. Drew managed to hit them both.

"Let's make it a little more difficult. I'll spin her around a few times and see what she can do."

He spun her until the entire arena swam before her eyes. "Two more pigeons," he called out.

She missed both of them.

"Guess I got her a little too dizzy, folks. I'd better set her down and let her head clear."

She had to grab hold of his arm to keep from falling. "I'm going to kill you for this," she said from between clenched teeth.

"I wanted you to know what it felt like last night."

"Your feelings are not my fault. I told you I didn't want anybody falling in love with me."

"Let's see what she can do with the balls I juggle in the air," Cole called out to the audience. "I just want a chance to talk to you," he said more softly.

"There's nothing to say," Drew said, taking aim. Cole started to juggle six balls. Drew shattered each as he threw them into the air.

"It's a good thing she didn't miss," Cole said to the audience. "I can't juggle worth a damn." The crowd laughed. "There might be, if you'd open up that closed mind of yours and give yourself a chance to feel something," he whispered.

"For my next trick," Drew announced, "I'm going to shoot over my shoulder using a mirror to see my target. I like you," she said to Cole when he handed her the mirror, "but I don't love you." She positioned the mirror and rifle, then shouted, "Pull!"

A clay pigeon sailed into the air. She hit it the first time.

"I think you do," Cole said. "You're just too stubborn and set in your ways to admit it."

She had spent most of the night lying awake, trying to forget everything that had happened in the garden, trying to convince herself it didn't change anything. But no matter how many times she went over the arguments against falling in love, she couldn't rid herself of the fear that she really did want to fall in love with Cole.

She had spent most of the morning trying to convince herself by ruthless logic it couldn't possibly be true. Having Cole guess what had been going on in her head and heart shook her badly

"Pull!" she shouted.

The untouched clay pigeon sailed out of sight. Damn, she had missed! If she didn't get herself under control, she would disgrace herself and ruin her career as a sharpshooter.

"It's true, isn't it?" Cole asked.

She ignored him, blocked out the sound of his voice, the image of his face. She thought only of the clay pigeon that would soon be released, of the necessity to shatter it into a million pieces.

"Pull!"

The clay pigeon sailed into the air and shattered at the peak of its arc.

She shouted "Pull!" three times in quick succession, and three clay pigeons disintegrated to loud applause.

"You didn't answer me," Cole said.

Drew refused to admit she'd heard the sound of his voice. She turned her back to the skeet shoot. "Pull three!" she called. At the sound of the three clay pigeons beings released, she whirled and shot three times. She hit all three.

"Are you going to keep refusing to answer me?" Cole asked.

She turned her back again. "Pull three!" She shattered three more clay pigeons, but she could feel her control slipping. Clay's words kept coming at her through the noise of the crowd. She refused to look at him, but each clay pigeon seemed to be a picture of Cole's face.

She dropped down on a bench, let her head hang over the end, and took aim upside down and backwards. This was her hardest trick. She couldn't allow herself to think of Cole or anything else.

"I still love you," Cole said. "One of these days you're going to have to stop running. You'll have to face yourself and ask why you were so afraid to let yourself be loved."

She wouldn't listen. She didn't dare. Inside her, everything was confusion. Only one thing was certain, her skill with a rifle. She had to hold on to that.

"It is fear," Cole said. "You know love can work. You see it all around you. Why are you so afraid to give yourself the chance for happiness?"

She couldn't hold on any longer. If she tried to complete her act, she'd embarrass herself. She closed her eyes and was shocked to feel them flood with moisture. She couldn't see with tears in her eyes, but she couldn't stop now. The audience was still, quiet, waiting expectantly.

She opened her eyes and the world swam eerily through the tears. She wiped them away, then closed her eyes again. Her vision was clear when she opened them, but she could feel the tears start to build up. It was now or never.

One more trick. Please, God, just one more trick.

"Pull!"

She didn't aim. She was useless, because she couldn't see. She pulled the trigger. She knew by the burst of applause, the cheering from thousands of female throats, that she'd made the shot.

"Thank you, God," she murmured as she got to her feet. She forced a smile to her face as she waved at the cheering audience. Then, without waiting for the usual challenge to the audience, she turned and ran from the arena.

"You can't run from me," Cole called after her. "No matter where you go, I'll follow until I find you."

She couldn't see at all now. Her eyes were blinded by tears. She ran into Myrtle's arms.

"What's wrong, child? Why didn't you finish your act?"

"It's finished," Drew said between sobs. "Everything is finished."

Cole was putting the props away when he heard a familiar voice.

"I couldn't believe it when I saw you enter that ring. My only son appearing in a vulgar sideshow."

Cole's stomach sank. On top of Drew not speaking to

him, he now had to contend with his mother. "Why did you come?" he asked, turning to face her. "You knew you'd be upset if you found me here." Sibyl accompanied his mother, providing the prop for her to lean on.

"I came because of that woman," his mother said.

"What woman?" Cole asked, certain he knew.

"The one you disappeared with into the garden last night. How could you do such a thing when you knew it would start such gossip? Then you ran off and left me to face it alone."

"You don't seem to be alone, Mother."

"Sibyl has been a true angel. She has stayed by my side the whole day."

"Why didn't you keep her from coming here?" Cole asked Sibyl.

"We couldn't very well continue denying what people were saying without seeing for ourselves," Sibyl said.

"Denying what?"

"It was Doreen who told me. She heard it from Sally Land, who heard it from—"

"Heard what, Mother?"

"That you worked in a sideshow and were infatuated with that woman, that you're with her all the time."

"We're in an act together. We have to be together a lot."

"Come home, Cole. You don't have to work in a place like this, or with people like her."

"What do you mean by *people like her*?"

"She's a show person, Cole, not one of your class."

"Her aunt has better social connections than you do."

"What kind of name is Drew? It sounds like a man's name. She's doing a man's job." She shivered dramatically. "How can you like a woman who shoots guns for a living?"

"Get to the point, Mother."

"Come home, Cole. Your father won't insist you learn his business. I won't even insist that you go to parties and balls if you don't want to, but you don't belong in a place like this." She looked around as though she were afraid something filthy, contagious, or just plain savage would jump out at her.

"Your mother's nerves have been shattered," Sibyl said. "She hasn't been able to hold her hand steady since you went into the garden last night."

"Men go into the garden with attractive women all the time," Cole said. "What is there to get upset about?"

"But not that kind of woman," his mother said.

"You didn't know she was in the Wild West Show last night," Cole pointed out. "You only knew she was the niece of a very wealthy woman with connections to the Vanderbilts."

"I never trusted that woman," his mother insisted. "From the first, I could tell there was something cheap about her."

"It certainly wasn't her jewels," Cole snapped.

"Anyone with money can buy jewels," Sibyl said.

"While a woman with a spendthrift father and brother can't. Is that right, Sibyl?"

Sibyl colored.

"Give up the idea I'll ever marry you or anyone like you," Cole said. "Give up the idea I'm coming back to Memphis to dance on the end of your string," he said to his mother.

"It's that woman," his mother wailed, clasping a dramatic hand to her bosom. "She's bewitched you."

"You're wrong," Cole said. "She tried her best to scare me off, but I'm in love with her and I want to marry her."

Sibyl went white. His mother let out a series of anguished wails that rose in a crescendo until Cole was certain everyone within a hundred yards could hear her. Several buffalo started to bellow. He could hear nervous whinnies from the direction of the horse corral.

"Be quiet, mother. You're upsetting the animals."

"The animals!" his mother practically screamed. "You're ruining my life, and all you can worry about is the animals."

"You should be ashamed of yourself for treating your mother like this," Sibyl said. "I would never have thought it of you."

"If you hadn't brought her here, you wouldn't have had to find out."

"You don't love me," his mother cried. "You don't care what happens to me."

"What's going on? I heard a scream!"

Drew came into the tent, followed by Myrtle and several old people.

"You!" Cole's mother pulled herself erect and pointed at Drew with a dramatic gesture. "Release my son. Let him come back to his family."

Drew looked from mother to son to mother and back to son, surprise, confusion, and dawning anger in her expression. "Is this your mother?" she asked.

"Of course I'm his mother," Mrs. Benton intoned. "I've come to save him from this awful place and women like you."

"You're rich," Drew said, ignoring Mrs. Benton and looking straight at Cole.

"He's the only son of the richest man in Memphis," Sibyl said. "He was born into the highest social circle."

"Are you here to save him, too?" Drew asked Sibyl.

"She's here to cause trouble," Cole said, "and hoping to find a way to convince me to marry her."

"I beg you to give him up," Mrs. Benton said to Drew. "I'll pay you as much as you want."

Drew turned her back on Cole. "You don't have to pay me anything, Mrs. Benton. I don't want him. I never have."

"You don't want him!" Mrs. Benton said, suddenly quite able to stand without assistance. "What right has a little tramp like you to refuse my son?"

"Every right in the world," Drew said, turning to Cole. "I want nothing to do with liars. Come on, Myrtle, we've got to finish packing."

Drew walked from the tent without a backward look. Myrtle and the others followed, but the looks they directed at Cole told him he was no longer one of them.

"I hope you're pleased, Mother. She'll probably never speak to me again."

"*She* not speak to *you!* I should think it would be the other way around."

Cole was tired. The woman he loved had refused to admit she loved him. Now his mother had given her every reason to refuse to see or speak to him. Getting her to admit she loved him was going to be harder than ever.

"Go home, Mother, and take Sibyl with you. Find her a nice husband, one you can approve of, one who will do everything in his power to please you. He doesn't have to be rich. You can give him all the money you were planning to give me. I don't want it or the life you want me to lead."

303

"But you can't want this," his mother said, gesturing at the tent and the boxes and props, "or her."

"I don't give a damn about the Wild West Show," Cole said, "but I can't live without Drew. Now you might as well go home and forget me. I need to finish packing. Then I've got to figure out how to make Drew fall in love with me."

"Where are you going?"

"Wherever Drew goes."

Drew was nowhere to be found. She wasn't in her hotel room, and she hadn't returned to her aunt. Neither Zeke nor Hawk would tell him where she had gone.

"You stay away from her," Zeke said.

"You bother her again, I cut your throat," Hawk added.

Cole considered the warning unnecessary. Hawk had unsheathed his knife the moment he set eyes on Cole.

"I just want to talk to her," Cole said.

"She doesn't want to talk to you," Zeke said.

"She never want to talk to you again," Hawk added.

"We have to talk," Cole said. "We have an act together."

"No more," Hawk said. "Drew shoot alone."

"But we still have several shows before New Orleans," Cole said.

"She's going to ask Jake to bring Will when he comes to New Orleans. He can take your place."

"But he doesn't know the routine," Cole said.

"He learn," Hawk said. "Now go. Drew do not want to see you again."

Cole didn't intend to give up this easily. He'd ask

around. If nothing else, he'd follow Hawk and Zeke. Sooner or later they would lead him to Drew.

But several hours later he still hadn't found Drew. Hawk and Zeke were working with the crew to get everything loaded on the train, but Drew was nowhere in sight. It was obvious Hawk and Zeke knew Cole was watching them. They didn't mean to catch up with Drew until it was too late for him to follow.

"Have you seen Drew?" he asked Myrtle.

Myrtle was packing costumes. She didn't look up and she didn't favor him with her usual welcoming smile. "Not since your mother was here."

By now everybody in the show knew he was the son of a wealthy businessman, and they had started to back away from him. Cole hadn't realized until now how much he had enjoyed the easy camaraderie that involved no elaborate social rituals, that required no classification of people according to ancestry or wealth. He feared it would be hard, if not impossible, to recapture.

"I've got to talk to her, but I can't if I can't find her."

Myrtle got even busier. "She was very upset with you."

"I know, but I can explain why I didn't tell her about my background."

"I don't think she wants to hear it."

"I know that, too. First she thought I was a drifter. Now she *knows* I'm a liar. She probably thinks I'm a drifting liar with a string of women behind me."

Myrtle looked up. "She doesn't think that."

"You heard what she said."

"She was upset."

"I was upset, too."

305

"What about?" She seemed less rigid, but she exhibited none of her former friendliness. Cole took a costume from her hands and forced her to look at him.

"I love her. I want to marry her, but she's certain she hates men, that she never wants to marry, that she wants to live on that blasted ranch by herself for the rest of her life."

"She's invited me to live with her when I retire."

"She's invited half the world to live with her, but she hasn't invited me to come within a hundred miles of the place. Hawk has threatened to cut my throat if I come anywhere near her."

Myrtle shook her head. "He wouldn't do that. He's a nice boy." She studied him for a moment, and cupped his cheek with her hand. "You don't look happy."

"I'm not."

She dropped her hand. "Drew looked unhappy too, more unhappy than I've ever seen her."

"That's because she really does love me, but won't let herself believe it."

"Are you sure?"

"As sure as I live and breathe."

Myrtle began to make nervous movements with her hands. "She said she didn't want to talk to you."

"She's just afraid her marriage will be like her parents'."

Myrtle was quiet a moment longer. "She did look very unhappy."

"Where did she go?"

"I'm not supposed to tell you, but I guess it doesn't matter now. She's going by steamboat."

Cole was on his feet and running in an instant.

"It's too late," Myrtle called after him. "The boat will have left by now."

* * *

The steamboat pulled away from the docks late because one of the wagons bringing barrels of tobacco had broken down. Cole jumped on the gangplank just as they were hauling it on board. It took him only a short while to find Drew's cabin, but he decided to wait until she had had time to feel she wasn't being pursued, maybe even to regret she'd run away. Then she might be more willing to listen to him.

But forcing himself to wait until Drew came out of her cabin was just about the hardest thing Cole had ever done. He'd never wanted anything so much in his life, and he'd never felt so helpless to get it.

He waited over two hours before she left her cabin. She wore a coat. She was going up on deck. Cole followed her at a distance until she reached the upper deck. She looked fore and aft, undecided, then turned toward the front of the boat. Cole waited, watching from the darkened stairwell, while she moved slowly toward the rail, reached out, and grasped it. She faced forward, letting the wind whip through her hair. She pulled her coat more closely about her shoulders. It was cold at night on the river.

Suddenly he saw her shoulders shake and her head drop. Then he heard the sound. She was crying. He couldn't stand to wait a moment longer. He was out of the stairwell and across the deck in a matter of seconds.

"Please don't cry. I never wanted to make you unhappy."

With a startled gasp, Drew spun around. Cole was certain he saw welcome and relief in her eyes, but caution and fear were quick to crowd them out.

"What are you doing here?" she asked. "How did you find me?"

"Myrtle told me, but she thought the boat had left."

"So you followed me even though you knew I didn't want to see you."

"Is that why you were crying, because you were so happy you wouldn't have to see me again?"

Drew turned away. "You have no right to spy on me."

"I have every right. I love you, Drew."

"You lied to me. You—"

"I had a very good reason. If you'll just give me a chance, I can explain everything."

The moonlight wasn't very bright, but he thought he could see relief, even hope, in her eyes.

"There's no excuse for lying."

"You may not agree with it, but there's a reason."

"Okay, tell me."

She squared her shoulders as if to tell him she wasn't going to believe him regardless of what he said. He took a deep breath and dived in.

"I'm the only son of a rich man and a socially prominent mother," he said. "From the moment of my birth, I had everything anybody could want."

"Then why did you pretend you were a drifter?"

"My mother wanted me to marry someone of equal prominence, settle down in some big house on the river, and raise a family."

"What's wrong with that?"

"Like you, I didn't want to get married. I especially didn't want to be part of Memphis society. I was bored, felt hemmed in and angered by all the rules of social etiquette. I come from a long line of adventurers. I guess I'm a throwback."

"Your mother must have been very unhappy."

"My mother is always unhappy when she doesn't get her way. She was furious when I joined the Texas Rangers. I didn't tell her what I was doing now because I thought she'd be happier not knowing."

"Why aren't you with the Rangers now? Did the wanderlust bite you again?"

"I was asked to become an undercover agent for the government."

"Doing what?"

"I'm not at liberty to say. But I can tell you why I joined the Wild West Show."

"So you didn't just *walk down out of the stands* one night."

"No. I'm supposed to find out who's behind a series of robberies. I wormed my way into your act so I could watch things from the inside."

"I don't know about any robberies. Has someone been stealing money from the show?"

Her obvious surprise was all the proof he needed to know she had nothing to do with the robberies.

"Several banks and business have been robbed over the last two years, and the Wild West Show has always been in the vicinity when the robberies have taken place."

"Who do you suspect?"

"That's what I'm here to find out."

She believed him, he was certain of that, but he had expected her to smile, relief to flood her body, and a welcoming smile to curve her lips. Instead she looked as cold and rigid as ever.

"I hope you find him."

"Is that all you're going to say?"

"What else do you expect?"

"I told you this to prove I'm not a drifter or a liar."

"I'm sorry I accused you of being either one, but you have to admit that's what you acted like."

"I don't care about that. I just want to know my not being a drifter and a liar makes a difference with you."

"Instead you're a manipulator, a schemer, a conniver, weaving a web to catch a thief. I was part of your web."

Cole couldn't restrain himself any longer. He closed the distance between himself and Drew, took her by the arms, and pulled her to him. "The Wild West Show was my web. You were something totally different. You were unlike any woman I'd ever met. You didn't care about money or social position. You wanted your ranch, and nothing else mattered. You were determined to earn the money to pay for it yourself because you wanted to feel it was truly yours. I didn't understand you, but I was drawn to you from the first moment. I fought it as hard as I could, but it didn't do any good. I fell in love with you."

"I don't want anybody to be in love with me," Drew said, but Cole could tell she didn't believe that anymore.

"Maybe not, but you can't stop me from loving you. I'm giving you fair warning, I don't mean to give up. I've never wanted anything in my life as much as I want your love. I'll pursue you with dogged single-mindedness. I'll follow you wherever you go. I'll give you no rest. I'll beg, plead, entice—"

"If you follow me back to the Broken Circle, my brothers will shoot you."

"I'll look so pathetic, so worn down to skin and bones, Isabelle will take pity and protect me. She'll take me inside and nurse me back to health. All the while she'll be berating you for being so coldhearted as to drive a wonderful man like me to the brink of madness."

He was certain of it. There was a definite twinkle in her eye.

"I always knew you had a glib tongue, but I never realized the lengths to which you would go to get what you want."

"Neither did I. You've inspired me to new heights."

"I think it's called depths."

"I've been there, too. When you wouldn't speak to me. When I couldn't find you. When I was afraid I'd never see you again."

"Cole, I'm not going to tell you I don't like you, but I've never considered being in love. It's come as a complete surprise."

"It's supposed to be wonderful."

"For a woman who's always insisted upon being in control, it's frightening. You have to give me time to try to figure out the true nature of my feelings."

"I will. You can. As long as I can be with you, I don't care how long it takes. . . . That's a lie," he said, grinning in spite of himself. "I will begrudge you every minute, but I will wait. Just allow me to—"

The steamboat shuddered, then lurched violently to one side, pitching Drew and Cole headlong into the icy waters of the Mississippi.

Chapter Twenty

The icy water penetrated Cole's clothing instantly, threatening to paralyze his muscles. He fought the cold and the drag of waterlogged clothes. He had to find Drew.

He broke the surface and drew a life-giving breath into his burning lungs. For one terrifying minute he couldn't find Drew. He turned in circles, scanning the surface made luminous by the moonlight but broken up by the steamboat's wake. Then he saw her several feet away, struggling to keep her head above water. With a lunge and a shout, he swam toward her. "Keep kicking," he called. "I'm coming." He was afraid if he didn't reach her quickly, the weight of her water-laden skirts and coat would pull her under.

As he cut through the water with swift, knifelike strokes, he was thankful that swimming in a lake had been a regular part of his summer activities while growing up. The steamboat continued on down the river, its huge bulk turned almost at a right angle to the shoreline. It must have hit a submerged sandbar, one big and solid enough to knock the steamboat sideways in the river. The captain would gradually right the boat and probably dock at the next town to check for damage. Only then would anyone discover they had lost two passengers.

In the meantime, Cole and Drew were alone in the river.

Cole had managed to shed his coat and kick off his shoes. He needed to get rid of his clothes, but he had to reach Drew quickly. He didn't know how long she could stay afloat. Any air trapped in her skirt and coat would help keep her afloat only for a few seconds. Once they were wet through, they'd pull her down like lead weights.

"I can't keep myself up," Drew called when he drew near her.

Cole reached out, caught her hand. "You've got to get rid of those clothes," he said.

They struggled in the water, performing acrobatics neither had probably performed before, but the waterlogged material of her coat clung to her dress as though they had been sewn together.

"Now your skirts," Cole said, when Drew finally managed to free herself of the coat.

"I can't without letting go."

"Can you keep yourself afloat for a few minutes?"

"I think so."

"I'll dive behind you and undo the buttons."

Cole had never realized how much he depended on his eyes to do even the simplest task. It took three dives to find and undo all the buttons on Drew's skirt and petticoats. When he resurfaced, she looked exhausted.

"I can't swim to the shore," she told him. "It's too far away."

"I'm not leaving you."

"There's no reason for both of us to drown."

"We're not going to drown. I'm a strong swimmer."

"The shore looks at least a mile away. Have you ever swum that far before?"

"Lots of times." He hadn't, but he figured this was one lie worth telling. "Relax and let me get a grip under your chin. No matter what happens, stay relaxed and don't fight me."

Cole secured a hold on Drew and started toward the shore, which seemed to be farther away than the last time he looked. He told himself to relax. He had a long way to go. It was crucial that he not expend all of his energy now. Both their lives depended on it.

Cole let the river carry him along. He hoped the current would transport them to a place where the river narrowed, but they were caught in one of those enormous, shallow elbows the Mississippi makes so often when it spreads out for miles before narrowing down into a deeper channel.

It soon became clear that his strength would be exhausted before they could reach the shore. He hoped for a sandbar, but though most of the river was too shallow for steamboats, it was too deep for his feet to touch bottom. Looking around for any possible help, trying to stem the feeling of desperation rising inside him, Cole spied the dark shadow of something floating in the river.

The trunk of an uprooted tree. He had to reach it before the current carried it past. It was their only hope.

Cole sighted a line where he hoped their paths would intersect. Then, summoning his remaining strength, he swam toward the path of the tree trunk. He was able to take hold of an outstretched limb before the log swept past them.

"Grab hold and don't let go," he told Drew.

She didn't waste energy talking. She hooked her arm over the log and held on.

"We have to swim this log out of the main current," Cole said. "Then we can get it to shore. Otherwise, we'll just be swept down the river. Hold on and kick."

For a time Cole feared their efforts would prove futile. The current, steady and strong, swept them along. Cole's muscles burned with pain. His lungs felt ready to burst, but he couldn't let up. Safety for him and Drew lay on the distant shore. He refused to let himself think of failure. That was not an option. He couldn't have found the woman he loved only to lose her.

"We're not getting any closer," Drew said.

"We're coming to a curve in the river," Cole said. "The current will push us toward the edge of the channel. When I tell you, paddle and kick for all you're worth." He didn't tell her this was their last chance. Only their constant swimming had kept their bodies from succumbing to the cold. But they couldn't last forever. If they didn't get out of the water soon, the river would win.

Cole waited, judging the strength of the current, the arc of the curve, guessing at the energy they had left. They would get only one chance.

"Now."

Cole kicked as hard as he could, but he could feel the weight of his wet underclothes pulling against him, draining strength from his muscles, stealing power from each kick. It could only be worse for Drew. But he was proud of her. She hadn't panicked when her wet clothes pulled her under. She hadn't given up, though he could tell from her ragged breathing, her strength was almost gone. They were both soft from spending too much time on trains and in hotel rooms. If they got through this, he would never let his muscles get this weak again.

Cole couldn't judge the width of the current, but he felt his strength draining away. He couldn't last much longer. Drew's breaths were coming in sobs. Neither of them had to speak to know the end was near.

Cole struck out with renewed energy. He couldn't stop. He couldn't give up. He felt the current release its hold of them. They floated into one of the quiet eddies that reached to the dark band of trees edging the river.

"We've done it," Cole said. "All we have to do now is get this log to the shore."

They clung to the log, forcing their nearly exhausted bodies to propel it closer and closer to shore. It was several minutes before Drew answered. "It looks terribly far away."

"Keep kicking," Cole said. "It'll keep you warm."

It was a long time before Drew spoke again. They were much closer to the shore, close enough to know they would make it to safety. "Isabelle said it wasn't ladylike for females to swim. Jake said I had to be able to swim across a river in case my horse went under, but I never swam across anything this wide."

"Neither did I, but we'll make it."

He was more worried about the cold now. They had discarded nearly all their clothes. The few garments they had left would be wet and cold, worse than having nothing at all. He would have to find some way to get her warm, but he had no means of starting a fire even if he could find wood. The forest that lined the bank of the river looked unbroken. There would be no plantation house with dry clothes and warm beds waiting for them when they finally struggled ashore. Just empty, cold, dark woods.

Cole felt as if he'd been in the river for most of his life when his foot finally hit something solid. It was only a sandbar, but it was easier to move their log by wading through chest-deep water than by swimming. The river bottom dropped away again, reappeared, and dropped away once more before they finally reached the edge of the river. They climbed out and collapsed on the narrow strip of sandy shore. Once they recovered some of their strength, they would look for a way to climb the high bank.

"I was sure I was going to die," Drew said after a few minutes.

"I wouldn't have let that happen."

"I knew you didn't have the strength to swim all that distance pulling me behind you."

"I wouldn't have left you."

"I know."

"Then why can't you believe I love you?"

"I do."

"Why did you run away?"

"I was afraid."

"Of me?"

"Of myself. I was afraid to be in love, of losing control, of putting myself in a position to be hurt."

Her voice trembled. He could barely see her where she rested in the shadow of the trees that overhung the river, but he was certain she was shivering. He moved next to her, put his arm around her, and drew her close. Both were too exhausted to do more than lean against each other. Wet, soggy clothes made their embrace awkward and uncomfortable, but he was glad to be able to put his arm around her at all. He'd come perilously close to losing her.

He leaned over and kissed her. Her lips were cold and stiff, but she kissed him back.

"Love is about giving, getting, and sharing. It's not about losing."

"Then why do I feel so frightened?"

"Because love is something you can't control. You have to surrender to it, but you don't have to worry. I won't let anything happen to you."

But Cole knew she had always tried to control every aspect of her life. It was going to be hard to entrust it to someone else.

"Come on. We have to get warm."

"How?"

"We'll worry about that once we find a way up the riverbank."

They walked along the shore, climbing over debris, wading or swimming when the tiny beach disappeared altogether. They didn't come to a break in the bank until they reached a small stream that emptied into the river. They waded up the stream until they found a place to climb up to the forest floor. Taking Drew by the hand, Cole helped her up the shallow bank.

The trees hadn't yet lost their foliage. It was virtually impossible to see anything in the stygian darkness. The thick carpet of leaves muffled their footsteps. Cole was trying to decide whether to go north, south, or head inland when he realized they'd wandered onto a place where the leaves had been trodden down.

"We're on a path," he said to Drew, his hopes soaring at their luck. "If we follow it, we're bound to come to a house soon."

Instead of a house, they found a small cabin that appeared to be used only by hunters. That didn't encourage Cole to think anyone lived nearby.

"We'll spend the night here," he said.

"What if the owners come back?" Drew asked.

"They're not likely to arrive in the middle of the night."

It was even darker inside the cabin. It took Cole several minutes of stumbling around, systematically searching each shelf and drawer, before he found a box of matches. The flare from the match showed a nearly bare cabin furnished with a small stove and one bed. He was able to locate an oil lantern before the match flickered and went out.

The sound of Drew's chattering teeth reminded him of the need for a fire. He lighted the lantern and discovered the wood box was empty.

"Take off the rest of your clothes," he said, "and wrap yourself in the blankets on the bed."

"How will you keep warm?"

"I'll manage. We have to get you warm first."

319

"You take one of the blankets. If you hadn't rescued me, I'd have drowned."

"That's okay. I—"

"No. After everything I've done to drive you off and the mean things I said, you risked your life to save me. I refuse to take the bed or the blanket and leave you with nothing."

Cole knew he couldn't survive sharing the bed with Drew. "I'll search the cabin. I'm bound to turn up something."

He made a thorough search while Drew undressed, but the cabin contained no firewood, food, or clothing. Apparently the owner brought everything he needed whenever he came. Or maybe no one came here anymore. Plantations were frequently abandoned when the soil became worn out from overuse.

"You have to get out of your wet clothes, too," Drew said.

Cole turned. Drew stood in the middle of the room, the blanket pulled tightly around her, her whole body shaking so hard she could hardly get the words out.

"I'm more worried about keeping you warm," Cole said.

"I can't be any colder than you. Get out of those wet clothes. I'll turn my back."

Cole could see no need for modesty. His underclothes clung to his body, revealing every contour. There were no sheets on the bed, just a second, very thin blanket.

"I'll strip after I look for some wood," Cole said. But a search outside the cabin revealed no pile of cut logs and no ax to cut new ones. He couldn't even find a fallen limb he could use. The forest floor seemed swept bare.

320

"I couldn't find anything," he told Drew when he returned.

"Then we'll have to use body heat."

Cole paused, hardly daring to believe he'd heard her correctly.

"I know all about survival," Drew said. "Jake wouldn't let any of us go on a trail drive until he was sure we could take care of ourselves."

"Are you sure? There's only one bed."

"We can sleep with our backs to each other."

Cole didn't know anything about Drew's self-control, but he was certain his would fall apart long before dawn.

"Why don't I wrap you in both blankets?"

"And let you catch pneumonia?"

"I'm not cold."

"You're lying."

"All right, I'm cold, but I don't know that I can control myself in the same bed with you."

"Of course you can. We're adults. We're not ruled by our urges like children."

Cole decided he must have regressed to his late teens. Despite being miserably cold and almost totally exhausted, the idea of lying next to Drew, their bare flesh touching, was having a very enlivening effect on him. He didn't feel nearly as cold or tired as he'd thought.

"You get into bed first," Cole said. He put a bar across the door. He felt uncomfortable going to sleep in strange country without a weapon.

"I'm ready," Drew said.

She lay facing the wall, the blanket pulled tightly against her, her body shaking from the cold. Cole set the lamp on a table within reach, put the matches next to it, then turned down the wick until the light went out. He stripped off his underwear. The garments landed on the floor with a soggy plop. He found his way to the bed in the dark and sat down on the bed.

"I'll put both blankets over us," he said.

But once in bed, lying back-to-back with the two blankets spread over them, Cole knew their bodies had too little contact to overcome the cold, which had penetrated all the way through them.

"I'm going to turn over," he said. "I want you to back up against me. The only way to get you warm is for our bodies to touch as much as possible."

Drew didn't move.

"I promise I won't touch you."

"How can you keep me warm if you don't touch me?"

"I'm trying to say I won't take advantage of you."

"I never thought you would. My brothers said the most desirable female is a hot one. I'm as cold as an iceberg."

Drew backed up to him. She hadn't exaggerated. She felt so cold, he wondered if even his body heat could warm her. He pulled her close, tucked his legs under hers, and wrapped his arms around her.

"Curl into a ball," he said.

She pulled her knees up to her breasts. He rested his arm across her legs and tried to will his body not to respond to her presence.

"What else did your brothers tell you?"

"They never told me anything. I had to eavesdrop if I wanted to hear."

"And what did you learn?"

"That they don't think much of women who give themselves to men."

"Most men feel like that until they meet the woman they'll love for the rest of their lives. Then they consider the sharing of her body her greatest gift."

"You would consider your wife more precious than sons?"

"I would if she were the one woman I would love for the rest of my life."

"How will you know when you meet her?"

"I already have."

She didn't speak for a long time. "How did you know?" she asked in a soft voice.

"I didn't at first. I had to have lots of signs before I figured it out. I found I was thinking of you all the time, wanting to be with you. I was jealous of the time you spent with Myrtle, jealous of the confidences you shared with your brothers. I couldn't imagine spending the rest of my life without you."

"How can something like that happen? You don't really know anything about me."

"I don't know. It just did. Did it happen like that for Jake and Isabelle?"

"No. They fought for weeks. But it was like that for Ward and Marina. Her father had arranged for her to marry Ward's brother. As soon as they saw each other, they fell in love."

"We're more like Jake and Isabelle. We were so busy arguing we didn't realize we had fallen in love."

"We?"

"Yes. You love me, too."

"How can you be so sure?"

"If you didn't, you wouldn't have tried so hard to run away."

She pulled her body into a smaller ball, hugged her legs tightly against her. "Does love make you feel confused?"

"Sometimes."

"Can it make you want the opposite of everything you've always wanted?"

"Yes."

"Can it make you feel miserable and unhappy?"

"Yes, but it can also give you unimaginable happiness."

"When does that start?"

"When both people admit their love and share it."

"Does it make you afraid?"

"It can certainly make you feel vulnerable. But if you trust the man you love, there will be no fear. Only happiness."

"There's so much to think about."

"Then think only of one thing, that I love you with all my heart. No matter what else happens, that will never change."

"I love you. I don't want to, but I do."

Warmth flooded Cole. For the first time since being thrown into the river, he didn't feel cold. "Is that such a terrible thing?"

In a flurry of movement, Drew uncurled her body and turned to face him. "Yes! It's awful. Everything's all mixed up. I don't know what I want anymore. I want to run my own ranch, but I want you helping me. I want to go home to Texas, but I'll follow you wherever you go. I've never wanted to cook and clean and have babies, but I'd do all that for you. But if I did, I'd hate myself."

"I'd never make you do anything you didn't want to do."

Cole was having a hard time keeping his mind on what Drew was saying. Her movement had caused his forearm to fall against the side of one breast, the other to lie cupped in his palm. He had a vivid mental image of the vee of her thighs, scant inches from his swelling manhood. In a few more moments, his body would be completely beyond his control.

"I'm not talking about you," Drew said, hitting his bare chest with her balled-up fist. "I'm talking about me. I feel like there are two of me inside, engaged in a fight to the death. I want both of them to win."

Her agitation caused her breast to move in his hand. Instantly his body became rigid with desire. It seemed incredible to him that Drew could be completely unaware of the closeness of their naked bodies while it was impossible for him to think of anything else.

"That's okay," said Cole. It really wasn't. He wanted Drew to love him so deeply everything else would seem unimportant, but he wasn't about to tell her she was the most cussedly obstinate female he'd ever met. "I won't ask you to make any promises until you've had time to decide what you really want."

He intended to do everything in his power to make certain she wanted him.

"But I want you to make hundreds of promises," she said as she huddled against him. "And I know that's unfair, since I'm not ready to make even one. Hold me close. Make me forget my head feels like it's got a cyclone inside."

"If you get any closer, I'm going to break every promise I've made to you and to myself."

325

"Are you excited?"

He laughed ruefully. "You could say that."

"When my brothers got in that condition, Jake would tell them to take a swim in the river and cool off."

"I've had all the swimming in the river I care for."

"I guess you have." She paused. "Are you still hot?"

"And getting hotter."

"Is it because of me?"

"Yes."

"Nobody ever got hot because of me before."

"I'm sure they did. Jake should have told you it's dangerous to get a man hot."

"Why?"

"We're not very good at controlling ourselves."

"Isabelle says a gentleman can always control himself."

"I'm reluctant to contradict Isabelle, but this gentleman is about to explode. I imagine your brothers would have felt the same way."

"Isabelle said they weren't gentlemen. She said Jake had ruined them all, teaching them to think it was natural for a man to go all crazy around women. Come to think of it, Isabelle said she didn't care a whole lot for gentlemen. She said they were usually so dull they caused their wives to cast longing glances at young cowhands."

"I've got to meet your Isabelle."

"I'm not too sure about that. If she ever finds out we slept in the same bed, she'll kill you—assuming Zeke and Hawk don't get to you first."

"I'm safe. I couldn't possibly get any sleep."

"Because of me?"

"For a woman with ten brothers, you are a strange combination of knowledge and naïveté."

"What do you mean?"

"You talk about men responding to women like it's old news, yet you seem surprised I can respond to you. You aren't at all embarrassed, either. You act like it's an ordinary topic of conversation."

"I guess that comes from being reared with so many brothers."

"Somebody forgot an important part of your education. Drive a man too far, and he becomes an animal."

"Are you going to turn into an animal?"

"I'm trying hard not to, but if you don't turn back around, I'm not going to make it."

"But I don't want to turn around."

"Drew!" It was an anguished wail.

"Isabelle said when I fell in love, I'd like a man's touch. I'd want him to touch me all the time. She said I wouldn't threaten to shoot his ears off if he didn't keep his distance."

A convulsive shudder passed through Cole. It took a minute before he could control his voice enough to speak. "What else did Isabelle tell you?"

"She said I'd start thinking about pretty dresses and new ways to fix my hair. She said the best part of the day would come when I crawled into bed at night and he put his arms around me and held me close."

Cole's body trembled.

"Would you hold me close?" asked Drew.

"No."

"Why?"

"Because I'm too excited."

"How will that keep you from holding me close?"

"It won't, not exactly, but it will get in the way."

"I don't mind."

"But I do."

"Isabelle said if a man loved a woman, he couldn't wait to hold her close."

"Isabelle was talking about a man and wife. You just said she'd kill me if she could see us now. She'd do something a whole lot worse if I do what I want to do more than anything else in the world."

"What's that?"

"Make love to you." There, he'd said it. Now she'd understand. Now she'd back away and give him a chance to hold on to his honor.

"Isabelle said I'd like that most of all."

Cole groaned, and felt the last of his control vanish. He put his arms around Drew and pulled her to him.

Chapter Twenty-one

Drew heard her words with as much surprise as Cole must have felt. She had practically asked him to make love to her. As much as that shocked her, it didn't frighten her. Rather, it seemed to release some kind of internal knot that allowed her body to relax into Cole's arms. She was still terribly cold, but she could feel a small core of warmth come into being somewhere deep inside her.

"This is a little awkward," Cole said. "On the physical side, we've skipped all the preliminary steps and gone straight to being naked in bed together. On the emotional side, we haven't even started."

Drew had never planned to let any man make love to her. But she hadn't expected it to be so complicated. From what her brothers said, it was quick and straightforward. But her brothers had been a lot younger then, and she wasn't sure they had had as much experience as they boasted of.

"What are we supposed to do?" she asked.

Cole laughed. "I don't believe this is happening."

"What's wrong?"

"Everything. But I'm going to do my best to change that. I'm going to start by kissing you. You like it when I kiss you, don't you?"

"Yes."

It felt strange to be lying in bed with Cole, something she'd never expected to do with any man. It felt even more peculiar to be naked and kissing, but Drew decided it wasn't bad. Unusual, but not bad at all. She really liked it when Cole kissed her. It was hard to explain why something as simple as pressing their lips together could make her world spin into a new orbit, but everything seemed different with Cole. Now she had even more reason to like kissing him. He loved her enough to risk his life to save hers. She knew she was probably dwelling on that too much, but how could any woman think about such a sacrifice too much?

When it caused her not to pay attention to the man who was holding her in his arms, who was kissing her, who was awakening in her body sensations she'd never experienced before.

One hand cupped her cheek as he kissed her gently, then more hungrily. His other hand cupped her breast. No one had touched her breasts. She was unprepared to find her skin so sensitive to his touch. She flinched when his thumb touched her nipple. The intensity of the sensation startled her.

"Did I hurt you?" Cole asked.

She shook her head, then recaptured his lips, greedy for the sweetness of their shared kisses. Isabelle had said she'd like it, but she hadn't said it would practically revolutionize Drew's whole way of thinking about men. She'd never thought they were all that necessary, but if they couldn't do anything else, she decided kissing was enough reason to keep them around.

She wanted to move closer to Cole, to press her body against his, but he kept her at a distance, his hands between them. Both were on her breasts, causing a new explosion of sensation. Cole's touch had opened the lid on the Pandora's box of her feelings, letting escape a world of sensations, feelings, experiences she'd never encountered. She began to understand why most of the women she knew talked about men as though they were an essential part of their existence. She would find it very difficult to face the rest of her life knowing she'd never be kissed again, that no man's hand would touch her body, make her skin burn with the heat of desire.

Cole broke their kiss. Her unhappiness was forgotten the moment she felt his lips touch her nipple. She thought she would rise straight up from the bed. Her breath caught in her throat, then poured forth in a torrent. Her body tensed, each muscle as rigid as dried sinew. Heat shot through her, driving out the cold that until now had held firm possession of her body. She felt like a banked fire, glowing hotter and hotter from the burning embers deep within.

The tension throughout her body built to such a level she couldn't stand it any longer. She pulled Cole's lips from her breast and recaptured his mouth with her own. She couldn't stand to keep her distance from him any longer. She wanted to feel the warmth of his skin, the hardness of his body. She wanted to wrap herself around him like a vine. She threw herself against him, only to discover the reason he'd kept them slightly apart.

His body was hard, erect, and pushed insistently against her.

Drew froze. She hadn't been prepared for that, but she didn't know why not. She had spent her entire life around breeding animals. She knew what happened between the male and female, yet somehow she'd never truly connected that to men and women. Maybe because she had never expected to take part in the mating ritual. Yet she now found herself in bed with a man she loved, naked, her body clamoring to be used as Nature intended.

But to Drew, this was about more than procreation, about more than the coupling of a man and a woman, whether for love or for pleasure. This was the ultimate surrender of her independence, the final goodbye to dreams of living her life without the need of a man. Despite the screaming desire that howled inside her, she felt herself tense, draw back.

"I didn't want to frighten you," Cole said.

"You didn't."

"Then what's wrong?"

How could she explain that it felt as though she was giving up, surrendering, yielding everything to someone else's control? She'd spent her whole life fighting for her independence. As much as she wanted to melt into Cole's arms, she couldn't if it meant accepting second-class status.

"You haven't answered me."

"I don't know how to say it."

"Whatever it is, just say it."

"This can't change anything. I mean, I still want my ranch. I still want to make my own decisions."

She felt Cole relax. "From what you've told me, marriage hasn't turned Isabelle into Jake's slave. It sounds like he gives in just as often as she does."

That was true, but she'd never though of a relationship with a man as being equitable. She'd fought every battle as though losing one would mean losing everything.

"Being in love is about sharing, Drew. If you don't give as much as you get, it won't work. I'd never tell you what to do."

Drew could hardly believe Cole's words. In her male-dominated world, men loved their women. Their wives doted on them, but the men ruled the world they lived in. Even Jake. She'd sworn that would never happen to her. But maybe she didn't have to win every time. Maybe sometimes would be enough. Cole had talked her into many things, but he'd never forced her. Now he was ready to love her unstintingly, her body and her spirit. Wouldn't that be worth the loss of just a tiny bit of her independence? She'd been independent for a long time, and it was lonely. She hadn't been lonely since Cole entered her life.

Her body had never felt one-tenth as alive as it did now. It appeared to be a case of giving up something she had to get something she wanted. An old-fashioned barter. Which did she want more?

Much to her surprise, she discovered that wasn't the question at all. She couldn't do without Cole. Just the thought made her want to bury herself in his embrace.

"Nothing's wrong," she said, truly meaning it this time. "I want you to make love to me."

"Are you sure?"

"If you don't, I'll have to make love to you, and I don't even know how to start."

Cole didn't need to be asked a second time. He took her nipple in his mouth once again, sucking and teasing it with his teeth until she thought she couldn't stand it any longer. His hands ranged over body, her back, her side; they cupped her bottom and pulled her close to him. She felt him pressing against her, hot and insistent. She felt an answering heat ignite in her belly and swell until it reached out to join Cole. All of her seemed to be on fire. It was hard to remember that just a short while earlier she'd been shivering from bone-chilling cold.

Cole's hand slipped down between them, across her abdomen, and between her legs. She felt herself tense, her legs clamp shut.

"I won't hurt you."

"I know." She did, but no one had ever touched her there. It was a bit of a shock. But Cole did something— maybe he found a particular spot, she couldn't be sure— that made her forget any reluctance to yield. A convulsive shudder shook her body and she grabbed hold of Cole as though she never meant to let go. He continued to massage that incredible spot inside her until she heard herself moan, then gasp for breath as the tension broke and flowed from her like liquid heat.

Almost immediately Cole raised himself above her, and filled her until she thought she could stretch no more. He began to move in her, slowly, steadily increasing the tempo until she felt the waves begin to whip her about like a late summer hurricane. Unable to lie still any longer, she began to move with him, forcing him deeper and deeper with each stroke, reaching for the kernel of need buried deep within her. It slowly expanded until it had her in its grasp and her whole body screamed for release. Though he was supposed to be in control, Cole seemed to be equally at the mercy of the need that enslaved her. He moved faster, his breath coming in gasps that alternated with her own.

One tremendous surge, and the tension broke. Cole's body went rigid, his movements uneven. Finally the breath left his body in a loud whoosh, and he collapsed beside her.

Drew lay awake long after Cole fell asleep. His soft breathing was a comfort to her. His arms and legs wrapped around her to keep her warm were a welcome proof of his love, while at the same time they were a symbol of the fetters that would hold her in bondage. Never had she been so much of two minds about anything as she was about this love they shared.

Though she knew love could work—she saw it in Jake and Isabelle's marriage every day—she couldn't forget her parents and the failure of their love to overcome the differences between them. She worried that she and Cole would experience the same problems. He came from a world of wealth and manners that was foreign to her. Worse, it was a world she hated. Suppose he decided he no longer wanted to rebel? Could she live in Memphis? Would he stay in Texas?

Even if he didn't want to go back to Memphis, would he want to spend the rest of his life on a ranch?

Drew buried herself deeper in Cole's embrace. Odd that the cause of her fears should also be the source of her greatest comfort. Despite all Isabelle had told her, all she'd witnessed in Ward's and Buck's marriages, she had never imagined it was possible for a woman to receive so much contentment and reassurance from the arms of a man. Despite the parade of fears her mind used to torture her, her feelings—or something that came from deep inside her—told her everything would be all right as long as Cole kept his arms around her.

Up until now, Drew had felt able to take care of herself in any situation. Now she felt vulnerable, lost, very much dependent on Cole to guide her. Normally that would have infuriated her. Somehow it didn't tonight. She didn't understand it. It was so unlike her. Yet even though she couldn't banish her fears, Cole's embrace made them powerless to hurt her.

She smiled. Isabelle would positively gloat over being right. The boys would kid her mercilessly. But she didn't care. She had found something with Cole that made all the rest seem unimportant, and she meant to hold on to it very tight.

Overton, Mississippi

"I'm sure your brothers are worried, but there was nothing we could do about it," Cole said to Drew. "We'll be back with the show in a few minutes."

It had been three days since they had been thrown off the steamboat. After a night in which they had made love three times, they'd set out the next morning to find help. They'd borrowed clothes from a farmer and his wife, who'd given them a lift in their wagon to a small town along the river. They'd begged another ride to a second town that had a telegraph, so Cole could get money to buy decent clothes and a steamboat ticket to take them to the next town on the Wild West Show's schedule. Drew had been more worried about her brothers than she had about getting back on a steamboat.

"I just hope they haven't telegraphed Jake and Isabelle," she said. "I'd hate for them to have been thinking I'm dead for the last three days."

Drew had insisted that they keep telegraphing Earl until he responded. When he replied that Zeke and Hawk had left the show to look for her body, she asked him to send somebody to find them and tell them she was still alive. She'd been so consumed with worry about her family, Cole hadn't been able to get her to concentrate on their future. He was beginning to understand that Drew worried far more about everybody around her than she worried about herself. It was an admirable quality, but it didn't leave much time for them. Cole made up his mind to do something about that.

They reached the field outside of Overton, where the Wild West Show had been set up, just as the show was about to start.

Myrtle was the first to see them. She let out a shout of happiness that sounded more like a scream of pain, and came running toward them. She threw her arms around Drew as though she never meant to let go.

"We didn't know what had happened to you," she sobbed. "The steamboat people said you must have been thrown overboard and drowned when they hit that sandbar."

"We telegraphed Earl several times. Didn't he tell you we were still alive?"

"Yes, but it was hard to believe anybody could be thrown into that river and survive."

"I would have drowned if it hadn't been for Cole," Drew

said, returning Myrtle's embrace. "He saved my life."

Myrtle released Drew and threw herself at Cole, smothering him in her thankful embrace. "I always knew you were a nice man," she cried.

Earl Odum came running up to Drew. "Thank God you're here." He gave Drew a push toward one of the tents. "Get into your costume. You go on in ten minutes."

"I just got back. I can't—"

"You've got to. Those newspaper reporters have made you into a star. The people will kill me if I announce you've canceled again." He pulled Myrtle off Cole. "Get out there and help Eddie set up the tricks. Hurry," he said when Cole didn't move immediately. "It's almost time to start."

Drew gave up and let herself be herded into the dressing tent. "I can get ready by myself," she told Myrtle. "Please find Hawk and Zeke and tell them I'm all right."

After the series of unprecedented events of the last few days, it was almost a relief to be back to her familiar routine. No questions. No uncertainties. Nothing new or unexpected. Wonderful, comforting familiarity. But that didn't last long. Before she finished dressing, Zeke burst into the tent and smothered her in a bear hug.

"I thought you were dead," he said, his voice suspiciously unsteady. "I didn't dare go home. Isabelle would have killed me, and Jake would have fed my carcass to the hogs."

Drew wriggled one arm free of Zeke's embrace so she could draw Hawk into the circle. His face was impassive, but when he hugged her so hard she thought her ribs would crack, she knew he'd been just as worried as Zeke.

"What happened?" Hawk asked.

"The boat hit a sandbar, and I was thrown into the water. I'd have drowned if Cole hadn't saved me."

"Where's Cole?" Zeke asked, the smile of welcome wiped from his face.

"He's setting up the tricks for the show." She noticed Hawk's expression had turned murderous. "Why? What's happened?"

"We kill him," Hawk said. "I slit his throat tonight."

"You can't. He saved my life. You ought to be thanking him, instead of wanting to kill him."

"He saved you so he can see you hang," Zeke said, grinding the words between his teeth.

"What are you talking about?" She knew both of them were upset, but they weren't making any sense.

"He's a federal agent," Zeke said.

"I know. He told me he was sent here to find out who was committing a bunch of robberies."

"He was sent here to prove we were committing those robberies," Zeke said. "To quote the agent who talked to us, he was sent here 'to infiltrate the gang, to get close to the leader any way he could, so she would confide in him.' Once he gained your confidence, he would talk you into giving him the proof he needed to put us all in jail."

For a moment Drew didn't feel anything. She couldn't believe it was true. Cole loved her. Yet this explained perfectly why Cole had come down out of the stands to challenge her, why he had worked his way into her act, why he had done everything he could to gain her confidence, why he had fallen in love with her despite her attempts to discourage him. Despite her happiness at being in love, despite her certainty Cole's love was genuine, these questions had waited, unanswered, in the back of her mind.

"Are you sure?" She could hardly speak the words. She prayed Zeke would have at least a tiny bit of doubt.

"I'm positive," Zeke said. "He's their top agent. They say he can insinuate himself into any situation."

Drew could attest to that. No man had ever come close to working his way into her affections or causing her to rethink her ideas on marriage. No man had ever made her want to make love to him. Cole had succeeded in doing all of these things.

Much to her surprise, she didn't feel a great sense of betrayal. Nor did she feel the agonizing pain that comes with the realization a cherished love is false. She didn't even feel like crying or throwing things. She simply felt cold and empty. She felt herself going through the motions of getting ready for the show, of responding to Zeke and Hawk like a well-oiled machine, with no emotion, no wasted movement. She felt disembodied, able to separate herself from the person who was about to enter the ring.

When she faced the man who'd betrayed her, she would call upon every ounce of pride to keep from showing that her ability to love had been slain before it could grow beyond its infancy. Better it should happen now. It would cause terrible pain as soon as she got over the shock, but it wouldn't hurt as much as if that love had been allowed to grow, as if she'd had time to build her life on it.

A boy stuck his head inside the tent.

"I've got your horse, Miss Townsend. It's time to go on."

Drew pulled her thoughts together. "I need more guns," she said to Zeke.

"Why?" Hawk asked.

"I'm going to give them a show they'll never forget. I'm not going to just hit every target. I'm going to make designs in them."

She draped gun belts around her waist and over her shoulders until she looked like a guerrilla fighter.

"Hurry, Miss Townsend," the boy urged. "Earl is about to give your cue."

"Are my rifles on the table?" she asked the boy.

"Cole saw to it," he said. "Please hurry. Earl will blame me if you're late."

"I won't be late. Help me up," she said to Zeke and Hawk. Each took an arm and lifted her effortlessly onto the back of the horse. "Get a good seat," she told them as she heard Earl announcing her entrance. "This is going to be a show to remember."

Cole had taught Drew the importance of paying attention to the fans, of trying to make a connection with them the moment she appeared. Drew was especially aware of them today. Though Overton was only a small town, the stands were full, mostly with women and children. Drew smiled and waved the first time around the ring. She wanted every woman in the stands to be cheering for her. As she circled around behind the targets, she got her guns ready.

She fired at all three targets in rapid succession, using four pistols, which she discarded the moment they were empty. The surprise on Cole's face only made her feel more determined. How dare he act like he was innocent?

As she circled around once more, Cole held up the targets for the audience to see. The bullet holes spelled out RIP. The audience applauded enthusiastically. Instead of shooting the second round of targets Cole had set up, Drew slid off the horse.

"What are you doing?" Cole asked.

"Get the candles ready," she said, and paraded around the ring smiling, waving, and graciously accepting the applause. She proceeded to go through the rest of her show, shooting candles and dozens of clay pigeons from every possible angle and position. She didn't miss a single shot. But rather than end her show by hitting three clay pigeons at a time, she turned and fired another round of bullets into the targets. Cole, looking even more perplexed, held up the three targets. RUN.

"What the hell are you doing?" he demanded.

"Giving you a warning, you lying, cheating bastard. If you don't turn tail this very minute, I'm going to fill you full of holes right in front of this audience."

"What are you talking about?" he asked.

"About you coming here to prove I'm a robber," she said, bowing and accepting the continuing applause, "about saying you loved me so I'd take you into my gang."

She didn't have to look up to know that piece of news had shaken him badly. Good. She motioned the audience to silence.

"Being able to shoot targets is fun," she said to the thousands of smiling and admiring faces, "but the ability to use a gun ought to have a practical purpose." Still facing the audience, she moved away from Cole. "Ladies, don't leave all the shooting to your men. You might need it for defense. Or you might need it for hunting." She checked her rifle to make sure it had a fully loaded magazine. "It's also a great opportunity to get away from the cook stove and the washtub. No reason the men should have all the fun and call it work."

A smattering of laughter came from the stands.

"But being able to shoot can be of particular advantage to you unmarried ladies. You can use it to drive off unwanted suitors."

A quick shot put a hole in the crown of Cole's hat. Cole looked stunned. The audience gasped, then laughed tentatively, as though unsure of what reaction was appropriate.

"It's especially useful for rich girls plagued by men begging for the privilege of worshiping them forever when all they really want is their money."

A barrage of shots sent Cole's hat flying through the air.

"That'll keep most of them away."

Cole's hand flew to his head, a startled expression on his face. The women in the audience laughed easily this time.

"But sometimes a man is particularly insistent," Drew said. "Your father, brothers, or uncles might be able to scare him off. But just in case he needs a little more persuasion, it's nice to be able to give it."

Four quick shots ripped holes in the loose-fitting sleeve of Cole's shirt. He backed up a couple of steps, fingered the tattered bits of his shirt, and looked in disbelief at Drew.

"What the hell are you trying to do?" he asked.

"But the worst kind of polecat," Drew said, still facing the audience, "is the man who comes pretending to do one thing when he's trying to do something altogether different. For example, a man who says he wants your help in solving a crime when he's really trying to convict you of it. He's the worst kind."

She turned and fired twice. Cole's belt buckle shattered and flew through the air. Cole grabbed at his pants. The spectators, men included, laughed heartily.

"I told my boss you didn't pull off those robberies," he said. "I made him let me come back so I could clear your name."

"A man like that will say anything to gain your confidence," Drew called out, now looking directly at Cole, who stood about twenty feet away. "If he lies about one thing, he'll lie about everything."

Several shots tugged at the other sleeve of Cole's shirt.

"I didn't lie about loving you," he said.

More shots tugged at his pants. Cole's clothes were shot to ribbons.

"And he'll keep lying until you believe him," Drew said. "A girl ought to be allowed to kill a skunk like that." More shots. "It ought to be legal for her brothers to bury his body deep or dump it into the river. Unfortunately, our laws are made by men, and a woman is not allowed to murder a shiftless rat, but she can scare the life out of him if she knows how to use a gun."

More shots. They were almost a steady tattoo now.

"I was sent here to collect evidence against you," Cole said, "but it didn't take long before I knew you couldn't have had anything to do with the robberies."

Drew had expected the sudden onslaught of bullets to send Cole running for cover. By now she'd reduced his clothes to tatters, the frayed edges as well as his untouched body a testament to her skill. But he just stood there, looking straight into her eyes, as if the bullets she was shooting at him weren't any more dangerous than a mosquito he'd slap away without a thought.

"I was going to tell you later, once we'd discovered who was really behind the robberies."

We! How dare he pretend he'd ever intended to take her into his confidence, to allow her to share in his investigation. He'd lied and manipulated her from the very beginning. Even telling her he was an undercover agent had worked to his advantage. She no longer believed he was a liar and a drifter. She'd actually thought he was noble, willing to risk his life so ordinary people might enjoy their freedom and feel safe in their homes.

He'd convinced her he loved her, that she was the most important person in the whole world. She'd have told him anything, done anything, believed anything, because she thought he loved her. He'd seen through her pretense, discovered she wanted love—was only waiting to be convinced she was loved before giving herself wholeheartedly to him—a weakness she didn't know she had. He'd pursued that weakness with the persistence of a fox after its next meal. He'd probably even arranged for the steamboat to run in to the sandbar and toss them into the water so he could save her. He must have known that after that, she'd believe anything he said.

"If you can't hurt a man's body, you can hurt his pride," Drew said.

Moving quickly, she maneuvered around Cole until she could get a clear shot at his boots. She shot the heels off both boots. Cole staggered, lost his balance, and sat down in the dust.

"After that, he'll leave you alone," Drew said. She waved and smiled at the audience. The spectators jumped to their feet, cheering wildly.

"I'll never leave you alone," Cole said.

"If you ever come near me again, I will kill you." Drew waved one last time and ran from the arena. She nearly stumbled into the side of a tent. Her eyes were blinded by tears.

Chapter Twenty-two

"I don't want to be in love," Drew sobbed in Isabelle's arms. "I hate it."

"You'd like it well enough if the man you loved loved you in return," Isabelle said.

"Even then it's an uncomfortable condition," Rose Randolph said. "It makes you do things you'd rather not."

"But you love your husband," Drew said, lifting her head.

"To distraction," Rose said.

"Then how can you say it's uncomfortable?"

"A woman distracted is not a woman in full possession of her reason," Rose said. "No matter how strong your convictions or your principles, you want to please your husband more than anything in the world. I find myself wanting to hit him over the head just about as often as I want him to make love to me. Isn't that true, Isabelle?"

Isabelle laughed. "Drew's heard Jake and me argue our whole married life." She kissed Drew's forehead. "But she knows I wouldn't trade one minute of it for the most biddable husband in the world."

"Nor would I trade George," Rose agreed. "However, if you know anybody willing to take a few of his brothers, I'd be happy to talk to them."

Drew had been back at the Broken Circle for three days, and she'd spent every one of them behaving like the kind of female she most despised. She'd cried and pouted and moped and sniffled. She'd been alternately angry with everyone and begging their pardon. She had no appetite and was starved to death, didn't want to see anyone and couldn't stand to be alone. She blamed Hawk and Zeke for not going with her on the steamboat, then defended them when Jake came down hard on them.

Half the time she wanted to see Cole more than anything in the world. The other half she swore if he ever showed his face again, she'd fill him with so many bullet holes, he'd practically disappear.

Rose Randolph and her husband George were spending a few days with Jake and Isabelle before all four left for New Orleans. They would travel to Corpus Christi and take a boat from there. Jake and George had spent most of their time riding over the ranch and talking cows. Hawk and Zeke had hovered between Drew and Jake, never feeling comfortable in either place but feeling guilty no matter where they were. Drew swore she'd never go back to the Wild West Show. Instead, she'd use what money she had to buy a ranch. It wouldn't be as big or as well stocked as she'd hoped, but she'd build it up. Zeke and Hawk offered to stay and help her.

But having confessed her foolishness to Isabelle and having decided what to do with her future hadn't brought Drew the relief she'd hoped for. Everything felt wrong, and it was all Cole Benton's fault. If she ever saw him again she *would* fill him full of bullet holes.

"You have to make up your mind what you want," Isabelle said. "Either you want this man or you don't."

Drew sat up straight in her porch chair. "I don't want him!" she said, indignant Isabelle could think she would even consider speaking to Cole, much less taking him back. "I can't be in love with a man who has lied to me."

"Of course you can," Rose said. "Women do it all the time."

"Well, I can't. And I wouldn't if I could."

"Fine. Then put him out of your mind and start thinking about what land would make the best grazing."

Drew had always liked Rose Randolph. She was a strong woman who didn't put up with any nonsense from anybody, especially men. It was a shock to discover she was apparently completely lacking in feminine understanding. How could she possibly talk about Drew's broken heart as though merely saying she didn't love Cole would cause all the hurt to go away, the feeling of betrayal to vanish? She was surprised Rose and Isabelle had been friends for so long.

"I agree with Rose," Isabelle said. "If you don't care for this man any longer—"

"I don't!"

"—and you don't think your relationship can be rescued—"

"I wouldn't want it if it could!"

"—then it's time to forget about him and focus your mind on your ranch."

Drew pulled away from Isabelle. It seemed neither woman could understand how she felt. They were both happily married to men they adored. They'd never been in love with anyone else, particularly not a man who'd won their love under false pretenses. Maybe Drew should have gone to stay with Marina instead. Even though she and Ward were happily married, there'd been a time when each thought they'd been betrayed by the other. Marina must remember what it was like to have a broken heart and know having her own ranch with all the cows and horses in the world couldn't fix it.

But Marina had a new baby. Isabelle said it wasn't fair for anybody to dump their troubles on Marina just now.

"I think you ought to start making plans for your ranch right away," Isabelle said. "Hawk and Zeke aren't going to stay around here forever. You'd better make use of them while you can."

"It'll give you something to occupy your mind," Rose said.

Drew decided she might as well have ridden out with the men. They couldn't have given her less sympathy and understanding.

"Looks like one of the men is coming back already," Rose said, indicating a rider in the distance.

"I'd know Jake and the boys at any distance," Isabelle said. "That's a stranger."

Drew looked up and her body went rigid. That wasn't a stranger. It was Cole!

She jumped to her feet, her body poised for flight—or to run straight into his arms.

She was disgusted with herself to know that her first response had been joy that he had followed her, hope he still loved her, and a willingness to do anything if he would only love her again. She had always considered herself a sensible woman, not subject to the volatile and foolish emotions that afflicted the average female. She could deal with men on an equal basis.

Yet here she was acting like the silliest of females, ready to throw herself at the man who'd lied to her, betrayed her love, broken her heart. She wouldn't be fooled again by Cole Benton. She wouldn't! She ran into the house.

"Who is that man?" Rose asked.

"I don't know," Isabelle said, looking at the house and then back at the approaching horseman. "But if I had to hazard a guess, I'd say it was Cole Benton."

Drew emerged from the house with a rifle.

Isabelle winked at Rose. "It's definitely Cole Benton."

"What are you going to do?" Rose asked Isabelle.

"Nothing."

Drew suspected she saw Rose smile.

"If you don't want to see him killed right before your eyes, you'll tell him to leave," Drew said.

"You know we always offer hospitality to strangers," Isabelle said.

"George likes it when a stranger rides in," Rose said. "It's a chance to get some news."

350

"He doesn't know any news," Drew said. "Besides, everything he says is lies."

"Do you know him?" Isabelle asked. Her expression was blank.

"That's Cole Benton, and you know it," Drew said, not mincing words. "You want to meet him, fine. But you'd better pick out a burial spot. He won't be around long enough for dinner."

Drew lifted the rifle to her shoulder and fired a shot into the ground in front of Cole's horse. The animal reared. Cole got him under control again and kept coming.

"Turn around," Drew called, "or I'll shoot you out of the saddle."

When he kept coming, she fired two shots that sent his hat spinning into the wind. Cole acted like he didn't even notice.

"Drew's a spectacular shot," Isabelle explained to Rose. "She could shoot the buttons off his shirt and not singe the material."

"I'm relieved to know that," Rose said. "I was thinking that young man was either a great fool or too much in love to value his own hide."

"His own hide is all he thinks about," Drew snapped.

She fired more shots into the ground before the horse. The animal reared again. He became so agitated, Cole dismounted, left him ground-hitched, and continued forward on foot.

Drew proceeded to riddle Cole's clothes with bullets.

"I thought Hen was a good shot," Rose said. "He can't hold a candle to this child."

"It's a gift," Isabelle said. "She could shoot better than

351

the boys from the start. It used to make Luke so furious he refused to shoot against her."

Drew felt deserted by everyone who should have cared for her. Jake and the boys were out entertaining George. Isabelle and Rose didn't seemed to be the least concerned that the cause of all her misery was rapidly drawing near. Cole didn't have the good sense to know he wasn't wanted. She raised her rifle again.

"You might as well quit shooting at me," Cole said. "I didn't run the first time, and I'm not going to do it now."

"She shot at you before?" Isabelle asked.

"In front of five thousand people," Cole said. "I looked like a rag doll. She even shot the heels off my boots. Caused me to fall down in front of all those people. It was humiliating, ma'am."

"I'm shocked she'd do such a thing," Isabelle said. "I taught her to have better manners."

"You also said it was okay to shoot thieves, no-good drifters, and lying coyotes," Drew cried, anger and frustration causing her voice to rise in pitch.

"This young man looks too presentable to be any of those things," Isabelle said.

"Thank you, ma'am," Cole said as he stopped before Isabelle. "Cole Benton at your service."

"Nice to meet you," Isabelle replied. "I'm Isabelle Maxwell, Drew's mother. This is a friend of mine, Rose Randolph. Drew has told us so much about you."

"All bad," Drew snarled. "Now get back on your horse and get out of here. I'd hate to splatter your blood all over Isabelle's new dress."

"I came here to talk to you," Cole said. "I'm not leaving until I do."

"I'm not interested in anything you have to say."

"You're going to hear it nevertheless."

Isabelle stood. "I think a cup of coffee would be nice right about now," she said to Rose. "Would you like some?"

"Yes." Rose stood.

"Don't you dare leave me with this lying, cheating sidewinder," Drew said.

"Please stay," Cole said. "I'd like you both to hear what I have to say."

Both ladies resumed their seats.

"You don't have to remember anything he says," Drew said. "It'll all be lies."

"I didn't lie about the most important thing," Cole said. "I love you."

"The son of the richest man in Memphis can't love a criminal. It wouldn't be socially acceptable."

"So you're *that* Cole Benton," Rose said. "My husband has had some business dealings with your father."

"I hope he's not a coiled snake, like his son," Drew said.

"I was sent to join the Wild West Show and work my way into your confidence," Cole said, directing his attention to Drew.

"See, he confesses to being a yellow dog."

"But I soon knew you couldn't be responsible for the robberies."

"But you weren't sure enough to tell me."

"I couldn't very well be an undercover agent if I told you."

"You could have trusted me."

"Did you trust me? As I remember, you did your best to get rid of me."

"I knew by instinct you were rotten to the core."

"When we were in Memphis, I tried to get my boss to take me off the case. He said I'd better stay on if I wanted to prove you were innocent, that anybody else would only be interested in proving your guilt."

"How could they do that when I had nothing to do with the robberies?"

"Because the people behind the robberies were using you and your brothers as a cover."

"How?" Isabelle asked.

"One of them is a woman who shoots well enough to be mistaken for Drew. The other two are men who're always masked, but that fits in with Hawk and Zeke being so easy to identify."

"That could be a lot of people," Isabelle said.

"The robberies always took place within a short ride of where the Wild West Show was playing, or in a town just after it left. One took place in a bank Drew spent half a morning studying."

"Your brother-in-law told me I ought to study the bank's customers before I decided where to deposit my money," Drew explained to Rose.

"That sounds exactly like something Jeff would say," Rose said. "He doesn't trust anybody."

"But the last robbery took place the night we were on the steamboat," Cole said. "That's positive proof you didn't do it. I was with you the whole evening."

"Good," Drew said. "You can tell your boss I'm innocent, and both of you can forget you ever heard of me."

"No, I can't," Cole said.

"Why not?"

354

"Who's going to believe me when I tell them the woman I intend to marry is innocent?"

"I'm not going to marry you!" Drew declared.

"They'll think a husband would naturally defend his wife."

"I should hope so," Isabelle said. "Jake and the boys would take it very unkindly if you didn't."

"George and his brothers wouldn't like it much, either," Rose added.

"I'm not going to marry him!" Drew virtually shouted. "Nobody has to worry about anything."

"I'm not so sure of that," Isabelle said. "That looks like Jake and the boys coming. From the way Zeke and Hawk are riding, I'd say they had blood in their eyes."

"Good," Drew said. "All the way home Hawk kept begging me to let him go back and cut Cole's throat. Fool that I was, I wouldn't let him."

"I knew you still loved me," Cole said.

"The hell I do!" Drew snapped. "I stopped him because I didn't want him to hang for removing your worthless hide."

"You say the sweetest things," Cole drawled. "Mama is gonna love you."

"I wouldn't go near your mama on a bet."

"I don't know how well she'll get along with your aunt, however. Mama's family is old Memphis society."

"My aunt is just as good as your mother. No, she's better."

"Of course my father is new money, but that hardly matters. If we live on your ranch, we won't have to see them more than once a year. This is a beautiful valley. Is your land nearby?"

Drew's temper had been stretched to the limit. Seeing Isabelle trying unsuccessfully to smother a laugh caused it to break. She marched up to Cole, shoved her rifle barrel against his chest, and pushed. "Git before I forget it's against the law to shoot society-bred skunks."

Cole calmly pushed the rifle barrel to one side. "This may be the way you greet lovers in Texas, but I prefer the way we do it in Memphis."

The rotten, low-down, belly-crawling traitor took Drew into his arms and kissed her ruthlessly, right there in front of Isabelle and Rose. He didn't even have the decency to ask them to turn their heads.

But she saved her most scathing thoughts for herself. After all the rotten things he'd done—horning in on her show, lying to her, suspecting her of being a thief, *waiting three days to follow her*—her treacherous body melted into his arms. Her lips kissed him back—*Kissed him back!*—as if they had no memory of his treachery. Worst of all, her muscles loosened their grip on her rifle, let it fall to the ground, then drew her arms around his neck. Then her heart and body combined to throw themselves into an embrace her mind screamed was a horribly blatant case of backsliding, a perfect example of a woman acting like a fool over a man, the precise reason why women hadn't taken their rightful place in the pantheons of power.

But her heart and body didn't give a damn about pantheons, no matter what kind they were. She was back in Cole's arms, and that was all that counted.

Drew felt Cole being ripped from her embrace. Zeke knocked him down and Hawk pounced upon him, a knife at Cole's throat.

"I kill him now," Hawk said.

"I think you ought to let him up," Isabelle said. "It'll be awfully difficult to introduce him to Jake and George with him lying on his back in the dust."

"I want to kill him," Hawk pleaded.

"He says he wants to marry Drew," Isabelle said, unable to repress a grin. "I think she ought to have first choice."

Drew had stood there, too paralyzed to move or speak. It was abundantly clear to her—and most likely to everyone else as well—that she still loved Cole. His treachery didn't make any difference. She wasn't any better than the women she'd scorned for so many years. She didn't care that her man had faults, what they were, or how many. She loved him, and that was the end of it.

Okay, she loved Cole. She couldn't do anything about that, but she didn't have to let that ruin her life. She would buy her ranch and throw herself into running it. She would be miserable at first, maybe forever, but she would at least have her self-respect.

But self-respect had never seemed so uninviting. Compared to the bliss of being in Cole's arms, of his kisses, it seemed like cold sawdust.

"What was all the shooting about?" Jake asked as he and George Randolph approached the group.

"Drew was welcoming her lover," Rose said, then burst out laughing. "I swear, she's just like Fern."

Drew had never met Fern, Madison Randolph's wife, but she'd heard plenty about the Kansas tomboy, and didn't appreciate the comparison.

"What's this about being her lover?" Jake asked, his brow creased with a deep frown.

"He wants to marry her," Isabelle said. "He'd just told her when you arrived."

"What was your answer?" Jake said, turning to Drew.

"She didn't get a chance to give one before Zeke and Hawk knocked him down," Isabelle said.

"Why would they do that?" Jake asked.

"Let him up, boys," Isabelle said to Hawk and Zeke. "Cole, this is my husband, Jake Maxwell, and his friend, George Randolph. This is Cole Benton."

Reluctantly, and with growls of protest, Zeke and Hawk drew back. Cole got to his feet, dusted himself off, and offered his hand to Jake. "Pleased to meet you."

"What's this about you wanting to marry Drew?" Jake asked as he shook Cole's hand. "She hates men. Says she doesn't mean to have one on her ranch."

"It's a long story," Isabelle said. "Why don't we move inside out of this sharp wind? I'll fix some coffee while Cole catches everybody up."

Drew felt helplessly drawn along, especially when Cole put his arm around her. After the way she'd melted into his embrace, it seemed pointless to push him away. Besides, if she was honest—she hated it when she had to be *this* honest—she liked it there. His touch, his kiss, the warmth in his eyes, had undone all her resolution. She loved him. She couldn't help it.

"That doesn't sound so terrible," Jake said to Drew when Cole finished explaining what had happened over the last few weeks. "You can't blame him for following orders, especially when he didn't know anything about you."

Drew didn't bother to explain she was just as angry at herself as she was at Cole. If she'd stuck to her principles, none of this would have happened.

"What happens now?" Isabelle asked.

"I want Drew to marry me," Cole said.

"No." Her answer was short and unequivocal.

"Why not?" Cole asked.

She couldn't tell him she didn't love him. She'd be doing what she couldn't forgive him for, lying. Besides, after the way she'd kissed him, nobody would believe her.

"I told you from the beginning, I didn't want to get married."

"But that was before we fell in love."

She wished he'd stop saying he loved her. It made it harder to stick to her resolution. "I still don't want to get married."

"Why?"

"I want to run my ranch without a husband telling me what to do."

"I won't interfere."

"Yes, you would. Men just naturally feel they've got to tell a woman what to do. They can't help it."

Isabelle and Rose smiled up at their husbands. George smiled in return, but Jake's expression remained serious.

"Besides, your mother doesn't like me. She wants you to marry that Sibyl person."

"I'm not marrying to please my mother."

"I wouldn't fit in with your rich friends."

"I don't know why not. If I'm any judge, your aunt is richer than just about anybody in Memphis. Not to mention Jake and Isabelle owning five or six valleys."

"None of that makes any difference. Look, Cole, it just wouldn't work. We're too different."

"You don't really know anything about me. I enjoyed working in Texas. I don't like Memphis society any more than you do."

"She doesn't want to marry you," Zeke said. "Get on your horse and ride."

"I make sure he go," Hawk offered.

"I think we ought to hear more about him," Jake said.

"This is not a group decision," Drew said. "It's between Cole and me. Since I refuse to marry him, there's nothing more to be said." She looked at Cole. "You might as well leave now."

"I can't leave without you."

"Why not?"

"I don't believe you don't want to marry me. I think you're still angry at me."

"You're damned right, I am."

"Before long, you'll stop being angry. I want to be with you when that happens."

"Why? Nothing will be any different."

"I believe it will. Besides, even if you're right, I still can't leave without you."

"Why?"

"Because you're still under suspicion."

"You said she couldn't have committed the last robbery," Jake said.

"I also said I'm not sure my captain will believe me. He knows I'm in love with her."

"Do you know who the robbers are?"

"I think so."

"Why can't you prove it?"

"Because all the evidence points to Drew. They've been using her as a cover. I have to catch them in the act. If she doesn't come back to the show, there won't be any more robberies. They'll get away with a couple hundred thousand dollars."

Jake whistled. "That much?"

"Maybe more. We can't be sure of all their robberies."

"How did you figure this out?" Drew asked. "When?"

"In bits and pieces," Cole replied. "Once I decided you weren't the robber, I looked around to see who was the most likely culprit. It was obvious it was somebody in the Wild West Show. It was also obvious that the two masked robbers could be almost anybody, but I couldn't figure out who the woman could be. You are the only sharpshooter in the show. One of the other women might have been able to shoot well enough to pretend to be you, but they were all either too old or had alibis."

"Why didn't you tell me this when we were on the boat?" Drew asked.

"Because I didn't know any more than that. It's not even a good theory, much less any sort of proof."

"Well, who is the woman?" Jake asked.

"I think it's Earl Odum."

The noise Zeke made was coarse and contemptuous.

"He's a man," Drew said. "And he can't shoot."

"He's a little man," Cole said. "And he's very pretty. With all the makeup and costumes readily available, it wouldn't be much of a problem for him to dress up as a woman."

"But he can't shoot."

"That's what everybody thought," Cole said. "Until you left."

"What happened?"

"He was auditioning a new sharpshooter for the New Orleans shows. The man is nowhere near as good as you. He said your tricks were impossible, that he didn't believe anybody could do them, especially a woman. Earl got so frustrated, he snatched up a gun and did one of the tricks himself. If I hadn't been setting up the tricks, I'd never have known."

"So arrest him," Isabelle said.

"I can't without proof. I need you to come back," he said to Drew, "so he'll attempt another robbery. We'll be watching him. He won't get away this time."

Drew didn't say anything.

"You've got to clear your name," Cole said. "All the evidence we have points to you. I'm positive Earl is the thief, but right now the captain considers it an unfounded suspicion. Unless we can lay a trap for him, you and your brothers are still the prime suspects."

"It looks to me like you don't have any choice," Jake said. "You can't leave that sort of thing hanging over your heads. It's not fair to Zeke and Hawk."

Drew felt as though she were sinking into quicksand. She knew she ought to refuse, was certain she wanted to refuse, but Cole had fixed it so she couldn't without appearing callously indifferent to the reputations of her brothers. "Is that all you're trying to prove?" she asked.

His gaze didn't waver. "No. I want the chance to prove you love me so much you can't take a chance on losing what we could have together."

"I'll only come back if you promise to leave me alone."

"I won't do that."

"Why not?"

"Because I can't."

Hell! She couldn't accuse him of lying to her now. He had laid it on the line right in front of everybody. But that didn't upset her as much as her reaction. Her heart beat faster; she could feel a flush in her cheeks. Regardless of what she believed in her mind, the rest of her was eager to give Cole the chance he wanted. She felt as if she were being torn into two pieces, each unable to tolerate what the other wanted.

"Okay, I'll go back."

"Zeke and Hawk will have to come, too," Cole said.

"We come," Hawk said.

"But I'm warning you now," Drew said. "You take one step in my direction outside that arena, and I'll shoot your ears off."

"Get your rifle ready," Cole said, that damned irresistible smile on his lips. "I never could stay away from you."

Chapter Twenty-three

"I don't understand why you don't want to marry him," Drew's aunt said. "He's a charming young man, and he adores you."

"He lied to me before. He could be lying now."

"You can tell by the way he looks at you he's sincere."

"Cole is an accomplished actor. It's one of the reasons he's so good at his job."

"I think you're being much too hard on him."

It was getting harder and harder to resist Cole's entreaties. He'd convinced nearly everyone he was desperately in love with Drew. They were equally certain she was just as deeply in love with him. She was, but she wasn't about to admit it to anyone. It was her own stupid mistake, but that didn't mean she had to share it with the world.

She'd known the minute she returned to the show that

she couldn't stay in the hotel with the rest of the performers. That would keep her in constant contact with Cole. She was a strong, determined woman, but she wasn't strong enough to withstand that much temptation. Dorothea had learned the Wild West Show was going to New Orleans. She was comfortably settled in a luxurious suite when Drew arrived. Drew decided to stay with her aunt rather than Jake and Isabelle. Not only did that save the cost of an extra hotel room, it saved her from being dropped into the middle of her parents' social schedule. Besides, Dorothea wanted nothing more than to spend all her time with Drew.

Unfortunately, she'd spent most of it trying to convince Drew to marry Cole. Drew had refused to see Cole except during the show, but Cole had made several visits to see her aunt. Dorothea was an enthusiastic convert after the first visit.

"Even Jake and Isabelle think he's the perfect young man for you," her aunt said.

"He lied to me, Aunt Dorothea. I can never forget that."

"Of course you can. I thought you were a sensible young woman, not one of these females who gets a foolish idea in her head and can't get it out again."

"I'm not being foolish." Jake and Isabelle had said the same thing. She was getting tired of everybody ganging up against her.

"The young man had a job to do that required him to keep his purpose secret. You can't hold that against him."

"Why not?"

"Because it's foolish, and you're not a foolish woman. He deceived a stranger for a perfectly good reason. When he fell in love with you, he told you the truth."

"Not all of it."

"He might have, if you hadn't been thrown into the river. Admit it, Drew, this has nothing to do with believing he loves you. You *know* he does, and it scares you silly."

"That's ridiculous."

"You think if you marry him, it'll be like your parents all over again."

"Why wouldn't it be? He's running away from his parents. I'm running away from you."

"You're not running away from me. You're running *away* from the life I lead and *to* that ranch of yours. Besides, it won't be the same. You're both more sensible than your parents. I loved my sister dearly, but she was a scatterbrained ninny. And your father was an idealistic fool. Neither one of them had an ounce of common sense. I doubt I've ever seen two more badly mismatched people. I thought you'd managed to avoid inheriting any of that. Now I begin to wonder."

Drew had endured a rough week since she'd gotten back to New Orleans. Cole's publicity efforts and the story of their surviving being thrown into the Mississippi had turned her into the star of the show once again. In addition to sold-out performances, she'd been called on to do interviews and hold shooting demonstrations. Cole had been present at every one, supporting her, protecting her, doing everything he could to make it easier for her. When reporters asked stupid questions, he deflected them. When they asked personal questions, he cut them off. When they seemed to doubt she could do what her press notices claimed, he handed out passes to the show so they could see for themselves.

She had endured this for seven days without the slightest indication that Earl—if it was Earl behind the robberies—was going to pull off another robbery. Cole had enlisted the members of the crew to help watch Earl. A second undercover agent had been sent to watch Earl's helpers, but Cole couldn't arrest anyone until he caught them in the act.

So Drew was forced to keep working with him, seeing him, talking to him, *wanting* him. The one time they'd found themselves alone together, she'd backed away from him.

"You don't have to run away," he'd said. "I love you, and I want to marry you, but I'm not going to force myself on you. I want you to want me as much as I want you."

He'd been as good as his word. So good, in fact, Drew wondered if he really did love her as much as he said. It nearly drove her crazy to be around him and not touch him, not let him hold her and kiss her. He didn't seem to be having any problem keeping his distance. Even Zeke and Hawk had relaxed their guard.

Earl was ecstatic to have her back. He was pressuring her to return next season. He'd already offered to triple her salary. If he'd quadruple it, she'd be able to afford the ranch she wanted and the cattle to stock it after just one more year. And she wouldn't have to depend upon Zeke and Hawk to help her.

But being self-sufficient was no longer a comfort. It made her feel cut off, lonely. She used to tell herself she wanted it because Jake and Isabelle had already given her too much, that she couldn't take anything else from them. But that was no excuse to refuse her aunt's little gifts or to shut her out of her life. She'd have preferred to shower Drew with clothes and jewels, to thrust her into the very center of high society, but all she really wanted was to be part of Drew's life.

That was all Cole asked, too.

Drew had always let people get close, then pushed them away before they got too close. She'd done it with Jake and Isabelle, her brothers, now her aunt. Even the old people in the show. It was okay for her to love people, to do things for them, to give of herself, but it wasn't okay for people to like her back.

Why?

She was afraid, but afraid of what? Being rejected? Hurt? Abandoned? Of becoming dependent? Of not being pretty enough? Not being feminine?

A hot feeling in the pit of her stomach told her she'd hit upon a live idea. She was afraid her own cussedness, her bossiness, would drive people away. But it was something more fundamental with Cole. She knew she was strong, capable, hardworking. She also knew she lacked feminine graces, style, beauty, all the little things that strong men looked for in women they chose to be their wives. She was more comfortable in pants than in a dress. A gun or a rope felt natural in her hand. A fan didn't. She didn't mind the smell of cows or sweat. She preferred the company of men to women. She had no graces and feminine wiles.

"Look at me," Drew said to her aunt.

Her aunt looked perplexed. "Why?"

"Do I look like any woman you've ever seen?"

"I don't understand what you're asking."

"I don't have flawless skin or seductive eyes. I don't simper, sigh, flutter my eyelashes, or make a fool of myself over men. I don't pine when they're absent or spend all my time thinking of ways to please them. I wear a gun rather than a gown, and boots instead of silk slippers. Hell, I can't be very charming and seductive if Earl Odum is able to dress up and pass himself off as me."

"This is nonsense," her aunt said. "Just because you've spent most of your life trying to look and act like a boy doesn't mean you can't be feminine when you want."

"I'm not sure I want to, but I'm positive I don't know how."

Her aunt's gaze narrowed. "When did you start worrying about being able to act feminine?"

"When I met Cole's mother and the woman she wants him to marry. I don't like Sibyl Owens, but she's beautiful, feminine, and stylish. Any man would count himself fortunate to have her as his wife. She'd know what to do in any social occasion. What man is going to want me when I not only look and act like a cowboy, but can do everything better than he can?"

Her aunt leaned back in her chair, a smile of satisfaction making her eyes dance. "You *do* love him. You needn't bother to deny it. It's in every word you say."

"Yes," Drew said, relieved to have finally divested herself of this momentous secret, "I do love him."

"Then marry him."

"I can't."

"Why not?"

"Because I'm not the kind of woman he wants. He's used to society, and pretty, soft women in fancy gowns and candlelight. What would he do with a female cowboy?"

"Cole strikes me as a man who knows his own mind."

"Isabelle says a man hardly ever knows what he wants.

He's liable to be attracted to a pretty ball because he likes its color or because it bounces high. But he'll become bored with it in a few days."

"Isabelle thinks you ought to marry Cole."

"She likes him, but she doesn't know him like I do."

"And what do you know that's so important?"

"Cole is rebelling against part of his upbringing, but not all of it. Eventually he'll be sorry I don't fit in."

"Then what are you willing to do about it?"

"What do you mean?"

"Do you love this man and want to marry him?"

"Yes." She had confessed everything now.

"Then you have to be willing to make yourself into the kind of woman you think he wants."

"I can't."

"You haven't tried. You don't know."

"I can't pretend to be what I'm not."

"I'm not talking about that. I'm talking about your willingness to make some compromises, to wear a fancy dress if necessary, attend a party, let him have the spotlight occasionally. If you're not willing to bend a little, there's no point in talking."

Drew started to say she didn't like fancy dresses, but she realized she'd never really worn one. Now that she thought of it, Rose said Fern had learned to wear gowns, go to parties, and entertain. Isabelle positively enjoyed all those things. It didn't seem like such a big sacrifice. She was sure she could still wear her boots and short skirts most of the time.

She wasn't so sure about mixing with the kind of people that made up Cole's social circle. She hadn't liked any of the women she'd met. But she hadn't met very many. That society had produced Cole. There was no reason to assume it couldn't produce other people she could like.

She didn't know how much of Memphis remained in Cole, but despite his years in Texas, she expected it was a lot. Rose said George had never stopped being a Virginia aristocrat, even though he'd been in Texas for years fighting Indians, rustlers, and carpetbaggers. Drew suspected Cole was the same. When she was honest, she had to admit that was part of what she loved about him. She might not be able to make the transition, but keeping Cole's love was enough reason to try.

"What do you want me to do?" she asked her aunt.

"I want you to turn yourself over to me for one night. Just one. Let me dress you as I like and take you to a fancy ball. I'll make sure Cole is invited. Then you can see for yourself if you can be what you think he likes."

Drew almost opened her mouth to refuse. She didn't see any reason to subject herself to public failure. She didn't really care what anybody thought, but the idea of losing Cole was too much. If she really tried, she could probably turn herself into the kind of woman he wanted.

She felt a tear roll down her cheek. It would be so much nicer if he loved her just as she was.

"He's doing it," Myrtle whispered to Drew.

"Who's doing what?" Drew asked.

"Earl. He's dressing up like a woman."

Drew was in the process of cleaning her guns; all her arsenal was disassembled and laid out on a long table. They didn't need cleaning, but she wanted to be close enough to Cole to see him without seeming to *want* to see him.

371

"Find Cole immediately and tell him," Drew said. What a time to be without a weapon!

"He's not here," Myrtle said. "A buffalo trampled on that man who was here to help him. Cole took him to the hospital."

Cole had recruited Drew's old people to help him, organizing them into teams to keep Earl under surveillance at all times. They were supposed to notify Cole the minute they saw Earl putting on his disguise. The government team would then follow him and make the arrest.

Only Cole wasn't here. It was up to Drew. If she didn't do something, Earl would get away with another robbery, and she and her brothers would still be under suspicion. Fingers flying, she started to reassemble one of her guns.

"Tell everybody to meet in this tent in two minutes, including Hawk and Zeke," she said to Myrtle. "Tell Eddie to find Cole and tell him what's happening. You see if you can delay Earl long enough for me to put at least one gun together."

Myrtle hurried away. Drew worked with feverish haste to put the gun together as quickly as possibly. She didn't know what to do. She could stop Earl, but it wouldn't help. He wouldn't rob any more banks, and she'd never be able to prove her innocence. She had to let him attempt the robbery and find a way to capture him in the process.

Zeke and Hawk were the first to arrive. Drew told them to follow Earl's two confederates.

"We can capture them now," Zeke said.

"No. We've got to catch them in the act."

"What are you going go do?"

"I'm going to follow Earl."

"I can't let you do that," Zeke said. "It's too dangerous."

"I won't be in danger. All my friends will be with me. Eddie has gone to get Cole. He can take over."

Zeke wanted to argue, but the others started to arrive and she sent him off, worried Earl's helpers would get away.

"What do you want us to do?" Myrtle asked.

"We're going to follow Cole's plan," she said. "We'll all follow Earl. Every so often one of us will drop off and wait to tell Cole how to find us. It's like leaving a human trail of breadcrumbs."

She finished putting the gun together. "Now, I need a purse to hide this in, and a huge, floppy hat to hide my face."

In minutes, Myrtle had unearthed both items from the trunks that filled the tent.

"Scatter and get your bankbooks," Drew said. "If we get caught, we can always say we're going to make a deposit. Now hurry."

Drew put her gun in the purse, jammed the hat on her head, and left the tent just in time to see a very pretty lady she didn't recognize leaving the field and heading toward town.

"That's Earl," Myrtle said.

Drew never would have suspected. Earl looked beautiful. Even graceful. Following him proved to be easier than Drew had expected, and much more boring. Earl made no attempt to keep out of sight. Apparently certain no one could penetrate his disguise, he didn't look behind him or take a roundabout route. He headed straight for the heart of the city.

Once there, however, he assumed a dawdling pace, looking in windows and even going into shops. The old people started getting restless. It had turned out to be one of the few cold, wet days in New Orleans, and their old bones were beginning to ache. Drew was certain they'd be a lot happier if they could slip into one of the cozy shops or restaurants they passed.

"Why's he taking so long?" Myrtle's husband asked when Earl entered his second shop.

"I guess he's supposed to meet his confederates at a certain time," Drew said. A terrible thought occurred to her. Perhaps Earl knew they were following him. He was leading them away from his henchmen, who would handle the robbery alone. Drew told herself to relax. Earl was too much of a control freak to let anyone do anything for him. Besides, Zeke and Hawk were following the other men. They were more than capable of handling them.

She just wanted Cole to arrive. She felt totally confident dealing with anything that had to do with a ranch, but this business of stalking and arresting robbers was out of her scope. It was easy with rustlers. You caught them in the act and strung them up on the spot. She was certain it wouldn't be quite so easy with a bank robbery in the middle of New Orleans.

"I'll bet he's looking for a bag to put the loot in," Myrtle's husband said when Earl went into a third store.

"Probably," Drew said, looking over her shoulder to make sure someone had dropped off at the last corner. A man who used to be an acrobat but now helped with the buffalo took up a position next to a tobacco shop. Drew turned her attention to a bookstore, watching for Earl's exit out of the corner of her eye. She hadn't been there more than a few minutes when a cry of "That's Drew Townsend!" caused her to spin around.

Across the street was the office of the *New Orleans Picayune*, the major newspaper of New Orleans. A horde of reporters had spilled out the door and were headed her way.

"What new tricks are you going to add to your show tonight?"

"Did you really feed your family by shooting game before you were ten?"

"Are you going to be with the Wild West Show next season?"

"I heard your parents were in town. Are they coming to see you?"

"My readers want to know the name of your assistant," a female reporter said. "They want to know if he's married."

"Where did you learn to shoot?"

"How old are you?"

"Tell us about your adopted family."

Drew had never realized how frightening reporters could be when she wasn't protected by Cole's presence. She knew it was useless to try to run away or avoid the questions. Her best bet was to answer as many questions as quickly as possible and hope they'd leave before Earl came out of the shop. Just then Cole rounded the corner at a run.

"Where is he?" he asked Drew.

"In that shop."

"What does he look like?"

"Myrtle can tell you. I have to talk to these reporters."

"Keep talking, even after Earl comes out and I follow him," Cole said. "I don't want any question about your alibi this time."

"Hawk and Zeke are following the other two men."

"Good. With David in the hospital, I'll need all the help I can get."

Drew was glad to be relieved of the responsibility of capturing Earl, though she didn't like being left out altogether. But of course it would be disastrous if the reporters guessed what they were doing. She turned to them, forcing herself to smile and appear relaxed. "I'll be happy to answer a few questions," she said, quieting the hubbub, "but I can only answer one at a time."

For the next ten minutes, Drew did her best to satisfy the reporters. But no matter how much information she gave them, they wanted more. Cole helped, but his attention was divided. She was halfway through an explanation of the kind of ranch she wanted when Earl emerged from the shop and headed off at a quick pace.

"Remember, keep them talking," Cole said as he and Myrtle ambled away in Earl's wake.

"I heard the police suspected you of being part of a gang of robbers," one reporter said. "What can you tell us about that?"

Drew didn't know where the man had gotten his information, but she couldn't ignore the question. It was obvious from the expressions around her that the reporters were much more interested in this answer than in anything she'd said so far.

"They don't suspect me any longer," Drew said, "but it's true there's a gang led by a woman pretending to be me. You'll have to talk to the federal agents in charge of the case if you want to know any more."

Drew had answered two more questions when a chorus of female voices raised in indignant protest caused everyone to turn.

"It's Sophia d'Elbe!" one of the reporters shouted. "The police must have raided her brothel."

In less time than it took to breathe, Drew found herself abandoned for a more interesting story. Female sharpshooters who manage to survive a dunking in the Mississippi might be interesting, but they couldn't compare to a beautiful madame who was reputed to be the mistress of the most powerful man in the city. When his enemies were angry enough to have her arrested, the reporters could scent enough scandal to fill their papers for weeks to come. Drew Townsend was forgotten.

Relieved, Drew headed after Cole.

Cole didn't know how he was going to arrest Earl. He'd come straight from the hospital. He had a weapon, but no backup. Earl had both. All Cole had was the element of surprise—if Earl didn't happen to turn and recognize him before he reached his destination. This operation had been cockeyed from the start. No reason to expect things to change now.

Earl hadn't gone half a block before he turned and entered the Louisiana Bank and Trust. It was eleven o'clock, exactly the time the bank opened. There probably wouldn't be any customers inside yet.

But before Cole could reach the bank door, a woman and her daughter came from around the corner and entered the bank right behind Earl. Fearful of what might happen, Cole broke into a run.

He stopped just inside the building. He looked through the glass doors that separated the inside of the bank from the lobby and his blood froze. Earl's two goons stood a little behind and to either side of him. Each held a gun pointed at the tellers. Earl, a charming smile on his face, handed his bag to a teller. He held the little girl by one hand. The other hand held a gun, which he had pressed against the woman's temple.

Cole couldn't decide what to do. If he went around and tried to come in through the back, he might be too late. If he could slip inside without Earl noticing, he could try to shoot the gun out of Earl's hand. He wasn't nearly as good as Drew, but he thought he could manage it at close range. Once he had disarmed Earl, he would have a chance for a successful arrest. He opened the door very quietly and eased his way in. He thought he'd been successful at escaping notice—Earl and his partners were too busy watching the bank tellers to notice him—until the little girl turned and saw him.

"That's the man from the Indian show," she cried.

At that, Earl turned and saw Cole. Cole aimed and fired. Then all hell broke loose.

Fortunately for Cole, Hawk and Zeke materialized from the back of the bank to overwhelm Earl's two helpers. Cole had succeeded in shooting Earl's gun from his hand, but Earl used the child and her mother as a shield to move toward the back door. The child and her mother were jumping about so much, Cole didn't dare chance a shot.

"Drop down," Cole called. "Fall flat on the floor."

They did as he asked, but it was too late. Earl had disappeared through a side door.

"Somebody look after them," Cole hollered as he ran past gaping tellers to the door through which Earl had escaped. It opened onto an alley. One way led to private homes that abutted the street. The other led toward the main square. Cole guessed Earl would try to disappear in a crowd, and he ran toward the square.

He emerged from the alley and ran into Drew.

"What happened?" she asked.

"We caught the others, but Earl escaped," he said, scanning the crowd for the familiar figure.

"Where did he go?"

"I don't know. There he is," he said, "over there, near the man selling rabbits."

Earl had hiked his skirts up so he could run faster. He would disappear into the maze of streets in the French Quarter in another minute. Cole held out his pistol to Drew. "You've got to stop him."

"That pistol isn't very accurate past twenty-five feet," Drew said. "Earl's more than twenty-five yards away."

"It's the only weapon we have."

"I can't shoot into that crowd," Drew protested. "I might hit an innocent bystander!"

"You have every right to be proud of your skill with a gun," Cole said, "but it's a worthless talent if you can't use it when you really need it. If Earl gets away, we'll never clear your name. You can do it, Drew. You make much harder shots in the ring every night. You just need to have faith in yourself."

Drew took the pistol form him, took careful aim, waited for the split second when she had a clear field of vision, and pulled the trigger. Across the square, Earl cried out, then fell to the ground.

"I shot him in the leg," Drew said. "Only a man would hike his skirts up to his knees in public."

Chapter Twenty-four

Wild West Show Star Foils Robbery Attempt

New Orleans, Nov. 17th—Miss Drew Townsend, the sharpshooting star of the Wild West Show that has been entertaining the people of New Orleans for the last week, aided federal agents in catching a gang of robbers that had evaded capture by government agents for the last two years. Miss Townsend, helped by several employees of the show, followed the gang leader and stopped him in the midst of the robbery. When he attempted to escape, she brought him down with a spectacular shot across a crowded square.

"I couldn't let him get away," Miss Townsend said when asked why she dared attempt such a dangerous shot. "Who knows what he might have done to the next woman or little girl who happened to get in his way?"

Earl Odum, the owner of the Wild West Show, had used Miss Townsend's presence in the show to divert suspicion from himself. He disguised himself as a woman, often displaying some feat of marksmanship so authorities would connect the robberies with Miss Townsend and her brothers.

When asked how she'd had the courage to attack him on her own, Miss Townsend smiled and said, "I knew I could shoot better than he could." Miss Townsend's fearless action prevented the villain from depriving the citizens of New Orleans of more than $100,000.

"Where is Cole?" Drew asked her aunt. "You promised he'd be here tonight."

"I don't know," Dorothea said. "He accepted the invitation."

"Maybe he is too tired," Jake said. "Running the Wild West Show for the last week must have taken a lot out of him."

The last week had been incredible. Demand for tickets had been so great that despite Earl's arrest, they'd had to schedule ten extra shows. The stands had been packed every night, the ticket sales exceeding even the most optimistic predictions. With Earl in jail, Cole had been asked to take over running the Wild West Show. He and Drew had barely managed to see each other for more than a couple of hours a day, most of it spent practicing or performing. The performers had voted to ask Cole to take over the show permanently. He'd promised to give them an answer by tomorrow.

Through the Randolphs, Dorothea had secured invitations to one of the most exclusive balls of the season. The weather had cooled enough so that the hundreds of candles in the three huge chandeliers and dozens of wall sconces didn't make the room too uncomfortable. A dozen huge mirrors and a highly polished floor reflected the light until the room seemed to glitter like a diamond. New Orleans society had turned out in numbers, with women dressed in lavish gowns and glittering jewels. Drew could at least take comfort in knowing she was dressed as expensively as anyone in the room.

She had allowed her aunt full rein to dress her for the ball. Dorothea had enlisted the aid of the finest dressmaker in New Orleans. And hairdresser. And jeweler. And what seemed like a dozen other people whose job it was to make Drew completely unrecognizable, even to herself. She wore a gown of emerald-green silk decorated with gold knots and lavishly trimmed with cream lace. Emeralds flashed at her throat and in her hair, which was piled high on her head in a coronet.

"Cole's probably trying to decide what he's going to do," Isabelle said. "Being asked to take on the show is a great honor, but it's a big responsibility."

Drew took no comfort from the thought that just as she had made up her mind what she wanted to do, Cole might be unable to decide what he wanted.

At least ten times an hour she had regretted her decision, been on the verge of changing her mind, but she didn't have the heart to ruin her aunt's happiness.

Don't lie to yourself. You're afraid this is the only way you could ever keep a man like Cole Benton.

Having Cole's mother and Sibyl Owen follow him to New Orleans made things even worse. Cole might not want to marry Sibyl, but she stood for all the women who were everything Drew wasn't.

"I don't see how you've had time to miss him," Jake said. "There's been a line of young men begging to dance with you all evening. You're a celebrity."

In addition to the robbery, the reporters had managed to discover that she was the adopted daughter of a wealthy rancher, the niece of a New York society matron, and heir to a New York banking fortune. It seemed every eligible bachelor and ne'er-do-well within a hundred miles had managed to wangle an invitation to the ball. She had been mobbed from the moment she entered. They said she was beautiful, captivating, breathtaking, and so many other things she couldn't remember them all. Even if every man had meant every word he said, it was meaningless.

Cole hadn't said those things.

While the orchestra took a break, she had retreated to a corner, shamelessly using her aunt, Isabelle and Jake, and Rose and George as a shield. She'd tried to get Hawk and Zeke to come, but they'd flatly refused. After a short twenty minutes, the musicians returned to their seats and began to tune up for the next dance. The line of would-be partners had already begun to form.

"I don't want to dance anymore," Drew said to Isabelle. "I want to go home."

"It won't be any better in the hotel, dear. You're a celebrity."

383

"I mean Texas. I don't want to see New Orleans ever again."

"You can't mean that," her aunt said. "You're the most beautiful young woman here tonight. Imagine what would happen if you let me take you back to New York."

Drew didn't have any thoughts to spare for New York. Her heart was in her throat. Cole had just entered the room. He stood for a moment, his gaze scanning the room. Drew was in the act of thrusting her arm up in the air to wave to him when two people entered the room behind him. His mother and Sibyl Owens.

Drew jerked her arm down and grabbed hold of Jake. "Dance with me," she said.

"Why? There are a dozen handsome young men waiting for the chance."

"I don't want to dance with silly young men who are more impressed with my aunt's money than they are with me. I want to talk about horses and cows, about the clean air and quiet nights. I *don't* want to talk about parties and listen to another compliment on my eyes, my hair, my dress, my—"

Her voice broke. If she didn't get control of herself, she was going to break down right there.

"Dance with her, Jake," said Isabelle. "I want to talk to Dorothea, and I don't want your long ears listening."

Drew didn't care that the suitors showed disappointment. She held tight to Jake, secure in the knowledge he loved her regardless of how she looked. She buried her head in his chest when they started to dance.

"You really love him, don't you?" Jake said.

"Yes."

"He loves you too."

"Then why did he get here two hours late?"

"I didn't see him." Jake turned his head to look. "Where—"

Drew reached up and turned Jake's head back toward her. "He's by the door, directly behind you."

"Then why don't you let him dance with you?"

"He brought his mother and his old girlfriend."

"A fellow can't ignore his mother."

"How about his girlfriend?"

"You're jealous, Drew. If you want this guy, fight for him. If not, do both of you a favor, and walk away."

"Is that what you did with Isabelle, just decided you wanted her and that was it?"

Jake grinned in a way Drew was certain had melted Isabelle's resistance so many years ago.

"No, I was just as big a fool as you. I had too much pride and too little common sense."

"Is that what you think, that I have too much pride?"

"Yes."

Drew froze. Cole's voice came from directly behind her.

"And no compassion for a tortured soul."

Jake executed a quick half turn. He released Drew and pushed her gently toward Cole. "You two work this out between you." He turned and walked off the floor.

"Are you going to dance with me, or just stand there in the middle of the floor?" Cole asked.

"I don't know."

"It's okay with me. I can look at you easier. Did you know you're beautiful?"

"There's a rumor to that effect, but I think it has more to do with my aunt's money."

"I have more money than I need. I'm talking about you."

"Not even the dress?"

"It's a pretty dress, but I think you look just as pretty when you come into the arena on horseback. It always makes me catch my breath."

It was tempting to believe him, but the masters of disguise had done their job so well, she doubted he could recognize her as the same woman. He probably only guessed because she was dancing with Jake.

"How about my hair?"

"It looks pretty all pinned up like that in a coronet, but I prefer it loose down your back."

Drew felt her muscles relax just a little. Maybe he did like a little bit of the real Drew.

"Why were you so late? I thought you weren't coming."

"Mother wanted to attend another party. She only agreed to come to this one when I refused to go to the other with her. Then she took so long getting ready, I threatened to leave alone. Sibyl had to run after me to stop me from leaving without them."

Drew's spirits soared. "I'm sorry your mother dislikes me so much."

"I'm not marrying to please my mother."

"Are we getting married?"

"You're damned right we are."

"I haven't said yes."

"If you don't, I'll kidnap you. I've already spoken to Isabelle. She thinks I've indulged you far too long."

"I won't go back to Memphis."

"We're not going to live in Memphis."

"Are you going to manage the show?"

"No. I'm going to marry a certain hardheaded, stubborn, obstinate sharpshooter I met a few weeks ago. I want to go into a partnership with her on a ranch in this little valley I know in Texas. I want to ride next to her over our land, go on roundup with her, even a cattle drive to Dodge. I want a woman as wild and free as the Texas breeze, as strong and self-reliant as a Texas longhorn, as tough as a Texas cactus. I never thought I'd find such a woman until I met you. Now that I have, I don't mean to let you go. After tonight I want you to put the dress you're wearing in the back of your closet and pull out my favorite outfit."

"What's that?" The words nearly caught in her throat.

"Flat-crowned hat, vest, short skirt, and boots. I fell in love with a female cowboy. That's the Drew Townsend I want to marry."

"You don't care if I'm not pretty and feminine?"

"You've always been pretty and feminine. This stuff you have on tonight just covers it up."

Drew forgot where she was. She threw her arms around Cole's neck and kissed him long and hard.

"You'll scandalize New Orleans society," Cole said with a chuckle when she released her hold on him. "They'll probably throw us out."

Drew let out a cowboy yell that reduced the entire room to stunned, immobile silence. "That ought to do it for sure," she said. "Can we leave for Texas now?"

Epilogue

Drew pulled up at the top of a ridge. She'd been riding over her new ranch for the better part of a day. Ownership of this land had given her the sense of pleasure she'd always hoped for. But she knew most of that was due to the man riding at her side. None of it would have meant anything without Cole.

"Are you happy with it?" he said.

"It's exactly what I wanted. Do you like it?"

"Actually I'd been thinking of something along the Pecos, you know, mostly desert infested with Comanches, rattlesnakes, and a few dozen Comancheros."

Drew smiled happily. "I should think a couple thousand cows would be exciting enough even for you."

"Maybe if you had bought longhorns, but you're buying some of those overly domesticated fat cows George

Randolph got from Richard King a few years ago. What's a cowboy to do for fun?"

Drew sobered. "I've got an idea about that, but I'm not sure you're going to like it."

"Shoot."

"You know you said it was time to think about hiring a crew."

"It's best to get them settled before the cows arrive."

"Suppose we don't get the ordinary kind of crew. Suppose we do what Jake and Isabelle did."

"Do you mean orphans?"

"None of my brothers would have had a chance without Jake and Isabelle. Several of them would be dead by now. There are other boys out there like that, boys whose lives are hanging by a thread. Girls, too. I know I can't help them all, but I want to give some of them the same chance Jake and Isabelle gave us."

"Are you sure? You might think differently when you have children of your own."

"Jake and Isabelle had Eden and it didn't make any difference at all. Just think how many boys we can help in ten, twenty, fifty years!"

Cole laughed. "Myrtle said you'd try to mother everybody. What are you going to do with the old people when they start arriving?"

"They'll make perfect surrogate parents for the boys. We can't give them all the attention they need by ourselves."

"Okay, bring on all the orphans you want, on one condition."

"What's that?"

"I'm not an orphan, and I don't need mothering."

Drew felt enveloped by something as close to perfect

happiness as humans are allowed. "I've got other plans for you," she said, giving Cole what she hoped was a perfectly wicked grin. She rode her horse up next to his and starting running her hands over his chest. "I've discovered I have an inordinate fondness for the male body, yours in particular, but without all these clothes in the way. I think I'll strip you naked right here and take cruel advantage of you." She slipped her hand a good bit lower and hooted with laughter when Cole growled in frustration. She dug her heels into her horse's side and was off at a gallop. "Beat you to the bed," she called out over her shoulder.

"The bed, hell!" her lover called after her. "If I catch up with you, a rock or a cactus patch will do."

Drew let out a yell of pure happiness as the wind whipped through her hair. She heard the sound of hoof-beats coming closer and laughed aloud. She had the faster horse, but this was one race she had no intention of winning. She had already won the only one that counted.

Author's Note

Buffalo Bill Cody's Wild West Show evolved from a kind of rodeo he arranged for a July 4th celebration for his neighbors in North Platte, Nebraska, in 1882. The following year he expanded his show to include Indians riding bareback, cowboys busting broncos, trick-riding, fancy roping, foot-racing, bison-riding, shooting on foot and on horseback, knife-throwing, and mock battles between Indians and scouts. The show was a sensational success and ended a triumphant season at New York's Coney Island. Buffalo Bill quickly developed the general format he would use over the next twenty years.

In each new city, the show would unload at the train station and parade to the exhibition grounds. Buffalo Bill, followed by the bandwagon pulled by six white horses, rode at the head of the line on a white horse, raising his hat to the cheering multitudes that thronged the sidewalks. Next came the Indians, feathered and painted, shrieking war whoops—Pawnees, Sioux, and Wichitas riding their barebacked, painted ponies. Next came a contingent of Mexican vaqueros in bright serapes and oversized sombreros. Annie Oakley rode in a special carriage by herself. Suddenly cowboys and scouts filled the streets, herding steers, buffalo, mules, and horses—filling the air with a cacophony of yelling, whip-cracking, neighing, braying, bellowing, saddles creaking, and horse hooves pounding. The Deadwood Mail Coach (bullet-riddled by Black Hills bandits) brought up the rear.

The exhibition itself was fast and furious. No sooner had the band serenaded the spectators into their seats than the show tunes changed to a loud fanfare. Buffalo Bill and the other featured performers galloped into the arena and pulled up their mounts in front of the packed stands. As quickly as they came, they disappeared, leaving Annie Oakley alone in the spotlight. With pistols, rifle, and shotgun, she shot at standing, moving, and flying targets from every possible position.

Then the scouts, cowboys, and vaqueros took over. Trick riders leaped from horse to horse, from horse to ground, and from ground to horse. They lassoed charging buffalo, swift-moving steers, and untamed horses. All joined forces in simulating a real Western roundup, cutting steers out of the herd, roping and branding them. The Indians and scouts put on a buffalo hunt, using blank cartridges and rubber-tipped arrows to "kill" their quarry. The Indians demonstrated their tribal dances, climaxing the demonstration with a war dance.

Next the Deadwood Stage lumbered into the light. A

band of Indians swooped down on the stage, but Cody and his scouts intercepted the charge and drove them into the hills. The bronc busters performed next. After that, the cowboys, scouts, and vaqueros rode steers, buffalo, even elk. The high point of the exhibition was a reenactment of the duel with Yellow Hand in which Buffalo Bill fought the Indian brave with guns, knives, and spears. The audience always cheered wildly when Buffalo Bill won.

The Wild West Show toured Europe for the first time in 1887. The cast was enormous, featuring as many as 250 actors and many more animals. The Wild West Show performed to worldwide success until it closed in 1917.

Annie Oakley joined the show in Louisville, on April 24, 1885, and retired in 1902. She was a star from the first, one of the greatest single assets the show ever had. The advertising rarely named performers, but after watching her first rehearsal, the business manager ordered seven thousand dollars' worth of printing featuring Annie on billboards and in notices.

Annie first gained notice for her shooting as a child by providing local hotels with game. Too small to carry a shotgun, she used a rifle. Chefs preferred her game because she was so accurate, she could kill squirrels, rabbits, and birds with a single shot to the head. Guests preferred them because they didn't have to pick buckshot out of their food.

By age sixteen, Annie had met and defeated Frank Butler, the man who was to become her husband and manager for the rest of her life. For three years, they traveled the vaudeville circuit, performing in theaters, practicing in hotel rooms, alleys, and back lots until she perfected the split-second timing of her act. When she joined the

Wild West Show, she was only nineteen, stood just under five feet, and weighed one hundred pounds. Sitting Bull adopted her and named her Little Sure Shot.

No woman in outdoor show business has been so long remembered. She was a consummate actress, with a personality that made itself felt as soon as she entered the arena. She entered bowing, waving, and wafting kisses. Her first few shots brought forth a few screams from the women, but they were soon lost in round after round of applause.

She could shoot an apple from the head of a trained dog, shoot a cigarette from between her husband's lips, hit a dime held in his fingers, and slice a playing card in two. After two clay pigeons had been released, she would leap over a table, pick up her gun, and bring down both targets. She could hit a dime tossed into the air from a distance of ninety feet. She was the most acclaimed marksman of her day. She never lost her skill and spent much of her retirement advocating that women learn to handle firearms and teaching them to shoot. She died in 1926.

LEIGH GREENWOOD
The Independent Bride

Colorado Territory, 1868: It is about as rough and ready as the West can get, a place and time almost as dangerous as the men who left civilization behind, driven by a desire for land, gold . . . a new life.

Fort Lookout: It is a rugged outpost where soldiers, cattlemen and Indians live on the edge of open warfare, the last place any woman in her right mind would choose to settle.

Abby: She is everything a man should avoid—with a face of beauty and an expression of stubborn determination. Colonel Bryce McGregor knows there is no room for such a woman at his fort or in his heart. Yet as she receives proposal after proposal from his troops, Bryce realizes the only man he can allow her to marry is himself.

Dorchester Publishing Co., Inc.
P.O. Box 6640   _5235-0
Wayne, PA 19087-8640 $6.99 US/$8.99 CAN

Name: _____

Address: _____

City: _____ State: _____ Zip: _____

E-mail: _____

I have enclosed $_____ in payment for the checked book(s).

For more information on these books, check out our website at www.dorchesterpub.com.
_____ *Please send me a free catalog.*

LEIGH GREENWOOD

The Reluctant Bride

Colorado Territory, 1872: A rough-and-tumble place and time almost as dangerous as the men who left civilization behind, driven by a desire for a new life. In a false-fronted town where the only way to find a decent woman is to send away for her, Tanzy first catches sight of the man she came west to marry galloping after a gang of bandits. Russ Tibbolt is a far cry from the husband she expected when she agreed to become a mail-order bride. He is much too compelling for any woman's peace of mind. With his cobalt-blue eyes and his body's magic, how can she hope to win the battle of wills between them?

SEVEN BRIDES
LEIGH GREENWOOD

**"I loved *Rose*, but I absolutely loved *Fern*!
She's fabulous! An incredible job!"**
—*Romantic Times*

A man of taste and culture, James Madison Randolph enjoys the refined pleasures of life in Boston. It's been years since the suave lawyer abandoned the Randolphs' ramshackle ranch—and the dark secrets that haunted him there. But he is forced to return to the hated frontier when his brother is falsely accused of murder. What he doesn't expect is a sharp-tongued vixen who wants to gun down his entire family. As tough as any cowhand in Kansas, Fern Sproull will see her cousin's killer hang for his crime, and no smooth-talking city slicker will stop her from seeing justice done. But one look at James awakens a tender longing to taste heaven in his kiss. While the townsfolk of Abilene prepare for the trial of the century, Madison and Fern ready themselves for a knock-down, drag-out battle of the sexes that might just have two winners.

___4409-9 $6.99 US/$8.99 CAN

Dorchester Publishing Co., Inc.
P.O. Box 6640
Wayne, PA 19087-8640

Please add $2.50 for shipping and handling for the first book and $.75 for each book thereafter. NY, NYC, and PA residents, please add appropriate sales tax. No cash, stamps, or C.O.D.s. All orders shipped within 6 weeks via postal service book rate. Canadian orders require $2.00 extra postage and must be paid in U.S. dollars through a U.S. banking facility.

Name_____
Address_____
City_____State_____Zip_____
I have enclosed $_____ in payment for the checked book(s).
Payment <u>must</u> accompany all orders. ❏ Please send a free catalog.
   CHECK OUT OUR WEBSITE! www.dorchesterpub.com

The Cowboys
PETE

LEIGH GREENWOOD

Pete rides up to the Winged T cattle ranch with one purpose: to retrieve his stolen money. A self-proclaimed drifter, he is not a man to get roped into anything. But within moments of his arrival he finds himself owner of a cattle ranch and husband to a charming woman. His new wife looks at him as if he were a cross between Paul Bunyan and Wild Bill Hickok—a lot of pressure for a confirmed wanderer. But when he takes the petite beauty in his arms, he wonders what it would be like to be tied to one place, to one woman. For though he came in search of his fortune, he finds something far more precious: the love of a lifetime.

___4562-1 $6.99 US/$8.99 CAN